2.50

Beauty

LEWIN JOEL

SIMON AND SCHUSTER · NEW YORK

This novel is a work of fiction. Names, characters, places and incidents either are the product of the author's imagination or are used fictitiously. Any resemblance to actual events or locales or persons, living or dead, is entirely coincidental.

Copyright © 1987 by Lewin Joel
All rights reserved
including the right of reproduction
in whole or in part in any form
Published by Simon and Schuster
A division of Simon & Schuster, Inc.
Simon & Schuster Building
Rockefeller Center
1230 Avenue of the Americas
New York, New York 10020
SIMON AND SCHUSTER and colophon are trademarks of Simon & Schuster, Inc.
Designed by Irving Perkins Associates
Manufactured in the United States of America

1 3 5 7 9 10 8 6 4 2

Library of Congress Cataloging-in-Publication Data
Joel, Lewin.
Beauty.

I. Title.
PS3560.0243B4   1987   813'.54   86-29663
ISBN: 0-671-60047-8

ACKNOWLEDGMENTS

Nothing truly worthwhile can be accomplished without help, and I am fortunate enough to have been on the receiving end of an overwhelming amount of it.

Without the inspiration, advice, and reputation of a wonderful writer and friend, Michael Malone, this book would probably never have been written, let alone published.

Many thanks also to my agent and friend, Molly Friedrich, and my editor, Patricia Soliman, whose encouragement and insightful suggestions helped to make *Beauty* the best it could be, as well as to Cheryl Weinstein and all the fine readers and copyeditors who polished it to a high gloss.

And to my family: Mom, Dad (glad you were here to see my dream come true), Vicki, Ross, Nana, Jack, and Aaron—for always being there.

And finally, thank you, Lauren: You are the frosting on the cake.

For DD, who never lost faith in me, even when I did.

FEBRUARY 1982

Her name wouldn't come to him. "You have beautiful eyes," he said. Karen, Catherine, Christine—it was something like that, something with a "K" or a "C."

"Thank you." Her voice was breathy, mildly embarrassed, as though no one had ever told her that before. He was sure many men had.

He held her tightly, bending over her as they stood, his right hand strong in the small of her back. Lynell Alan looked into those deep, oval blue eyes, down at her full glossy lips so close he could see the fine vertical striations beneath the dark lipstick, could smell the waxy Revlon smell. "Nice lips, too," he said, parting his own and tilting his head so that his mouth would meet hers in the perfect kiss, though their lips would probably never meet.

"Thank you," she said again.

She was a professional and he hoped the compliments, though he meant them, didn't embarrass her . . . or himself. She was very pretty and very young, with even white teeth and sandy blonde hair that was clean and shiny and reflected the light in silver highlights. Her nose was straight and narrow, and her smooth, pale skin stretched taut over prominent cheekbones, hollow cheeks, a wide strong jaw, and an engagingly cleft chin. She was only a few inches shy of his own six-feet two, and he had seen her body when she came into the large open room wearing the soft, green, low-cut dress. Her breasts were not large but were high and perfectly shaped, and he tried not to watch them

11

when she reached the top of the stairs out of breath and he could see the veins tracing thin blue wisps beneath her translucent skin. He tried not to stare at the nipples, peaked against the flimsy fabric that was too light for the cold room.

But the klieg lights had warmed her, he noticed as he released her and saw that the fabric had smoothed over her chest. He'd not had to think of Aimée this time only of . . . whatever her name was.

With each *pop-crackle* of the flash bulb, each *zip* of the Nikon's automatic film-wind as her mechanical cue, the young woman flipped her head back regally and altered her pose: thick, wavy, waist-length mane curling down the middle of her back; a smile, a half-smile, a pouting dreamy stare; full face, full profile. She changed angles with an instinctive, feline grace that at first settled Lynell Alan, then prompted him; that encouraged him, then excited him; and that took him far away from a frigid studio on West Twenty-eighth Street.

"What a way to meet people," she laughed to him, but loudly enough that they could all hear. They did and joined her.

"One more roll," Mike Dudley called jovially, breaking the mood, "just in case. What you were doing was perfect, real romantic," he said, beaming and thrusting the light meter between them as he tested the exposure. "Just do the same thing again." In the background his wife/assistant frantically changed rolls. Lynell Alan had worked with Mike Dudley several times before. The photographer was thorough, if bumbling, the consummate pro who was acutely aware of his own shortcomings, always taking twice the number of shots he needed "just in case." At $250 an hour, Lynell thought, he could take as long as he wanted.

When he'd changed agencies less than a month ago, Cline Models had immediately raised his fee from $150 to $250 an hour, and though he wasn't yet working as regularly as he hoped to be, he had made more in modeling fees in that time than he'd made the previous three months with his former agent. Yes, he was on his way. Cline Models had the power to make a career. And the way they had brought him along in only a short time suited him just fine.

"I haven't seen you in ages," the young woman said. "You're with the Munson Agency, aren't you?" Her teeth smiled perfectly. He wondered if she'd felt it, too, the electricity of that lost moment.

"Not any more. I was with them for a year or so, but as a matter of fact, I just joined Cline a couple of weeks ago."

"Didn't you like Munson?"

He paused for half a beat. "I wasn't working." It had occurred to him to lie, as he was sure most models would have—something about their "look" not being right for the agency or testing the waters for a change of scenery—but his whole life was a game. Why play it with a virtual stranger?

"You'll like LeeAnn. I've had a few dealings with Gretchen." She paused briefly, as though weighing his sensibilities. "Fucking bitch!" The "F" word didn't quite go with her perfect face.

"You got that right," he agreed. Gretchen at Munson, LeeAnn at Cline—all bookers were full of shit. If he wasn't smart enough to have gotten out of this damn business by now, at least he was smart enough to have learned that.

"Okay, Cathy, Lyn, once more with feeling," Mike called from behind the lights.

"Cathy." He repeated the name softly to himself as he watched her take her place. He was usually good with names because he tried. The chill of the draft that slipped through the studio was beginning to get to him. He hoped Dudley had gotten it right on the first roll, because the second take wouldn't be as good, wouldn't be as spontaneous. He'd gotten into the first one: Cathy in that dress, in his arms. It would show as a good, professional job. But the emotions that had made the series what he was sure it would turn out to be, flickered like a candle in the icy February draft seeping into the studio. He felt the others in the room around him, and as he took her in his arms again he tried to lose himself in thoughts of Aimée.

Catherine Ward was wiped out. Six weeks ago, as the post-New Year's rush began, she had called LeeAnn and booked out for this week, swearing she wouldn't accept a job for anything or anyone. Monday through Wednesday had gone according to plan: awake at ten in the morning, curled up in bed with the *New York Times* until noon, a two-hour stroll window-shopping along Fifth Avenue, afternoon "soaps," an early dinner alone by the fire, television or a movie, and back into bed by midnight. She didn't call her answering service; she didn't call the agency. Life was bliss. That was, until last night when Mike Dudley had called.

"It's that Halston job, the one we started last month, so it has to be you, Cathy. What can I say? I fucked up and let it slip my mind. Now I've got to have the shots in on Monday, and the only way I can make the deadline is to do it tomorrow. I've got a guy for the clinches, and he's promised to keep the day open. I'm at your mercy. Any time you

13

say. Midnight if you want. I'm on a tight budget, too, so it's not a full-day booking; I can only pay hourly. It's $250 an hour, but it should only tie you up for a few hours."

It was not her practice to give her home telephone number to clients, but Mike had been one of the first good photographers to take an interest in her that was purely professional. He was from the old school. Though he was extremely successful he refused to surround himself with the trappings of success, preferring to remain in the same drafty studio he'd occupied for over twenty years and never using his position to take advantage, but only to help. It seemed in the early days when she was struggling to make ends meet—days that had been, thankfully, short-lived—Mike would always come through at a critical time with a decent job, no strings attached. Now that she was in demand, she wasn't about to turn her back on him.

Imagine, she thought: Catherine Ward, a twenty-year-old high school drop-out, and she'd have turned up her nose at $250 an hour . . . *an hour!* . . . if it hadn't been Mike. She would earn more in a few hours than most people earned in a week. Thank God for a society's warped sense of values that would probably pay her $250,000 this year—with a little luck even more—when it would pay a high school teacher $15,000. Not that she didn't work hard, damned hard. From the first of January to the middle of February she had been booked seven days a week, eight to twelve hours a day, in the busy whirl of fashion shows and catalogue shootings for the upcoming spring and summer seasons—not to mention her increasing television commercial commitments.

What sometimes made her feel guilty was that the hard work was backed more by luck than by brains or talent. Though she considered herself intelligent enough, she knew it wasn't brains that earned her a six-figure income. She didn't think of herself as all that great looking, either, but she was the right size: 5'11" and 125 pounds. And she did like her nose: straight and narrow and with a sort of natural flare to her nostrils. She had always wished her breasts were a tiny bit fuller, but they were well-shaped and, fortunately, clothes hung better on a smaller bosom. With the aid of professional makeup and hairstyling and the gorgeous clothes she wore (Halston, Dior, Blass, Givenchy), not to mention the work of talented photographers like Mike, Scavullo, Penn, and Avedon—well, she couldn't argue with the results. With all that help she was photogenic even if the end product didn't always look to her like . . . well . . . like her.

Being photogenic was the name of the game. What mattered was not so much what you actually looked like, but what you looked like in photographs, on tape, and on film. She'd seen models, especially print models, who were eccentric-looking in person but absolutely dynamite in black and white—all interesting angles and exotic planes—and runway models who positively blossomed onstage in front of an audience. So who could tell? And what was so bad about being a model, anyway? Sure, models sold their bodies, but so did carpenters—and considerably more cheaply. And all of those brainy people who looked down their not-so-attractive noses at models—weren't they just as lucky to have been born with brains as she had been to have been born with looks? And their brains couldn't have caused them the heartache her looks had caused her.

Perhaps she was just tired because she hadn't expected to be working today. Three hours certainly wasn't a grueling day. She walked to the dressing room mirror. Milt Myles had noticed the deep circles before he had applied the first stroke of base. "Not getting enough sleep, dearie?"

Maybe she had been getting too *much* sleep. She peered closer into the mirror, admiring Milt's work—a real artist, that Milt. She looked the picture of health, though she hardly felt that way. She felt like a wet rag, she had the sniffles, and she was depressed.

Crossing her arms in front of her, she grasped the pale green Halston original at each hip and drew it over her head as she turned from the mirror. She was standing that way, naked above her translucent beige panties, arms extended over her head and hands clutching a now-reversed fifteen-hundred-dollar dress, when Mike Dudley strolled casually in.

Though she was used to the immodesty of a profession in which she often shared a dressing room with a dozen other half-naked models, male and female, flinging off clothes in a frenzied attempt to keep a live fashion show going with no dead time, Catherine was nonetheless frozen for a moment by the unexpected intrusion. Mike's eyes widened in surprise and rested for that moment on the smooth rise of the young woman's shimmering breasts.

The picture of a Santa Claus in jeans who had himself received a belated Christmas present, the rotund, white-haired, and blushing photographer chuckled self-consciously. "Sorry, Cathy," he said with a shrug. "I thought you'd be dressed by now."

"Ever think of knocking, Mike?" she asked without malice, dropping the dress back over her shoulders and smoothing it against her slim hips.

"Thanks for coming, kid," he said, quickly changing the subject.

Catherine shrugged and smiled demurely. "Any time, Mike . . . *ex-*

15

cept tomorrow," she added with a laugh. Then she walked behind a long portable rack on which hung a dozen gorgeous evening gowns— gowns that she would have been hard-pressed to afford even on her salary. As Mike sat in the room's lone chair, a comfortable-looking Salvation Army reject with half its stuffing spilled on the floor, she positioned the rack between them and again lifted the dress over her head.

"Ever worked with Lynell before?"

"No. Why?" she asked as she changed dresses in the brisk and absent flurry of an experienced runway model. When she had hung the Halston neatly at the end of the rack and stepped out from behind the row of dresses, she was wearing a clinging burgundy jersey-knit that drew Mike's admiring smile.

"No particular reason. Jayne thinks he's wonderful, but I don't think he works too much. He's always available when I call—even at the last minute."

"So am I," she shot back sarcastically. "I hope you don't tell people *I* never work."

"Good point," he agreed.

"Anyway," she continued, wondering as she did why she felt the sudden need to defend Lynell Alan, "he's only been with Cline for a couple of days, and he did just earn $750 from you."

"So, you like him."

"He seems nice, and he's very attractive," she said noncommittally.

In fact, she remembered Lyne Alan from an audition the previous summer for a television commercial for Gillette. She had gotten the job—really just as a prop for the man in the advertisement. Lynell had been turned down and she hadn't been surprised. It was a razor blade ad and he simply was not the macho type. But in a room crowded with men, many of whom were more classically handsome, he had stood out and, in that instant she had first seen him, had taken her breath away. She had distractedly dropped her portfolio, and had fumbled on the floor like an amateur trying to retrieve the scattered pictures. Her initial response to him was one she rarely had with men: sexual. Actually, sensual was perhaps a better word. She'd felt a warm attraction to him, as though they could easily have been friends; as though he could have been one of the few men she'd met in New York who would have been worth knowing.

Her heart had skipped involuntarily each time his eyes met hers. A playful tangle of loose brown curls framed his oval face. Severely high cheekbones cast hollow shadows across his wide jaw and accentuated the pouting fullness of his lips. His long nose was ever-so-slightly

16

crooked, and when, in the midst of helping her gather her scattered portfolio shots, he had suddenly swung back toward her and caught her staring, he smiled with even teeth and she felt the disconcerting impact of his deep-set, teal-blue eyes.

The total impression was of strength and yet weakness, of power and yet vulnerability, of desire and yet need. He was charming, seemingly sensitive, and . . .

"He reminds me of my father," she said to Mike Dudley without knowing she was saying it and immediately wishing she hadn't.

Jayne Dudley followed her own light knock into the small room, her long gray hair flying loose behind her. Catherine backed away from the clothing rack instinctively as the older, Levi's-and-sweatshirt-clad woman threw a protective sheet over it. "Cathy, you were fantastic, as always. You and Lyn are some handsome couple." Jayne wheeled the rack toward the door as Catherine moved to the mirror and daubed away the excess makeup. "And the guy is so darned polite I thought I might get his mother's address and send my kids for a refresher course." She hesitated at the door. "Mike, let's give the kid a little privacy." She walked out, jerking her head as a signal for him to follow.

Mike stood and ambled to the door. "Cathy, you look as tired as I feel. I'm sorry I had to impose on you."

"That's okay, Mike," she said, smiling sincerely.

He took a long, concerned, last look at her. "Take care of yourself, kid," he said with a smile as he turned and shuffled out the door.

In the empty room she felt her headache returning. She eased a thumb and forefinger around the bridge of her nose and into the corners of her eyes and tried to pinch the throb away. The job was over. The euphoric rush of performing was gone, replaced by what seemed an ever more cavernous depression. A pleasant thought beat back the blues momentarily. She hurried to the door and stuck her head into the studio. "Mike, is Lyn gone?"

"Yeah," Mike called over his shoulder. "He hustled into his dressing room, changed, gave me his voucher, and was outa' here. I don't think he even bothered to take off his makeup."

"Thanks." She shook her head at her foolishness as she backed into the room and closed the door. What was she going to do if he hadn't left? Invite him in? What would she have said? "Lynell, I'm kind of lonely and depressed. Would you talk to me?" Men were men and he'd have probably taken it as an invitation, she thought cynically. *Lynell, I'm kind of lonely and depressed. Would you fuck me?* But somehow he didn't seem like most men.

Her nose was running again—it seemed it was constantly running.

17

She reached into her purse for a handful of tissues and was gripped by an intense fear that wrenched her gut like a tightening fist.

She thought again of Lynell Alan. She could have told him how cute it was that he had gotten an erection during the last take when she had worn the green Halston. Actually it had been disconcerting until she realized he was so into the mood he hadn't seemed to notice. And it *was* cute when the shooting was over and he'd stuffed his hands into his pockets and fairly raced off the set. But she was only trying to distract herself now as she raised the wad of tissues to her nose. Her eyes were still closed when she slowly pulled her hands from her face with a fear as crimson as the tissues.

A smile spread across Aimée Harris's face as she replaced the receiver on its cradle. She looked up from the papers in front of her, put her elbows on the desk, and rested her chin on her fists dreamily. "I know it's only three o'clock and you might be too busy," Lynell had apologized, "but I was just in the neighborhood and I thought I'd drop in if you have a minute."

So she sat in her office on the forty-second floor of 747 Fifth Avenue and gazed out over the gray skyline, waiting for him to appear. She loved him more, she was sure, than he knew, though precisely why was sometimes still a mystery even to her. There had been so many men before him, so few since—and there needn't have been any. He had so much to give and at times he gave it all: the talking, the listening, the caring. He made her know she could do anything, be anything. And when he loved her it was an effortless extension of their interpersonal relationship, and neither had happened overnight. Oh, they had liked each other right away, had seen the potential right away. But emotionally *and* sexually it had taken years to perfect: touching, feeling, responding. But the sex was easier. Emotionally it still wasn't perfect. Maybe it never would be. Maybe it never could be.

He made love to her with a gentle, unrestrained ease that danced with his fingers, with his lips, through every fiber of her; with a needing and feeling that drifted her into a tactile dream, floated her into a weightless abyss of not caring, not worrying, not thinking, not focusing, of her skin tingling so her whole body, every inch of her body, slipped gently into a blurred delirium, and she would awaken to wonder how long she had been writhing beneath him, slick with their perspiration, focusing white-hot, clutching, sobbing, staying inside her forever into the night, until he was always inside her, was inside her now.

The buzz of the interoffice phone snapped her back, flushed with an excitement out of place in these sterile surroundings. "Ms. Harris, Lynell Alan to see you."

"Send him in, please." The thought edged its way back. . . . But he could be so moody—had been for a couple of weeks now. She prayed he would break out of this funk soon.

"You just don't understand, Aimée," he'd said. "I enjoy modeling—the excitement, the people I meet, the whole aura of glamour—not to mention the fantastic opportunity I have now that I'm with Cline. But even with Cline, the most prestigious agency in the world, not even the top two or three men have the luxury of being booked more than a couple of weeks ahead. Unless I continually land more bookings, when I finish my next few jobs I'll be out of work, unemployed. And it will probably always be that way, no matter how successful I'm lucky enough to become. I face the constant worry that I may never get another booking. You just don't understand the insecurity," he'd finished with a shake of his head.

But she did understand. That he could give her so much made her all the emptier when he took it away, made her desperate that she would never get it back, left her emotionally unemployed.

"You look great!" he said cheerfully as he leaned over the desk to kiss her. "I'm going to have to start setting my alarm to make sure I get up with you every morning. No man in his right mind would let a woman out of the house alone looking that good." He leered playfully at her and winked suggestively.

"Well, everyone knows *you're* not in your right mind."

"Touché," he said dryly, hanging his coat and the shoulder bag that contained his portfolio over the back of the chair opposite her and sitting heavily.

"Praise be to the all-American boy with his Shetland sweater and faded blue jeans."

"Today was all-American-boy day."

"I see it took you a pound of makeup to achieve the effect."

"Oh, shit, I forgot," he said, stroking his cheek, looking at his bronze-stained fingers and wiping them on his pants. "Well, my all-American-boy days are a few years behind me." He looked appraisingly around the small office. "Couldn't Mortimer & Snerd splurge on a bigger office?"

"It's Morton & Stearns, and I haven't been here six months and this office is fine and why are you so full of it today?"

"I just earned you another seventy-five dollars," he said, waving his copy of the job voucher in front of him.

"Be still, my heart." She beat the left side of her chest lightly with her right hand. "Lynell," she said, "I don't want it. I don't need it. I . . ."

"I know. You earn twice as much as I do in a good year. But with a little luck—and a lot more hard work—that could change now. And besides, we made a bargain and I'm sticking to it. If it weren't for you I wouldn't be making anything in this business. You earn your ten percent."

"But that's just it. I don't earn it." It was hopeless, she knew. She wished he wouldn't give her the money. He needed it more than she did. He had been dipping into the special account of his for years, the one he kept for taxes, retirement, and what savings he could muster. Now that the money was starting to come in he should be replacing it. But she had long ago resolved her internal conflict about the money by opening a trust account in his name, with herself as trustee. If someday it ever accumulated significantly, she had already decided on a perfect use for the money. One thing was certain: it was not her money and she would never spend it on herself—ever. For once she was thankful for the interruption of John Hayes, an associate in the firm who, though barely Lynell's age, looked ten years older.

"Hey, Aimée," he called, sticking his head in the open door. "You tell him it's two hundred dollars an hour?"

"Jesus, it's only twenty-five in Times Square."

"Lyn," she told him, "don't be fresh."

The two men harbored a thinly veiled dislike for one another that, of the three of them, only Aimée had considered long enough to recognize as territoriality. Hayes looked from his watch to Lynell and sneered, "When are you going to get a job, Alan?"

Lynell turned and looked over his shoulder at the squat, balding man. "On the day you get a hair transplant, Hayes."

"Now, boys," Aimée intervened, putting her palms up like traffic cop. "John." She nodded to Hayes as if to say, Be patient with him, he's only a child. "Please . . ."

Hayes grinned sheepishly, returned her nod, and left without another word.

"God, I hate that guy," Lynell said. "He's such a creep."

"He's never done a thing to you, Lyn."

"It's not what he's done to me, it's what he wants to do to you. Look, Aimée, all three of us know he's had his eye on your pants since the day you started here. Anyway, isn't being a creep enough reason to hate the guy?"

20

"Come on, he's harmless."

"Yeah, that's what the czar said about Rasputin."

She laughed in spite of herself and shook her head slowly. He was so much like a child sometimes. She moved to change the subject. "So, what have you done today besides make me rich beyond my dreams?"

"Jesus, maybe you *should* take up with Hayes," he joked. "As I said on the phone, I was in the neighborhood and just thought I'd stop in to say hello and ask you out to dinner. How about the China Pavilion?"

"I don't think I'll get out of here until seven, seven-thirty. I've got this case to prepare," she said, indicating the mountainous paperwork in front of her.

"Perfect. I'll meet you there. Is it a date?"

"It's a date."

As he left he passed Aimée's secretary in the doorway. "What a hunk," the young woman said instinctively after he was gone. Then she looked at her boss apologetically.

"Yes," Aimée agreed as she slipped on her glasses and signed the papers the young woman had placed in front of her. When she was alone again, Aimée took off her glasses and the adolescent grin returned to her face. At the time she and Lynell had met in Boston three summers ago, she had been dating a classmate at Harvard Law School for several months. Todd Thornton was from old money. He was sophisticated and attractive and the son of a Boston real estate magnate. They had planned to rent an apartment together in the fall. She had liked Todd, maybe even loved him. But that was a big maybe, and her relationship with him hadn't kept her from a string of casual affairs and one-nighters that ran the gamut from straight sex on the baseball field with a teenager who washed dishes in the university dining hall to giving head to a middle-aged law professor in his library while his wife entertained her bridge club in the next room.

It was often difficult for her to believe that girl had been Aimée Harris. It was like looking through a haze of years at another woman's youth. Sex then had been like a game—like *watching* a game, really: watching the urgent, taut striving of a boy or a man, then exulting in some victory she could never quite comprehend. It was as though she was helping someone else to celebrate, cheering for a touchdown or a home run but never *being* cheered. The irony was that it always left her so hollow and unfulfilled she had to be needed all the more, had to share in yet another victory.

But with Lynell the applause was hers, was theirs. For the first time

21

the cheers were for her, too. The day after she and Lynell first slept together she had called Todd Thornton. "I'm sorry, Todd, but there has been a change of plans."

That summer there was only Lynell. And her final year at Harvard Law School there was only Lynell. And there would still be only Lynell, if he just didn't force her out of his life like this. Then the cheering stopped, and the silence would become so deafening she would remember the way it used to be.

She shook herself out of her gloomy reverie. He was on his way up the ladder. Maybe if he could climb the last few rungs he'd finally realize it himself; and at least if the ladder was pulled out from underneath him he had his family's business in Connecticut and a soft place to fall. Either way he could get off this emotional roller coaster once and for all—and she with him. He had seemed in a good mood. It had to hold through tonight, to the China Pavilion and into the days ahead. It had to—for her sake.

Lynell Alan was back on the street, $750 richer, but on paper only. Lord only knew when he'd be paid; he sure as hell didn't. At Munson, by the time the agency had billed the client, was paid itself, then fiddle-fucked around before paying *him*, it was usually at least two months and sometimes as long as six.

He hurried across Thirty-ninth Street, turned right until he reached Lexington Avenue, then headed north into the teeth of a damp, blustery, late-February wind. What a bleak place New York City was in winter, he thought as he watched discarded papers swirling in eddies around the oncoming pedestrians. Everything noisy and filthy. He longed for the sudden, unexpected, and tantalizing April heat wave, when underdressed young women blossomed like the flowers in suburbia, unveiling their delicate petals for the first time since the Indian-summer days of early October. As he approached the Forty-second Street subway entrance he felt as far from those days as he did from success. For in spite of the fact that *he* was now a Cline model, he wouldn't delude himself into thinking that alone would cause bookings to fall into his lap. He'd still have to go out and hustle. And that was the hard part, the demeaning part.

Three steps down the stairway he changed his mind about returning to the apartment. True, he'd worked from ten to twelve and one to two, and earned a pretty fair day's pay. But after deducting the twenty percent commission the Cline Agency skimmed off the top and the thirty percent he put aside for Uncle Sam, health insurance, and per sonal retirement savings, he figured about fifty percent was actually his. Forty percent: he'd forgotten the ten percent he paid Aimée for her role in his "discovery" and her ongoing legal advice. But he didn't have the money now. And as long as he could keep racking up the modeling fees—and showing the agency he could earn his keep—he had to keep pushing himself, because who knew when it would all end? He had climbed aboard the last train for the big time when they had taken him at Cline. Now he had to ride it for all he was worth.

"Shit!" he said disgustedly. He couldn't afford to go back to the apartment. (He could never quite think of it as "home.") What he had to do was impress his new agent with his diligence. Maybe he'd make a few rounds before five to renew some contacts and try to escape the graveyard that was filled with models who'd changed agents. Because if a client still didn't know he'd switched agencies and called Munson looking for him, Gretchen would sure as hell tell them he was dead, retired, or in Denmark having a sex-change operation, and she'd have a replacement on the job in a minute.

So he would drop in, report on today's booking, and hand in his voucher in person. He'd keep his face in LeeAnn's mind, his name on the tip of her tongue. Some models treated bookers like dirt, but he knew they were the most important people in the agency. He'd be nice to LeeAnn, and when a call came in for his "type," maybe she would think of him.

He pulled his scarf tighter around his neck and slogged on. The cold grayness of the day was mirrored in the faces of the passersby. Only in this city would he not have bothered to remove his makeup after the day's shooting.

He quickened his pace, hoping it would warm him. He should wear a hat, he knew, but it would crush his curls and he always had to look his best, keep the "product" in shape. The thought reminded him and he shook his head in exasperation. He'd have to run in the dark again tonight. Always keep the product in shape. At least he enjoyed running. That he did on weekends, too. But trying to look his best? Anyone who'd ever depended on it for a living knew what a burden it could become. Whenever weekends were his—and they weren't always— he'd look like a slob, dress like a slob, go unshaven.

"It's amazing that someone who can look as *good* as you can, can look as *bad* as you can," Aimée had once complained.

"Do you carry a briefcase on Sunday?" he asked.

She had never mentioned it again.

"Hi, LeeAnn." God, did it sound too cheery to her, too? "Here's my voucher: Lynell Alan." He articulated his name carefully, as he had

23

each time he had come in, giving it not so much to take *her* off the hook as to take his own *ego* off the hook in case she didn't remember him after such a short time with the agency. There was, after all, a constant turnover among the perhaps fifty Cline Men, and she couldn't be expected to remember them all at any given time. And in this business there was plenty of rejection to go around without inviting it from your own booker. "Three hours with Mike Dudley for Halston."

"Great, Lyn. How'd it go?"

"Fine. Just clinches," he said, pantomiming embracing a lover. "I've worked with Mike before so it was no sweat." It didn't seem to matter that he referred to himself as "Lynell," always introducing himself with the full name. He'd never escape being called "Lyn" except by his few close friends, who knew his intense aversion to the nickname, to all nicknames. Aimée only called him "Lyn" when she was pissed off. "Oh, LeeAnn, I almost forgot. Here are those composites you wanted." He handed her a stack of the five-by-eight calling cards the agency would circulate to prospective clients and that he would hand out to almost anyone who would take one.

"These are good, Lyn." After admiring the full-face photograph on the front of the top card, she flipped it and checked the two prints that shared the back side with his physical details—height: 6'2"; weight: 175; waist: 32; inseam: 32; suit: 40R—and the agency's name, address, and telephone number. Nodding with approval, she flipped it again to the front.

She was thumbing through her messages. He could tell without asking that she was a former model: the trim figure, perfect teeth, large brown eyes, and fine angular features. But at what he guessed to be her early forties—though she was still an attractive woman—her face had been falling for a good fifteen years since her prime. He wondered if she'd been big and had squandered her money, or if she'd never quite made it. He wondered if Albert Cline had used her in her youth, was still using her now. And he wondered if he'd ever meet The Man and The Woman who owned the biggest modeling agency in the world, who probably knew only a handful of their entire stable of models even existed: the "superstars," the "franchise-makers," like the Christie Brinkleys and the Jeff Aquilons and the Cheryl Tiegses. Albert and Mary Cline certainly didn't know Lynell Alan existed. But they would, Lynell decided as LeeAnn looked up from her desk. He suddenly felt intensely sorry for her, for himself. By God, he wouldn't struggle to the end of the rainbow just to find there was nothing there.

24

"I'm sorry, Lyn, but there doesn't seem to be anything here I can send you on. Nothing in your age range."

Lynell wondered what LeeAnn considered his "age range"—probably twenty-five to thirty-five. Though he was thirty-one, he had written twenty-seven on the information card. (Or had it been twenty-eight? He couldn't remember.) He was fairly sure he could pass for that . . . most days . . . after 10 A.M., anyway. "That's okay," he said. "I just wanted to stop and check in, and leave these composites for you." He wasn't at all disappointed. After all, he had worked a few hours today, which already made it better than most days at Munson. "I'll see you tomorrow," he said, slinging his bag over his shoulder and heading for the door.

Outside on Lexington Avenue Lynell thought briefly of Gretchen over at the Munson Agency. He hadn't yet notified her of his defection, either in person or by telephone. The reason was not that he was afraid to face Gretchen or that he had any doubt at all that he was now precisely where he wanted to be. In fact, he would have loved nothing better than to visit Munson's seedy offices one last time just to tell Gretchen off, as he had wanted to since his first day in New York over a year ago. But that sudden emptiness had flooded through him again. He had no written contract with Cline Models and he wanted to make damn sure of his position with them first. One of his mother's favorite expressions echoed in his brain: "Never burn your bridges." *Play it smart,* he thought as he began walking south. *You don't owe Gretchen or the Munson Agency or anyone else a damn thing. Practically every penny you earned over there you earned on your own. Let them find out you dumped them the same way. But for now, you just might still need them.*

At the corner of Fiftieth Street the row of pay phones caught his eye, and guilt and fear rose up in him simultaneously. It was a dangerous game, playing one agent off against another. Too dangerous. He had to be on the up and up. He owed it to LeeAnn for putting her faith in him. He owed it to himself. And it was something he'd been waiting over a year to do. On impulse he stopped, dialed.

"The Munson Agency," came the all-too-familiar tone of superiority. "Gretchen speaking."

And he told her. Simply. Directly. Politely. With none of the venom that had been building up inside him for so long. "Gretchen, this is Lynell Alan. I've decided to go with another agency."

"Really?" she said haughtily. "Well, maybe you'll have more luck with someone else. You certainly haven't put too many filet mignons

25

on *my* dinner table." Then, almost as an afterthought, as though it didn't matter in the least to her but only to him, she asked, "What agency are you going with? In case a client calls for you."

Lying bitch to the end, he thought. She would let them rip her fingernails out one by one before she would tell a client who he was with. But he was proud of being with Cline, no matter how short-lived the association might turn out to be, so he told her.

"You'll get lost in the shuffle over there," Gretchen said with bitterness creeping suddenly and viciously into her voice. *"You just haven't got it!"*

He sighed, then hung his head slightly, but only because she couldn't see him. "Maybe you're right," he said softly. His eyes momentarily lost their focus, his ears shut out the sounds of the traffic—screaming whistles, blaring horns, screeching tires—and he concentrated only on the future. But the picture wouldn't form in his mind. "Maybe I haven't got it," he continued. "But at least now I have a chance to really find out."

There was a long silence at Gretchen's end of the line, so long that at first Lynell thought she might have hung up on him. When she finally spoke again she was uncharacteristically contrite. "I'm sorry, Lynell. It's not you I'm angry with. It's the system. We find them. Mary Cline steals them. I don't blame you. And just to show you there are no hard feelings, I have a last go-see for you. Let's see . . . here it is. Franco Canero called a couple of times. He's doing some testing over at his studio today. He used to be pretty big-time, Lyn. If he likes you and wants you to test, he could probably still open some doors for you. And I promised him I'd send you over. If you do get a job out of it you can tell Mary Cline she owes me a favor."

Lynell was immediately suspicious. Gretchen doing a favor?! Actually, it wasn't much of a favor. Testing was demeaning to an experienced model. He could rationalize that he needed to change some of the shots in his portfolio and that it could eventually lead to a job. But what it usually came down to was working for free. It was invariably an experiment—either unusual lighting, a new camera, or an innovative technique—and the photographer needed a free model, a guinea pig. Sometimes a bastard would even have the balls to charge him for a print of a shot he wanted. Lynell usually requested at least one print if only to justify the time spent, or so he wouldn't insult the photographer's work. He rarely used them in his book, though. He preferred tearsheets—actual advertisements he clipped from magazines, newspapers, and catalogues—to show that he worked. "The more you work, the more you work," was a basic truism of this, as much as any other, profession. Oh, well, what did he have to lose? An hour of his time? Every go-see was a long shot anyway. And if this one paid off . . . "What's the address?"

"He's at 281 Madison, between Thirty-ninth and Fortieth, the penthouse."

"What time does he want me there?"

"Two hours ago. But you can run over there now. He'll be there until five. I'll call to let him know you're coming."

Walking south along Madison he remembered he still hadn't removed his makeup. He'd meant to do it at the agency. The lingering memory of LeeAnn made him feel old and very tired. He took his time getting to Canero's studio, inhaling deep gulps of what passed in Manhattan for fresh air, its chill somehow making it seem less putrid. It was turning out to be a very long day.

Gretchen Saczynski hung up the telephone and looked across the reception room at her own smugly grinning reflection on the mirrored wall. Every reputable agency in the city had stopped dealing with Franco Canero years ago. Lynell Alan would find no job there. He would find only a down-on-his-luck has-been and—at the very least—a demeaning experience. Gretchen began to laugh out loud at the thought. It was a cruel laugh, a frightening laugh, a laugh worthy of all the rancor in her heart.

For Lynell, running had over the past ten years become a religion— like daily weigh-ins and crash diets after eating binges. Sometimes he longed to be an overweight and out-of-shape Connecticut dirt-farmer like his father and his father's father before him and not give a damn, just so he wouldn't have to keep abusing his thirty-one-year-old body like this.

It was early evening by the time he got to run. He dodged the pedestrians along Third Avenue and cut across to First, where the foot traffic was less dense. He hadn't felt much in the mood for running today. He was tired and depressed. Tired because since it was still well before five when he had left Franco Canero's studio, he had dutifully called the agency again and LeeAnn had gratefully sent him off to Bloomingdale's. He had literally run the twenty-one blocks to make the curtain on a fashion show, and even though it was as a fill-in for a no-show, it was another hour and a half of work and lots of appreciation from LeeAnn and the fashion directors at Bloomingdale's, and contacts, contacts, contacts.

But he couldn't erase Franco Canero from his mind . . . or the nagging anxiety that weighed so heavily on him—the anxiety of being so close . . . so close he could almost touch it. Nor could he erase all the sleazy things he'd had to do to get here. God, the pressure to succeed. It was strange, but when he was back with Munson it just hadn't been there. Just schlep along merrily from job to job, doing the best you can. And always, always, there was the outside chance you could catch on with one of the better agencies . . . maybe even the *best*. And now he was with the best. And he was scared shitless. Scared because there was nowhere left for him to go. No longer could he blame his failures on his booker or his agency. The opportunity was there, and he *had* to deliver or he was through.

Ironically, it was on days like this that running felt best—afterward, of course—days when he never quite got his second wind, days when it hurt from the first step to the last and he covered the entire ten miles on guts alone. It was on days like this, when he was out of sync for the whole hour and five minutes, that his mind raced at a feverish pitch and he was able to remove himself as far from the pain in his body as was humanly possible.

He had no idea what Aimée expected of him. In fact, he had no idea what he expected of himself. If on the outside chance he made it to the top, fame would certainly be fleeting. On the other hand, if he didn't keep working more and more he'd be out of business, replaced by a younger, better-looking man. Either road pointed back home to the family nursery-business in Pine Orchard. And Connecticut, after all, wasn't such a terrible fate. He'd just wanted so desperately to break the mold. Funny—Aimée, with her youth and indomitable spirit, had once been his link to that break, but now, as she gained more and more responsibility, she had become instead his link to stability.

Their apartment building loomed through the twilight and again pain seared his thighs. Just when he was sure he couldn't take one more step, he picked up his pace, knowing he would make it because he always did. Life should be this easy, he thought as he lowered his head and broke into a final lung-bursting sprint.

Book 1

1

Catherine Ward was living proof of the adage "You can't judge a book by its cover." To her, being 5'11", 135 pounds, 36-24-36, and a chisel-featured natural blonde had been an almost lifelong curse—albeit one that had allowed her to escape Ames, Iowa, for New York City at eighteen with the hope of becoming the world's next Christie Brinkley.

Though convinced that she was not gay, that she would be interested if Mr. Right ever came along, she rarely initiated her own sexual fantasies with a man. That just brought back painful memories. Rather, she was constantly confronted by everyday lechery—the stares, the whistles, the lewd remarks from the anonymity of the crowd. "How'd ya' like a piece of that?" "Bet she gives great head." And the overt passes. Then came the repulsive images of hairy, muscled, acrid, sweat-smelling bodies relentlessly invading her.

For all her looks and money, Catherine had no love in her life. But she neither wanted nor needed another lover. What she wanted was a friend. What she needed—and needed desperately—was help.

It had been fourteen years since February 5, 1968, the day her father hadn't made the rotary known as Kenilworth Circle, on the outskirts of Morgan City, Iowa. The end of William F. Ward's life had marked the beginning of Catherine Ellen Ward's nightmare.

It was as though Catherine had had two separate childhoods. The faded memories of her handsome young father—memories all but lost without the dog-eared family portrait she carried in her wallet—still tied a painful knot in her stomach after all these years. Somehow the sense lingered that the man with the wavy brown hair and penetrating blue eyes had let them down by removing his bright presence from their lives, had let her and her mother down by not being there to love and protect them, had let them down . . . by dying.

Catherine's father was a big man, six-feet, four inches tall and well over two hundred pounds. Except for the four years he studied agriculture at the University of Minnesota, William Ward had spent his entire life on his family's northern Iowa farm. He was attractive in a pleasant, bearish sort of way, though by thirty his face was as craggy and weathered as the arid stretch of farmland he and his small crew of men worked tirelessly from sunrise to sunset. With the anxiety of each new harvesting season, his curly brown hair gathered more and more flecks of silver. "The land makes a man grow old before his time," he often told his young daughter.

If Catherine was to inherit her father's height, then it was certainly from her mother that she would get her striking good looks. Pamela Olson was a slim, lanky, statuesque blonde in the finest Scandinavian tradition. An orphan from St. Paul, she earned a scholarship to the state university in 1960 when, at nineteen, after interminable rounds of preliminary beauty contests, she was selected as Minnesota's representative to the Miss America Pageant. Pamela, eventually voted Third Runnerup, was the type the television audience guesses will win on looks alone, yet never does. But her real consolation prize was meeting Bill Ward at the university. They were married in 1961 and Catherine was born a year later.

Life was a continuous adventure for a small child growing up on a farm. Though there were few neighbors Catherine's age for her to play with, she had her family. As she grew older, there were more and more light chores for her to do.

Ironically, once Catherine entered school her loneliness only intensified. A skinny, gawky girl, she already towered over her classmates, who were unable to decide if she was more comical standing in her knock-kneed, self-conscious crouch or prancing about awkwardly on her spindly legs like a whooping crane. Inevitably, her nickname in school became "Stork." But to her doting father she was only "My Beauty. Oh, you're going to be something, Beauty, truly you are—prettier than Marilyn Monroe. But when all the boys start coming around, don't you leave your Daddy, okay? Because I'll never leave my Beauty."

"I won't, Daddy," she would say bashfully.

"Promise?"

"I promise, Daddy."

But it was her Daddy who had left her when his battered pickup truck slammed into a utility pole, killing him instantly. Five-year-old Catherine would never recover from the blow.

Helen Warshaw, a junior high school classmate and next-door neighbor, was Catherine's first real friend. She was half a foot shorter than Catherine and, though the same age, had already begun to fill out. Catherine envied her not only her relatively slight stature but the sensuous roundness of her breasts, which seemed to attract every boy in school.

During the summer of their thirteenth year, in the small, muddy pond that abutted their two farms, Catherine and Helen shared their first sexual experience, a tentative and innocent groping inside bathing suits, that spoke more of curiosity than of sex. It was the kind of fumbling discovery that transformed their relationship from one of two little girls into one of two young females crossing into womanhood. And for Catherine, after all those years as a loner, there was finally someone with whom she could share the insecurities of adolescence.

They talked about everything teenage girls talk about, and more. They gossiped about school and their teachers, about rock stars and movie queens and, of course, about boys. It was also to Helen that Catherine recalled the nightmare of her father's death.

But the real nightmare was still three years away. It arrived one Saturday afternoon wearing a grease-stained, olive-drab jumpsuit with a red star and the name "Bobby" sewn on the pocket. It came to fix her mother's car. It never left.

Why Pamela Olson Ward married Bobby Stillwell was a mystery to Catherine, unless her mother had experienced some mid-life rejuvenation in the company of a man whose age was roughly halfway between the twenty years that separated mother and daughter. He had a dark complexion and thick black hair that was only slightly thinner on his heavily muscled arms and legs than it was on the top of his head. His mouth dipped at the corners into a cruel smirk that even a neatly trimmed moustache couldn't hide, and even on the mornings when he bothered to shave, his face bore the dusky blue shadow of a full day's growth. A leer was the closest Catherine could ever remember that mouth approaching a smile.

But it was his hands that bothered her most. They were thickly knuckled and rough with calluses, and his fingernails, no matter how closely he chewed them, were perpetually underlaid with a thin black

33

crescent of grease. Catherine shivered at the mere thought of his touch.

"He's always pawing me," she told Helen with disgust, brushing her friend lightly in intimate places in imitation.

"Yech!" Helen said and they shivered in unison. "Your mother could do so much better than that creep."

"Don't I know it."

Gooseflesh rose along Catherine's arms at the mere idea of him, her thoughts redolent with the memory of stale cigar smoke and cheap alcohol. He looked at her the way the boys in her high school were beginning to look at her—in a way that made her wish her growing breasts and gently curving hips would disappear, made her wish she were less conspicuous, wish she were . . . shorter.

"Oh, excuse me, kid," he apologized halfheartedly after lurching into her room one day without knocking. Then he turned away, feigning embarrassment, and closed the door behind him. She stood frozen on that spot in the middle of the polished wood floor, because he had *seen* her little rounding breasts and the sprouting down. He had *seen* her and *looked* at her so that those private places were private no more but were seared white-hot by his lascivious stare. Catherine vowed she would always keep the door locked. Then she slumped her shoulders as the tension drained from her, and he stuck his head back into her room and slowly slid his narrow eyes up and down along her naked body as she stood riveted to the floor. "Nice," he whispered with an appraising nod, and she ran to the door and slammed and locked it against him, but it was too late.

And that night she was alone with him because her mother was working late again. "You be a good girl and mind Bobby and help around the house."

She should have told her mother she was afraid of Bobby. But her mother loved him, and after all, what was there really to fear? So she lay in her bed, cool in her pale blue nylon nightgown, warm in her bed, but cold in the pit of her stomach. The television was too loud. It was keeping her awake. But as long as Bobby had forgotten she was there . . .

Oh, God, was that Bobby trying her door? No, it had to be something on TV. "Hey, kid."

Fear squeezed her heart to a stop.

"Open up." Bobby rattled the doorknob with a rising anger. "Come on, I just want to say g'night."

She could almost smell the whiskey through the heavy pine door.

34

"I'm in bed," she whispered in a small voice that was not her own. She brought her hand to her mouth and felt ice-cold perspiration drip from her armpits, though the August night was sultry.

His pounding reverberated through the door and thundered in her chest. "I said open the fucking door, you little whore!"

She should have opened the door before he got angry. Oh, God. Mother, please come home. Would he rub against her again? Kiss her like her father had never kissed her? "Movie star kisses" like she and Helen practiced, stroking each other's breasts, sometimes touching between the legs like they did in the R-rated movies they sneaked into at the Center Cinema on Saturday nights. But it was exciting with Helen because she wasn't afraid of Helen.

When he shouldered through the door the wood splintered, sending pieces of the broken lock sliding across the floor. "You little cunt! Who the fuck do you think you are? The Queen of England? I tell you to open the door, you open the fucking door."

She pulled herself up stiffly against the headboard, the sheet gripped tightly against her shoulders. The light from the television washed the side of his face a deathly blue-gray. She wished she had surrounded her bed with burning candles like they had in *The Zombies Return*, but there was nothing to keep him from coming to her.

"Hey, kid, I'm sorry." He sat on the edge of her bed and stroked her hair with a pathetic, fumbling gentleness. "I just want to say goodnight, to be nice."

"Goodnight," she whispered.

"You're not afraid of Bobby, are you?" His hand stroked her hair, her throat, her bare shoulder. "You're a real woman, aren't you, kid?" He snatched away the covers before she could react.

"No," she said. How many times in her life had she protested, "I'm not a little girl"? And oh, how she wished she were now, so there wouldn't even be these tiny sloping breasts for him to look at, to touch, so her father would still be here. "Please," she sobbed.

"Please what? Please do it to me, Bobby?" he slurred drunkenly.

"No."

"It'll feel good. I promise it will."

"No." She began sniffling.

"Okay, okay," he said nodding reluctant agreement. "You win." His hands slid up over her a final time, once more cupping each small breast through the sheer nylon before continuing up over the neckline of her nightgown.

Thank God that was all. But she would tell her mother this time.

When he grabbed her nightgown and tore it to her waist, it was as terrifying as the moment when he had stuck his head back inside her door and said, "Nice."

"No," she screamed, but James Garner was screaming louder from the living room. She scrambled instinctively over the bed, past Bobby's shadow. Her hot tears splashed on her cheek as the back of Bobby's hand ripped across her face, stunning her and sending her sprawling onto the cold pine floor. He was beside her, his hand tight around her slim throat.

"Now, you shut up or I'll hurt you, bitch. You fight, or scream, and I swear to God I'll get a fucking razor blade and slice that perfect nose right off that perfect little face." He emphasized each verb by slamming her head against the floor and she knew through her semi-conscious daze that he would do it. Her muffled sobs shook her, as the shadow of a nightmare lowered itself over her. She heard a distant ripping, felt a searing pain, smelled the whiskey, heard a deep, guttural groaning, and when he rolled her limply onto her stomach she fainted.

Only his heavy work-shoe digging into her ribs brought her back into the nightmare. He stood over her laughing, zipping himself, and she knew in her soreness that he had violated her again, unthinkably.

"Clean yourself up. And you tell a soul, I'll make it so's you ain't pretty no more, kid." He slammed the door behind him, but it wouldn't close all the way without its lock. Catherine lay paralyzed. When she sat up she hated her compact breasts, hated her flat stomach, glistening with his pungent sweat, hated the dark, moist rise. God, would she bleed to death? she wondered in panic, just before she began to pray that she would. But she hadn't bled to death and the rest was too painful to remember, too shameful to remember. But she had to remember. Always she had to remember.

Helen had sensed the change in her friend and felt the involuntary flinch when she touched her even casually, as though touching was no longer enjoyable for Catherine. At the same time as Helen was developing an ever-increasing interest in boys, with whom she now spent the majority of her time, Catherine seemed to be developing an inordinate fear of them. Even in school she was withdrawn. From time to time, one of her teachers would be impressed by her diligence and try to coax a bit more class participation from her, and occasionally a boy would be so taken by her striking looks and rounding figure, he would forget the disparity of their heights and risk almost certain rejection from the icy loner. But otherwise, her closest human contact was with Bobby

Stillwell, who for almost three weeks came to her bed. Who could she tell? Not her mother. Who could possibly share her humiliation, her degradation, her pain?

Ultimately, of course, it was Helen she told. Helen, who would understand, who would sympathize, who might find some miraculous way to help her out of this purgatory, and who would, above all, guard her shameful secret.

But when the tale was finally, mercifully over, Helen held her sobbing friend in her arms and vowed inwardly that, no matter what she had promised, she would tell her own mother and they would see Bobby Stillwell hang by his lousy balls.

Two days later Kurt Weiss, Morgan City's Chief of Police, drove up to Kelsey's Texaco Station on West Main Street with his deputy and quietly placed Bobby Stillwell under arrest.

Mortified. It was the perfect word—the only word—to describe how Catherine Ward felt. That anyone else knew what Bobby Stillwell had done to her was almost more than she could bear. She had trusted Helen, and because of her betrayal everyone would know. Her mother would know. She wanted to die, but the dozen Valium she found in her mother's medicine cabinet only succeeded in landing her in the hospital and adding fuel to the rumors already rampant in the small village.

"Disloyal" was, amazingly, the word her mother used. "This is a family matter and you should have had the sense to keep it in the family. My God, Catherine, that man is my *husband*. He's your step-father. Maybe he made a mistake, but we don't need the police to correct it. Damn it, they've got him down there in a cage like a common criminal. And I suppose you're going to say it was all his fault? He's just a man! Haven't I warned you about parading around half naked? About leaving your bedroom door open? For heaven's sake, what did you expect? Bobby isn't a child molester. Look at you. Just *look* at you! You're sixteen years old—almost a woman. This whole business is as much your fault as his. Can't you see that, Catherine? You've humiliated me in front of this entire town. What are people going to say?" Never, not once in the thirty minutes her mother was in her sterile, ether-smelling room, did she ask, "Catherine, are you all right?" Not once.

The police wouldn't allow Pamela Stillwell to speak with her husband immediately, and when she saw him for the first time in the presence of his attorney, the prosecutor, and a police officer, she kissed him fondly and passed him a note which the police officer intercepted and which the prosecutor was shocked to find read, *Catherine's sorry. I still love you. Can't wait until you're home again.*

But Bobby Stillwell never came home. Though Kurt Weiss— against his better judgment—was forced to release him for lack of evidence when Catherine refused to repeat the story she had told to Helen Warshaw, neither Catherine nor her mother ever saw Bobby Stillwell again.

What he did was jump into his dusty pickup truck and head west, leaving his meager belongings behind. What Catherine did was live quietly with her mother, anesthetized to the gossip, lurching like a feral cat at each unfamiliar sound. All of her spare time she spent alone, consumed with reading, but even the people she met and the places she traveled to in books couldn't dig her out from under the crushing burden of loneliness and despair.

For her mother she felt nothing at all. She saw her only as a stick of furniture that you move from room to room, knowing all the while that eventually you'll throw it out because it doesn't seem to match any of your new things. For Helen Warshaw she felt unreasoning rage, for although she had removed a nightmare from her life, it had been replaced by another that Catherine feared almost more: her most intimate secrets had been revealed to an unsympathetic world. In a perverse sort of way she almost missed Bobby Stillwell. He might have degraded her, but sometimes, sometimes he had whispered the word "love."

It was early in the autumn of her senior year that Catherine arrived home one afternoon to find her mother hanging from the rafters in the master bedroom of their century-old ten-room farmhouse. In their euphemistic media vernacular, the local newspaper reported that Pamela Stillwell had "died suddenly." But although the manner of her death was indeed sudden, it could have been truthfully reported, as Catherine noted it had been for a sprinkling of senior citizens who shared the obituary page with her mother, that she had died "after a long illness." For as surely as those seventy- and eighty-year-olds had gradually disintegrated from the ravages of cancer or hardening of the arteries, her mother had since the death of Catherine's father been suffering from an equally insidious disease: a broken heart. It had just taken her twelve years to die.

For Catherine, her mother's suicide brought no anguished sense of loss, not even the gnawing and instinctively selfish question "What will become of me?" Catherine had experienced the loss months ago, as though her mother had already died, and she had been asking herself that question ever since she could remember.

But the answer was out of her control. On September 30, 1979, the day before her seventeenth birthday, her paternal grandmother, Constance Ward, arrived to take Catherine home with her to Ames, where she had moved after the death of her husband. She found her granddaughter alone in the old farmhouse, sitting pensively at the kitchen table. She clasped the young child's shoulders firmly, kneading the tightly knotted muscles affectionately. When Catherine looked up over her shoulder into her grandmother's eyes, the old woman wrapped the child's head protectively in her arms and held it to her breast. So much hurt in those sad young eyes, so much disillusion. "You know I'll always be here for you, dear," she whispered. "You'll always have your Nana." It was the same promise her father had made so long ago.

And one more time Catherine Ward awoke in the middle of the lonely night to the street noises of Manhattan clanging below, and she knew sleep would not come again. She thought again of Bobby Stillwell and wondered if it would ever be different for her.

She opened the drawer of the low bedside table and took out a package of Gillette razor blades. She slid one shiny, new, metallic-blue blade from the package, turned it thoughtfully in her fingers, and briefly pondered the irony of having so recently done their television commercial. Some day she would have the nerve to sit back in a warm bath and run the blade smoothly across her wrists. She would leave the hot water running and pull the plug, and her life would pour down the drain and into the sewers of New York City where it belonged. But tonight she reached back into the drawer, removed a small, square mirror and a tiny vial, and shook a practice-measured mound of the vial's contents onto the mirror. Then she used the blade to chop the snowy crystals into a fine white powder and to form the powder into two thin parallel lines. Blocking one nostril, she leaned down and snorted one line. Then she blocked the other nostril and snorted the second line. She fluffed her pillows behind her head and leaned back, smiling as she recalled her first days in this dirty old town, sniffing and feeling the rush, momentarily forgetting the panic that had possessed her this afternoon at Mike Dudley's studio when she had blown her nose and once again found the tissues soaked with her own blood.

* * *

Catherine had arrived in New York City with lofty ambitions and a small inheritance. She checked into the Doral Inn on Forty-ninth Street and Lexington Avenue, and on her first full day set out to find both a job and an apartment, optimism running high.

After three days the only job she'd found paid slightly less per month than the cost of the only apartment she'd found. Each night she returned to the cramped room at the Doral—for which she was paying a to-her-amazing forty-five dollars a night—smoked a joint, and watched the picture on the wall television set flop sickeningly as she tried without success to steady it.

New York's awesome facade has a way of eroding even the brashest self-confidence, and though Catherine had been told for years that she was pretty, it obviously wasn't going to be enough to achieve her dream of breaking into modeling. She passed *hundreds* of pretty girls each day on the streets and most of them seemed to be carrying port-folios. Here in New York her life was starting over, but *she* had to start it. There was no family here, no one to call, no one to cry to. There was only Catherine Ward.

Her first real break came on her fourth day. When she saw the advertisement in the *New York Times* classified section, she left her expensive half-eaten breakfast at the Doral Coffee Shop and hurried to Third Avenue, knowing in her heart that the apartment would be taken as all the others had been before. She suspected they were taken even before the ads were placed and that the landlords had only advertised them to comply with local housing laws. But she had to try. She didn't waste a telephone call. Maybe if she was the first one to show up she'd have a better chance. And if the renter was a man he just might be sympathetic to a young woman alone in the big city. But a little flirting was as far as she would go. She had already decided *that* coming in. This was a new life, and she would *not* take the easy way out.

At 323 Third Avenue she buzzed 10F. "I'm here about the apartment advertised in the *Times.*"

A woman's voice answered. "Come on up."

Catherine allowed her hopes to soar as she rode the slow, rickety elevator. The woman wouldn't have bothered to invite her up if the place was taken. Three hundred fifty dollars a month for a studio apartment was the cheapest rental she had seen so far. *Oh, please,* she thought as she stepped into the hallway, first checking to see that, indeed, one Thomas Davis, or Davies, had inspected the elevator only four months ago. A lot could happen in four months, she knew only too well, but if she landed this place she'd take the risk of riding

Thomas Whoever's elevator or maybe she'd even take the stairs instead just for the exercise. After all, she was going to be a New York fashion model—of that there was not the slightest doubt.

Even empty, the room was small. But it was perfect: bright, airy, and clean. She took in the entire apartment in a single sweeping glance. It was just four barren, off-white walls. In a recess along the wall to her left were a stove, a sink, and a three-foot-wide swatch of linoleum that passed for a kitchen. There was a minuscule bathroom with only a basin, toilet, and shower. She'd have to give up her luxurious baths, but it would be a small sacrifice.

"It's still available?" Catherine asked hopefully, trying not to sound overly anxious.

"Sort of." The woman was plain, thirtyish, and dressed in an expensive gray-tweed business suit. "I've had a couple of people express interest, but I can afford to be choosy."

"I should say," Catherine agreed pleasantly. "It's lovely."

"Well, let's get down to business. It's three hundred and fifty dollars a month. I'm subletting, so you would be paying me directly. I'm getting married and moving to Paris," the woman offered with a self-satisfied smile.

"Oh, congratulations. How exciting."

"Yes, but a royal pain in the ass, too. My fiancé is off in Paris while I'm left to tie up loose ends here—and there are a lot of them. Anyway, as I was saying, it's three hundred and fifty dollars a month, first and last months' rent and two months' security; one-year lease with an option to renew for another year. That's fourteen hundred dollars, and you could move in immediately."

Catherine hoped the shock didn't register on her face. Fourteen hundred dollars! For a $350-a-month apartment! Just to move in! "Um . . . at the end of the . . . um . . . lease . . ."

"You would, of course, get your security deposit back, plus four percent interest by law. That would mean the last month's rent, in effect, would be prepaid." The woman was very understanding. "So, you see, though it's quite expensive up front, you'll get it all back when you move out." She shrugged her shoulders. "It's standard real estate practice. I've got to protect myself."

"Of course," Catherine reluctantly agreed. Fourteen hundred dollars. After the plane ticket and the Doral, Catherine had just under five thousand dollars left. This would leave her with thirty-five hundred. But she *would* get the security deposit back some day—with interest—and it would seem like a windfall then. And if it was standard

41

practice . . . Christ, she could live in Ames for a year on fourteen hundred dollars. "I want it," she willed herself to say.

"Well, I shouldn't be sexist, but my other two offers were from men, and it's tougher in this town for a woman alone—especially a pretty one," she added admiringly. "If we don't look out for each other, no one else will." She smiled and extended her hand, and Catherine took it eagerly.

At 1:00 P.M. Catherine returned to 323 Third Avenue as instructed with a teller's check made out to herself. Marianne Johnson met her outside the front door. *Good,* Catherine thought, *one less trip on that elevator.*

"I thought I'd buy lunch," Marianne offered. "Maybe take a little of the sting out of the deposit."

Over lunch Catherine endorsed the check, and both women signed the original and a copy of the lease. When Marianne Johnson slid the two apartment keys across the table it signaled the end of their meeting.

"That's it?" asked a beaming Catherine.

"That's it," Marianne nodded. "My new address in Paris is on the lease, and I'll send you my telephone number as soon as I have one. John is too busy for details like that," she said sarcastically. "I hope it doesn't take you too long to get settled here."

"I'm sure it won't. All I need is a few items of furniture."

"Enjoy," Marianne said when they were back on the street.

"Oh, I will. Thank you so much. That's one thing I don't have to worry about anymore. And thank you for lunch."

"It was the least I could do," Marianne Johnson said, and she turned and disappeared into the afternoon crowd.

Catherine covered the six blocks to her new apartment as though on a cloud. This morning no apartment, this afternoon a beautiful little place all her own. Things happened fast in New York City, for sure. It wasn't such a cold, impersonal place, after all. Marianne Johnson was testimony to that. She'd buy an inexpensive bed later today, check out of the Doral, and tomorrow she would have a job—she was sure of it. As she walked she thought about the way she would decorate her first home: a small rubber tree here, a fern there, a chair, a sofa, an end table. Rust and muted browns would match the tan carpet perfectly. An anticipatory smile stretched across her face from ear to ear. Her life was finally turning around.

When the first key didn't slip easily into the lock on the glass door, she stepped back in a mild panic as she checked the gilded numbers: 3–2–3. Then she plunged her fist into her purse and retrieved the sec-

42

ond key, somehow already knowing it wouldn't fit, and Marianne Johnson's grinning image flashed across her brain.

She tried each key eight times each way—teeth up and teeth down—though in her anxiety she wasn't counting. Then she pushed the button below "Super."

"Ten-F . . . I'm subletting . . . from Marianne Johnson."

"Easy. Calm down, lady. You'd better come inside. I'll call the manager," he said in his heavy Puerto Rican accent.

The walls of the superintendent's one-bedroom, first-floor apartment were cluttered with crucifixes, and the air was thick with the pungent aroma of Campbell's vegetable soup. His telephone call took less time than it had taken her to endorse a check and hand over fourteen hundred dollars of her late mother's hard-earned money.

After he hung up, he turned and delivered the knockout punch in his thick accent. "*Muchacha*, the apartment is owned by a Mr. John Winslow. He move out a month ago. It's on the market for sixty-nine thousand dollars, and the manager ain't never heard of no Marianne Johnson, and I ain't neither. Unless you've got sixty-nine thousand, I'm afraid you've been taken good."

It knocked the wind out of her. "But . . . I have a lease," she protested, waving the document impotently. "I need a place to live . . . Fourteen hundred dollars . . . My God, what will I do?" She stood in the middle of the small room, shivering in spite of its heat, and tears of desperation streaked her windburned face.

"I . . . might . . . be able to . . . let you stay here for a while," he offered tentatively, suggesting far more than free hospitality.

In her self-pity she had nearly forgotten he was there. When she looked up, his leer was almost more humiliating than being fleeced of fourteen hundred dollars. "*No, thanks*," she spat, and he had to duck to avoid being hit by the pair of useless keys that chunked a thumbnail-sized piece of plaster from the wall between his head and a plastic Sacred Heart of Jesus.

She lunged out the door and wobbled shakily from wall to wall along the narrow hallway, making her way desperately toward the fresh air beyond, wanting only to escape the sickening smells that followed her down the corridor.

She pushed her way out of the building, and before the door closed behind her she caught the final insult. "Hey, *muchacha*, welcome to New York!"

That was it. Somehow, after all that had happened, that was *it*. She whirled and wielded her heavy purse on its shoulder strap, slamming it like a mace into the large gilded "2" between the two "3"s. The clatter of splintering glass in the hallway brought the super on the run, wide-eyed with shock and anger. Then her outraged scream stopped him in his tracks. "Fuck you!"

She was reborn.

Catherine hadn't been raped but she felt as though she had been. She stormed along Third Avenue against a frigid, blustery wind, oblivious to the passersby.

"Hey, beautiful, you broke my bottle of wine!"

She hadn't even heard the smash, and when she turned, the tall, well-dressed young man stood with his arms spread, leather-gloved palms to the sky. She briefly considered an apology. "Tough shit!" And she turned with a half-smile—for which she would later feel overwhelmingly guilty—and continued her march north.

She left her room only once that evening—to pick up a hot pastrami sandwich and a bottle of beer at Tiny's Deli and a copy of the 1981 *Madison Avenue Handbook* at Weinblum's Bookstore. It was raining heavily again, and before she left the deli she stuffed the paper bag inside her down parka, hefting the small package to be sure the jacket's elastic waistband was snug enough to hold it securely. She gathered her long hair and dropped it inside the collar of her coat. Then she re-zipped the royal blue parka and turned the collar up to meet the bottom of the Minnesota Twins baseball cap she wore pulled down to her ears.

The jacket was water resistant, but even the mad dash across Lexington Avenue and into the bookstore didn't keep her Levi's from getting drenched by the freezing rain. Once inside the enormous store, she walked directly to the "Handbooks & Pamphlets" section in the rear, and slipped between a pyramid of books displaying a new runaway best-seller and the wall-rack where she hoped to find what she was after.

Catherine was no longer the clumsy, coltish girl she had been in adolescence. In fact, if given sufficient space, she was downright graceful. It was just that over the past few years she had grown so rapidly she hadn't had quite enough time to adjust to how far her arms and legs extended from her body. So even though she could see the pyramid of books beside her as she thumbed through *The Madison Avenue Handbook*, when the paper bag with her sandwich and bottle of beer slipped out from under her jacket and fell to the floor with an embarrassing clatter and she turned and bent to pick it up, she misjudged

44

how close the display was. As she spun to catch the teetering rack, she stumbled and fell full against it, and wound up sprawled face-down atop a scattered pile of hard-cover best-sellers.

From her station at the checkout counter at the front of the bookstore, Peggy Markle heard the crash and winced. She quickly thanked her customer for his purchase and hurried toward the noise. Two minutes before closing time and the store was almost empty. Just her luck: some asshole had picked closing time to give her a problem. As she rounded the corner she saw Catherine still sprawled on the floor.

Oh, well, it would give her something to do to start the morning shift tomorrow. She immediately changed her mind about the tirade she'd intended to launch. From the back the guy looked like he might be kind of cute: tallish, broad shoulders, trim waist, and a few strands of blond hair peeking from underneath his baseball cap. His rear end was low and round, a little on the feminine side, but with a decent face he'd have definite possibilities.

"Hey, pal?" she began, with good-natured sarcasm. "You buying? Or just browsing?"

From the floor Catherine spun her head around indignantly, simultaneously removing her cap and shaking her long, wavy blonde hair out over her shoulders. "I'm *very* sorry about this," she apologized sincerely. "But I most certainly am *not* your pal!"

As Catherine rolled onto her back and extended her hand, Peggy Markle was purely and simply overawed.

"Would you mind giving me a hand up?"

"Oh . . . sure," Peggy stammered, recovering from her confusion. At barely 5′2″, Peggy Markle considered anyone over 5′5″ to be tall. As Catherine unfolded herself to her full height, Peggy tilted her head back slowly. "Holy shit," she gasped. "What did your mother feed *you?*"

"Corn," Catherine answered sardonically, "and the weather up here is fine. Any more clichés?"

"Hey, I'm sorry," Peggy said, backing away so she wouldn't have to crane her neck. "But you're so . . ."

Catherine nodded fatalistically.

"It's not fair," Peggy said. "I feel like a dwarf."

"I insist on helping you with these books," Catherine broke in. She did want to help, but she wanted most to change the subject.

"Nah." Peggy gave a wave of dismissal toward the pile of books. "I'll pick them up tomorrow morning. It'll give me something to do."

"Well, then I'll come back in the morning to help you."

"No, no, you don't have to."

"But I insist."

"Listen," Peggy said. "All I want to do right now is get out of this place. I'll tell you what you can do for me. Buy me a cup of coffee?"

Catherine hesitated a moment, thinking of Marianne Johnson. Then she relented. It was only fifty cents this time. "Deal."

Apparently the only topic Peggy Markle was conversant with was men, because it was all she talked about for two hours. She discussed this lover and that lover as candidly and as explicitly as though she had known Catherine forever. After initially being unnerved by it, Catherine found Peggy's frankness refreshing. She was self-deprecatingly funny, discussing her own physical features and Catherine's as though comparing a child's finger painting to a Picasso.

"It takes me two hours just to get my hair to look *terrible*," Peggy complained, holding a frizzy mass of it away from her scalp. But Catherine guessed that when Peggy wanted to make the effort she could be quite pretty. True, her hair was the unmanageable type. And her figure was perhaps a tiny bit stout for her small size. But even though her nose had an obvious hook it wasn't unattractive. All Peggy needed was a good haircut, makeup, and the right clothes. And it would help to lose those awful horn-rimmed glasses. But she had what Catherine considered to be the two most important features: beautiful teeth she showed off in an almost constant smile, and large, oval brown eyes, with whites as clear and sparkling as a sunny day. Make that the three most important features: the third was an infectious good nature.

"Have you found an apartment yet?" Peggy asked as they left the counter at the Doral Coffee Shop.

Though Peggy had bared her soul to her, Catherine had found it impossible to draw more than the most sketchy outline of her own life, including her recent arrival in town. She couldn't even imagine telling Peggy how she'd been taken in by "Marianne Johnson." The wound was all too fresh.

"No. Actually I haven't had much time to look yet." Catherine hoped she was only blushing on the inside. She quickly paid the bill and they walked out onto the sidewalk.

"Where are you staying?"

"Nearby," Catherine evaded.

"Well, I spend just about my entire exciting life at the bookstore. Come back and see me, Catherine—soon." Then she held out her hand and smiled her beautiful smile. "But promise you won't *touch* anything."

They shared a laugh while they shook hands, then Catherine

watched Peggy Markle disappear down the brightly lit street, missing the warm, savvy young woman even before she was out of sight.

She wouldn't move to a cheap fleabag hotel, she simply wouldn't. If she could keep her other expenses under ten dollars a day, Catherine figured she could last about forty days at the Doral and still have enough money left for a deposit on an apartment. Forty days—it seemed prophetic, she thought as she munched her no-longer-hot pastrami, sipped her warm beer, and listened to the rain pelting the window.

The optimism of youth is quickly rekindled and by ten o'clock she had reassessed her position. In fact, she hadn't been raped or stabbed or murdered. Fourteen hundred dollars was fourteen hundred dollars, but it was, after all, only money.

As she thumbed through *The Madison Avenue Handbook* she remembered an article she had once read in *Vogue*. It was an interview with Esmé, who admitted she had been turned down several times at the Wilhelmina Model Agency before they had finally signed her. "If you know you've got it, keep trying," she had advised aspiring models. The other advice Catherine remembered was to visit no more than two agencies a day. A woman selling her beauty had to look fresh at all times. So tomorrow she would start at the best; and she would hit them all in time. And then, if she had to, she would hit them all again. And she *would* make it. But she wouldn't get discouraged along the way. Today this city had declared war, and she was going to show it what she was made of. She might have lost the first skirmish, but she had a lot more fight left in her.

The authors of *The Madison Avenue Handbook* make no pretense as to their opinion on where the center of the world of advertising and fashion is. The first 174 pages are devoted to New York City listings: photographers, modeling agencies, advertising agencies, television and film studios, and art supply stores. There are 20 pages on Los Angeles and a total of 76 on Boston, San Francisco, Chicago, and the rest of the world.

The following morning at eight Catherine donned her one suit, a businesslike gray wool skirt and jacket, and set out to conquer the world, albeit a little more warily then the day before. But first she stopped for what was intended to be a brief visit at the local police precinct to abashedly report her gullibility. Between disconcerting

47

stares at her legs, the desk sergeant informed her that she was not "Marianne Johnson's" first victim and that there was little chance of apprehending the woman or of effecting the return of her money, "Do you want to make out a formal complaint anyway?"

"You bet your ass I do!" It was her only form of satisfaction, impotent as it was.

The vehemence of her response both surprised and amused the sergeant.

It was ten-thirty by the time she descended the precinct steps. The brisk walk to Fifty-ninth Street and Lexington Avenue revived her, and she stepped off the elevator on the twenty-third floor fresh and confident. Bronze letters on a huge oak door at the left end of the corridor announced "CLINE MODELS." She took a deep breath, exhaled slowly, and walked in, feeling a cold sweat rise on her forehead and upper lip.

She·was greeted by an empty reception desk. Behind a high counter to her right, two well-dressed middle-aged women were discussing their divergent views on the masculinity of a hairdresser named Jacques. As Catherine approached, they saw but ignored her.

"He's a flaming faggot," said one, a tall, attractive, salt-and-pepper-haired woman who had obviously been a model in her prime.

"I happen to have it on good authority that he's balling every one of those little tarts who works for him," said the other.

When a polite *ahem* failed to interrupt them, Catherine understood that the conversation would end only when it ended. She sat and waited. Their five minutes of patient indifference to her seemed like five days.

"Do you have a book, dear?" the heavy, less attractive one finally asked from behind the counter.

"Umm . . ."

"Pictures? Eight-by-tens?" the woman prompted impatiently.

"No." Catherine was at the counter, smiling her perfect smile, but the woman wasn't looking. Instead she turned and picked up the telephone receiver, punched a button, and dialed.

"You've got to have pictures," the woman said into the ringing telephone. "We're not taking any new models until June, anyway. Get a book together and come back then." Then, just as quickly, Catherine was forgotten as the woman spoke into the phone. "Jacques? Is that you, sweet?"

Catherine was stunned. The Hindenberg hadn't crashed any more precipitously than her ego. She spun and blindly made for the door. In the hallway she stumbled and the attaché case was on the floor. She bent to pick it up. "I'm sorry. Forgive me. I wasn't watching where I was going," she apologized profusely. Catherine handed the leather Etienne Aigner case to its owner, a small, homely, gray-haired woman.

"Are you a model?" the woman asked, ignoring Catherine's fumbling.

"Yes. Well, no, not exactly."

The woman looked at Catherine with silent appreciation, as though inspecting an unfinished Rembrandt. "If you're interested, lose ten pounds and come back and see me. In a week. Same time. Right here." She motioned toward the sign that said "CLINE MODELS." Then she extended her hand with stiff formality.

Catherine was astonished. She accepted the hand passively.

The woman took it, shook it firmly, and introduced herself.

Catherine Ward was still standing dumbstruck in the hallway when the huge oak door closed behind Mary Cline.

2

Lynell Alan arrived in New York City within weeks of Catherine Ward, in late January of 1981. His road to a modeling career had started out relatively smoothly in Boston two years before, but soon after his arrival in New York it lay in front of him flat and wide and visible for miles—a highway to nowhere. However, that he was a model at all, given his physical appearance and lack of self-esteem in his early years, was nothing short of a miracle.

Twenty-nine years before he met Aimée Harris, Lynell Oliver Alan was born in New Haven, Connecticut, to a family that had for thirty extremely successful years been the reigning royalty of the nursery business in New England.

Conn-Tree, Inc., had been founded by his grandfather, Oliver Alan, Sr., in 1921 on a ten-acre tree farm in Hamden, Connecticut. By the time Lynell was born, his grandfather's guidance and foresight, along with a generous infusion of federally subsidized farm loans and cheap Puerto Rican labor, had turned Conn-Tree into a multimillion-dollar business and the largest non-governmental owner of real estate in the state of Connecticut.

Since Oliver Jr. had joined the company in 1945 upon graduation from Dartmouth College and Harvard Business School, his business acumen and financial expertise had seen Conn-Tree more than double its real estate holdings while expanding into all areas of wholesale and retail distribution of plants, trees, shrubs, soil, and landscaping ser-

50

vices. It was, by 1950, a $10-million-a-year operation. In short, Lynell Oliver Alan was born into a family that was dirt *rich*.

His sister, Veronica, older by two years, was incomparably beautiful. She possessed the perfect amalgam of her parents' features: her mother, Liz's, long fine throat, slightly uptilted nose, and sparkling blue eyes; Oliver's plump, rosy cheeks, fair complexion, and white-blond hair that thickened as rapidly on her as his thinned.

"She should be in Gerber Baby Food ads," friends invariably said as they lifted the netting over the baby carriage to admire her.

Liz's second pregnancy was easier than the first. In fact, during the final trimester the fetus's inactivity caused her considerable anxiety. "Don't worry, dear," said a clearly worried Dr. Salinger as he patted her womb reassuringly. "I detect a strong, even heartbeat."

"A fine, healthy boy," Dr. Salinger announced with satisfaction.

Liz watched the doctor expectantly as the nurse handed her the bundle, but this time there were no comparisons to Cary Grant or Gary Cooper. As Liz pulled back the white hospital blanket that partially hid the baby's face, Dr. Salinger grasped her wrist firmly. "He's responsive and has all the right parts, Liz. That's the important thing."

As Liz took her first-ever look at young Lynell—a family name she and Oliver had chosen for a boy—Dr. Salinger continued, nodding paternally, "Their features tend to even out in time."

Dr. Salinger did not add that, true as it had been that Veronica was at least one of the prettiest babies he'd delivered in his forty-three years of obstetrics, this one was unequivocally the ugliest. The baby had a face that, as they say, "only a mother could love."

"He's not that bad, after all," Oliver decided after a long study of his year-old son's face.

"May I have another piece of Lynell's birthday cake, Mummy?" Veronica asked from across the table. All round red cheeks, white-blonde hair, and stars that sparkled from her darting blue eyes, she was as thoroughly spoiled as she was beautiful.

Disposition was the single area in which Lynell compared favorably with his sister. While Veronica cried and wheedled and demanded, Lynell played quietly, often alone, seldom spoke, and never cried. By the time he entered school in the fall of 1955, the family had moved from Lake Whitney in Hamden to a waterfront home in Pine Orchard. Veronica, the irresistible extrovert, had gained immediate admittance

51

to the almost endless rounds of Pine Orchard birthday and holiday parties and had, in turn, received no fewer than thirty-five excited friends into her own home to celebrate her seventh year.

But in Lynell's case the serene disposition that made him such a manageable child combined with his shyness to render him almost an outcast among his peers. Even among his teachers, though he was perfectly behaved, he suffered in the inevitable and constant comparison to his bright and beautiful sister.

"Do you think he's retarded?" Oliver asked Lynell's school counselor on parent/teacher conference night.

"No," Hannah Lincoln said with a vigorous shake of her head. "Definitely not. These IQ tests aren't infallible, but Lynell tests out at 165. He's a *very* bright young man. Just a little shy. He'll get over that. It just takes time. And he's such a dear boy," she added as she led Liz and a pleasantly surprised Oliver into the waiting room, where Lynell grinned quietly into Dr. Seuss's *The Cat in the Hat.*

And then she said it. Six years and someone finally said it. "Cute, too," Hannah Lincoln said with a grin only Lynell could match.

"He *is* cute," Liz stated flatly as though trying to convince herself. Through the kitchen window she watched the children playing as the whitecaps boiled angrily on deserted Long Island Sound. "He may never be Clark Gable but he's awfully huggable with all those beautiful curls."

As Oliver reached the window and draped his arm over his wife's shoulder, Veronica was snatching a Matchbox firetruck from Lynell's hand without resistance or complaint. The boy simply replaced it with a Chevy on the narrow sand road.

"He's got no . . . spark," Oliver said, shaking a fist impotently into the air.

"Why? Because he doesn't haul off and sock her?"

"Yes."

"Well, I don't agree. He's a nice little boy and I love him just the way he is." If she analyzed it, which she tried not to do, Liz would have had to admit that perhaps she loved Lynell just the tiniest bit more than Veronica—but only because he needed it so desperately, and to make up for the little bit less that his father seemed to love him. "Someday he'll find something worthwhile to fight for and you'll be proud of him." At that moment Veronica snatched away the miniature Chevy and Liz thought, *Go ahead, sweetie, sock her.* But he didn't. He only smiled and put his head in his hands and watched his sister play. Liz turned to Oliver with tears in her eyes. "He is cute, isn't he?"

52

Oliver surveyed the dramatic features that had at last found some symmetrical plan on his son's face, then looked at the flawless face of his daughter and sighed. "In a homely sort of way," he conceded.

Disappointment, loneliness, and confusion followed Lynell throughout his youth, but never did he feel more rejected than when he was sent to boarding school in September of 1964. The Choate School, with its sprawling campus and equally sprawling alumni endowment fund, is the envy of many a college and university. The chronology of campus buildings is best determined not by the dates etched in their cornerstones but by the height to which the ivy has climbed their hallowed walls. Indeed, parents consider "The Choate Experience" to have been less than a success if their children do not proceed directly to Harvard or Yale, or at the very least one of the other half-dozen venerable Ivy League institutions—and the rate of success is high.

Lynell made few friends at Choate. In spite of his feelings of rejection, and quite possibly because of them, he devoted his entire energies to his studies, at which he excelled.

When the first term ended in mid-December, Lynell arrived home at Christmas break ranked second in his class.

"Maybe next term you'll be first," his father said. Lynell, who had naively assumed that his being second out of eighty-five would please his father, was crushed.

By the time he left Choate behind for the last time at the end of that school year, Lynell had left behind a good deal of his adolescent awkwardness as well. By the age of fifteen, having gained a phenomenal seven inches and 30 pounds during his nine months at Choate, he was now 5'10" tall and weighed 165 pounds. But his growth in those months was not limited to physical measurements. An important question was answered for him that school year, but a difficult one was also raised. The answer came from a faculty wife; the question from his next-door neighbor in Memorial House.

The object of his fantasies was none other than the wife of Dean Paul White, around whose dinner table a dozen boys were rotated on a weekly basis so that Dean White would have an opportunity to become acquainted with each.

Sally White, twenty-five years her husband's junior, was a slim, pale, dark-haired woman of thirty who despite no more than passable looks was, by virtue of being one of the three females on campus between the ages of ten and fifty, the object of much lustful fantasy. A hot-blooded young woman, Sally bore up admirably under the frustration of having a palpable corner on that untouchable hormone market. Over the years Sally had had several discreet affairs, but mostly she amused herself with lighthearted flirtations with the boys. All strictly innocent, of course, but she enjoyed their blushing when she caught them ogling her as they passed her table on out-of-their-way excursions to the kitchen to refill their empty platters. And she especially enjoyed the squirming discomfort of her week's dinner companion as she passed him a quiet double entendre with the fried eggplant and rare roast beef.

"I don't remember seeing you before," she lied when Lynell finally revolved to her side one Sunday night.

Six days ago he had arrived at their table in a tight-fitting sport coat that even now, when he shrugged, she thought might split down its madras seams. She was taken by his shyness and athletic grace, by the severe facial features that were softened by a head full of brown, bedspring curls. His loneliness had reached across the table and joined hands with her own. She wanted to hold him, to tell him he would be all right. She wanted him to be her son.

Lynell thought the Dean's wife was infinitely sophisticated and incredibly beautiful and he tried not to stare from across the table. The days passed excruciatingly slowly as he made his way to her, seat by seat, and when he finally arrived next to her he was sure his heart would stop beating.

That Sunday evening Sally White's thigh and bare calf pressed against Lynell Alan's leg. After enjoying the comfortable warmth through his pantleg for a heartbeat, he wanted to move it, sure that she must think it was the table leg she rubbed against. But he couldn't. What if she were offended that he hadn't moved it immediately? He was consumed by such a flood of sheer panic that, in spite of the lack of an erection or any apparent sexual arousal, he experienced his first-ever involuntary emission—there, amid five hundred roasters with razor-sharp skewers at the ready.

"Mrs. White, may I please be excused? I don't feel very well." And indeed, his ashen face glistened with perspiration and his breathing was alarmingly uneven.

"Certainly," she said with maternal concern. "Perhaps I should take you to the infirmary." Eleven boys waited with hushed anticipation, each praying for the same mysterious sickness to engulf him.

"Thank you, but I'll be okay. I'll just go to my room and lie down. I don't want to be a bother." He slipped out of his jacket, held it across his lap, stood, and hurried from the dining hall.

For Lynell the pain of seeing her again the next evening was excruciating. Her hand covered his and a look of concern crossed her face. Six more dinners with her. Six more dinners he could only eat, because not to eat would surely draw her attention. Six more dinners he vomited into the toilet on the fourth floor of Memorial House.

He was incapacitated by the mere thought of her, blinded by the sight of her, the fantasy of her naked body reclining on his narrow bed. That he could, in the final two weeks of a three month term, plummet from first in his class to tenth was testimony to her unflagging power over him. He walked into people, excusing himself absently. He lost weight. He lost his starting position on the junior-varsity baseball team.

But the worst symptom was his nearly constant state of arousal. He would awaken in the middle of the night in his small single room tucked into the eaves of Memorial House, and there would be only one way to ease his near-physical pain. Between classes he walked with his hands stuffed into his pockets, his books tucked between his elbows and his ribs, and if there was time and he was close enough, he would fly up the stairs by fours, lock his door, unzip himself, and stare at Donna Michelle's Playmate of the Year breasts until he could close his eyes and they became Mrs. Sally White's and the tension had left him again.

Once again he stood in front of that centerfold, feeling the inexplicable guilt and depression that always seemed to follow. As he began to snap the fly on his pajamas, the door to his room suddenly popped open.

"Oh, excuse me," Larry Mansfield said, quickly reclosing the door behind him.

Lynell lay on his bed in a fear-induced trance, waiting for Larry's inevitable return and the equally-inevitable humiliation. He would have to survive one more week here. Then he would never return—never!

"You awake?"

Even as his eyes adjusted to the light filtering through the row of small dormer windows, Lynell could barely make out Larry's features on this moonless night. He tried to calm his heavy breathing, afraid to give himself away.

"I'd never tell," Larry promised as he sat on the edge of Lynell's bed.

55

Lynell immediately took the defensive. "What's to tell?"

"I do it myself." Larry paused in the thick silence. "I think everyone does, though they would never admit it, of course."

"Does what?"

"You can make *sure* I won't tell anyone, you know," Larry continued.

The bed shook lightly. Lynell was cold with fear and the fear pulsed excitement through him. "No," he managed to whisper. Lynell shook his head unconsciously as he felt Larry's hand take his. "I couldn't do that." Even as he felt Larry's hand draw his nearer; even as he knew he wanted to, knew he *had* to; even as he felt the odd, detached stiffness in his hand and heard Larry suck in his breath at the touch of his fingers closing around him.

When Larry Mansfield left that night, fifteen-year-old Lynell Alan considered suicide for the first time. It would not be the last.

When he was alone Lynell stared blankly through the open window at the mist sweeping in over the empty playing-fields, and the chill of that emptiness grew inside him like a malignancy. With his luck the four-story drop wouldn't kill him—it would paralyze him for life.

He searched his desk drawer in the darkness until he felt the cold steel. Opening the long scissors, he held the thinner blade against his chest and knew he couldn't pierce the sternum. As he pressed it into his stomach the stinging pain came with the first warm trickle of blood. The scissors clattered to the floor. There must be an easier way—and he would find it.

"Let's put in for a room together," Larry Mansfield suggested as he shook Lynell's hand on the last Friday after exams.

"Sure, Larry . . . that would be great," Lynell agreed hesitantly.

"I'll send in the application next week . . . roomie," Larry added over his shoulder as he strode toward his father's waiting Mercedes.

As Lynell watched him walk away, he wondered if Larry would be placed with a "suitable" roommate in the fall when he didn't show up. Because if Choate hadn't seen the last of him—the world had.

"I won't go back to Choate," Lynell announced, which shocked Oliver to his shoes, though it shouldn't have. His son had been disappointing him since the day he was born.

"What do you mean you're not going back? Choate is the best boarding school in the country and it's practically in your own back yard."

"I hate it."

"What do you mean you hate it? You did so well and you can do even better next year. Of course you're going back. The baseball coach says you'll probably even make the varsity team. And you'll be able to play football this year. Look at the size of you." He clapped his strapping son on the shoulder as though sure that the young boy's sanity had wavered only momentarily.

"I hate it," Lynell repeated with a shrug. "And I won't be number one or number ten or number eighty-five, because I hate it. And I won't make the baseball team, because I don't want to make the baseball team. And I don't *want* to play football."

"Well, you're going to go back and that's that."

But he hadn't gone back, because he had promised as much effort at Pine Orchard High as he promised lack of effort at Choate. The one condition Lynell had submitted to was that he agree to return to Choate the following year if he didn't fulfill his promise. And after all, what could Oliver do? Chain him to the pillars in front of Memorial House?

By February of 1968 Lynell Alan was a guard on the Pine Orchard High School basketball team. He was a sturdily-built six-footer whose facial features had not only "evened out," as Dr. Herbert Salinger had so optimistically predicted some seventeen years earlier, but had actually become attractive.

Even so, it was not until the autumn of his senior year in high school that Lynell had his first steady girlfriend. He continued to be nagged by a strong, though increasingly erroneous, image of himself as plain, if not downright homely, and couldn't imagine what a beautiful girl like Stephanie Nelson could possibly see in him. So afraid was he of alienating her affections by boldness that it took him more than two weeks merely to kiss her. It was three days before Christmas when she slipped his hand inside her blouse and he felt a girl's naked breasts for the first time.

"I love you, Lynell," she said, and as she sat in the gymnasium the next night cheering him on, he lunged for a rebound with just a little bit of extra effort *for her* because she had said he was *handsome.* When the elbow hit him he was sure he had been shot.

"You've ruined your looks," she said callously while visiting him in his bedroom, where he was recuperating with twelve stitches that repaired the three-inch gash on the inside of his mouth. Their conversation was brief and awkward, and she wasn't the same girl who had offered him her breasts less than a week before. He regarded her from

57

behind a broken nose, two purpled eyes, and a chipped front tooth, and she seemed not to know that her four words had hurt him more than a stranger's bony elbow and would leave deeper scars.

Lynell entered Dartmouth College in the fall of 1968 with 813 other incoming freshmen—only eight others of whom had received dual admission to both the college and graduate business school—and, for a reason that he would have been hard-pressed to recognize himself, quit.

First he quit studying any more than was necessary to scrape by. In the winter he tried out for the freshman basketball team but quit after three days of practice. In the spring he failed to show up for baseball tryouts. At an age when most young people have found at least a piece of themselves, Lynell Alan had found nothing.

Dartmouth in the late sixties and early seventies was an insular male society in which being "dressed up" meant your jeans and sweatshirt were clean and having "class" meant not throwing up on your date. Lynell had no one to dress up for and precious little opportunity to display class. He was as apathetic as his freshman roommate was active, as uninvolved as the other was involved.

For all of their pride in their deserved reputation as animals, most Dartmouth men were intensely interested in *something*: maybe it was only women and beer, maybe physics and chemistry, or track and football. Most at least had something, and most had goals, dreams. They wanted to be doctors, lawyers, or bankers. They wanted to find "Miss Right" ("a gorgeous nympho"), eventually get married and have a family, live in Scarsdale or Grosse Point or Westport.

Lynell had no dream, only a future that was etched in stone. His goal was to graduate from Dartmouth with as little effort as possible, when he would return to Pine Orchard and become the next president of Conn-Tree, where he would, he expected, die of boredom well before his fortieth year. He wandered between the college and the business school in a semi-fog for most of two years, making few friends at either branch of the school while virtually raising mediocrity to an art form. A report of his grades was an electric typewriter run amok: CCCCCCC.

A meal at Dartmouth's Thayer Hall, like those at most college dining halls, contained enough starch to run a Chinese laundry for a week, but it was the only place on campus where Lynell's attendance was perfect. Because of that and his lack of participation in athletics, and though he had reached his full height of 6'2" by age twenty, Lynell had gained twenty-five pounds since high school and by the close of his sophomore year weighed a beefy two hundred pounds. Occasionally the additional poundage and lack of fitness made him physically uncomfortable, but as to their impact on his appearance, he was indifferent.

Two fortunate decisions intercepted Lynell on his way to obesity. The first was when he and Peter West, his roommate and best friend, resolved no longer to eat at the college dining hall but to share the cooking chores in the Alpha Theta fraternity kitchen. The second was in the summer of 1970 when he defied his father's edict that he begin learning the business at Conn-Tree and instead took and passed the lifeguard test at Hammonasset State Beach.

By September, after nearly three months of the rigorous physical regimen required by the job, he had not only shed fifteen pounds, but was more fit than he had ever been in his life. Even he would have had to admit he looked pretty good. And he felt great. When he returned to school he made a vow to keep control of his weight and remain as fit as he could. It was his first goal since arriving at college—the first he had ever set for *himself.* He continued to do stretching exercises, pushups, and situps, but for the three-mile run in the sand and the half-mile swim, he substituted a daily run of five miles, which he usually extended to ten miles on Saturdays.

By November Lynell was a lean, fit 180 pounds, and his body was tight and muscular. But the thing that astounded him was his face. It had bones! High, severe cheekbones; a wide, square jawbone; and cheeks with shallow, dark hollows. He had a little trouble breathing through his broken nose but despite his mother's insistence absolutely refused to have it "fixed." It look fine, he thought, and the slight bump was visible only under the closest scrutiny. He had Veronica's large eyes, but in his a bright blue border surrounded dark, jagged stars. His hair had always been curly, but now, with the styles longer, it was *curly.*

He especially loved the way he looked when he sweat: clean and tough and agile, and in the privacy of his room he stood in front of the mirror, the famous athlete just off the field, being interviewed after yet another victory—the papers always referring to him as "the handsome Lynell Alan."

But after years of playing the Beast to Veronica's Beauty, he had no idea just how handsome he had become. And though he felt better about himself physically, was healthier and no longer lost his breath climbing the stairs or jogging across campus, he retained his lingering insecurity about women. Meeting Ellen Barnes went a long way toward changing that.

When Ellen Barnes stepped off the chartered Trailways bus at Hanover, New Hampshire, with her classmates on that late November day in 1971, she could have had her pick of the dozens of young men who gathered competitively around the girls. The event was Dartmouth's annual freshman mixer.

Unknown to the neophyte freshmen who waited impatiently in the gymnasium, smuggled spiked drinks in their fists and randy gleams in their eyes, the upperclassmen, including Lynell Alan, lingered outside to "scoop" the best of the year's crop as they arrived from Skidmore, Colby, Smith, Mount Holyoke, and Ellen's own Simmons College.

Spurred by the two strongest forces in nature—social pressure and horniness—Lynell crunched quickly across the narrow, snow-encrusted path and stepped between Ellen and a young man already propositioning her on behalf of his own fraternity. "I can make a better offer," Lynell said softly, barely audible over the indignant protests of his outraged competitor. "Would you and your friends like to come to a party with me?"

After conferring with a group of half a dozen girls, Ellen took Lynell's arm possessively and he led them across the college green, admiring the beauty of the whitewashed buildings of Dartmouth Row under a light dusting of newfallen snow. Ellen's enormous eyes glowed in the light of a full moon that sparkled off the snowy landscape, and in the blue-gray twilight her face was nothing if not exotic.

Peter West held the door and waved them ceremoniously into the warmth of the large clapboard-and-brick house. A fire blazed in each fieldstone fireplace of the twin living rooms flanking the foyer, and the sounds of rock music and boisterous laughter and conversation filtered up from the basement bar.

"I'll tell the guys you're back," West said, hurrying for the basement stairs. "Got a pretty good crowd building."

Moments after West had disappeared down the staircase his enthusiastic voice echoed over the rising din. "Lyn's brought seven!" A lusty chorus of cheers ensued.

"Are you the bait?" Ellen asked as she unbuttoned a calf-length raccoon coat that had already been stylishly moth-eaten when her father wore it at Yale in 1945.

Peter West had reappeared beside Ellen with a handful of unkempt young men who buzzed around the girls, taking coats and offering welcome. "He's our face man," West explained.

Ellen Barnes looked into Lynell's eyes for a long moment, was still looking into them when she spoke. "Well, he's sure got the *face* for it, hasn't he?"

"Holy shit," Lynell whispered inaudibly as an unnoticed fraternity brother whisked away Ellen's family of raccoons and he saw her—really saw her—for the first time.

"What?"

"Oh, nothing," he said, regaining his composure and taking her arm with renewed interest. "Let's go downstairs and have a drink."

They spoke animatedly in a small booth as the party whirled noisily around them, and Lynell was hypnotized. The severely angular planes of her face would to many men, he guessed, not be pretty. But her face was so interesting he could only take his eyes from it for an occasional brief, clandestine glance between the open lapels of her pale yellow Oxford blouse at her impressive cleavage.

At precisely 9:45 P.M., with an innate sense of timing and a keen awareness that Ellen's bus left for Boston at midnight, Lynell suggested adjourning to his room on the second floor "for a nightcap." As she preceded him up the spiral staircase and he followed the line from her racehorse thin ankles (the left enticingly encircled by a delicate gold anklet) up along the shapely calves to her swaying bottom, he hoped he wouldn't make a fool of himself.

In his darkened room, with the door locked surreptitiously behind them and the light of a setting moon pouring through the uncurtained window, he clumsily made his move on the rusty-springed couch.

He pressed his lips to hers and she drew his tongue into her warm mouth and sucked it firmly and he stiffened painfully as though *it* were being sucked and he fondled her full, firm breasts through cotton and lace and as she reached to unbutton his shirt her hand brushed over his crotch and he thought it might be over before it started.

Ellen Barnes stood in the hazy luster of moonlight that filtered through her tousled hair and slowly unbuttoned her blouse, slipped it over her broad shoulders, and hung it neatly on the back of the chair at his study desk. He couldn't believe his luck. Then she pulled the bra off over her head and dropped it to the floor. Her breasts were larger than any he'd ever seen out of the pages of *Playboy* and unbelievably beautiful in the phosphorescent half-light. When she came to him his hands were on them and his lips were on them, and when he reached between her legs and pressed the wide-wale corduroy skirt against her in delirium, she pushed his hand away.

61

"I have my period," she whispered, and she wondered why she was always so goddamned viciously horny when she had her period and wondered whether she would be doing what she was about to do if this guy wasn't so nice—not to mention so goddamned good looking. And as she pushed Lynell back on the couch she hoped he wouldn't be disgusted tomorrow when he remembered how easy she had been, because she really liked him. But right now she didn't care, and she didn't even give him time to be disappointed at her revelation as she unbuckled his belt and carefully unzipped his Levi's while he ran his fingers gently through her hair.

He pressed his heels and elbows against the couch to raise himself as she worked his pants over his hips, his penis snapping free from the elastic waistband of his shorts and slapping smartly against his stomach. He was sure she was more experienced than he—which wouldn't have been difficult—when she hiked her skirt and, without removing her panties, straddled him and lowered herself, pressing his stiffness between her and his stomach. She leaned forward and kissed him gently as he took a breast in each hand. She kept her body forward, supporting her weight on her strong arms as she rocked back and forth smoothly, her clitoris rubbing along the length of him through the sheer nylon. They were deaf to the rhythmic squeaking of the rusty springs.

"Don't come," she begged as she rocked faster, pressing his penis against his stomach with ever-more-rapid thrusts that he eagerly returned. "Please don't come." And she inhaled in short, choking gasps, "Oh, God, oh, God, oh, God." He tried to hold back, thinking of how much work he had to do to catch up in Professor Selznick's calculus class, wondering if she did this the first night with every man, imagining himself skewered by a rusty spring.

Then she was writhing against him in almost painful, spasmodic jerks and she cried out in a great, glorious anguish of ecstasy. "Now! Come now!" she commanded, and he obeyed as eagerly and as promptly as any student ever obeyed a teacher, grunting huge sighs of pleasure with each pulsing, thrusting release against her.

When it was over Lynell Alan beamed in the darkness, suddenly knowing he had brought a woman to orgasm for the first time. And it was satisfying even though, admittedly, his role had been minor.

As the couple's breathing evened, five young men in the adjacent room, with empty beer-glasses pressed against the paper-thin wall and painfully full erections pressed against their jeans, stifled laughter as Lynell and Ellen unknowingly provided them with the first of what would be almost a year of vicarious thrills.

"That was *wonderful*. . . . Let's do it again," they all heard her whisper, as clearly as though each was lying on the couch beneath her.

After graduation from Dartmouth Lynell accepted a position with the accounting firm of Arthur Young & Company in Boston, putting off his father's offer to join the family business for "a year or two" while he acquired necessary business skills.

Having opted for the suburban life, Lynell discovered a suitable community twenty miles north of Boston on the rocky Massachusetts shore. Marblehead, its steeply gabled, white, two- and three-centuries-old houses, with uniformly black shutters and slated roofs, surrounding Old Burial Hill and a harbor area dotted by Abbot Hall and the oldest church in the Commonwealth, was the very picture-postcard image of the quaint New England village. The town, which had in the first half of the twentieth century been a summer playground for the super-rich, had become by the midseventies a year-round playground for the once super-rich, against whom inflation, a sagging economy, and an accelerated tax-rate had conspired to reduce to merely rich.

He scoured the village and was fortunate to turn up a secluded barn which had been converted into a large apartment. The barn sat between a salt marsh and an apple orchard, north and south, a thick wooded section to the east, and the landlord's main house across one hundred yards of lawn to the west. The dirt driveway wove a quarter of a mile through the orchard to a paved side road off Green Street. The ground floor was a barren thousand square feet of linoleum with a functional kitchen and a bar in one corner, behind which a spiral staircase wound up to a second floor covered with cheap wall-to-wall carpeting and furnished in an interesting mélange of pieces whose state of disrepair was indicative of how long ago each had fallen from the landlord's favor.

Lynell's first purchase was an expensive, steel-framed, king-sized mattress which, to his subsequent embarrassment, the deliverymen were unable to fit up the narrow staircase. However, the magnificently comfortable queen-sized mattress and box spring he traded it for proved more than adequate to entertain a stream of Arthur Young & Co. secretaries and Boston-area coeds over the ensuing years. But even his stimulating sex life couldn't stave off the day-to-day boredom of his job or the growing realization that he was fast running out of excuses not to return home to his father's business.

And then suddenly out of nowhere came a new nightmare that made all Lynell's other problems pale in comparison: for no apparent

63

reason he couldn't "get it up." Like death, it had never occurred to him that at age twenty-eight it could happen—or more precisely *not* happen—to him.

Once he had seen a doctor and ruled out physical causes, he began privately to explore the emotional. Was it lack of commitment? Nagging insecurity? Guilt? Fear? Or a combination of the above? Whatever the reasons, there he was in the naked embrace of a pretty Boston University coed he had met on the return commute on the P & B bus, and a lack of confidence overcame him in waves at the moment of entry, waves that began in his chest, numbing waves that sent ever-widening ripples down along his stomach, his abdomen, down . . .

For three nights in a row she returned before finally giving up on him. He spent a week of his vacation time shut inside his barn, the shades drawn, the telephone unplugged. He grew morose and, though he doubted his nerve ever to go through with it, suicidal.

Weeks passed, months, and his only enjoyment was relaxing alone at the beach, where in spite of his efforts to ignore the problem, without the immediacy of the pressure to perform he would watch the women in their skimpy bikinis and fantasize himself into that longed-for condition. But always there was that nagging doubt, and in one of the cruel ironies of life, just when Lynell was sure things could get no worse, they did.

"Excuse me." The young male voice was apologetic. "I'm just visiting this area and a friend told me there was a bar in Nahant Beach called The Pub. You wouldn't happen to know how to get there?" He knelt—like Lynell's vexing problem, uninvited—on the corner of the faded, threadbare olive blanket, his yellow hair rippling in the soft off-shore breeze, perfect weightlifting-defined upper torso a deep brown in contrast to his pale cut-off jeans.

"Sorry, I don't. Nahant is that way," Lynell offered, pointing south. "That's the best I can do for you."

"Mind if I sit for a minute? I've been riding this damn bicycle all morning," he added when Lynell offered no immediate response.

"Sure," Lynell answered reluctantly. He thought momentarily of his mother, shaking her head and clucking her tongue from some appropriate vantage point. His mother, who had read every published volume on self-assertiveness and extolled its virtues even as she bent with the wind. He doubted that he, either, would ever learn to say "no."

"Carl Howard . . . I'm a dancer in 'Don Quixote,' playing at the North Shore Summer Theater . . . one of the horsemen who rape Dulcinea . . . Actually the part was miscast—I'm gay. . . . I know. If you were, you'd have picked up on The Pub. It's a gay bar. . . . Don't

64

knock it until you've tried it. . . . What have you got to lose? . . . Anyway, come and see the play. It's great, really. . . . I'll leave a ticket for you at the box office. . . ."

A ticket—as in one. Jesus Christ, why now?

But he went to see Carl Howard in his three-minute role in "Don Quixote" and it was good. And after the performance he went back to his small, shadowy dressing room, and left feeling like a gay summerstock groupie. And late that evening he stood in front of his full-length mirror—wearing clean underwear for his mother—and held a Gillette Blue Blade in his hand. But that was too messy. Then he took the vial of Percodan—left over from his wisdom-tooth extraction the previous year—out of the medicine cabinet. But that was too risky (Lynell was convinced that the most pathetic thing a human being could do was bungle a suicide). And his guilt and self-revulsion were absolute. But three days later Aimée Harris threw him a life preserver. And three nights after that she saved him.

3

Blue blood impressed Aimée Harris. Perhaps it was because hers was as blue as the ocean that connects the Plymouths old and new. But whatever the reason, nothing seemed to intoxicate her more than the prestigious narcotic of heritage, and she was always quick to point out to worthy company that Mother's family had arrived in America on the *Mayflower*.

Aimée was reared in a spacious, five-bedroom, three-hundred-year-old colonial home which was one of the oldest in Marblehead and part of Massachusetts' historic Heritage Trail. It was a showplace adorned with only the finest Hitchcock furniture, Waterford crystal, and seventeenth- and eighteenth-century heirlooms. The men of the family wore Brooks Brothers suits; the women shopped at Talbot's, Bonwit Teller, and Lord & Taylor; and Aimée was deprived of nothing but affection.

As a child, though Aimée was considerably smaller in stature than most girls her age, she was exceptionally bright and cheery, with icy blue eyes and shiny, straight-as-string hair so fine and translucent that the sunlight filtered through it like copper. Indeed, she was possessed of charms ample enough to melt even the most frigid of hearts. And in her early years she tried to be a "good girl" in what proved to be a vain attempt to intercept Father's attention on its way to the office.

Nonetheless, Aimée remained undaunted. Father, a senior partner in the law firm of Adams, Hudson, Green, Harris & Adams, P.C., obviously respected education, so she took to her elementary studies with a fierce persistence. Miss Dowd, a sixth-grade teacher who but for a "y" would have been aptly named, and who was the president of the local chapter of the Audubon Society, adorned paper after perfect paper with stick-on robins, orioles, and cardinals, the avian equivalent of stars, which Mother dutifully displayed, gathering a flock so dense it would have daunted even Hitchcock. But, never a bird watcher, Father remained unimpressed.

Nor did a pubescent spurt of growth improve her status, for by that time two brothers and one sister, ranging from one to five years her junior, seemed destined to make her the runt of the litter. The only thing that could temper her growing jealousy was the knowledge that, with the notable exception of Lawrence, Jr., her siblings had escaped Father's notice as thoroughly as herself.

Unlike Father, Mother paid all of her offspring strict attention. But it was an antiseptic attention born less of affection than duty. She was the perfect mechanical mother, responding with precision to her children's needs: maintaining a transportation service to rival the MTA, praising good deeds and admonishing bad, and taking proper note of trends.

One such trend was the correlation between how rapidly young Aimée outgrew her bras and the lateness of the hour she returned home from dates.

"I think you should speak with her, Lawrence," Nancy Harris finally announced courageously.

"Isn't this something you could handle a bit more delicately, dear, 'woman talk'?"

"What I say doesn't seem to carry any weight. Please, Lawrence."

Lawrence Harris could never remember having "spoken with" his daughter before, and he would soon wish he could forget this time.

"Anything we do, we could do *before* 10:30," fifteen-year-old Aimée said with a disinterested shrug, spinning on her heels and leaving the den to an appalled Father, whose first and last piece of paternal advice stuck in his throat a decade too late.

"Well?" Nancy asked expectantly.

"She's a tramp," Father pronounced. "I wash my hands of her." And he folded the Boston *Evening Globe* under his arm and returned to the den with his martini, almost as disappointed in his wife as he was in his daughter.

Though even at thirteen Aimée was virtually a sexual magnet, she remained a "technical virgin" well into her sixteenth year: "technical" because at fourteen she had felt for the first time a male's stiffness through the friction of two layers of nylon as he dry-humped her on the beach, in their private little nook of Sandy Cove in the shadows of the cliffs below Ambassador Millard's estate; "technical" because by fifteen she had mastered a hand-job that the locker room grapevine described as "better than fucking Marion Comstock."

Aimée was experienced yet discriminating, and it amused her that a larger-than-average bustline on a smaller-than-average body—which in spite of her almost conscientious neglect remained hard and muscular—could overpower young men literally twice her size, or thoughtful men more than twice her age.

But it was more than her body that attracted them. It was a face that was not sharp-featured and gorgeous, but pretty; not classically beautiful, but cute. It was a disposition that sparkled like her auburn hair in the bright summer sun. It was her bearing, her attitude toward them. It was her consumption of them, her reveling in them, the touch of them, the feel of them, the smell of them: those mysteries so long unknown. It was her insatiable desire to please them, to be accepted by them, to be wanted by them.

By her mid-teens she had been reading Father's *Law Journal* religiously for four years, along with selected decisions from the *Massachusetts Reports.* She joined the debating club at Marblehead High School and *became* the debating club. At first, of course, these interests had been spurred by an unabated desire to win Father's approval. But very soon, and quite surprisingly, she found that she enjoyed them, enjoyed everything about them. She loved words, loved their subtle nuances, and became almost sexually aroused when she knew instinctively that a specific word would fit precisely here and she was able to pick it dextrously from her brain without breaking stride. She loved a good, stimulating argument, having put to use a tenet she'd overheard from Father as he heatedly explained to Mother why he brought so much work home from the office: "A good lawyer spends ten hours *out* of court in preparation for each hour he'll spend *in* court." It was a fine piece of advice and she wished she hadn't had to *steal* it.

Though she found her high school studies relatively unchallenging, Aimée's interest never flagged, and by the end of her junior year, at age sixteen, she had been accepted for admission to half a dozen colleges, including Harvard and Yale, but chose Stanford, which she entered in the fall of 1974. In the three years it took her to earn her degree, Aimée became as confident and adventurous sexually as she was academically.

In California she was no longer an extension of Lawrence and

Nancy Harris and a sister of Harriet, Chester, and Lawrence, Jr. She was Aimée Harris, period. She could wander about the panoramic Palo Alto campus and finally be treated as an adult. And if through no design of her own she continued to attract men like a human electromagnet, at least now she could deal with it openly and as she chose.

At Stanford Aimée joined the debating club, then quickly dropped it as old hat, preferring to concentrate on her pre-law studies and her rapidly maturing social life, whose focal point was not *a* man, but men—*all* men. Her measure of a man was not necessarily chronological, though the qualities she sought she often found in men much older than she. Of course, she wasn't above yielding to the obvious advances of a college farm-boy or a local high schooler in the interests of a healthy, energetic fuck, but it was men with brains who interested her, serious men, sensitive men, men who challenged her mentally, who loved a stimulating discussion. To boys she sometimes gave her body, but to men she gave her all.

Aimée grew to love Palo Alto's mild climate and its distance from home; Stanford, with its clean, Spanish stucco architecture; and the law school in particular, with its brilliant young professors and dedicated students. Even so, she never once considered any other law school but The Law School: Harvard Law School, a noble goal, but one, she was sure, that was shared with equal enthusiasm by every pre-law student in America. Thus, she was careful not to allow her social life to interfere with her main priority and, after earning three consecutive years of high honors at Stanford, was in the fall of 1977, at nineteen, the youngest of the 23 women and 131 men in the entering class of Harvard University Law School.

In Cambridge she lived in a tiny single room on campus, which she transformed into livable condition with a variety of plants, including ficus, African violets, pepperomia, and other hearty strains, and a six-foot rubber tree placed judiciously to hide a water stain on the wall at the head of her small bed. She worked long hours, spurned many advances, and quickly shed her awe of both the competition and her tormentors, a group of the most outstanding law professors ever assembled and which even included, in a Harvardian display of liberality, a handful of women.

During the summer between her first and second years, Aimée took her first vacation since high school and quite possibly the last she would be able to afford in the foreseeable future, since the next spring the mad scramble would begin for apprentice jobs with prestigious law firms. Such a job, if she was fortunate enough to land one, would occupy the summer between her second and third years. After her third year would come preparation for the bar exam and in the fall—hopefully—a full-time job.

She enjoyed the first week of freedom from routine, sleeping regularly until late morning, lying snugly sunk into the feathers of the old mattress on her antique brass bed. Her room at home was warm and cozy, full of fine memories and twice the size of her dormitory room at Harvard. The walls were cornflower blue, her favorite color, freshly painted by Mother just the week before in a dutiful "welcome home" gesture. In that room she was surrounded by old friends: Betsy Wetsy, a worn and tattered Poor Pitiful Pearl, and a like-new Ken and Barbie, whom she had outgrown years before Father had given them to her on her twelfth birthday. On sunny days she took a sandwich and a beer, sat by the neighbors' swimming pool, and read novel after pulpy novel until she became so horny she wanted to scream.

On a sweltering afternoon late in June, Aimée, like the heroine in one of her paperback novels, lay on her back on the diving board, still burning with the excitement of making love with a stranger. And she was also thinking, remorsefully, of Todd Thornton—attractive, bright, wealthy Todd, whom she'd been dating back in Boston for the past three months. She was beginning to wonder if things would work out with Todd or if she would need a new man every day to survive the growing ennui of the next two months at home, when she was suddenly and rudely interrupted.

An hour before he first saw Aimée Harris, Lynell Alan was sweating in the fifth-floor suite of offices occupied by the accounting firm of Arthur Young & Company at Boston's 10 Post Office Square. It was the first remarkably uncomfortable day of the summer, hot and steamy, and in a tribute to American technology the building's central air conditioning was inoperative.

For six months Lynell had been sharing the ride between Boston and Marblehead with one of the firm's senior accountants. Today, after leaving work early as a concession to the intense heat, they rode in the air-conditioned comfort of Richard Ferris's new Mercedes.

They covered the twenty-five miles north to Marblehead, ninety minutes in rush hour, in just under half an hour. Ferris pulled up alongside the eight-foot brick wall that hid his house and swimming pool from the road, not bothering to turn into the steep driveway. "I'll get you a bathing suit and you can hang out here this afternoon, Lyn," he offered, stepping out of the car.

"I don't want to impose, Richard."

"No imposition at all. You'll have the place to yourself. I'm just going inside to grab a clean shirt. Then I'm going to run over to the country club to join Barb and the kids."

"Well . . ."

"Just step outside and tell me you want me to drive you home."

Lynell could feel the muggy air wafting in through the open door. It was a Turkish bath in contrast to the controlled climate of the Mercedes. "I'm convinced."

It was the first time he had been inside Ferris's home. The sturdy, two-story brick structure was built into the side of the hill, so near the road that part of the wall that ran behind the sidewalk was the south wall of the house. They entered the lower-floor kitchen from the driveway. There was a large family room off one side of the kitchen and a small laundry room opposite, between the kitchen and garage.

Ferris walked into the laundry room, took a neatly folded shirt from the shelf, and tossed Lynell a brief piece of nylon. "Here you go. Might be a bit small, but . . ." He shrugged. "Don't wear it if it's uncomfortable. We won't be back until five-thirty, six o'clock. I'll toot the horn if you're modest."

"Thanks."

"The pool is up the stairs, across the living room, and through the porch. The wall goes all the way around and we keep the gate locked from the inside, so you'll have complete quiet and privacy. Help yourself to the beer," he added, gesturing at the refrigerator as he passed it. "Make yourself at home." And he was out the door and gone.

Lynell went into the family room to change. He folded his gray suit neatly and balled his wilted shirt around his socks and underwear. Speedos were not his personal choice, stylistically. He preferred baggier bathing suits—cutoff Levi's were his favorite. And Richard's suit had to be two sizes too small. He had seen men wearing them. When they were wet they left nothing to the imagination. But then, he'd be alone. He hoped he'd have the nerve to swim in the raw.

He was on the screened-in porch and reaching for the door to the patio before he saw them at the far end of the pool, the shallow end; there could be no doubt as to what they were doing.

Her back was toward him. The first glimpse he ever had of Aimée Harris was of her naked, white behind. The man, fully two heads taller, was facing the porch but was too preoccupied to notice that they were no longer alone; Lynell was too preoccupied even to look at the man's face.

Lynell flushed with the guilt of his discovery, recalled the shock of a

71

boy walking in on his mother and father. He wanted to escape, wanted to stay.

Her legs were wrapped around him; their hands held each other's hips desperately; and as they pushed against each other, her bottom—that sweet, round perfection—moved hypnotically, bobbed above the water line, then below, until the young man pulled her roughly to him, held her fast, in his deep, shuddering climax.

When their light laughter floated to him, Lynell felt that sudden lonely emptiness, that wanting-to-sneak-away-in-the-night sensation he had felt the few times he'd slept with a stranger.

"That was good," the young man sighed finally as they held each other.

Lynell was still riveted to the porch floor when she pulled away, turning so he could see her breasts, not large but bigger than he had expected, white against tan.

He backed slowly into the living room, closing the door gingerly, still unable to take his eyes from her. He watched from his clandestine vantage point as she paddled languidly to the edge of the pool, stood in the waist-deep water, and snatched up the small pile that was her bikini from the side of the pool, letting the bottom float in front of her as she slipped into the top and tied it behind her. While the still-naked young man swam toward the deep end with long, lazy strokes, she dipped her headful of cinnamon hair under the surface and stepped into the bikini bottoms, and Lynell seized the opportunity to retreat across the living room and down the stairs to the safety of the kitchen.

The now-exaggerated tightness of the Speedo was at the same time physically uncomfortable and psychologically reassuring. It was the first time since . . . He shook off the thought, went to the laundry room and found a pair of Richard's tennis shorts, struggled out of the Speedo, and put them on. They were snug but a big improvement. Then he grabbed a beer from the refrigerator and sat at the counter, picked up the copy of *Sports Illustrated* he found there, and tried to think of other things. He couldn't.

He'd wait an appropriate interval before arriving at poolside—fifteen minutes should be enough. He'd climb the stairs slowly, making a monumental racket this time. God, with her, he knew once wouldn't have been enough for him. What a wonderful body—and he was so lonely, much worse now. The whiteness of her still burned the inside of his retina.

Three paragraphs into a story about the antique collection of the St. Louis Cardinals' baseball player Ted Simmons, he decided he couldn't possibly confront the couple at poolside and maintain his composure.

He was ready to slip out quietly and walk the two miles home, when he heard the young man whistling past the screen door of the kitchen, up the steep driveway, and out of earshot down the road toward the Summer Theater. I'd be whistling, too, he thought. He guessed the young man must be about twenty. At twenty-nine, Lynell suddenly felt fifty-nine. *So that's what the college kids are doing these days while I'm out working?*

He finished the baseball article and his beer simultaneously and went to the refrigerator for another. Feeling somehow excited that the young woman would be alone and flushed with the glow of sex, and filled with the unreasoned logic that in her arousal she would want him, too, he actually removed two bottles before checking his libido and his memory, judiciously returning one.

Most of each breast spilled tantalizingly out of her pale yellow bikini, and the smooth, dark rise of her nipples was visible through the two tiny triangles of sheer nylon. She lay face up on the diving board, with her feet toward him. He stood over her, eyes drawn along the length of her—her thighs, up, inside them, stopping, heart beating heavily for her, sitting quickly in a pool chair lest she should awaken and see his obscene wanting. "Mind if I join you?" he asked, announcing himself as he sat. The young man had left. Singing had seemed superfluous.

"Oh!" She bolted upright. "You startled me," she said, embarrassedly re-covering the breast that had fallen exposed. But then, she didn't know. He found it mildly amusing. "Who are you, anyway?" she demanded, her misinterpretation of his smug grin at her exposure quickly transforming her embarrassment into anger.

For the first time he saw her face. She wasn't beautiful, certainly not in the classic sense. But there was something about her . . . something . . . what was the word? There was something . . . captivating . . . Yes, there was something incredibly captivating about this woman, and now he couldn't take his eyes from her *face*. "Lynell Alan." God, he hoped this wasn't the fifteen-year-old daughter Richard was always raving about. "I work with Richard. He invited me to spend the afternoon. He didn't think anyone would be here, though. I'm sorry. I'll leave if I'm intruding on your privacy," he offered, standing. But he had already done that to a greater degree than she would ever know.

"Oh, no, that's okay. I'm sorry I snapped at you. I had no right. I was just startled."

"That's my fault. I thought you'd hear me coming."

"Well, you got a free peek," she said irritably as she tightened the knot behind her.

He couldn't understand how the small bra stood the strain. "I didn't do that on purpose," he apologized, blushing self-consciously. *Christ, why would I? I just saw you get your brains fucked out,* he wanted to say, but didn't.

"Okay . . . truce," she offered, smiling behind teeth of exaggerated whiteness in contrast to her tanned face, teeth perfect but for a narrow gap separating the front two. "Aimée Harris. My family lives next door." She stood, stepped down from the diving board, and extended her hand.

"And where do *you* live?" he asked.

"Cambridge." Perspiration glistened over her body, rolled down her flat brown stomach. She was diminutive in stature, but that body: perfectly proportioned and with the faint, delicious aroma of coconut oil. He would have liked nothing more at that moment than to sink his teeth into the tight bronze flesh at the curve of her hip. When she turned her back to him his heart stopped. She dived into the pool, slipping gracefully under the surface without a splash. "Come on in," she called up to him, "the water's great."

He put his beer on the diving board, took an eager step toward the edge, and looked down at her. Seeing her there in the pool for the second time, he suddenly remembered what he had seen the first time and stepped back. "No, thanks; maybe later."

For Lynell Alan, Aimée Harris would prove at first to be a cure, and then a disease.

The voice had come out of her dream. But it wasn't Todd's voice, and she only noticed how sexy-looking the man was after she had snapped at him.

When he introduced himself, Aimée was convinced that her once keen, analytical mind was slipping. Of course this would be the locally famous—or infamous—Lynell Alan, the handsome, young bachelor whom Mother had had occasion to meet briefly earlier in the year. "He's *so* charming. And he seems not to notice that *every* female between fifteen and fifty is simply *mad* about him," Mother had said in her inimitable style.

He might be handsome and charming, Aimée thought, but he sure was slow. In the hour they had chatted he never so much as hinted at making a pass at her, even after a good bit of subtle prompting, such as her talk of how boring Marblehead was and how few available men there were.

"Have you ever been to a square dance?" she had asked finally, as they climbed the steep driveway separating her parents' property from the Ferrise's.

"Never."

"A friend of mine is having one Friday night at eight—to celebrate a barn raising, really. They've rebuilt the one that burned down last fall." She stammered like a schoolgirl. "Maybe you'd like to try one?" she blurted, immediately wishing she hadn't. If he'd wanted a date he'd have asked, wouldn't he? He probably lived with someone.

"Love to," he had answered, flashing that charming smile. "Should I meet you there?"

"No. Pick me up at seven-thirty." Christ, he was hopeless.

At the dance Mother was extraordinarily attentive and Aimée thought that Father might even have noticed, though he successfully kept any judgment from registering on his stoic face. As the festivities neared an end, Aimée was sure that, if anything, Mother had underestimated Lynell Alan's charms—fifteen to fifty didn't cover it: *every* woman was charmed by him and not least of all she. Not only did he seem to be totally unaware of that but also of the lusty rumors that trailed him around town, fed by his aura of remote sexuality.

They strolled the beach and he held her hand, and the silence wasn't an empty first-date silence but was filled with the new intimacy that passed between them. She wondered what she would do if he wanted to sleep with her, because she wanted more than anything the closeness of that closest act. But somehow she would have been disappointed if that was what *he* wanted more than anything, because she knew, as corny as it seemed to her, she knew that she was in love with him. It was curious how, the first time, it was so much easier to sleep with someone you didn't care about, and she cared about this man and wanted him to care about her.

She loved the way he always referred to her—to every adult female—as a woman rather than as a girl. But he could have *called* her anything; he made her *feel* like a woman.

"You are such a serious woman," he said as they walked.

"I'm in serious competition," she answered, sounding more defensive than she had intended. "This summer is my final fling and I'm going to enjoy it."

"I thought you were bored."

"I'm not bored now," she said, squeezing his hand warmly.

"Neither am I," he agreed. "But on Monday I'll be an accountant again. God, an accountant: it even sounds boring."

They stopped for a nightcap at the Red Lion Inn, a local establishment dripping colonial atmosphere and packed to its two-hundred-year-old oak rafters with boisterous young Marblehead sons and daughters returned to the womb for the summer. She apologized.

"For being home and reminiscing?" he asked. "Don't be silly."

At her front door she held both his hands in hers. "Thank you for coming, Lynell. Square dances and high school friends—I hope you didn't feel left out."

He tucked her hair back over her ear and lay his warm palm against her cool, smooth cheek. "May I kiss you good-night?"

"I'd like that," she whispered, and when he bent low they were lost for those few seconds in the warm softness of each other's lips.

Inside the house Aimée leaned against the door, trembling, then quickly walked to the stairs and sat on the thick carpet. Blood pounded in her temples, and she knew that Lynell Alan's rumors would soon include her.

During the next six months, Lynell and Aimée enjoyed a near-idyllic life in an apartment they shared at the Kenmore Square end of Commonwealth Avenue in Boston. It was a spacious, one-bedroom apartment on the second floor of an old brownstone and had two bay windows with window seats perched high above the sidewalk. Beautiful refinished hardwood floors and a large working fireplace added to its romantic charm. The only drawback, from Aimée's point of view, was its proximity to Fenway Park, where Lynell dragged her every weekend through September when the Red Sox were home.

"Finally," Aimée sighed when they had signed the lease. "An apartment where I won't be sleeping in the kitchen."

"*Or* in the living room," Lynell said with a laugh. "Although either could easily be arranged," he added with a lecherous grin.

In a brief fling at domestication, Aimée convinced a reluctant Lynell that they should adopt a calico kitten from the litter of a beautiful black cat owned by a family on the first floor.

"C.C.," Lynell answered with a disinterested shrug when Aimée asked him to suggest a name. "You know, Calico Cat—C.C.," he explained.

Lynell became more attached to the animal than he cared to admit, and when, on his way home from work two weeks later, the woman downstairs passed him carrying an anemic gray-and-white kitten, he inquired jovially if this was the last to be adopted.

"We haven't had any luck. I'm taking her to the vet."

"He's going to find her a home?" Lynell asked naively.

"Um," she answered hesitantly, "in a manner of speaking."

Lynell looked at her cradling the pathetic ball of gray and white fluff in her arms, and his eyes widened with sudden comprehension. "Oh, no, you're not," he blurted in spite of himself as he snatched the doomed animal from her grasp.

"L.C.," he said, this time to a disbelieving Aimée. "Little Cat." He stroked the pathetically skinny animal lovingly.

"You continually amaze me, Lynell. Continually."

There were many reasons why they loved each other then, and there was no need to analyze them. Aimée was happy at school and at home, and both worked and played hard. For Lynell, on the other hand, the evenings with Aimée made up in a great measure for the tedious days at Arthur Young & Company. But those days were also the source of his sometimes desperately black moods, during which he shut out everything and everyone, including Aimée. More and more his outlet became—literally—running himself into the ground, and not surprisingly, he began to lose weight.

During the Christmas season of 1979, something happened that would change their lives; ironically, it grew from a seed planted and nurtured by Aimée herself.

"Jesus, Aimée, I haven't been to a cotillion since high school."

"It'll be fun, Lynell. Anyway, you can never tell when you're going to need a tuxedo."

"Right. I'll take this one," Lynell said. "Forty long, 32/32 pants," he announced proudly, remembering the new size he'd had to buy when all his old suits had begun to fall off him.

"Just a minute," Aimée grasped the salesman's arm lightly, then immediately let go and turned back to Lynell. "Madras? You're going to buy a *madras* dinner jacket? You're joking." She turned to the young salesman. "He's joking. Black."

"Wait a second," Lynell called after him. The salesman stopped a few feet down the aisle as Lynell spoke to Aimée. "Hey, at my last cotillion madras was a smash."

"Yeah? I want to see the pictures."

"Okay, so I didn't wear madras. But this is a special occasion."

"Your mere presence at the Park Plaza will antagonize Father enough. Madras would be overkill." Aimée turned to the impatient salesman a third time and said with an air of finality, "Black."

The young man gave an exasperated shake of his head. All he really wanted was to go on his lunch break.

"Why doesn't your father approve of me, anyway?" Lynell whispered when the salesman was out of earshot.

"Because you don't respect him."

"I don't respect him, Aimée, because he doesn't respect *you*."

Aimée smiled broadly and absently fingered the top button of her blouse. "Ah, but if he doesn't respect *me*, Lynell, maybe it's because I live with *you*."

"Touché," he said, licking his index finger and notching her score invisibly in the air between them.

The Christmas cotillion Lynell had attended at the Pine Orchard High School gymnasium and this one at the Park Plaza ballroom were separated by ten years—but they were ten light-years. For this one he hadn't rented a tuxedo from Grimaldi's Department Store. For this one his date didn't wear "Blue Velvet" and nylon stockings that drooped on her heavy ankles. No, for this one Lynell wore a crisp, new, $175 Robert Hall tuxedo that might fall apart at the seams or stain his underarms blue-black if he perspired, but that, while it lasted, fit him like a glove. His date wore a floor-length satin Halston, slit almost to the hip and hugging her as tightly as black skin. It must have set Mother back three times the price of his suit—for one-tenth the material. And the guest of honor was James J. Adams, Mayor of Boston and, more significantly, Aimée's maternal uncle.

The price of a ticket had inflated—to one hundred dollars a couple—but so had the atmosphere: from crepe paper and balloons to a thirty-foot Christmas tree decorated with antique ornaments and a thousand tiny white lights; from Southern Comfort-spiked Hawaiian Punch and five bush-leaguers from East Haven to French champagne and the Benny Goodman Orchestra. It was a gala event, and Lynell whirled Aimée across the polished wood floor, rubbing elbows with and stepping on the polished patent-leather feet of Boston Brahmins.

He had never before seen Aimée in this light, in *her* light, and she literally glowed in it. Her cheeks flushed with excitement and she flitted from table to table, introducing Lynell to people with names out of history books and the front page of the *Boston Globe*—including its publisher, and Mother and Father's next-door neighbor, Donald Moncrief. Everyone was there.

They met Lawrence and Nancy Harris seated among a dozen dignitaries, including Jeremy Thornton, whose sleazy but immensely profitable real estate deals were legendary in Suffolk, Essex, and Plymouth Counties, the legality of which had for decades been seen to—or the illegality of which had been circumvented—by Aimée's father's law firm of Adams, Hudson, Green, Harris & Adams, P.C. While Mrs.

Harris introduced Lynell around the table with stiff politeness, he felt a spasm of jealousy twitch like an open nerve as the land baron's attractive son led Aimée to the dance floor, encircled her waist, and held her close.

When the introductions were complete, the Thorntons and Harrises and Adamses and Greens and Hudsons returned to their interrupted conversations, leaving Lynell to wonder what was the inconspicuous thing to do, the polite thing to do, the *right* thing to do under the present circumstances. Should he return to their table and wait for Aimée to be "delivered" by young Thornton? Or should he wait here so as not to leave her unescorted?

"You look uncomfortable," she said when he looked over his shoulder in response to her tapping. "Would you like to dance?"

"I'd love to," he sighed with relief.

"My name is Janet Shupe," she said as they danced to "Sentimental Journey."

"Lynell Alan." He stepped back to offer his hand. Though she obviously utilized every feminine wile to rise above the description, Janet Shupe was extremely average looking. Spike heels could only raise her average height to around five feet, six inches. Perfectly applied makeup highlighted her intense brown eyes and softened the severe planes of her long, narrow face but was barely able to nudge her into the "attractive" category. Her hair was frosted and closely cropped, and an obviously expensive, shimmering, full-cut gown was draped from throat to ankle over what Lynell suspected was no more than an average figure. He guessed she was in her late forties but she could easily have been ten years younger . . . or ten years older.

She danced beautifully, and for the first time he was grateful for the two years of lessons his mother had forced on him so long ago. Together they slipped artfully into "Mood Indigo." In spite of the cynical attitude he always adopted when he attended such pretentious affairs, Lynell had to admit he was enjoying himself. Janet Shupe followed him as surely as a tuning fork humming sympathetically to his vibrations. The music carried him away and he loosened his grip, which he noticed was too firm.

"God, this music is romantic," he said wistfully. "It's not too difficult to figure out why there was a baby boom in the 1940s."

Aimée and Todd Thornton waltzed through his daydream, and his expression altered when he noticed them in close, private conversation, alone among 250 other couples.

"I'm sorry?" he said when he realized Janet Shupe had spoken to him.

"Men. You're all alike," she began, and he expected an admonition about dancing with one woman and thinking about another. "What I said was, 'you know, Lynell Alan, even in that cheap suit, you're gorgeous.'"

He threw back his head and laughed, then looked down into those serious brown eyes. "I'm at a total loss, Janet. Should I say I've never been so insulted or never been so flattered?"

"The former, because I'm sure the latter would be a lie."

"Well, then, I've never been so insulted," he said with mock hauteur. "I paid a hundred and seventy-five dollars for this suit."

"You were robbed." Then her smile turned serious. "But it fits you wonderfully. May I ask what size you are?"

"Size?"

"Suit size."

"Janet, I can't imagine where this is leading, but . . ."

"Don't worry, Lynell." She watched Aimée and Todd Thornton dance by, lost in the crowd. "I can't compete with her." Then she looked back at Lynell and, as if reading his mind, added, "And he sure can't compete with you."

"My jealous streak is that obvious?"

She nodded. The orchestra finished "Mood Indigo" with a flourish and Lynell thanked her with a ceremonious bow.

"My pleasure," she said. "Forty long, right?" When her meaning didn't register, she prompted him. "Your cheap suit. Forty long."

"Yes, but . . ."

"And with your elbows slightly bent you could probably fit into a forty regular," she said. Slipping her purse from under her arm, she produced a small business card and held it out to him.

"Are you a haberdasher, Janet?" he asked, winking impishly.

"Just call me if you get a chance." She started to walk away but stopped and turned as though knowing he would still be standing in the middle of the quickly emptying dance-floor, holding her card quizzically in front of him. "By the way, Lynell, if you don't mind my asking, what do you do for a living?"

His face twisted with distaste. "I'm an accountant."

"Funny. You don't look like an accountant."

"Yeah? This is probably a set-up, Janet," he said with a wince, "but I'll bite. What *do* I look like?"

"You look like a model." And she disappeared into the crowd.

* * *

80

He had made dinner, passable beef Stroganoff. Aimée had arrived home late from a *Law Review* meeting, so he had eaten alone and she had allowed him to keep company with his thoughts.

In the window seat he leaned back with his feet up, sipping a glass of his favorite two-dollar-a-bottle Czech wine and stroking a purring L.C. curled comfortably in his lap. He watched the thinning foot-traffic pass below in the leaden dusk of another late winter day and again wondered sadly why C.C. had taken to the rooftops over a month ago, never to return. No loyalty, he thought. L.C. missed her, too.

From the kitchen he could hear the tap water and intermittent bursts of the garbage disposal as Aimée went about *his* usual job. She was a good cook and he normally didn't mind doing the dishes. But tonight he was glad for the change, any change. God, any change at all.

Her words and his spring-weight khaki jacket hit him with a simultaneous thud, and L.C. scrambled angrily to the floor. "Let's go," she said tersely.

"Gee, Aimée, I'm not really in the mood to go out tonight. Where did you want to go, anyway?"

"It's where *you* want to go, Lynell. You've been putting it off for three months. You'll never know unless you try," she said with a shake of her head. Then she read from the small card that had been tacked up on the kitchen message-board for three months: "Janet Shupe, Montage Models, 2757 Newbury Street, Boston, Mass., (617)383-0078."

"It's eight o'clock at night, for Christ's sake."

"They have open interviews every Thursday night from seven to ten." She grinned with self-satisfaction.

He looked up at her with a pained expression.

"What can it hurt?"

They shared the small anteroom with nine other aspirants—seven women and two men—and it was fifteen minutes before they could sit in one of the five leather chairs. From behind where Aimée sat in the V between his legs, Lynell took in the scene and got his first taste of humility.

The women were young and beautiful, the men were young and beautiful, and they came in a steady parade that soon stretched far into the second-floor hallway. He wondered which had come first, the agency name or the montage of advertisements and fashion layouts

81

that papered the walls, fighting each other for attention with splashing colors, flashing teeth, and bone structures as breathtakingly angular as the exotic panoramas. As he looked from those perfect, frozen smiles to the smooth-skinned faces around him, he silently asked himself the question he would ask again a million times over: *What the fuck am I doing here?*

The disappointed hopefuls entered and exited the inner office with embarrassing speed, and Lynell prayed they wouldn't just stop him at the door. "Are you kidding, pal? Don't waste your time or ours."

A graying former pretty-boy stopped in the doorway and did a double-take in their direction, and in the flash before the man continued on his way, Lynell's heart stopped. He's probably checking out Aimée or wondering what someone my age is doing here, Lynell thought. By the look of it, they don't get many twenty-nine-year-old beginners.

"Next."

"My God, you have great bones." The former pretty-boy, whose name Lynell was too nervous to catch, sat them at a high, round glass table on wicker barstools. "Come here, Cara," he called excitedly, as a brunette woman left a strikingly beautiful twenty-year-old man at the door.

"Not exactly our type," she was saying. "Just a sec, George." Then to the young man again, "Maybe you should try Copley Models or A-R-T."

"This is the man I told you about a few minutes ago, Cara."

"Yes, I can see, the one with the bones. Beautiful," she said, surveying him as though he were a prime cut and she was deciding on the right government stamp.

"I'm just his moral support," Aimée said when Cara eyed her suspiciously.

"With bones like that, he doesn't need any support—moral or otherwise. Do you have any pictures?" she asked, taking the reins from George.

"No."

"First thing you've got to do is get some pictures taken: head shots—smiling and serious, profiles, full lengths—one in a bathing suit or shorts so we can see the body, and one in a business suit. We've got to see if those bones come across in black and white. By the way, how tall are you?"

"Six two."

"A little tall. Not bad . . . Weight?"

"175."

"Suit?"

"Forty long. But I can easily fit into a forty regular," he added quickly.

She nodded with apparent approval. "What do you think, George?"

George smiled and peered at Lynell as Picasso would at an empty canvas. "Shadowing right here," he said, running an index finger along each side of Lynell's nose. "Narrow it a bit. Pull the eyes out, shadow the cheeks and . . . *love* those cheekbones."

"Is your hair naturally curly?" Cara asked.

Lynell nodded. "But I can straighten it easily."

"Good. I think we can use you. But we've got to see some pictures first. And have a few taken with your hair straight." She handed him a photocopied list of names and addresses. "You can use one of these photographers, or if you know anyone you'd prefer . . . Try to get back to us within two weeks, okay? I'll tell you right now, Lynell, and this may sound stupid, but my only reservation is that you may be too up-scale for the Boston market."

"Upscale?" Aimée asked. Lynell was too stunned to speak.

"Classy. High fashion. Too good-looking. The Boston market is mostly young executive stuff: Route 128, engineering, high tech. Lynell's the perfect age range, but he might look *too* good in a suit. You know: unbelievable to the consumer. Some advertisers in this market are scared off by models who might steal attention from the product." She used her hands in a calming gesture. "Just bring back some pictures. We'll take it from there."

As they passed from the inner office through the anteroom, Lynell was the center of the rapt attention of the expectant crowd.

When they were alone in the hallway, Aimée turned and hugged him. "I feel sorry for those schnooks," she said. "You're going to be a tough act to follow."

He looked down at her with a grin and winked his eyebrows playfully. "I know," he said, wishing he were as confident as she was. They celebrated flirtation with success over dinner at the Chart House.

To have his ego crushed was one thing. Lynell refused to have it cost him an arm and a leg in the process. For the time involved in setting up and taking the shots he needed, the fees of the three photographers he called from the Montage list were upward of $400 each. Aimée had a friend, Jeff Foster, a photographer for the *Globe*, who would do it for $125 plus the cost of processing the film.

Lynell's first impression—that Foster was a lightweight—was quickly dispelled by the seriousness with which he took the job.

"Do the makeup yourself?" Foster asked as Lynell and Aimée stepped into his tiny, unkempt Back Bay apartment.

"No. I did it," Aimée answered, preempting what she anticipated would be an acerbic remark by Lynell, who, she knew, already felt like a flaming queen.

"For a woman who never wears makeup, you know what you're doing."

For the standard shots Foster brought them to his small studio on Boylston Street. Then they drove south to Cohasset. Lynell was overwhelmed by the number of shots Foster took in each of the set-up situations. "You don't think Cheryl Tiegs looks great in *every* shot, do you?" The only time Lynell balked was when Foster told him to strip to the waist for a full-length macho shot with the Atlantic Ocean as a backdrop.

"You're kidding. It has to be thirty-five degrees out here."

"Don't be a pussy. This is man's work. Freeze in the winter, sweat in the summer. Now take your fuckin' coat off and let's get to work. If you stiffen up, I'm sure little Aimée will take care of you." He turned to Aimée, who had followed them unobtrusively throughout the day.

Aimée glared at Foster with mock affront. "If I thought you were smart enough for puns, I'd slap your face."

One hundred twenty-five dollars didn't seem enough for what Jeff Foster had done for him. He had made him feel at ease in front of the camera—something he had feared no one would be able to do. He had made him feel as though smiling into that lens, or shooting it a steamy stare, was the most natural thing in the world.

"If anyone ever tries to tell you that what you're doing is foolish or faggy, man, just think of the seventy-five dollars an hour they pay for decent models in this town—and there aren't very many of them. Not bad pocket money."

"I'm exhausted," Lynell said, when he and Aimée arrived back at their apartment just before midnight. He flopped on the bed without taking off his clothes.

"It's been a long day."

"Not to mention expensive. One hundred twenty-five dollars, plus thirty-five for processing and a hundred for dinner at Locke-Ober's."

"He's good. Anyway, it's a write-off." She was standing by the bed, undressed to the waist. "You're the accountant."

"Don't remind me."

She dropped to her knees at the side of the bed, ran her fingers through his soft curls, and said excitedly, "You're going to be a star, Lynell. I can feel it in my bones. Don't ask me how I know, I just feel it. You're going to be a star." But he didn't hear her. He was sound asleep.

The ten contact-sheets with two dozen negative-sized prints on each arrived in the mail three days later addressed to Aimée. Lynell was sitting in the window seat with the unopened manila envelope in his lap when he saw Aimée walking toward him across the intersection of Massachusetts and Commonwealth Avenues three blocks away. He began waving the envelope madly when he saw her.

"Open it! Open it!" she screamed when he met her at the door.

Jeff Foster's note said it all: "Aimée, I'm good, but I'm not *this* good. The guy hardly takes a bad picture. I don't know, Aimée, but there's something about him. For what it's worth, my advice is to hook on with Montage or someone else in town and get some experience. But send some prints to New York agents, like Wilhelmina, Ford, Elite, or even Cline—it can't hurt. Don't ask me what it is, but he's got it. Give a call when you decide what shots you want printed. I've X'ed the ones I like, but it's your money. And Aimée, some more advice—don't let this guy out of your sight. Jeff."

The timing was perfect. After the abrupt end of the tax season on April 15, Lynell was able to fit in time off for "go-sees"—visits to photographers and firms who hired models—but the mounting costs were beginning to seem like a waste of money: Jeff's $260, the $150 to Montage to be included in their headsheet, which he learned was a compendium of the agency's models that they sent to prospective clients. And, finally, $175 for his own individual composite. All he had gotten for his money after a month with Montage was a lot of encouragement, an increasingly annoying number of solicitous "darlings" from Janet Shupe and the other people at the agency, a mimeographed sheet of names of people to see, blisters on his feet, and more rejections than the Elephant Man at the Playboy Club.

His first job wasn't much. In fact, it was downright embarrassing. It was a promotion for a Father's Day sale at Filene's and was euphemistically referred to by the agency as "live modeling." Because it wasn't print it paid only thirty-five dollars an hour, but Lynell was suddenly overawed that someone was actually going to pay money for his looks.

On the Thursday night before the holiday, Lynell and another man walked the department-store floor for four hours, dressed in various sale outfits and passing out free samples of Ralph Lauren perfume.

Lynell's prayers were answered: no one he knew saw him, and when the job dragged ploddingly to an end, he signed his first voucher for $140, less Montage's ten percent commission. One hundred twenty-six dollars: not bad for riding escalators for four hours; and he hadn't even had to wear the orange jumpsuit. Joe Martone had been stuck with that one and had looked like a cross between Steve Canyon and an inflatable life raft. Indeed, there was only one panicky moment for Lynell.

"Do you have much experience 'freeze modeling'?" the manager of the Men's Department asked.

"Experience? I don't even know what it is!" Lynell announced proudly. After having briefly considered faking it he had changed his mind—only because the phrase "freeze modeling" conjured up images of something he'd sooner not become experienced in.

"We just put you up here in place of the mannequin," the manager explained from behind an almost visible cloud of body odor. "You stand perfectly still, and when the people aren't looking you change your position slightly. It's great fun if it's done correctly, and quite effective. Some people will stare for minutes and minutes, trying to decide if you're real or not. It's a good gimmick. Well, we may try it later in the evening, depending on how things are going."

Ten minutes before closing he dropped what remained of his Ralph Lauren perfume into a receptacle in a second-floor Men's Room and rode back down to the basement.

"Where the hell have you been?" snapped the manager. "You missed the last two changes, and Joe here had to do all of the freeze work."

"Gee, I'm sorry, Joe," Lynell said with feigned remorse. He did feel badly for Joe, but not badly enough that he'd have traded places.

"No sweat, it's kind of fun. And they gave me an outfit as a bonus." He smiled broadly as he displayed his selection: the orange jumpsuit. Well, at least he wouldn't get lost.

Then Lynell turned to the manager. "I tried to get back a few times, but I was so busy passing out this stuff . . ." He held out his empty basket. "Didn't you have a lot of customers? I kept heading them down this way." He didn't like being deceitful, but neither did he want to be a flop on his first job.

"Well, we did have a pretty good turnout," the manager said apologetically. "Good for you."

From the items he'd worn Lynell picked a simple white LaCoste tennis shirt. It was the least expensive choice, which assuaged his own guilt and at the same time seemed to please the relenting manager—and it wasn't polyester, so maybe he'd get some wear out of it.

Lynell's second job was a fashion show at Jordan Marsh, and it didn't come for over a month. He was nervous and excited and flushed with a thrill he used to feel when he anticipated a big basketball game. He hemmed and hawed in his anxiety over whether or not he wanted Aimée to go, but they both knew she wouldn't miss it for the world.

Benji, Jordan's fashion coordinator, was as effete as his name, and as he flitted from model to model he gushed compliments. He stopped halfway down the line and daubed the sheen from Lynell's face. "Jesus, I wish I looked just half as good in that thing," he said, adjusting the shoulders of the light-weight, charcoal-gray, pin-striped Halston suit. Lynell wore it with his elbows bent slightly, as Janet Shupe had instructed, so that his long arms would fit the standard-sized forty regular suit. "Listen. Catch one woman's eye and play to *her*. Give her the 'We're-going-to-do-some-serious-fucking-tonight' look," Benji advised him.

The women danced beautifully to the sounds of "Macho Man," as did several of the men with varying degrees of success. Lynell was simply himself. He caught Aimée's eye and he did give her his "serious fucking" look. Once over his initial stage fright he was able to get into the aura of the experience, and it was wild and frenetic and exciting. It was an orgasm of self-celebration he had never before experienced: the beautiful clothes, the beautiful people, the electricity of the audience. It was a completely professional job, and for the first time he felt like a professional model.

Each of the two forty-minute shows per day was a nonstop extravaganza of summer fashions. Lynell had six wardrobe changes: from the Halston suit to Fila tennis clothing to a skimpy Jantzen bathing suit. While half the models were strutting down the runway in a steady stream, the other half were in the wings throwing off clothes haphazardly, sometimes being helped into their next outfit so there would never be a break in the constant flow of models along the runway.

Lynell's first taste of the complete immodesty required of the runway model had come early on the first night, at dress rehearsal. Because of the logistic problems, all of the models—twelve women and five men (Lynell would soon come to learn that one of the difficulties for men in modeling was that they were in so much less demand than women)—had shared the single small dressing room nearest the auditorium. Lynell had flung off his Halston suit with the giddy rapture of a child inexplicably given permission to mess up his room, when he suddenly found himself in a quandary: if he pulled the tight-fitting bathing suit on over his underwear, even the thin outline of the Elance briefs would be visible. *When in Rome,* he thought, and looked up quickly to see what the Romans were doing, only to find himself sandwiched shoulder-to-shoulder between two stark-naked women, one black and one white. He was momentarily transfixed by the sight of the full-breasted, almost skin-headed black woman stepping into her bright-yellow bikini, her large round breasts bouncing to attention as she stood.

"I've seen you around," she said nonchalantly, extending her hand as though they were meeting on the busy corner of Washington Street six floors below. "I'm Mandy. I'm with Montage, too."

Her face was exotic; her skin, chocolate silk. He raised his hand haltingly. She shook it and, sensing his embarrassment, quickly snapped her bra in place.

"You'll get used to it," she said, but he knew he never would. "Better hurry."

That first time at dress rehearsal he'd worn the bathing suit over his underwear.

"Not a bad weekend," he said to Aimée as they left Jordan Marsh and crossed Park Street, and he fingered his pink voucher-stub. "Seven hundred fifty dollars for two days' work."

"You call that work?"

"I had to be there for five hours yesterday and five more today. Not to mention dress rehearsal Friday."

"Not to mention. Poor baby. Most of the time you just sat around waiting. You actually *worked*—if you call changing clothes with naked women work—for a grand total of about three hours."

"Have you ever tried it? It's harder than it looks."

"I'll bet," she said sarcastically.

He put his arm around her shoulders as they walked through the Common, and it seemed to him that the birds sang louder and more sweetly than they had in years. The yellow-green buds struggled to life on the trees around them, the park tingled with the aroma of spring, and people smiled and said, "Nice evening," transporting them to a Boston of a simpler time.

Paddle boats whisked over the pond, and as they crossed the trellised drawbridge in the fading light, he stopped and held her gently, feeling the warmth of her shoulders through her light-weight jacket. "I love you."

"I know."

His tender kiss was not of passion but of companionship, of respect, of thanks.

They began walking again, more slowly, and they drank in the sights and sounds of evening Boston coming alive.

"How about if I take you to the Bay Club for dinner? The view over the harbor from up there will be fantastic tonight."

"Wow. Big spender."

"Hey, I'm in the chips," he said, crinkling the voucher again.

"You think they'll accept that at the Bay Club?"

"Not if they're smart. I haven't even been paid for the job last month at Filene's."

"Lynell, did you see me?"

"What?"

"When you walked down the runway with that sexy, flared-nostril stare. With the glare of the lights I couldn't tell. Did you see me?"

"Aimée, I saw you even when I wasn't looking at you."

"Lynell?"

"Yes?"

"Before we go to the Bay Club for dinner?"

"Yes?"

"Let's go home and fuck."

"I thought you'd never ask."

The Jordan Marsh fashion show is an annual spring rite of Boston fashion. The models are experienced and gorgeous, the music and scenery are professional, and the clothes are exquisite. Corporate buyers normally fill at least the first three-dozen rows, gathering from all eighteen Jordan Marsh stores to make the big fiscal decision: which ensembles are practical enough to sell to the conservative housewife in rural Pittsfield, and which will appeal to the more cosmopolitan Bostonian? Curious shoppers jam the remaining five hundred seats to capacity and beyond, craning for a glimpse of the new styles.

Gretchen Saczynski attended this particular show for a different reason. "My God, who *is* that *man*, Janet, dear?"

"Oh, he's new with us—very green," Janet Shupe answered with feigned disinterest.

Gretchen Saczynski was in Boston "whackin' the bushes," as her boss and long-time lover, Kevin Munson, disdainfully put it. Well, he might think it was a waste of time, but hadn't they found Gloria Mitchum here? Or, rather, hadn't *she* found Gloria Mitchum here? And hadn't Gloria been one of their bread-and-butter girls until the ungrateful little slut had jumped to Cline last year? It didn't matter what Kevin thought, anyway. *She* was the Munson Agency of New York now and everyone knew it—everyone but Kevin, that is, which was just as well. He'd find out soon enough. And she owed everything, all her success, to the little triangle she was sitting on right now. Men! They were all the same: brains in their dicks. But women were different. No matter how intimate, they always kept business and pleasure separate. She eyed Janet Shupe cautiously. She was shrewd, all right, and Gretchen would make no mistake about that. Janet knew she had something here, and she was going to hold onto him for as long as she could—milk him dry in the Boston market until her clients started thinking he was over-exposed. Well, that was fine, but *she* would be right there when that happened—maybe before.

That night over dinner at the Ritz Carlton Gretchen thought of how much better suited women were for business than men. In an intimate moment Kevin Munson would tell her anything, offer her anything. But with Janet she would have to bide her time. All things come to those who wait.

She didn't have to wait long.

The Montage Agency was aware of Lynell's work schedule at Arthur Young & Company and tried to arrange his bookings for late afternoons, evenings, and weekends. But there were an ever-increasing number of calls for him, and Janet Shupe began to wonder how long they'd be able to juggle clients. By summer Lynell had taken another leave of absence and his employers at Arthur Young & Company were growing obviously disenchanted.

"That modeling stuff is fine, Lynell," Richard Ferris warned him, "but this is your job."

"I know," Lynell answered. "I know." But by the fall of 1980 he was modeling steadily at one hundred dollars an hour: sweating in heavy fall and winter clothes under hot lights in Newbury Street studios; pinned and taped and stuffed like a Thanksgiving turkey for department store catalogues; posing for Sunday newspaper advertising supplements; breezing through weekend fashion shows; and standing over "secretaries" at IBM word-processors, Xerox machines, and Wang computers. Not only did he love every mindless minute of it, but he was actually making more money modeling part time than he made as an accountant full time.

He didn't read magazines anymore; he only looked at the advertisements, studying all the techniques of the established models. Each ad was a source of inspiration. He experimented with stances, arm and hand positions, and "looks," and he worked to become a good, versatile Boston model.

It was Aimée who remembered Jeff Foster's advice and acted on it. In mid-July, without giving much thought to where it might lead and how it might change their lives, she sent a Lynell Alan composite to each of twelve New York City modeling agencies, with a short note under his name. Only one wrote back. But all it took was one.

"You have a great commercial look, Lynell."

The offices on Fifty-second Street and Third Avenue had seen better days. Gretchen Saczynski was a pale, fiftyish woman, lean and stringy, with hair too russet and cheeks too mauve. She was extremely self-assured, and that self-assurance began to infect him. He tried to hold his trust in reserve, but he wanted desperately for this to happen.

"We don't do much fashion work at Munson, mostly commercial. If you're willing to work, I think you can be very successful."

"It would be an awfully big gamble for me to take: to quit a steady job and leave Boston on a chance," Lynell said apprehensively. But in his heart he knew he had already decided. Gretchen was offering him an escape, and it hardly occurred to him that he would be wise to find out first what the difference was between commercial modeling and fashion, and what the accepted "looks" were in each.

"No one ever made it in anything, Lynell, least of all modeling, without taking risks. There are no guarantees, just my experience, and that tells me you can do very well for yourself—and for us, of course. I wouldn't bother if I didn't think you'd make money for us. And I think you can." She ruffled several three-by-five cards through her fingers. "I have ten hours of work right here that can be yours over the next few weeks. At $150 an hour, that's $1,500. What do you say?"

"I say, when do I start?"

4

Ice cream wasn't Catherine Ward's only vice, but it was the only one she had to give up on an instant's notice, so it was the only one she thought about day and night for a week. She began each morning with a decent breakfast of dry toast, eggs, and black coffee at a small, relatively inexpensive diner. The rest of her days were filled with water, walking, and reading. On an almost daily basis she stopped at Weinblum's Bookstore for another paperback—historical novels were her favorite—and each time she and Peggy went out for lunch. (Actually Catherine drank Perrier and watched Peggy eat.) And their friendship intensified.

At her height—she could make 5'11" only if she slumped a tad when she was being measured—Catherine had long considered 135 pounds slim. But even though she had no scale to judge herself by, when she slipped into her once skin-tight jeans the following Friday, she knew she had lost the ten pounds and quite possibly one or two more. Otherwise, she wouldn't have noticed but for the fierce craving she had for Häagen-Dazs Chocolate Chocolate Chip.

"Yes, your face is noticeably thinner." Mary Cline nodded with approval as she ran the thumb and forefinger of her right hand gently along the side of Catherine's finely chiseled nose, from the corners of her large, oval, sky-blue eyes high over her cheekbones, down into the hollows of her cheeks, and out across her broad jaw. The tips of her fingers barely touched the soft skin. "How are your teeth?"

Catherine pulled back her lips and touched her teeth together, and for a moment her father was inspecting her brushing job—but only for a moment.

"Hands?"

And the inspection went on. For the first time in her life Catherine felt like meat on the hoof, but she wanted this so desperately that if the woman had raised three fingers Catherine would have scratched the floor three times with the toe of her shoe and whinnied.

"Are you wearing underwear?"

"Why . . . yes, of course," Catherine answered haltingly, wariness creeping into her voice.

"I'd like to see your legs," Mary Cline explained.

Catherine squirmed out of her jeans self-consciously, wishing she had had the foresight to wear a skirt.

"Thank you," Mary said noncommittally. "How long have you been in New York, Catherine?" Mary asked when the young girl was dressed again.

"Ten days."

"From Nebraska?"

"Iowa."

"Yes," Mary Cline said. "We New Yorkers are extremely provincial. Everything south of Staten Island is Miami and everything west of New Jersey is Nebraska. Sit down, Catherine . . . please." The woman's smile was sincere. She indicated the leather couch against the side wall.

Catherine took a deep breath, exhaled slowly, and sat, noticing for the first time the opulence of her surroundings. Mary Cline's desk was dark-stained teak and was surrounded by plush brown leather chairs and the matching couch on which Catherine now sat. The wall to Mary Cline's left was glass from floor to ceiling, offering a spectacular view of the teeming East River. Over the couch hung a painting Catherine recognized as a Cézanne, though she wouldn't have guessed it was an original.

Mary Cline was in the business of selling people and she prided herself on recognizing the product. She rose from her seat behind the desk where she had been sitting almost since Catherine had arrived. Now she sat on the couch beside Catherine, and the formality that had surrounded them evaporated.

"Catherine, you are an extremely beautiful young woman, as you are no doubt aware. Unfortunately, this business, by its very nature, attracts many unscrupulous types. I would tell you to trust no one, but if you took that advice you wouldn't trust *me*. So, I will instead cau-

93

tion you to trust only those who prove worthy of it. I hope that I will. And . . . mind you . . . the standards of measuring that worthiness are distinctly different here than they are in Nebraska." She tilted her head and smiled. "Iowa."

Catherine wanted to say, "I know," but then she might have had to explain. The woman's voice was warm and soothing and concerned.

"The girls said you have no pictures. That's first. We have to see if that wholesome, all-American glow comes across in print. You could get some hand, teeth, hair, and leg jobs," she added, squinting into her imagination. "Unless everyone in Iowa is blind, you've done some modeling?"

"Yes. Fashion shows when I was younger."

"We book some live fashion, but only with our print people. Now, I'm going to give you a list of photographers, and I want you to pick one and get some shots taken. These people aren't all Richard Avedon or Francesco Scavullo by any means, but they'll get the job done at an affordable price. But before I send you out there—a few rules:

"First: always, *always* wear underwear—panties *and* bra. You're going to be wearing other people's clothes.

"Second: you'll need one underwear shot for your book. That's it—one. Never be photographed in your underwear unless you are specifically booked for it at a minimum of double your rate. And never, never be photographed nude for anything or *by* anyone—not even your boyfriend. You have a boyfriend?"

"No."

Mary Cline's face betrayed the hint of approval. "Third: if anyone asks you to pose nude—or more—refuse and go on with the job like the professional you will be. If they insist, you leave—and pronto—and report it to the agency. Once is tolerable. Boys will be boys, after all. But insistence is definitely not. Now, where are you staying? Have you got an apartment yet?"

Catherine flinched. "No. I'm staying at the Doral on Lexington Avenue."

"Ouch! If we decide we can do business we'll help you out. But for now, get out of the Doral—unless you can afford it?"

Catherine shook her head vigorously and her wavy yellow hair shimmered like sunrise on the Atlantic.

"I'll give you the address of a place with weekly rates. It's not up to the Doral's standards, but it's clean—and cheaper. As for pictures, you'll need . . ."

* * *

94

So where would she get an evening dress? Where would she get a tennis outfit? Where would she get a bathing suit? Shoes? Lacy lingerie? Where would she get anything, on *her* budget? Mary Cline had an answer for that, too. "But never let on I told you," she said with a conspiratorial wink.

Friday afternoon Catherine called one Matt Vine, who was, quite simply, the photographer whose studio was closest to her new room at the Barbizon Hotel for Women. "No relation to the modeling school," Mary Cline had said with a smirk. Catherine made an appointment with Vine for Monday at 10:00 A.M.

Saturday she shopped and felt every bit the queen: Givenchy evening gown at Bloomingdale's ($395) with matching Gucci shoes ($147); cosmetics at Macy's ($84); Jantzen bathing suit and Norma Kamali sun dress at Bergdorf's ($140); Ellesse tennis ensemble, complete with Donnay racquet, at Herman's World of Sporting Goods ($257); and a final Saturday afternoon treat, a trip across Thirty-fourth Street to the top of the Empire State Building ($5, and the only thing besides the cosmetics she paid cash for during the entire day's shopping spree; oh, and there was the $1.99 for the masking tape she'd use to keep from scuffing the soles of her shoes).

Accessories pushed her dangerously close to her $1,000 Master Charge limit. But that didn't matter compared to how disappointed and smarmy she'd feel when she returned everything but the makeup and the bikini after she'd gotten her photographs.

"Oh, well—look out, world, here I come!"

If she'd expected all photographers to be fruits, then she was sadly mistaken. Matt Vine was as horny as an eighteen-year-old and made little attempt to conceal his intentions. He was an attractive, craggy man of forty-two who had fallen into fashion photography twenty years earlier, while serving a brief stint at Benton & Bowles as the assistant to the assistant to the account executive working on the Chanel perfume account. They had hired several high-fashion models and a photographer to do the print advertisement layout, and when Vine had seen how close the photographer had gotten to all that ass he was instantly sold on photography as a career.

He had stayed with Benton & Bowles for only as long as it had taken to finance a few necessary photography courses, set himself up in a small studio on South Park Avenue, and moonlight his way into enough jobs to quit the agency. He'd starved for nearly five years, but not for pussy. He had never married. Why should he? He had all the

95

advantages of marriage and none of the disadvantages. And anyway, in his first five years he and his Nikon had been to enough weddings to last him a lifetime.

Now the jobs came in so regularly he could turn down work that didn't interest him. But he always had time for an eager young thing anxious to break in. And it wasn't for the money. It was for the way he could make them look, the way he could make them feel. Matt Vine could make them look as good as it was possible for them to look. He could make them *feel* sexy. Matt Vine knew the relationship between a woman and her photographer could be an unbelievably sensual one—urging, encouraging, touching. When he got a woman into the flow the eroticism was infectious. No, it wasn't for the money. It was for the way it made him feel to bring out the woman in them— in print. And if there was a carry-over—well, he'd take what he could get.

"Oh, that's it. God, that's sexy." He told them all the lies they wanted to hear, and then some. "Jesus, that face, that body." Especially receptive were the plain ones with voluptuous breasts that alone take them out of that class of women who designers see as perfect coathangers for their clothes, women whose families and boyfriends had for years told them how gorgeous they were, women without a chance to make it. With him, for an hour, they did make it—and what was so wrong with that? He was clever and subtle, never insistent. The new ones needed the money they'd save when he didn't charge them—more than they needed to protect their long-lost virginity.

Then there were the handful who would achieve a degree of success as models. And finally the one-in-a-million who had a chance to be a blockbuster. Matt Vine knew one the moment she walked into the studio. Along with a "look," they possessed a certain inner confidence that made them more than just another pretty face. There was almost an animalism about them, something predatory that told you they would go after it with a vengeance. Catherine Ward was such a woman, and he knew from the moment he saw her that he had to have her.

"Don't worry, Catherine, we'll work something out," he said with a sincere smile when she inquired about his fee. "I don't want my models worrying about money. It makes them too tense. Let's see how these come out. Maybe we'll be able to help each other."

Her instinct told her to leave. But her spirit of competition told her to stay. *You can't win the game unless you play.*

Vine was good—very good—though there was that nagging question of the final price, which she was beginning to guess.

96

He saved the lingerie shot for last. It was a white, translucent lace camisole that left her midriff bare above her panties. When he stood behind her and adjusted her hair, he stroked it in a decidedly unprofessional manner and flicked one shoulder strap down to "make this one really sexy." She shivered when his stare dropped to her taut red nipples against the lace, and he made no attempt to hide the outline of himself against his tight wool slacks.

Two days later Catherine sat on the worn couch in Vine's studio and peered through the small magnifying glass at the contact sheets while Matt Vine looked on, admiring her and at the same time his own work. From what she could tell, squinting through the small glass with an uneducated eye, the results were good. But there was something about them that bothered her, something she couldn't quite pinpoint.

"I printed these two," he said, handing her a pair of eight-by-tens. "My own personal favorites. I'll give you any prints you want, though," he added. Then his eyes met hers. "And no money need change hands."

She flinched when he touched her. The top shot was one of the dozen or more camisole shots he'd taken, and it was nice but for the fact that she was exposing so much breast that a dark crescent of areola peeked above the thin material. In the second she was in her sleek, red, one-piece, French-cut Jantzen bathing suit, and it was flawless except she had been changing positions so her legs were spread too far apart, leaving even the least imaginative viewer to wonder which of the Kama Sutra positions she would be demonstrating next.

But there was something else that disturbed her even more. It was something in her face, something she had seen on all of the contact sheets. There was a tautness at the corners of her mouth, a strain of anxiety in her eyes. Her mind had been somewhere else. On what Matt Vine had planned for her? On how she would get the pictures if she was right about his motives? And, as now, on who the hell she thought she was kidding if she was thinking he wanted anything but her.

She stood abruptly and the contact sheets slipped from her lap onto the floor. She decided to go for his ego. "These aren't as good as I had expected, Mr. Vine. I'm worth a lot more than this." She dropped the two eight-by-tens into his lap. "As you can plainly see."

She stormed to the door, as angry with herself as she was with him. At least *he'd* made his intentions clear from the outset. It was *she* who had been dishonest. But she was learning. At the door she spun, and as much to reinforce her own scruples as to add the final punctuation to their brief association, she said: "No deals, Mr. Vine—not *ever*." And as she slammed the door behind her and strode proudly away down the hall, she was sure she meant every word.

Catherine was disappointed but realistic. Some of the pictures were very good and no one was going to see them but Matt Vine. She shuddered to think what he'd use them for.

She spent the next three days doing what she should have done in the first place. She called photographers from the list, more or less at random, and told them—or their assistants—what kinds of photos she wanted and what for, and asked the price.

"He could do it for ninety-five dollars an hour plus ten dollars' processing for each print you want made," one woman answered. "I'm Mike's wife, Jayne. We have some time Saturday morning if you want to get right to it."

Most prices had been, in the way of Manhattan, either in the same modestly high range or totally outrageous, with nothing in between. For no particular reason other than the woman's raspy, agreeable voice, Catherine had been ready to make an appointment. The fact that this photographer had an assistant who was also his wife had sealed it.

The studio, on lower Seventh Avenue at Twenty-eighth Street, was on the upper two floors of a four-story brownstone that must have been gorgeous eighty years before but now appeared on the verge of becoming part of Mayor Koch's city reclamation plan. Inside, the huge loft was cluttered but cozy. It was filled with ancient props and dusty ottomans and was flooded with natural light from a skylight that covered half the arched roof.

Mike Dudley was an enormous, shuffling, white-haired man, with a florid complexion and a terminal case of bags-under-the-eyes. His old dungarees and denim shirt were worn beyond color, and he exuded a homespun flavor that was almost comically unsophisticated in his cosmopolitan surroundings. He clasped her hand, shook it firmly, then turned to welcome her in with a sweep of his hand, at the same time tripping clumsily over a light stanchion. Catherine had to stifle a laugh.

If her first break had been running into Mary Cline—something of which she was not at all sure at this point in her "career"—her second was meeting Jayne Dudley.

"Come on in, Catherine dear," Jayne said, pulling her into the studio. "Did Mike offer you a cup of coffee? No, of course he didn't." She answered her own question as though Mike weren't there, and in fact

98

he no longer was, Catherine realized when she heard the distant tinny clatter of metal hitting the floor. Jayne Dudley rolled her eyes heavenward. "Half our income goes into the trash in little pieces," she sighed impatiently.

Jayne was an attractive woman in her mid-forties who had managed to keep her figure and made her husband seem younger by association. She led Catherine to a re-covered couch that looked as though it had been mortally wounded and had staggered into the corner to die in a pool of cotton stuffing.

"I don't have too much money," Catherine managed tentatively when there was a brief lull in the conversation, which was a rarity with Jayne Dudley. "I don't mean to be impolite," she continued apologetically, "but I was kind of hoping to be able to do this in an hour or so."

"Not to worry. The conversation is free. Hey, Mike, Catherine wants it done in an hour. Can you manage that, you think?"

"An hour it is," he called back. Something metal fell and rolled noisily to the wall. "Is she going to charge me if I go overtime?" he asked with a laugh.

"You're too tense. Relax, for heaven's sake," Mike said when they began shooting. Catherine didn't have the heart to tell him her tension was the result of a run-in she'd had in the dressing room with a cockroach roughly the size of a Pekingese.

"Thank you," she said when they had shot for an hour.

"What's your hurry? Got another appointment?" Mike asked. He wore a hurt expression that did something Catherine would have thought impossible: it actually inflated the bags under his eyes.

"Well . . . no . . . but . . ."

"But nothing. It's ninety-five dollars plus ten for the shots you want. End of story. If it'll make you feel better, pay me the ninety-five right now and let's get it over with."

"It would make me feel better."

She counted out the money and Mike wrote out a receipt. They exchanged. "Now . . . relax . . . and let's get to work."

"She's an awfully nice kid," Jayne said to Mike, when Catherine had walked down the hall to make a change.

"Too nice for this racket, I think."

"Yes, but she's got a lot of spunk, Mike. Don't you think we could use some good fashion shots to update your book?"

Mike looked at her and shook his head softly. "Christ, what I don't break, you give away. Okay, *okay*, I get the message."

99

She walked over to him and hugged him affectionately.

The day with Mike and Jayne Dudley was like a family outing. The natural light was good, muted as it was by a heavy overcast, so they took to the streets. Mike treated them to a ride around Manhattan on the Circle Line and caught Catherine with the New York skyline as a backdrop, then the New Jersey Palisades. But it was only when he developed the pictures that he noticed something.

"Look at these," he said to Jayne when they were alone in the studio on Sunday afternoon. "The kid's got a natural talent for mugging. The shots I got when she *knew* I was shooting are even better than the ones when she didn't. She plays to the lens—already. Imagine what a little experience will do for her."

Mike Dudley printed every shot in which Catherine hadn't blinked or the wind hadn't blown her hair across her face or the light hadn't been wrong, or that wasn't a duplicate. The processing alone cost him $175.

"She doesn't *take* a bad picture," Jayne said. "Both profiles are absolutely perfect."

"Thanks," Mike said, with mock hurt in his voice.

"Honestly," she continued, ignoring him. "She doesn't have a good side. She has two perfect sides."

"Yeah, I wish I could take credit for these," he said dejectedly.

"Oh, Mike, I can't afford all these," Catherine told him the following morning through a rising panic that threatened tears.

"Hold on, kid," he said. "Just professional curiosity. How many were you going to get?"

"Half a dozen or so, I guess."

"How about eighty dollars for the lot of them?" Jayne broke in. Catherine was a good kid, but business was business and at least they should break even.

Catherine brightened with the same spark that ran through her photographs. She hugged each of the Dudleys affectionately. "I don't know how to thank you."

"Some day when you're rich and famous you'll do *us* a favor," Mike said, and he joined his wife in a grin and a shrug that said her friendship was payment enough.

Catherine sat in her small cubicle at the Barbizon and slowly thumbed through the three dozen photographs again and again until she could have memorized their order in the pile. Then she shuffled them and thumbed through them again and remembered Matt Vine's

100

photographs. Gone was the tension from her large, oval eyes, replaced by a sparkling all-American vitality. Gone was the anxiety, replaced by the bright glow of optimism.

On Monday morning she waited three hours at the agency for Mary Cline to arrive. "I didn't think I'd see you for three or four weeks," the older woman said as she ushered Catherine into her office.

"I don't *have* three or four weeks," Catherine answered, placing the eight-by-tens in a neat stack on the teak desk.

"Who took them?" Mary Cline asked as she sat and adjusted herself comfortably in the deep leather cushions of her swivel chair.

"Mike Dudley."

"Mmm." It was fifteen minutes before Mary Cline spoke another word. "My God, these are incredible," she said evenly.

"If I only *looked* like that," Catherine said to break the sudden tension.

"Ah, but you do, Catherine." Mary Cline held up a shot taken on the East River against the Manhattan skyline. Catherine's head was tilted slightly and a coyly seductive smile edged across her porcelain face. "You look *exactly* like that."

In the three days that followed, the Wilshire Printing Company did a rush job on a five-by-seven fold-out card for their best client, Cline Models. The front shot was a reduction of an eight-by-ten full-face of what was to become Catherine Ward's primary "look": a coy, seductive smile. The other eight situation shots and profiles showed her in all of her guileless charm and displayed a versatility of emotion that ran from childlike playfulness to seething sensuality.

Catherine spent too much of her dwindling funds on an expensive brown leather case she purchased at an art supply store along with ten transparent acetate sheets into which she inserted, back to back, the twenty shots Mary had selected to start her book. Dressed comfortably and, on Mary's advice, wearing a pair of "sensible" shoes, Catherine began the next week with her portfolio under her arm, stuffed to bursting with fifty copies of her new composite.

"There's no sense going on rounds unless you have something to leave behind," Mary had said when Catherine was eager to start seeing people with her book alone. "Photographers, art directors, advertising executives—they're all very busy people. I tell our models that if they don't have a composite they'll be forgotten as soon as they're out the door. I don't think anyone will soon forget *you*, but the comp leaves them a name and a way to reach you through the agency."

Catherine organized the Cline Agency's rounds list systematically into geographic sections of the city. At first she called to make appointments but quickly learned that when she explained she was a model, even a "Cline Model," everyone was suddenly too busy to see her.

"Just send in your composite," they would say with varying degrees of civility. The more blunt just said, "Don't call us. We'll call you."

So she began ringing doorbells and dropping into offices and an obvious pattern soon emerged. When she was greeted by a man, she was invariably invited in and her book as well as her figure were given a thoughtful once-over. Both were occasionally circulated through the studio or office, and she was thanked politely and asked to leave a composite. Twice she was told that a studio would surely be able to use her soon, and each time the promise was followed by an invitation to dinner. At least six other dinner invitations weren't preceded by such a promise.

In contrast, when a woman answered the door, Catherine was, more times than not, flatly turned away. It was an altogether disappointing day which was to be followed by what seemed to her an endless string of equally disappointing days.

"You can't afford to get discouraged," Mary told her. "Just keep plugging and always have a positive attitude. Always maintain an air of confidence in yourself, because no one will believe in you unless you believe in yourself."

The advice, as is most, was easier given than put into practice.

By moving from the Doral Catherine had managed to cut her daily expenses, but the start-up costs were more than she'd bargained for. There were the $175 for Mike and Jayne Dudley, $85 for her portfolio case, $350 for a run of a thousand composites, and $250 for inclusion on the soon-to-be-coming-out Cline Models headsheet, a book containing a headshot and two or three situation shots of each of the fifty male and one hundred fifty female models at the agency. The competition for jobs, she realized whenever she thought of those numbers (and those were just the models at this agency), was depressingly overwhelming. Her set-up expenses alone were nearing $1,000 and *she* was nearing insolvency.

"It's an investment in yourself," Mary told her. "Think of it as a fairly inexpensive means of starting your own business."

After three straight weeks of eight-hour days spent walking the streets of New York, with nothing to show for it but thickening calf muscles, blistering feet, and a string of propositions that would have kept her on her back for a year, even Mary Cline's words of encouragement couldn't keep Catherine's ego and optimism from being totally decimated.

She had made a mistake. Catherine knew it now, but it was too late. She'd put too much time and effort into a chancy business when she should have gotten a job long ago. As February rolled into March she altered her priorities and began looking in earnest for steady employment. But before she could find anything, LeeAnn Schneider, Cline's booker, called with her first booking.

"Ten to two with no lunch break. Corona Studios." LeeAnn reeled off the address and phone number in a businesslike monotone. "Five hundred dollars. Do you have vouchers?"

Catherine was speechless. She had a job. "Sorry?"

"Vouchers? Do you have them?"

"Oh, yes," Catherine answered, regaining her composure. "LeeAnn, how long will it be before I get paid for this job?"

"Low on cash, huh?" LeeAnn asked, softening her tone. "We can advance you your fee at a five percent surcharge to cover the contingency that the client doesn't pay us. That's twenty-five percent total to the agency. Otherwise, it's usually anywhere from one to three months."

Catherine figured it quickly. "I'll take the $375. And thank you."

She arrived at Corona Studios the following morning at 9:30 with her portfolio and makeup kit and an award-winning case of the jitters. She was shown in by the young receptionist and introduced to Harrison Marx, the account executive from Chase Manhattan Bank, for whom she would be posing for an in-house promotional brochure.

"My, you're early," Marx commented, surreptitiously appraising her figure as he checked his watch. "We're still setting up. I'm sure we told the agency eleven o'clock."

"I told them to have her here by ten," a vaguely familiar voice broke in. "So I could run through the storyboard with Catherine, show her exactly what I want from her."

"Oh, good. You'll take care of her then?" asked Marx as he bustled off. "I have work to do."

"Yes," Matt Vine said, "I'll take care of her."

Catherine flinched but did not resist as he took her arm gently. Fear and revulsion rose up inside her and Mary Cline's warning swam around in the distant corners of her brain. But what would she do? What *could* she do? She was trapped. It had taken her almost a month to get this job. She had already spent the $375. Question: How could she possibly pay back the agency? Answer: There was only one way.

Matt Vine turned to her then and spoke softly. "I believe we have some unfinished business." And Catherine Ward followed him pas-

103

sively, accepting the fate that had perhaps been hers since the moment she had met him.

She spent the next three days very, very stoned. But she could never get stoned enough to forget.

A thousand times during those three days, she thought about taking the bus back home. A dozen times she began to pack her bag. Once she got as far as the door. But the fight in her made her want to stay, made her *have* to stay. On the fourth day something happened that, she realized, should have broken her siege of depression but somehow only served to deepen it: LeeAnn Schneider called her with a full day's booking at a thousand dollars for the day. So she had sacrificed her self-respect for nothing . . . for nothing. When would she run out of lessons to be learned? Or assets with which to pay the price?

On the street she checked the unfamiliar address again and took the elevator to the third floor. But after waiting, then pressing the "3" frantically several times, the door still didn't open. Panic flushed her cheeks before she saw the doorbell and pressed it. Her cheeks were still hot when she heard the answering buzz and pushed her way out of the claustrophobic elevator and into the empty foyer.

"In here," a man's voice called from the other side of an open doorway to her right.

"I'm Catherine Ward from Cline Models," she said, extending her hand.

A gnome of a man stood behind a long table, examining a series of drawings. He looked up when she entered the room, but didn't take her hand and, in fact, didn't even seem to see it. Instead he stared up at her with a comical look frozen on his face.

His large round head was topped with a thinning blond down, and even with a dumbstruck expression his smooth pink face was filled with such affable innocence that Catherine had an overwhelming maternal urge to sweep the overgrown infant into her arms.

Martin Bennett, author of countless pulp novels, was the originator and, to his knowledge, sole practitioner of a game he called "Titles," many of which he later used for his novels. Some people appreciated natural scenes for their beauty or sensuality. Some fantasized mundane human encounters into intriguing dramas and bizarre sexual liaisons. Martin Bennett gave them titles, and had he been observer rather than participant, he would have entitled this encounter "Beautiful Jungle Amazon Meets Pillsbury Doughboy." He entitled it "Angela Stark."

"I must be a better writer than I thought," he said, when her self-conscious smile broke his spell.

"What?" Catherine asked, puzzled.

"If the agency sent *you*, I must be a better writer than I thought. You *are* Angela Stark. Angela Stark," he repeated when he received no reaction. "*The Face That Lied?* You must not be one of the five million people who read it," he said proudly. "Anyway, you are Angela Stark. She's the heroine, and we're doing the cover and some promotionals today for the second book in the series. On the first cover she wore a mask—sort of like the Lone Ranger. Now we want to show the readers what she looks like. You're perfect."

The Manhattan Yellow Pages list over seven hundred photographers, and Catherine, by her own estimate, had already visited nearly a hundred of them. But as she followed Martin Bennett along the corridor, she recognized the clatter from the studio as surely as she'd have recognized his voice, and a smile spread quickly, across her beautiful face. "Hi, Mike!"

"We haven't even started shooting and he's already cost us seventy-five dollars," Jayne Dudley said impatiently as she came in from the dressing room with Catherine's wardrobe.

"I got my first job!" Catherine called excitedly as she rushed into Weinblum's Bookstore waving the $750 advance check, which she had only collected *after* completing the day's shooting. (To her, that *Angela Stark* shooting with Mike Dudley and Martin Bennett would always be her first job.)

"Good," Peggy answered as she snatched the check and read it. "I don't want a roommate who's on welfare."

"What?"

"I said, Do you want to be my roommate? What, are you deaf?"

That evening Catherine moved, which meant throwing her suitcase, a cardboard box full of paperbacks, and a few accumulated odds and ends into the first cab that passed the Barbizon.

The apartment Catherine shared with Peggy was in an old brownstone in a not-bad neighborhood on Park Avenue South and had a mountainous doorman on duty every evening from 6:00 P.M. until 2:00 A.M. The day after she moved in she bought a bed, which she had delivered, and she gradually began acquiring the other necessities—a bureau, a wicker chair, and a small black-and-white TV—as she could afford them. At a consignment shop in Greenwich Village she bought a rolltop desk that she refinished in sections as she found the time. Much later she would invest in an antique brass bedstead like the one she'd had as a child and which she chronically polished to within an inch of its life.

Catherine was the perfect roommate—neat, quiet, and unobtrusive—and Peggy especially appreciated those qualities when she returned to the apartment with a man and Catherine retreated discreetly to her bedroom with her latest book, if she wasn't already ensconced there. Whereas she initially was concerned about whether Catherine might have a preference for women over men, Peggy was now concerned that she seemed to like—or at least associate with—neither. In fact, she almost never went out at night.

Peggy, on the other hand, had a voracious appetite for men that was equally puzzling to Catherine. "I made a decision when I was fifteen," Peggy explained, one rare celibate evening as the roommates finished a quiet and increasingly infrequent dinner at home.

"Yes, and what was that?"

"I decided that I wouldn't even consider settling down until I had dated at least a hundred men."

"What are you going to do *next* week?" Catherine asked.

Between the Dudleys—who had recommended her for the *Angela Stark* job—and their friend Martin Bennett, Catherine was kept busy through February and was booked almost solid through March. But though her professional life was booming, her personal life was a bust. On March 2, Martin Bennett called and timidly invited her to dinner. She accepted with pleasure.

Martin proved to be the perfect companion, not only because of his glib manner and because his presence kept the wolves away, but because he was the ideal man for Catherine at that point in her life: he was gay.

For his part, Martin Bennett was a realist. As a writer he wasn't so flushed with self-importance that he considered himself an artist. Realistically, what he did was earn over $500,000 a year writing stories people wanted to read. There was nothing particularly romantic about it. It was hard work. And he understood from his Columbia Business School days that packaging and marketing made a product, whether that product was a widget or a novel. So when he had gained a position of respect in the publishing field, he had gradually insisted on approval of jacket design and promotion for all his books.

He was also realistic enough to know that, though he enjoyed a somewhat vague—and disturbing—sensual attraction to her, he and Catherine Ward would never be more than friends. But neither would they ever be less. There had never been a cover more perfect, more enchanting for a Martin Bennett novel than the one for *Angela Stark*, because there was never a face more perfect or enchanting than Catherine Ward's.

Work generates work, and as a direct result of her cover with Bennett, Catherine was booked for an editorial layout for *Gentleman's Quarterly* to be shot in Nassau during the last week in March. Editorial rates were the poorest, the agency explained, while reassuring her the exposure would be invaluable. She couldn't have cared less about money or exposure. It would be her first time out of the United States. Hell, it would be her first time south of Missouri.

There were fifteen in their party: the photographer, a surly young prodigy named Jake Donovan; his assistant, Tom Connolly, who, though barely thirty, was five years older than Jake; Sam Bowen, the art director from *GQ*; three other models—two male and one female; a makeup artist named Molly Falk; and seven various technicians and "gofers." All of them flew first-class to the Bahamas.

The descent into Nassau was the most exhilarating feeling Catherine had ever experienced. The ocean below them undulated above the latticework of dark reefs, and boats bobbed on the surface like Popsicle sticks in a crystal-clear green puddle.

They shot at first light the following morning, and Jake Donovan's detached, professional manner did nothing to relieve Catherine's initial anxiety or her feeling that Kristen, a gorgeous, pale-eyed brunette, was not only infinitely more experienced than she but also markedly prettier.

By 9:30 A.M. Jake announced that the sun was too high for further shooting. "Be back here at 4:30 in makeup," he said as he dismissed them. "And be careful of this damned sun," he added, swiping the back of his hand across his sweat-beaded upper lip.

Catherine had never been so soothingly warmed by the sun. She lay on the beach in front of the Paradise Island Hotel and blossomed like a tropical orchid, soaking the rays like moisture into her skin. When she opened her eyes a boy in his early teens was at her feet gaping.

"Lady, you're getting kind of red," he warned her. "I'd get out of the sun if I was you."

"Oh, thank you," she said, apologizing with a bright smile for what she had been thinking. But she needn't have, for his stare had rested

107

long enough on her slim body—on the mound between her long, willowy legs, and the gently rounded white flesh that spilled from the sides of her bikini top—for him to display the beginnings of a mammoth erection.

Molly sat on the shaded balcony of their third-floor suite, sipping a glass of iced tea and reading a paperback novel. "Oh, my," she said as Catherine stepped onto the porch. "Look at you. You look like a boiled Maine lobster."

"I'm beginning to feel like one, too," Catherine said. She sat, flinching as the icy iron of the seat painfully seared the backs of her thighs. "And I wasn't out there for more than forty-five minutes."

"Take a cold shower right away," Molly advised. "It'll feel good, and it's supposed to cut down on some of the burning that comes later."

Catherine was willing to try anything so she followed directions. But she didn't think it helped much. After her shower she slathered her body with cooling Oil of Olay, but she was still burning up.

Molly left at four o'clock. "I'll tell Jake to shoot around you. Just stay in bed. I'll bring you something to eat."

"Thanks, but I'm not hungry," Catherine said when Molly returned with a roast beef sandwich. Catherine was still stretched out on the bed, moving as little as possible. She was on her back, naked but for a sheet draped modestly across her from upper thigh to chest.

"I got you this, too," Molly said with a smile, placing a bottle of Noxema on the table between their beds.

"Oh, God, I don't even want to move. How did Jake take it?"

"He was pissed off, but fuck him. The others covered for you. From the look of those eyes I don't think you'll be ready tomorrow, either. But we shouldn't lose any time. They can do the rest of Kristen's shots with each of the guys. Then as long as I can make you look fairly human by Thursday, they'll still have two days for you and two for the group shots. It'll be no sweat."

"Thanks a lot, Molly. I feel like an idiot."

"You'd do the same for me." She looked at Catherine's crimson skin and shook her head. "If I was as reckless as you are," she added with a chuckle.

Catherine struggled to sit up, as though her raw, delicate skin would tear with the effort. Then she eased back into the two pillows she'd carefully propped against the headboard. She barely noticed the sound of Molly's deep sniffing from the bathroom. It reminded her of the same one she'd made herself the previous night as she stood on the

108

balcony and inhaled her first breaths of the cool, fragrant, tropical air. But now she concentrated on her stiff motions as she spun off the top of the blue jar and dipped three fingers into the pungent menthol paste. She sucked in her breath between her teeth with a painful hissing sound, then exhaled an orgasmic *ahhh* as she applied the cool salve to her tender shoulders.

The bed bounced lightly as Molly sat, shaking back her long, glossy black hair and regarding Catherine through sympathetic jade eyes. The sash of her short robe was tied loosely, and she sat immodestly with one leg on the floor and the other underneath her, making only an absent attempt to wrap her small round breasts under the red silk as she handed Catherine the open compact case. "Here. This will make you feel *much* better," Molly promised.

"I don't know, Molly," Catherine said, but her reluctance was quickly consumed in a fire that spread across her skin from the bottom of her feet to the top of her forehead. She remembered the first time she had smoked marijuana and how little it had affected her.

"It just keeps getting better," her friend Helen had said then, but Catherine had had to fake the mellow giddiness half a dozen times before she finally experienced anything approaching a high.

But this was different. She inhaled, and after stifling a sneeze, she sat back and her head swam with stars as it had when she was a child in the schoolyard. Inhale deeply. Exhale. Inhale deeply. Exhale. Inhale deeply. Hold your breath and force the pressure to your head. And she'd known she wouldn't faint then, as she knew she wouldn't get a kick from the fine white powder now. But she had fallen to the ground in the schoolyard, with the same sparkling rush that swept over her now. Only now there was nowhere to fall, and instead of waking to an aching lump on her head, she woke to a flicker of pins and needles that riffled over her skin like rice paper in the wind.

"Here, let me do that for you. On your stomach." The words rolled to her out of a thick, erotic fog, and Catherine's flesh twitched again like an exposed nerve as she obeyed the gentle command. The menthol aroma stung her nostrils as Molly's soft, circular strokes spread the cooling cream that was at once anesthetic and aphrodisiac.

The soothing salve seeped deep into her shoulders as the delicate strokes slid gently into the small of her back and slowly to her waist. Catherine noticed but did not notice when the sheet slipped from her bottom and upper thighs. The backs of her knees stung deliciously, and the smooth strokes covered her calves, then rose above the backs of her knees to her thighs and the curve where her thighs met her round buttocks. She was drifting into a dream, into a beautiful dream in which her entire sensitive body pulsed with eager, aching excitement.

Catherine was lost in the erotic tension, and the incredible intense rush exploded from between her legs like a sweeping tide. When she was urged onto her back her legs parted to expose a desire beyond experience.

The gentle strokes on her throat and chest were the teasing torment of fingers. The moist warm suckling on her taut nipples was the torture of lips. From high above her a voice moaned, "Please, please," and it was her own voice. And when she thrust her hips forward and the tongue rimmed her, it was as if the earth had opened to swallow her. Suddenly she was falling, slowly falling, and she clutched for the ecstasy that was life but instinctively she knew that she would die. It was an agonizing death and the pain was unending, wonderfully unending, and she held the whole earth tightly in her hands but it only fell with her, and she floated in a pleasure so intense it was pain. She cried out and clutched again for the earth but it fell away . . . farther and farther away until it was only a distantly glowing satellite . . .

The depression Catherine awoke to was more debilitating than any she had ever experienced, even before she saw her puffy, purpled eyes in the bathroom mirror. The only heartening thing was that her skin didn't look or feel quite as bad as it had the night before.

Her head was unbelievably clear and when she brushed her teeth and splashed cold water on her face she actually felt not bad—physically. But mentally? Her first big job and she'd blown it. How unbelievably stupid! And after having been warned about the sun in Nassau. Oh, God, and last night. How could she have let *that* happen?

The note by the bed brightened her spirits: "Stay out of the sun. I've convinced Jake we're on schedule. Don't worry. Molly."

By ten o'clock she was bored to tears. She pulled on her jeans, an "I Love New York" T-shirt, and her dark sunglasses, and topped the ratty ensemble with a wide-brimmed straw hat she had bought the day before. Her first stop was at the hotel gift shop, where she paid $18.95 for a $5 long-sleeved black sweatshirt with "I Saw Nassau" in white across the front. It was tacky and overpriced, but functional in keeping her forearms from being exposed to the sun.

A leisurely stroll to the pier eased her cabin fever. She climbed aboard a glass-bottomed boat and sat under the awning, out of the intense rays. A dozen faceless vacationers joined her for the half-mile trip to the mainland, and as she watched the colorful sealife slipping be-

110

neath the boat, she felt acutely the absence of love, of family, of something—anything—to hold onto.

As she window-shopped along the main thoroughfare, she found herself drawn almost magnetically to young couples, especially young couples with small children. Lingering in the background, she would see a mother's loving caress or overhear a father's gentle reprimand, feeling at the same time closer to home and yet so very far away. Once a tiny girl with downy blonde hair and huge blue eyes engaged her in conversation, and Catherine sat on her haunches, held the child's hand in hers, and found herself laughing for the first time in weeks. But a moment later, alone again, she stood crying into her hands. She was living on the cutting edge of her emotions.

Her only purchase was two postcards of Paradise Island Beach, one she sent to Peggy and the other she mailed home to Nana in Iowa. She ate a light lunch in the elegant British Colonial Inn. After lunch she hired a cab for a tour of the island, then had a cocktail at the Bama Club before returning to Paradise Island at dinner time.

As the small boat glided across the bay, she admired the soft pastels of the low stucco homes dotting the beach, and again that indescribably empty ache rose inside her and a reluctant tear slid over her cheek.

That night and the next Molly returned to their room in the early evening, and each time Catherine at first refused the finely cut, innocuous-looking powder, then inwardly reproached herself as she sucked it eagerly into her nostrils. Each time, it washed away her depression. Each time, it made her know she was the most beautiful, sensual woman alive. And each time, she and Molly made love in an uncontrolled frenzy of need.

Two days later Catherine's skin glowed the healthy red-brown of burnished wood. When she arrived at the shooting she was bursting with the anxiety of a woman with an ugly new haircut. She clenched her teeth and awaited the sarcastic remarks. But they never came.

"My God, you look marvelous," was all Jake Donovan said. "Kristen, go back to bed. We'll do Cathy's shots today."

The styles were loose-fitting in cream, beige, and taupe. Mark was an incredibly striking blonde with a perfectly proportioned body, and if the proposed cover shot of him in a bathing suit, leaning casually against a cabana, didn't sell to every woman and gay man in America, Catherine would have been astounded. Joe was the dark, hirsute European type and served mostly as a prop for Mark and Catherine. Both men were experienced professionals, with such a sure sense of timing and anticipation that Jake rarely offered more from behind his lens

111

than, "That's it. Fine. Great. Now relax for a sec while I change film."

Catherine watched, and listened, and reacted. There was more to all this than being beautiful. There was versatility and anticipation—producing the right "look" at the right time. There was ease in front of the camera. And there was something Catherine seemed to have naturally: a way of playing off the other models that made the whole production look not like three people working their asses off under the intense tropical sun, but like a carefree trio of intimate friends romping ecstatically in the sand. And there was, finally, something that grew in her from that very first morning: the confidence that the other models could successfully play off *her*.

She resolved she would always pay strict attention—that she would try to learn something from each shooting for as long as her career lasted. But there was something she didn't have to learn—something, in fact, that she could never have been taught—and that something was magnetism, charisma. When she looked languidly up into Mark's eyes he was her lover. But it was a pure, clean, wholesome love. Even seated on a sea-wall with one arm thrown loosely around Mark's neck and her other hand resting casually on Joe's hairy thigh, Catherine radiated a coy and sleepy innocence that lifted her from print; that made men want her and women want to *be* her; that made her three-dimensional. In print she came to life.

Back in New York Catherine's days were occupied with rounds and occasional one- or two-hour jobs that kept food on the table and paid the rent. Martin Bennett seemed busy and preoccupied, and on the one occasion she met him for dinner he spent half the meal looking over his shoulder. Perhaps there was a jealous lover in the wings?

When after two weeks she hadn't heard from Molly Falk, she dialed her number. Somehow she wasn't at all surprised that a man answered.

"This doesn't mean we can't still see each other once in a while," Molly whispered into the receiver.

"Sure," Catherine answered noncommittally, laying the receiver softly in its cradle. Suddenly she wondered what the Dudleys wanted from her, what they were after, and she immediately chastised herself for the thought. She wished Peggy were home. She was a good listener and talking to her always seemed to help. But Peggy had found another "steady" boyfriend and spent more and more of her evenings at his apartment. Often now they didn't see each other for days at a time.

For the next week Catherine didn't go on rounds and left her apartment only for the few jobs the agency had booked her for. Then she called Molly again and went to her apartment, where she paid five hundred dollars for a surprisingly small vial of cocaine and where she also spent the night. She felt considerably worse about the latter than the former. As for the drugs, well, that was all right. She'd stop after this. Christ, who could afford it?

From the moment GQ hit the newsstands Catherine Ward was in almost constant demand, and although it would be some time before she would, under the careful orchestration of Mary Cline, cross over from print to television, at any given time she could be seen in numerous magazines and catalogues, advertising skin creams, toothpaste, soft drinks, and an amazing variety of products. There were rumors that she sometimes didn't show up on time, and Mary warned her about it. But to the clients her magnetic, sultry innocence was worth any small amount of trouble she might be. So she was a prima donna—*she sold the product!*

By the autumn of 1981, within nine months of her arrival in New York City, Catherine Ward had become one of the five most sought-after print models in the city.

5

New York modeling agents are funny, except of course if you happen
to be a struggling model. Each agent aspires to cover the talent market—"talent" being the industry euphemism for looks. As a result,
most agencies are oversubscribed, and most models underbooked.
From the agent's point of view, if a job requires a certain "look" and
he has five models in that category he can send to the go-see, the
agency will have five times as great a chance of landing the job. Of
course, every other agency employs the same logic. The result is that if
six agencies are called, instead of the six agencies sending six people,
the six agencies send thirty. The odds for each agency remain the
same, but the model is overwhelmed by what is known in the business
as the "cattle call," and unless he hustles—and often even if he does
hustle—he will soon be left in the swirling dust of his own agency's stable. All the agency risks is a few disgruntled models. Their answer to
that: Go find another agent.

The Munson Agency was neither better nor worse in that regard
than any other. Gretchen Saczynski saw potential in Lynell Alan, and
she merely wanted to take advantage of that potential. If he made
money for the agency, wonderful for everyone. If not, she'd never have
to say, "Sorry, young man, it just hasn't worked out the way we'd
hoped." No, as long as he kept paying to have his pictures included on
their headsheet, the Munson Agency wouldn't lose money; in fact,

they'd make a few bucks. Gretchen Saczynski could just smile and say, "Keep hustling," and it was entirely up to him to decide when to quit. Hell, it was a shot in the dark. Every model should know that, and if they didn't—was it her fault?

If agents never lie—which is at the very least debatable—they are often misleading. "If we're going to take a chance on you, we've got to be sure you'll stay with us long enough to make it worth our while."

"I don't know, Lynell," Aimée had advised when he returned to Boston after his New York visit. "This is an exclusive contract. It commits you to stay with the Munson Agency for a year, but it doesn't specify any minimum amount of promotion they'll do for you. It's awfully one-sided."

"You must have an agent," Gretchen countered, "and if you're going to be a model, why do it half-assed? New York *is* modeling."

When Lynell continued to balk at the suggestion that he sign the exclusive and come to New York, Gretchen promised him ten hours of immediate bookings at $150 an hour and offered to ease his move by finding him an apartment. It clinched the deal.

The apartment Gretchen arranged for Lynell was along the river in the fashionable East Seventies. He arrived in midafternoon, when its two other occupants were, no doubt, scouring the city for work. But as they were also models at the agency, Lynell imagined they were booked solid, as he soon would be.

The living room was a Euclidean nightmare in black and white, all rectangles and triangles and steel and glass that made the small room expand and contract in a dizzying optical illusion. When he closed his eyes the shapes spun on his eyelids. But at least the place was clean. Clean? It was sterile! He guessed the tiny cubicle that was the kitchen hadn't seen a roach during the entire tenure of its present occupants. In New York, that was nothing short of a miracle.

Although he had already sent the two men his third of the $1,500-a-month rent, he would have felt uncomfortable poking about the apartment curiously. Instead he sat inhibitedly in the living room on a plumply cushioned black leather chair and recalled his visit to the agency earlier in the day.

It had disturbed him greatly when Gretchen had seemed not to know him, but then it had been over a month since he had seen her and she *had* been quite solicitous when he jogged her memory.

"Yes, the boys got your check and are looking forward to meeting

115

you. You'll love Tommy and Dan. They're such darlings. Ned was sweet, too. We hated to lose him, but he wanted to try his hand in L.A. for a while, so we arranged for him to work with Nina."

Her manner of speech was more haughtily superior than Lynell remembered, but he didn't have to like her. And he didn't, he decided, when she handed him the reminder slip on the upcoming bookings and he saw that it was for five hours at $150 per hour, not the ten hours she had promised.

"It's only five hours?" he asked with a puzzled look.

"I don't control the whim of the client," Gretchen snapped defensively.

"No problem," he said. "I was just wondering." He didn't have to like her, but he couldn't afford to alienate her, either. "Just anxious to get to work," he offered, along with his most infectious grin.

"Well, there's a good deal more to it than that," she snapped again. "When I have a moment I'll clue you in."

So he'd waited in the small reception room, trying with all his resolve to mask his temper. For almost an hour he listened as Gretchen answered the telephone with such a total lack of diplomacy that he wondered how the agency remained in business.

Occasionally models strolled in and Gretchen fawned over them with varying degrees of intensity, which Lynell quickly judged bore a direct correlation to the amount of money they brought in. The bustling atmosphere, at least, was a good sign.

The female models, if they weren't primping in front of the mirror that occupied the entire wall to his right, or too hurried to notice him at all, sometimes offered an acknowledging nod in his direction. The males, and specifically the two who were roughly his "type" and in his "age range," threw him dark looks, as though they'd caught him picking their pockets—which, as they saw it, was exactly what he was trying to do.

Lynell decided then, albeit a bit late, that sitting around the reception room for an hour or two had to be the best way in the world to judge an agency: the atmosphere, how they treated their models, *and* how they treated their clients. At his next agency—and there would be, had to be a next agency—he would do precisely that before joining.

By the time Gretchen deigned to bestow upon him the full three minutes she could afford, Lynell Alan hated the suddenly sycophantic woman and everything about her with a passion he could barely conceal. But he smiled sincerely as she spoke, and his mouth went dry at the realization that this self-important bitch controlled his future.

"You've got to get in to see these people again and again," she said,

116

handing him a photocopied list of names and addresses, "and come into the agency every single day you're not booked out of town. I have to remember who you are, so when a client calls for someone with your 'look' I'll think immediately of . . ."

"Lynell Alan," he filled in quickly, articulating the name precisely before she had time to draw the blank space into a humiliating slight that would tell him better than words how unimportant he was to her—to them. He thought of Aimée and the comfortable apartment on Commonwealth Avenue, and hating his old accounting job just didn't seem quite as important any more.

"Always show up on time," Gretchen went on, "and don't take rejection personally. No matter how attractive you are, you may not fit the image the client sees for his product."

"How about fashion shows? I really enjoy those."

"We don't do much fashion—practically all commercial: products and services. It doesn't pay quite as well as fashion, but there's more work and . . . quite frankly . . . I don't see you as the fashion type. Your look isn't right."

"Can't I do both?"

"There's some overlap, but mostly it's fashion agencies like Cline, Ford, and Willy who have gotten more and more into commercial, not the other way around. Here, you might want to look through our headsheet." She handed him a thick, eight-by-ten, gold-covered book. "Give me a call any time if you need help. But it's best to drop by in person. The rest is up to you."

As she returned to her desk he thanked her and started for the door, but Gretchen interrupted her vilification of her young female assistant to call out to him. "Look at that *here*, please. . . ." Her tone was reminiscent of his second-grade teacher. "They're too expensive to have *models* running off with them."

She said "models" the way *he* said "cockroaches." The woman was unbelievable.

I paid $433 to be included in the next one, you bitch, and I think that entitles me to this lousy $2.50 piece of crap, he ached to shout. "Oh, sorry. I misunderstood," he said, and he returned to the sofa to thumb quietly through the volume, which he realized was something else he might well have done *before* he came to New York and joined the Munson Agency. Jesus, almost thirty-one years old and he still did everything backwards. He had a lot to learn. Why did he insist on learning it the hard way? Maybe his father was right: dreamers always did.

The book contained literally pages and pages of photographs of men

117

whom, he surmised, any casual observer would find indistinguishable from himself.

"Thanks again," he said, laying the book on the counter in front of her when he'd finished. His manner was a little more obsequious than he liked. "I'll keep in close touch."

Lynell had prepared himself for virtually every conceivable possibility, and still he was totally unprepared for Tommy and Dan.

Tommy was fair-haired, frail, and on the small side for a model, with delicate features that would have been stunning in a woman but were almost too pretty in a man. After an apparently boffo start, his career had gone into remission, and he now supported himself by working the four o'clock to midnight shift at the clerk's desk of a seedy midtown hotel and through the good graces of his roommate.

Dan was literally as different from Tommy in appearance as black is from white. He was at least as tall as Lynell, but with the rippling muscles of a bodybuilder, and he was one of the most booked black men in the business. He was obviously body-proud and enjoyed parading around the apartment, sometimes with only a towel draped around his pencil-thin waist, sometimes completely naked—which Lynell found disconcerting. The man did have the type of body, like a well-conditioned prizefighter, that even another man could appreciate. But what made Lynell really uncomfortable was that Dan was hung like Goliath, and Lynell kept telling himself his eyes only drifted to that amazing appendage as they would to any remarkable feature: a perfect smile, high-crested cheekbones, finely tapered legs—all of which Dan also had, but none of which recalled the insecurities of youth—hell, the insecurities of adulthood.

It didn't require a college degree to deduce that Tommy and Dan were lovers. That they gave their new roommate the single bedroom wasn't the determining factor. And it wasn't their appearance. Lynell knew better than to make judgments like that—especially in New York. Nor was it the fact that whenever Dan wasn't out of town on a job he went out to walk Tommy home from work. The evidence wasn't nearly as circumstantial as all that. It was the muted sounds of love that drifted through the walls of the small apartment after the trio had retired for the evening. It was the sound of the two men's laughter from the shower, laughter that invariably rose to a crescendo before it fell to stillness behind a curtain of intimacy.

Lynell considered the relationship of the two men almost comfortingly devoted. In fact, the only thing about their relationship that

118

really bothered him was the same thing that bothered Aimée on her first visit, almost a month after Lynell's arrival in the city.

"What the hell was *that*?" she whispered into the darkness, having been awakened from a sound sleep by the commotion in the next room.

"Huh?" Lynell asked through a tired yawn. "Oh, that. Playful scuffling."

"Playful?" she repeated. "What does it sound like when they're mad at each other?"

Within three hours after he had taken Aimée to Penn Station on that Sunday and seen her off on the two o'clock train, Lynell Alan sat alone in his apartment on the hard kitchen floor, knees tucked up under his chin and arms wrapped around his shins, and wept. He wept because he'd had to borrow seven hundred dollars from Aimée to pay his March rent and to keep food on the table for another few weeks. He wept because his lover was returning to her apartment (and what had been *their* apartment) two hundred miles away, and the only place in Manhattan he could ever hope to afford he had to share with a couple of S & M freaks. And he wept because he was an abject failure.

"I'll pay you back, Aimée. Maybe not for a while, until I start making more money, but you *own* ten percent of me. Ten percent of nothing," he added ruefully.

The promised ten-hour shooting, which by the time he'd arrived in New York had shrunk to five hours, had ultimately become, by the time he had finished his one job to date, three hours. The rest of his time he spent slogging through snow or sleet or freezing rain, only to face rejection after ever-more-unceremonious rejection. In one month he had gone, by his conservative count, to approximately three hundred clients—photographers, advertising agents, art directors—on rounds he chronicled precisely in his diary, down to the time of day of his visits and the exact words spoken, especially if they were encouraging—which was all too seldom. Roughly one third had been unavailable; one third were available but not to him or, he suspected, to any model; and the final third had invited him in and looked briefly at his book with varying degrees of disinterest. Not one had a specific booking for which they were interested in him. Several made vague references to the possibility of future work: "Keep in touch. I'm sure we'll be able to use you soon." But increasingly he began to see that as the modeling industry's polite brush-off. He almost preferred the more direct "You're definitely not our type," and the hurtful but no-false-promises "I hope you kept your full-time job," which sent him reeling back into his old ugly-duckling insecurities.

On an almost daily basis he checked in with Gretchen, who invariably kept him waiting for as long as an hour before acknowledging him. "Oh, darling Lynell. No call for a gorgeous hunk today. Keep at it, though. Things are bound to break soon. Ta ta."

God, he hated Gretchen, and the venom that rose in him when he thought of her surprised him. But he should have thanked her, because in a distorted way she was what kept him going. For he was determined he would make it, if only for the satisfaction of making it big enough to be able to tell her, "I quit. I'm going with another agent."

But now as he sat dejectedly on his kitchen floor, with tears streaming down his face, the image of success was impossible to conjure. Anyway, how could he break his exclusive contract with Munson? The agency, and more specifically Gretchen, had him by the balls, owned him for a year, until January 1982—a lifetime.

In the weeks that followed Gretchen threw him a few bones, and though he needed the work and couldn't afford to turn it down, he resented the last minute calls that told him as clearly as words the jobs were only offered because someone else, or several someone elses, either weren't available or had turned down the weekend bookings. But maybe if he showed his willingness . . .

So he had canceled trips to visit Aimée in Boston, to work instead in fashion shows at G. Fox & Co. in Hartford and at Bloomingdale's (not the Bloomingdale's in Manhattan, where the "stars" worked, but the Bloomingdale's in the outback of White Plains, where nobody wanted to go); and to do a catalogue at Aspetuck Country Club in Redding, Connecticut. Still it was fun just to be working. When he worked he was exhilarated. Work was a small corner of the dream. The beautiful clothes, the beautiful people, the flashing lights and winding film pumped new blood into him. It was the unbelievable, self-indulgent high that enabled him to endure all the lows.

It was difficult for him to be separated from Aimée for such long periods of time, and he almost bought a bus ticket from Hartford after a Saturday fashion show as visions of bare-breasted women in their underwear bounced feverishly through his head. But he checked his libido. He wasn't so naive that he didn't entertain the possibility Aimée might have made other plans. It wasn't that he liked the idea. He just understood it. Maybe he should take greater advantage of the opportunities around him, too. His relationshp with Aimée would remain strained until she moved to New York, as she planned to do in the fall.

So he had taken the return train to New York and sat watching

Casablanca on Channel 2's Late Show, getting stoned and melancholy and turned on by Ingrid Bergman. He was immensely pleased that Muhammad Ali and Joe Frazier had apparently left the apartment to him for the weekend.

When he heard the key in the lock his spirits sank further. The movie had at least another half hour to run. Maybe by then Dan and Tommy would have quieted down and he could go to sleep undisturbed. But Dan came in alone, lumbering past him and into his room with barely a nod. Strange, Lynell thought. Since he'd arrived they had treated him not like an intruder, but as though he had been there with them all along.

Lynell finished his joint and clumsily rolled another. The shower sizzled in the background like steaks on the grill, and for the first time in hours thoughts of food replaced the thoughts of sex that had occupied his mind since early in the afternoon.

He went to the kitchen and scoured the refrigerator and cupboards but came up only with graham crackers. He went back to the living room, sipping a glass of water.

"Great flick." Dan sat on the couch, legs crossed Indian style. With only a towel draped around his waist, the inside of his thighs and that incredible machine were visible in the flickering gray light of the television. Lynell tried not to look, but it was truly amazing.

"Where's Tommy? Working this late?"

"Nah. He's in Jersey, visiting his folks for the weekend."

Lynell sat on the floor again and passed the joint back over his shoulder, offering Dan a hit.

Bogey was sending Bergman away again, but no matter how many times he'd seen it, tears still welled in the corners of Lynell's eyes. "We'll always have Paris," Lynell said sadly.

"How about some of this, Lyn? Cheer you up." Dan slid down to the floor beside him and held out a small ampoule that looked like an oversized sinus remedy.

"What is it?"

"What it is, is beyond description, my man," Dan answered, and before Lynell could react, Dan had crushed the ampoule under his nose.

Though the gas had a sharply pungent odor, the initial sensation was not unpleasant, rather harmless.

"Deep breaths," Dan said. "That's it." Then Dan held the capsule under his own nose and sniffed lustily.

Lynell wasn't exactly sure what happened next and he wasn't sure that he cared. He might have blacked out momentarily. When he regained consciousness, the plane to Lisbon was rising into the cloud cover over Casablanca and casting wavering gray shadows over the long, sleek legs that stretched out beside him. He ached for Aimée to be there.

"Sexy broad, Bergman." Dan's voice echoed in his swollen head.

Lynell wanted to draw his knees up to hide his stiffening erection, but his legs were leaden and he could feel the blood pumping through them, pumping through his entire body, inflating his cock as he watched helplessly. "I'm going to bed," he said, and he struggled to shake himself conscious enough to stand.

"Why waste it, man?" Dan murmured as he pulled the towel from around himself.

Lynell was gripped by an almost choking fear. He wished to God he weren't so drugged out, because if Dan forced himself on him, he'd be helpless.

Lynell's past reared up before him. "You're not touching me with that thing," he gasped. Through a fog Lynell pulled himself to his feet with a great, straining effort. His leaden legs moved heavily, but somehow he propelled himself resolutely toward his bedroom.

A nightmare awoke Lynell from a sleep like death, to a strange bed in a strange room and a stranger aura of doom. But with his own familiar clothes hung over chairs and strewn haphazardly across the floor, he shook away the cobwebs and remembered where he was—remembered grass, strange capsules of gas, and Dan. He swung his legs to the floor and began gathering his few belongings, glad it was not yet seven o'clock and that Dan would still be sleeping soundly, as he himself should be. After a fast shower he dressed and slipped out of the apartment, leaving his key on the kitchen table with a note: "Thanks a lot for the hospitality. Sorry I had to leave on such short notice, but here's a check for a month's rent in advance to cover any inconvenience. Hope you understand. When I get settled I'll have you over for dinner. Thanks again. Lynell."

Out on East Seventy-third Street he walked briskly into the bright, crisp April morning, a man trying to escape his past. At the corner he reached into his pocket. He barely had enough money left for the train to New Haven.

122

6

Until *Gentleman's Quarterly* came out in July, Catherine Ward's progress in her career was at best modest. But she did not allow herself to become discouraged.

"The GQ layout will do wonders for you, Catherine, but until then we aren't going to just stand still. When something happens I want us to be ready." It always gave Catherine a warm, secure feeling when Mary spoke in terms of "we" and "us," as though Mary really cared about what happened to her beyond her potential to make money for the agency.

So on Mary's advice—and her own money—Catherine had enrolled in a ten-week commercial acting course at the Lender/Stebbins Studio on West Forty-fifth Street. It was the most high-yield investment she would ever make. Catherine hadn't the least doubt that the experience she gained there landed her dozens of commercial acting jobs, eventually returning her 285 dollars thousands of times over.

Joan Lender and Valerie Stebbins were a pair of middle-aged former models whose personas dripped success as ostentatiously as their digits dripped diamonds. There were two other potential actors, a man and a woman, in Catherine's weekly three-hour class, and the minute she walked in the door she was forced to shed the top layer of her self-consciousness.

"You're on in one minute, dear," Joan Lender informed her before she had even introduced herself. Valerie Stebbins handed her a half-

123

page script simultaneously as she bustled past her to adjust the camera angle and focus.

"But . . ."

"Welcome to the real world," Valerie said from behind the camera.

So Catherine sat and practiced reading to herself for the full sixty seconds allotted her before Joan Lender indicated her place behind a table whose gold-speckled white Formica surface was empty but for a familiar green bottle of 7-Up.

"When I snap the clapsticks," Joan instructed, "Val will ask you to 'slate.' You give your name and agency and go right into the spot. Here, I'll take the script. You won't need it. Val will put up the cue cards. Okay, relax. Here we go. Diet 7-Up. Take one."

"Slate."

"I'm Catherine Ward from the Cline Models." She looked directly into the camera and smiled: " 'Whenever I asked for a diet soft drink, I always got something I didn't ask for . . . diet soft drink aftertaste.' "

She was trying not to look at the cue cards, knowing the camera would catch the angle of her eyes the way it did in so many of those amateurish commercials she saw on late-night TV. But she was so nervous she could barely remember three words at a time. " 'Well, now I've said bye-bye to aftertaste for good. 'Cause I'm drinking delicious Sugar Free 7-Up.' "

She picked up the bottle as instructed in the cue card margin and held it up to the camera. " 'Sugar Free 7-Up. It has a beautiful, fresh, natural flavor . . . without any aftertaste. So, when you say hello to Sugar Free 7-Up, you can say bye-bye to aftertaste. Bye-bye!' "

It was dreadful. When Valerie played back the tape on the monitor, Catherine wanted to crawl under her chair. But instead she had to sit and face the music, as Joan Lender and Valerie Stebbins dissected her performance like a biology lab frog.

"Too fidgety, Catherine," Joan said, "right from the start."

"You'll lull the audience to sleep with that monotone delivery," said Valerie.

"The midwestern twang has got to go." It was Joan again—or was it Valerie? She'd lost track during the rapid-fire criticism.

"Too fast. You've got to give it the proper pacing."

"The product. The *product.* That's what you're selling. You're just a prop. You could be standing backward as long as the product label is facing the camera."

Joan was standing in front of her now. " 'Whew! Am I glad that horrendous ordeal is over'—that's exactly what you look like you're saying to yourself on screen, as though you'd just endured an unbeliev-able torture."

"Then I must be a good actress," Catherine muttered disappoint-edly into her hands, "because that was *exactly* what I was saying to myself." The small consolation for Catherine was that, even with the lessons of her tape behind them, the other two students weren't signifi-cantly better than she had been.

During one of her stops at the agency during the week after that first class, Catherine had an opportunity to speak briefly with Mary Cline. "We had a commercial audition call for you yesterday," Mary admitted.

"And?" Catherine asked expectantly.

"And I told them you weren't available just now. You're not ready, Catherine. When we go on an audition I want us to have a chance to get the job. I won't be eaten alive just because we don't know the ropes. There's plenty of time."

Again the "we" and "us" mollified her. Of course Mary was right, and Catherine attacked her classes with renewed vigor. Gradually her life settled into a routine. Her daily rounds were sprinkled with an oc-casional print job and every so often a fashion show at one of Manhat-tan's ubiquitous department stores. But what she really looked forward to each week with growing anticipation was her Friday afternoon class. She literally threw herself into her hypothetical roles as the enthusiasti-cally brimming young housewife: " '*Beat* the summer heat with *Howard Johnson's frozen* macaroni au gratin. Just remove the cover . . . place the package in the oven . . . and in a matter of *minutes* . . . *you* can serve the family the *best-tasting* macaroni au gratin they've *ever* had! That's *Howard Johnson's* . . . *delicious* . . . *frozen* macaroni au gratin. Pick up a package at your grocer's when you shop . . . *tomorrow!* ' "

As the sophisticated, upscale, young suburban career girl: " 'Want a *medium*-sized car with *big* car *luxury*? That's *Seville* by *Cadillac*. Se-ville is *small* enough to fit into those *tight* city parking spaces . . . yet *big* enough to afford *Cadillac comfort* and *styling*. And with the op-tional *sunroof* you can let the *sun* in by day and *stars* in by night. Do what I did—make an investment in *economy and luxury*—get a *Seville* . . . built by the *Cadillac* of automobiles . . . *Cadillac*.' "

And as the femme fatale with deliciously understated elegance and seethingly overpowering sensuality: " '*All* my men wear *English Leather* . . . or they wear *nothing at all*.' "

She quickly learned how to mark a script to highlight what they called in the business "color words," like "delicious," "best-tasting," "luxury," and "sumptuous," so she would remember to emphasize them during her mock auditions; to note the appropriate places for a pause; to double-underline the product for the dual purpose of remembering what it was she was selling and to ram the name home to the imaginary consumer; and to imagine herself in a real-life situation so the scenario would come alive for her. Unless it came alive for her, it hadn't a chance to come alive for her audience.

She practiced extending her lower jaw and relaxing her lips to round out *aw* words and *ah* words, so that "wall" now came out *waul* instead of *wool*, and "Wisconsin" came out *Wiscahnson* instead of *Wiscansin*. She practiced at home in front of her mirror. She delivered her lines to her roommate until Peggy surrendered absolutely: "Okay, okay. I'll go out and buy a bottle of the shit right this minute if you'll just give it a rest!"

Catherine put all her energy into becoming a commercial actress. She worked at it until she was completely comfortable in front of the camera. She learned proper pacing and phrasing. She learned how to make someone else's words become her own and how to deliver them with the kind of unobtrusive, semisuppressed excitement that is the trademark of a good salesperson.

Mary Cline was right about the GQ layout. The magazine had been out for only two days when Catherine got her second call, this time for a preliminary interview for an Oil of Olay commercial. Mary Cline had also been right to wait until Catherine was ready. When Mary Cline took a personal interest in a "talent" everyone knew it. Mary made sure when speaking with clients that she sprinkled her conversations with savory tidbits such as, "Oh, I have a lovely new girl who might be right for you once she has the proper seasoning. A bit green right now, but we're bringing her along."

Holding Catherine back until the time was right compounded her future value as surely as though she were a mother lode of precious stones—and Mary Cline headed the cartel that controlled the supply. When Donald Harvey, the casting director from Oil of Olay, called the Cline Agency looking for young blondes, Catherine was in her eighth week at Lender/Stebbins Studios. Mary immediately telephoned her old friend, Joan Lender.

"Yes, I think she's ready . . . at least for some battlefield experience. She may not get the job, but she could use the experience and she certainly won't embarrass herself . . . or you. I'd give her a shot if I were you."

126

Catherine's performance began the moment her eyes met Donald Harvey's. "Good morning, Mr. Harvey. I'm Catherine Ward from Cline Models. Thank you for seeing me." She handed him her head shot, an eight-by-ten glossy, with a copy of her resume attached. Even though it listed her agency, her vital statistics, her training, and all of her print credits, it was still less than two thirds of a page long.

"I see you have no commercial experience," Donald Harvey said after scanning the photo and resume. But he was thinking that he had heard this young girl's name before—perhaps more than once—and that she must have something if she was a Mary Cline prodigy.

"No, but I have a great deal of experience in front of a camera. I'd like to read for you to give you a sample of my qualifications."

Donald Harvey was impressed with the young woman's presence. She was self-confident, yet not cocky. She was also unbelievably gorgeous. "Here. Try this on for size," he said, handing her a sample script.

"Thank you. Do you mind if I take a moment to look it over?"

"Be my guest." He tapped the ashes from his pipe thoughtfully as he watched her remove a pencil from her purse, read, and then mark the passage for pacing and emphasis. He was unable to suppress a smile. The kid was well organized, he'd give her that. With a bit of makeup she could be made to look a little older . . . say twenty-five. He suddenly realized that from the moment she had walked in the door he had hoped she would be good.

After less than a minute Catherine looked up from her lap, and Donald Harvey indicated a black-framed certificate on the wall behind him and to his left. "That's your camera lens. Any time you're ready."

" 'I used to wonder *how* I would keep my skin *smooth* and *healthy-*looking . . . *dry* air in the winter or *hot* sun in the summer . . . the *weather* is *rough* on your face. Then I discovered *Oil of Olay* . . .' "

Catherine Ward was a natural: nice, soothingly low voice and a hint of a midwestern accent—but there was nothing wrong with a hint. Though she had studiously marked the script, she only consulted it once as she delivered her lines. Donald Harvey found himself mesmerized by the beautiful, deep-blue eyes that caressed the "camera," by the gentle smoothing of her fingers over her angular cheekbones as she spoke: " '*Oil of Olay—nature's moisturizer.*' "

"Thank you, Catherine. I'll be in touch through the agency."

"May I take this copy of the script?"

"By all means."

When she was called back the following week, she made sure to arrive early for her 10:30 A.M. appointment, doing her best to look more mature by dressing in a crisp, off-white linen suit she'd purchased (charged), along with a white silk blouse, specifically for the event.

In the waiting room she nodded greetings to the few other women she recognized, picked up a copy of the script, and walked out into the hallway to practice again, noting the one phrasing change that had been made since her previous reading. Let the rest of them chitchat. She was taking care of business.

When she was called, Catherine walked directly to her mark.

"Give me a level."

She responded to the sound man's voice with practiced efficiency, reading the opening sentence from the teleprompter as it scrolled the first several lines of copy above the camera lens. Even though she had no experience with the electronic device, she was nonetheless prepared for it. At the Lender/Stebbins Studio, she had learned there were even teleprompters that ran the copy across the lens—sort of a one-way glass—so the performer could read the lines without looking off camera.

"You all set?" Donald Harvey asked as he broke from a conversation with a female assistant.

"Yes, Mr. Harvey," Catherine answered. She had taken great care to remember his name from her interview. "I'm ready when you are."

"Slate for us, will you please, Catherine?"

So he remembered her, too. It was a good sign, and it buoyed her confidence as much as did knowing she was prepared to do her best. As Harvey's assistant approached her with the clapsticks, Catherine asked in a calm, conversational tone, "Mr. Harvey, would you like me to include the take number or just my name?"

"Just your name is fine."

The woman leaned in. "Action!" and the simultaneous *clack*! of the clapsticks sent the adrenaline pumping through Catherine's veins.

"Catherine Ward." She paused, smiled, took a deep breath, and exhaled slowly: " 'I used to wonder,' " she began, delivering once again those lines she had delivered a hundred times in front of poor, beleaguered Peggy and another thousand times in front of her mirror. Somehow it was even easier in front of a camera and half a dozen strangers.

"Thank you for coming in, Catherine," Donald Harvey said, walking to her side and offering his hand.

"My pleasure, Mr. Harvey," Catherine answered in his same evenly-measured cadence. When they made eye contact their manner was like that of clandestine lovers desperate to hide their intimate and unspoken secret beneath a veil of professionalism. But like those lovers, theirs was a secret that could not be kept. Catherine Ward *had* this job. But even after she had thanked them all politely and left the studio, that tacit understanding translated into an awestruck silence that was finally broken by the sound man.

"Wow," he breathed, with an appreciative chuckle, "where can I get my wife a gallon jug of that stuff?"

Donald Harvey's voice broke gently through the laughter. "Play back the tape, Phil."

The cameraman rewound the tape and they all watched in silence. When the 60-second spot ended, Harvey was still tapping his pencil on his bottom front teeth in thought. "Let's have the woman's point of view."

His assistant nodded. "She was very convincing," she agreed.

So Catherine got the job, but that was far from the end of it. The commercial was shot at Claiborne Farm in Lexington, Kentucky. She was the only actress in it, and still the production crew totaled some two dozen people. There were the stylist who had fit her in New York and was responsible for the wardrobe, the makeup artist, the hairdresser, three sound men, two grips to take care of the heavy work, a set designer, the "gaffer" or head electrician and his assistant, the director and assistant director, two cameramen, the film company's manager, and the script girl. Also on hand were the account executive from Benton & Bowles, the copywriter in case it was necessary to make any final script changes, the art director to see that his images were re-created faithfully, and the agency producer. Finally, two men and two women executives from Oil of Olay were there to cover any other eventuality.

Catherine felt right at home back on a farm. The scene called for her to dismount from a silky-coated palomino, keep hold of his bridle, and stroll with him to a split-rail fence. There, she would stroke his muzzle affectionately, turn to the camera, and begin her lines. She had to be perfect; the horse had to be perfect; the sky behind them had to be perfect; the lighting, her sweater, leather vest and slacks combination . . . *everything* had to be perfect. They were in Kentucky for six days.

After the film was processed and edited back in New York, Catherine was called to the sound studio for another day to dub the lines over the tape until the lip-sync was exact. And finally, the commercial was "in the can." Before it ever reached the air, her contract had earned her $1,500 in session fees, $500 in travel time, and another $750 in meal and other allowances (most of which she didn't understand but which were standard requirements by the Screen Actors

129

Guild, her new union). Even less the agency's twenty-percent commission, that was $2,200. When it did air in test markets just prior to the fall of 1981, Catherine had her first glorious experience with that coveted phenomenon among actors called "residuals." At first the checks were small: $250, $275. Then they got larger: $545, $750, as the ad reached the bigger markets. They would peak at $3,712.25—*one check*—before beginning a gradual decline. When the contract cycle of thirteen weeks of use expired, Oil of Olay anxiously renewed it for another thirteen weeks. It was an extremely popular spot. Before year's end Catherine would earn almost $45,000 from that commercial alone—for less than two weeks' work.

But the money was only part of Catherine's compensation, and a comparatively small part at that. The real benefit she derived from the exposure, for that summer she was auditioned in rapid succession for Closeup toothpaste—which she got; Playtex bras—which she didn't get, but who referred her to the print department, which booked her for over twenty hours of print advertising at double her usual hourly rate (which was now $250); Selsun Blue Shampoo—which she also didn't get (no one, the casting director reasoned, would believe that this woman would have *anything* undesirable, let alone something as mundane as dandruff), and Gillette, a role she got as a prop smiling suggestively at the man who used Gillette Blue Blades.

All in all it was a successful summer—professionally. Personally, her life was empty, and never had it been more obvious than at the Gillette audition where she had met her first really nice, eligible man (she couldn't count Martin Bennett) since she'd arrived in New York City. In the waiting room she had broken her usual rule: Instead of picking up a copy of the script and walking off by herself to practice, she took the seat next to him. She had left him a small opening, but he hadn't seemed interested. Just her luck. And almost worse than his patent lack of interest was the reminder of how desperately alone and homesick she was.

7

For six months, until October of 1981, Lynell Alan lived in his old room in the eaves of his family's large Victorian home in Pine Orchard, Connecticut, and commuted daily to Manhattan on the Conrail train out of New Haven. It was an hour-and-a-half trip on a good day—and there weren't many good days.

He rose before his parents at six and moved about in a quiet bustle, having to catch the seven o'clock train in order to be fairly sure to make the city by nine. At least once a week he could count on the train taking more than two hours.

His days were spent making rounds, with a growing sense of impotence and frustration. Getting a job blind—walking in off the street— was a one-in-a-million shot, and Lynell's number never came up. That summer and fall he rang more doorbells, shook more hands, and was slobbered on by more watchdogs than he cared to remember. And he felt the sting of more rejections than a human being should have to endure in a lifetime. The only thing that kept him alive was a biweekly job posing for Sunday newspaper advertising supplements for K-Mart Department Stores and another job posing for photographs to be made into illustrations for a series of Bantam paperbacks, the latter with a genial photographer named Mike Dudley. Both those jobs and the few other one- and two-hour bookings he was hired for he got without any help at all from Gretchen.

Three or four days a week he managed to steel himself sufficiently to stop at the agency, sometimes with a small bouquet of flowers or a cup of coffee for Gretchen and Donna, her beleaguered assistant. His practiced obsequiousness became a game for him—the only way he could tolerate it—and Gretchen favored him with an occasional unproductive go-see.

On one particularly hot and humid late afternoon in August, after another day of pounding the pavement in search of the ever-more-elusive booking, Lynell was passing through the midtown Madison Avenue neighborhood on his way to Grand Central Station, and the train ride back to Connecticut, when it began to rain. To avoid getting drenched he ducked inside the nearest building. While waiting in the foyer for the rain to stop, he noticed on the building directory the familiar names of Bill Blass and Dior and Halston, along with a list of others he didn't recognize; anesthetized as he was to rejection, he decided to tour their distinguished offices in a final shot of the long, steamy day. At the offices of the names he knew, the receptionists haughtily informed him, "We only use Cline models." Another half-dozen firms, those whose names he didn't know, also turned him down, though more politely.

At Maria Kim, Inc., the receptionist made a call and buzzed him into a rear workroom, with row upon row of middle-aged Korean women stitching, sewing, and ironing in a modern, air-conditioned, well-lighted version of the all-American sweatshop. He brightened when a tiny, well-dressed young woman with the face of a China doll approached him and bowed formally.

"I'm a model from the Munson Agency," he began his monotonous spiel, hoping he'd wiped the hang-dog expression from his face, knowing the client could read the self-fulfilling prophecy of doom.

"Yes. Try on please." Her "l" was an "r," so that "please" came out "prease." She stood no more than five feet tall and had the body of a twelve-year-old girl, with breasts that barely rose against her crimson silk blouse. Even so, he couldn't resist an inconspicuous peek as she handed him the cotton sweater and drawstring slacks, and the shallow V-neckline fell away from her chest. As she swung her head and pointed to an unmarked door along the corridor behind her, her hair fell over her shoulder in a single billowing sheet of black silk.

When he returned, wearing the sweater and slacks, she measured his shoulders, sleeve length, waist, and inseam, uttering a professionally automatic, "Excuse me," while performing the latter.

She was so small, so delicate, and when she bent forward he could see without effort below the neckline of her filmy blouse. He never

132

would have believed that such an undeveloped chest, breasts merely dark, smooth nipples above the gentlest swell, could have been so erotic, and he was relieved when she was finished and stood again.

"You are medium?"

"Yes, I wear medium."

"We pay you fifty dollars per hour to try on."

"My agent . . . ," he began, but she cut in.

"Sorry, agent up to you. We pay *you* fifty dollars per hour or part of hour."

Her bearing alone forced a smile across his face. She looked as though the slightest harsh word would crack her down the middle. But who would speak a harsh word to this doll?

"You interested?"

"Yes, I'm interested," he answered, knowing that if the agency found out they would fire him, but suddenly not caring.

"Good. Suzy Yun," she said, holding out her hand.

"Lynell Alan."

"Rynerr Aran," she said with some difficulty. "Rynerr," she repeated slowly. Then, nodding, she looked up at him, smiled pleasantly for the first time, and added fatalistically, "It's never Sam."

Through the summer months he averaged four hours a week at Maria Kim—avoiding falling helplessly in love with Suzy Yun only because of the amazingly young-looking woman's all-business attitude; wedding ring; son, seventeen; and daughter, twenty-one. The amount he earned was barely enough for transportation and entertainment expenses—and the entertainment was infrequent.

Aimée was able to visit Pine Orchard several times during the summer, but Lynell always sensed that though they welcomed her as a member of the family, his parents never completely warmed up to her. In fact, the senior Alans found it impossible *not* to like the attractive, charming, and obviously bright young woman. What they resented— especially Lynell's father—was the ease with which she was accepted by the members of the Pine Orchard Yacht and Country Club, acceptance which they still felt was not completely theirs after two decades of membership. It was as though the snotty bastards could *smell* her lineage. It was as though Aimée Harris and *her* family, not the Ludlows and Whitings, had erected the fences east and west of their home on Pine Orchard Road when the Alans had first bought into the Connecticut Gold Coast some twenty-five years before. (For her part, Aimée found it positively unbelievable that Lynell could spurn all of this. There were the two gorgeous three-bedroom homes overlooking Long Island Sound. There was the prestigious, well-paying job with a solid-gold future. There was the nearby city of New Haven, in which she could easily imagine herself finding employment with Wiggin & Dana or one of half a dozen other top law firms, or maybe even striking out on her own. There was, in short, everything.)

As the daily treks to Manhattan became increasingly arduous in the wilting days of August, Lynell spent more and more time lounging on the beach. Unless he had an appointment with Suzy Yun at the offices of Maria Kim, he found it practically impossible to face the grinding disappointment of rounds. Occasionally he accompanied his father to his office at Conn-Tree, Inc., and each time he did the elder Alan made him the same offer. "Thirty-five thousand to start and an expense account."

Each time Lynell's answer was a noncommittal, "Let me think about it, Dad." But each time he did think about it, more and more.

"Think about it?" his father would ask incredulously. "Thirty-five thousand a year and an expense account versus pimping yourself in that shit-ass city for peanuts? Christ, I thought *you* were supposed to be the smart one!"

"I've got to get it out of my system," Lynell explained, each time with less conviction. "I've got to give it my best shot or I'm afraid I'll always regret it."

"Well, you've got to put more into it than *you* do."

So it was in answer to his father's challenge that, after calling the agency at noontime one late August day, he dropped everything and hustled into the city for a three o'clock cattle call for a shaving commercial.

He arrived at 2:45 and sat in the mirrored waiting room with forty other models, roughly two-thirds of them women, who filed in and out of the studio for their brief taping sessions. His nervousness and anxiety at never having auditioned for television fairly overwhelmed him.

By four o'clock he had long since stopped assessing his meager chances of getting the job and, with five men still ahead of him, had instead begun weighing the narrowing odds that he'd make the five o'clock train back to New Haven.

The entrance to the suite was at the opposite end of a long, narrow corridor that connected the studio to the waiting room. Lynell strained to pick up snatches of conversation that might give him even the slightest inkling of what to expect. His heart sank for the three women who still waited when he heard someone of apparent authority call from the studio to greet a new arrival. Unable to see down the hallway, he could only guess from what he heard that the new arrival must be "somebody."

"Cathy, darling, so glad you could make it."

"Hello, Paul, John, Susan. I told the agency I'd try to get here if I got out by four. So, here I am."

"Wonderful, wonderful. We know you're terribly busy, so come right in. This won't take five minutes."

Lynell looked around the small room at the rest of the disgusted, insulted faces.

"Thank you, John. That's awfully considerate of you. But I see there are others waiting. I'll just wait my turn. I'm sure I'm no busier than anyone else."

As her footsteps echoed toward them along the bare hardwood floor, the other models looked toward the hallway expectantly and Lynell recalled the words of his high school basketball coach. "Never watch the competition during warm-up drills," he had always said. "Let *them* watch *you*." This woman might be a "big cheese" and she might have made a nice gesture, and maybe he wasn't competing directly with her, but he'd be damned if he'd join the rest of these tools and stroke her ego more than it had just been stroked.

So he rested his gaze on the pages of *Ulysses*, the latest novel he carried to fill these inevitable idle hours. He had read the same paragraph three times, when he felt her standing over him.

"Excuse me. Is this seat taken?"

When he looked up, she did something he'd have expected himself to have done were their positions reversed: she flushed momentarily, and the forgotten portfolio she held across her chest with both arms fell to the floor with a resounding crash, splitting its frayed binding and sending her ten-by-fourteens sliding unceremoniously across the floor.

A multitude of words could have been used to describe her: beautiful, gorgeous, stunning, striking, perfect, elegant, statuesque, blonde, sleek, dimpled, familiar. Only one word said it all. The young woman was exquisite. Not sexy. Not like Aimée Harris or Suzy Yun or, God help him, Dan Buford, all of whom reeked of sexuality; no images of her sweat-soaked body clasped with his in blissful carnal union, in some mystic, sylvan paradise. No, she was not sexy at all, not really.

The word was exquisite. She was tall and slim as of course she would be, though the precise contours of her body were well hidden under loose-fitting, pleated khaki slacks and a shapeless navy blue V-necked pullover. Her hair poured over her shoulders in golden waves, and her teeth sparkled when she smiled her demure smile with award-winning dimples offsetting perfectly the narrow cleft of her chin.

The woman—she was a kid really, not more than twenty—was a goddamned walking amalgam of television commercials, all of which he'd seen her in: Closeup smile, Oil of Olay complexion, Herbal Essence hair, and large, round, ice-blue eyes with the sincere honesty to sell them all.

Though the three remaining women wilted in her presence, the men bloomed. Lynell knelt from his chair to gather her photographs, but he wasn't a great deal of help, picking up one to her three as he scanned each appreciatively—except the panty and bra shot, which he covered quickly with another of her in a fur coat as though it would embarrass her to have him see her in her underwear. It did embarrass him, though half the population of the United States had seen her in that Playtex advertisement.

She thanked him and sat, and he returned to James Joyce and read the same paragraph three more times. An uneasy silence sat between them.

"May I look at yours?" she asked softly.

"Hmm?"

"Your book. You've seen mine." She indicated the pile of photographs she had straightened and stuffed as best she could back into her broken case. "May I?"

"Oh, sure, of course. It's not in that class, though."

She studied each photograph as no one ever had. There were only twenty shots, but it took her nearly that many minutes to silently peruse them. "Very good . . . ," she said as she zipped the leather case and handed it back, leaving the "good" dangling off her lips without support.

"But?"

"It's very good," she said evenly, softly, so the conversation wouldn't be overheard. The room was still filled, several new men and women having arrived to replace those who had gone.

"Look," he said, using his hands to define his seriousness, while matching her conspiratorial stage whisper. "It's obvious from all these tearsheets that you work—a lot. So tell me the 'but' you wanted to tack onto the 'very good' before you decided I couldn't take it. Believe me, I can. And I'd appreciate it."

"It's not that I think you couldn't take it," she began hesitantly. "It's just . . . Who am I to criticize?"

"Who are you? You're the only person besides my mother who's

136

ever taken more than thirty seconds to fan through my portfolio and not act like it was an unwelcome intrusion on their day—including my agent. Believe me, that's enough."

"Catherine Ward, Bill Weber." The young male assistant stood in the doorway and read the names from the separate sign-up lists he kept on his clipboard. "Margda Andresson? Lynell Alan? You're next." Then as abruptly as he had appeared, he slipped back down the hallway.

Lynell stood outside the studio and watched intently as the three Gillette representatives put Catherine Ward and Bill Weber through their paces while the cameraman rolled the tape. He noted the fundamental mechanics: when the cameraman's assistant called "Slate!" the models smiled into the camera and gave their names.

"Catherine Ward."

"Bill Weber."

From then on they spoke no lines. One of the men from Gillette played a tape recording of the voice-over, and Catherine Ward and Bill Weber brought it to life. Bill Weber was good—very good. He was big, swarthy, and raw-boned, with thick, wavy brown hair and the seething chip-on-his-shoulder look of youth bound to conquer.

"Macho Shave," the voice-over began, and Catherine Ward had Lynell's rapt attention; he *knew* Bill Weber's cheek was smooth, because *she* brushed it appreciatively with the back of her delicate hand.

Each time she looked up between takes, she found Lynell's eyes and blushed self-consciously, and each time they rolled the camera again, her composure returned intact.

"Do you two have a few minutes to wait?" one of the Gillette men asked when they had taped three takes.

Even their "Yes" was perfectly timed.

"That's a hard act to follow," Lynell complimented them as the two passed him in the hallway.

She grasped his biceps in a gesture of friendship. "Break a leg."

"I probably will," he said with a touch of sarcasm, as he heard his name called. "But please don't watch."

"Sure."

He and Margda did three run-throughs that must have taken five to ten minutes but were over in an anxious, clouded blur, and he almost fainted when they asked him to wait.

"I'm sorry I wasn't better for you," he apologized as Margda left.

"Hey, it's not your fault. They took you. But thanks."

It was nearing 4:30 and there were few new arrivals. Catherine

137

Ward and Bill Weber were standing in the middle of the waiting room talking, but when Lynell came in she excused herself and again took her seat next to him.

"You were good," she said enthusiastically.

"You watched?"

"I figured the important thing was that you didn't know I was watching."

"I guess," he said in a forgiving voice.

"And you *were* good. They *did* ask you to stay."

"Yeah, but you and Mr. Macho were perfect," he said in a grudging whisper from the corner of his mouth.

"Thanks. My name is Catherine Ward."

"I know. Mine's Lynell Alan."

"I know."

When she smiled, he had to chuckle and shake his head softly. That ingenuous smile—all dimples and flashing ivory teeth—and those hypnotic eyes that invited you past the exquisite face and inside her head, invited you to share what she was thinking. He was beginning to like this kid, really like her. She was too young for him and didn't particularly turn him on sexually, and in spite of her looks she hadn't bombarded him with that "come hither" attitude, even seemed to present herself as though she wished someone would disregard her looks. He had had very few female friends in his lifetime. There was always the pressure of sexual involvement, usually from the start. With Catherine Ward he felt no such pressure. He felt . . . well, like he felt with his sister, Veronica.

"May I see your book again?"

"Yes. My book. You were saying before?"

She took it again and thumbed deliberately through it. "It's all sexy looks and hard stares. They're nice but . . ."

"There you go with the 'buts' again."

"Well, remember, this is just my own feeling. I could be completely off base. But I don't see that as you." She looked up from the portfolio and folded it closed in her lap. "You have a nice, sincere face and a beautiful smile—with or without showing teeth. I think you need more smiles, more different kinds of looks. Show your versatility. I'm surprised your agent hasn't told you that. Who are you with?"

"Munson."

"Oh."

"Bad news?" It was the way she'd said "Oh."

"No, but they're mostly commercial, aren't they? I see you more as the high fashion type."

138

"I wish you people would get together. They tell me I'm commercial."

"Have you been to the other agencies?"

"A couple." He felt guilty. He'd meant to see more.

"You should try some of the fashion agencies: Wilhelmina, Elite, Zoli, Ford, Cline."

"I have an exclusive with Munson."

"Oh," she said fatalistically. "How long?"

"Until the first of the year."

"Well, you should still look around. If someone's interested now, they'll be interested in a few months. It's not that far off, you know."

The conversation flowed easily, though she seemed reluctant to talk about herself, except to say that she was from the Midwest.

In the hour since his audition the traffic between the waiting room and the studio had completely subsided, and only Bill Weber sat across from them, thumbing through the pages of an old issue of *Time*.

When the young assistant reappeared with his clipboard, Lynell for the first time considered the upcoming scenario. They had decided on Catherine—that was easy. In fact, he was surprised they hadn't already decided on Bill Weber, too. But they'd asked him to wait, so they must be going to give the thing one more run-through with each of them before deciding. It was his first real chance. Christ, a Gillette commercial on TV—and residuals! It didn't seem fair that with few exceptions, for print work a model got his hourly rate for a job—period—no matter how often or in how many places they used the shot. He'd give this his best shot. If he got it—great; and if he didn't—well, there would be other chances . . . maybe.

"Catherine, Bill. John would like to speak with you about returning with a few other couples for next Tuesday's callback," the young man with the scruffy beard said. "Lynell, thanks for coming in."

Lynell looked at Catherine and tried to hide his disappointment. "Hey, that's great," he said with a wan smile.

"That's shitty," she spat venomously. "They kept you hanging around for over an hour to tell you that?" When she shook her head he was watching her wavy golden hair bouncing on a nineteen-inch screen, and for the first time in his life, he believed it just might be possible for a woman's hair to have "body." "That's really shitty," she repeated.

"Hey, it's a shitty business," he said, standing, shoving his portfolio under his left arm, and extending his right.

She stood and took his hand.

139

"And don't get yourself into any trouble with them over this," he added, nodding toward the studio. "You look like the stubborn type. It's not worth it. Anyway, for me, the hour with you was an hour well spent. Thanks for the advice, Catherine."

Their eyes held momentarily in warm, budding friendship, and in that moment something had to be said, some new ground broken, to change the nature of this relationship from professional to personal. He wanted to say it, but in his insecurity hoped that she would. In the hesitation the moment was lost, and they hadn't made the transition each had so desperately wanted, needed, to make—to real friends.

It occurred to each simultaneously that they had been holding hands, not shaking, and they awkwardly released their grasp and were suddenly chilled by the cool breeze of unfamiliarity.

"See you," he said with a nod, as he turned to leave. With each step down the long corridor, he thought not of how callously he had been rejected but of how good it would be to have a friend in this city, in this business where the competition was so cutthroat it almost preempted friendship. He could still go back, he thought as he rode the elevator to the street, tell her straight away, "I'm not one of those guys you probably meet ten times a day who just want to get into your pants. In fact, I have a lover. I just want to be friends." By the time he reached the street it was, conveniently, too late. By then she'd be talking business and have forgotten him.

He who hesitates, he thought, *is not only lost but lonely—very, very lonely.*

But Catherine Ward did not forget Lynell Alan. She wished to God she was better with people. She was pleased to have gotten a callback for this job so easily, but in truth she'd rather have been turned down. The rest would do her good. And so, she thought, would Lynell Alan. If they had been rejected together, they could have gone to the nearest bar and commiserated. As it was, she had wanted to say something, but what? "Can you wait another hour, or God knows how long, until I'm finished here?" Who was she kidding? The guy just wasn't interested. Period. Exclamation point. He probably had half a dozen women—lovers *and* friends; what did he need with her? She was pretty well-known in the business, so maybe he had even heard she was gay. After all, since the Bahamas she'd been approached by several other women models, and though she had turned them all down, she had made no pretense that it was because she was not gay, only that she

140

was "involved." It seemed the pragmatic thing to do and so far had worked out to her satisfaction.

Most of the people on the hiring end, for whatever reason, were men, and in a buyer's market the buyers availed themselves of every possible fringe benefit—as she knew only too well. By her own rough estimate, perhaps fifty percent of the men were heterosexual, and as any woman knows, men have voracious egos to feed. They may want a woman to sleep with them in exchange for a job (or even the chance of a job), but they have to be able to convince themselves that she'll *enjoy* it, too. That they thought she was gay eliminated a substantial amount of harassment.

On second thought, she was glad nothing had come of her meeting with Lynell Alan. She had liked him, liked the way he looked, but it would only have led to disappointment—disappointment if he had, predictably, made a pass at her and perhaps even disappointment if he hadn't.

There was only one lover that could reverse her deepening depressions, that could get her up, get her off, erase her fears and inhibitions; only one lover that could make her feel like a woman, a beautiful, desirable woman; only one lover that could make her forget, that could ease the pain of her separation from the one person who really mattered. Her lover was cocaine.

As summer turned to fall the intense heat and humidity began to ease, but Lynell's anxiety didn't ease with it. Summer was traditionally slow, as they had told him at the agency. Anybody who was anybody left the city for as much of the season as they could afford to be away. Fall fashions were shot in the late winter and early spring; winter fashions, in early fall. Summer was as dead as the spindly, defoliated maples lining Manhattan's streets, as dead as Lynell's dream.

His family kept a roof over his head, and Suzy Yun kept him busy enough to earn pocket money and save for the security deposit on the apartment he and Aimée would share when she arrived in October. But he had no pretenses about what he was: a fifty-dollar-an-hour coatrack who, except that he could raise his arms and say, "It's a bit snug," could have been easily replaced by a mannequin.

Finally, one mid-September afternoon, he suffered the ultimate irony. When he entered the tenth-floor offices of Maria Kim, Inc., he found the porcelain-faced Suzy Yun hard at work fitting a sweater to a headless dummy, rotating its arms effortlessly over its head.

141

"Rynerr." She bowed her lithe body gracefully, and he sneaked what was to be a last peek at her soft nipples beneath the ubiquitous silk V-necked blouse. "I am sorry, but Maria has informed me that we can no longer afford the services of a professional model at this stage of the fitting process. It has been a pleasure working with you, and if we need you again we will call. I have a check for your trouble today."

"Thank you," he said numbly. He had come to count on the work, though in spite of Suzy Yun's unusually respectful treatment, it was as demeaning as anything he had ever done.

As Suzy Yun bowed again and went back to her work, Lynell smiled broadly, and when he burst into laughter she looked up at him as though he were touched. Americans were so strange. She would never understand them, no matter how long she lived here.

Lynell Alan walked out laughing only because there was nothing else to do but cry. He had to admit that his headless replacement was the perfect man for the job.

8

In spite of Catherine's having neither a lover nor any prospects, Peggy had talked her into taking the pill, "just in case." Catherine felt foolish popping the tiny pink things each morning and her enlarged breasts were sometimes sore and sensitive, but at least there was one small advantage: her periods, which since adolescence had been annoyingly erratic, had become as regular as clockwork.

Through the spring and into the summer, Peggy remained as "busy" socially as Catherine was idle. Her appetite for men was the same as it was for food—insatiable. She loved men, adored them—all sizes and shapes, all religions and races.

At first the sound of Peggy's squeaking bedsprings was an annoyance to Catherine, to the point where she occasionally contemplated violating the sanctity of her friend's room to apply a dose of A–1 All-Purpose Oil to the overworked steel coils. But eventually she found the rhythmic creaking soothing, cathartic, and, once Peggy had met a man named Phil Symonds, even stimulating.

Catherine liked Phil Symonds, which was more than she could have said for any of Peggy's previous lovers. Phil was a gentleman. He never looked at Catherine the way most of the men did, ogling her whenever Peggy turned her back—not even the night the pair had come home unexpectedly early and caught Catherine lolling about in her flimsy summer nightgown. No, Phil had more respect for Peggy than that. In fact, Peggy confessed with some concern—though, due to the thinness of the walls in their apartment, she needn't have—she had literally had to drag him into her bedroom. But only the first time.

By the end of the summer two situations had conspired to put Catherine almost completely out of touch with Peggy. One was her own increasingly hectic schedule. The other was that Peggy and Phil often spent the nights at his apartment, particularly when Peggy was aware Catherine had to be up early for a job. Even so, the fact that they lived together was comforting to Catherine, because though she spent more and more evenings alone, she knew that eventually she and Peggy would be together again, sharing a bottle of wine and conversation.

One evening at the beginning of September, Peggy arrived home alone from a dinner date, tapped excitedly on Catherine's bedroom door, let herself into the darkened room, and flung herself onto the bed.

"What's going on?" Catherine asked, reaching to snap on the bedside lamp and lazily rubbing the sleep from her eyes.

Peggy only splayed her left hand against her cheek. "Oh, nothing."

"Where's your date?" Catherine asked suspiciously, still not having noticed the rock that sparkled insistently from Peggy's ring finger.

"He's got to go to Cleveland on business. Leaving on the red-eye."

"What happened? Big Boy dump you?" Catherine asked. Then the diamond caught her eye. "Oh, my! You're not . . ."

"Yes, I am. Phil has asked me to marry him."

Catherine sat up, then sighed and threw her arms around Peggy. "Oh, Peggy, I'm so happy for you. So, Phil is Mr. Right?"

"No, dear. Phil is Mr. One Hundred."

That she would miss Peggy was something Catherine never doubted; however, it was a little while before she realized just how much. Peggy's outgoing, effervescent personality—style, really—had dragged Catherine into sociability. Not that Catherine was unfriendly. She simply had a nearly unbroken record of not knowing *how* to make friends. Her waiting posture, along with her extreme good looks, made her seem aloof at best, snobbish at worst.

After a party that Peggy took her to early in their friendship, of which Peggy had as usual been the life and Catherine the wallflower, Catherine had asked dejectedly what was wrong with her. "People always seem to look right through me—like I'm a piece of the furniture."

"It's because you look so damned unapproachable."

"How can I look approachable?"

"You?" Peggy shook her head and shrugged her shoulders. "I don't know, babe. Don't look so damned gorgeous?" Then she shrugged again. "I know it's not your fault but"—her voice lowered and she winced slightly, almost as though she were telling Catherine she were a monster—"you're kind of scary, to men *and* women."

"But not to you," Catherine noted defensively.

"Oh," Peggy answered, making her point by gesturing with her index finger, "but I'm a secure, self-satisfied bitch."

It was something that had crossed Catherine's mind innumerable times but that she had never before heard articulated. She was a freak. People stared at her the way they stared at dwarfs and the grotesquely fat and deformed, quickly and self-consciously averting their eyes when she looked up. She was a monster as surely as though she had a bolt driven through her temples. Not only did she have no lover, but except for Peggy she had no friends. And that relationship was destined to change very soon. The wedding wasn't until the first of November, a month after Catherine's birthday, but Peggy moved out in mid-September.

Catherine's work had kept her busy through the summer, and she earned enough money to send her grandmother several hundred dollars a week on a regular basis. She made a point to visit home at least twice a month—even if it was only overnight—but no matter how often she visited, it never seemed enough. And even the money didn't make up for that.

When she worked, even if it was only on an hour or two print-booking, Catherine focused her entire day on that, anticipating the look and style the photographer would call for, doing everything she could to present herself at her best. For 9:00 A.M. jobs she tried to get to sleep early the night before, but that was difficult as recently she had begun to suffer from chronic insomnia. When the job was from 3:00 to 5:00 P.M., she spent the day preparing, sometimes only napping to catch up on lost sleep, never wearing herself down, physically or—almost as important—mentally, by pounding the pavement making her interminable rounds. On the few days she didn't work, she steeled herself to the rejection, the humility that went with knocking on doors unannounced: photographers, advertising agents, art directors, anyone who might remember her when a job came up. Though on many days it would have been easy to say "to hell with it all," she treated it exactly like what it was—her nine-to-five job—and tried to face it with fresh enthusiasm each and every day.

More and more she began running into people a second and third time, and along with her television exposure, it began to pay off. Catherine's was, after all, not the type of face or body one could easily forget, and she began gradually to imprint herself on the memories of a variety of potential new clients.

At first Catherine had planned to try to find a new roommate, but no one could ever replace Peggy. The overwhelming majority of people she met, she met on rounds, go-sees, and shootings, and none of those situations was the kind that spawn lasting friendships. The unrelenting pressure of competition and the professionalism she expected of herself on the job preempted any chance of that. If the right person fell into her lap—which she doubted would happen—maybe. But for now, as long as paying the rent by herself was a luxury she could afford, she would continue to live alone.

Catherine still met Peggy once a week for lunch or dinner, and those dates amounted to the sum total of her social life. As the wedding day approached, it became increasingly difficult for Peggy to break away. Though she had always considered herself a loner, Catherine felt isolation begin to bear down on her like the fearful darkness of sleepless nights. She had only three things to occupy her time: her work, her books, and a dream—an impossible dream that somehow she could reunite her fragmented family.

Catherine hadn't been with a man in months, and as a joke Peggy gave her a vibrator for her birthday.

"Don't get too attached to Studley there," Peggy facetiously warned Catherine when she unwrapped the thick, eight-inch-long pink machine and sat eyeing it in shocked embarrassment. "He's unbelievable in bed and he won't bore you to death with idle chitchat. But he absolutely refuses to help around the house, and he just might electrocute you if you decide you want to get one off in the bathtub. Anyway," she said, a bit more seriously than she'd intended, "he's no substitute for the real thing, Catherine."

On shootings Catherine breathed sexual fire, but the inferno often raged on long afterward, sometimes out of control. The men she worked with seemed not at all interested in her, though her all-business attitude, she realized, must surely put them off. In one respect she was disappointed, but in another it was what she wanted, so she couldn't complain. It was only that sometimes, just sometimes, she felt the aching and unfulfilled need to have someone beside her; to have someone to tell her she was beautiful—not physically beautiful, but *really* beautiful—to have someone need her.

"You've got to break into new circles," Peggy told her during her last lunch as a single woman with Catherine. Peggy was—as she had

146

confided in her fiancé—frankly worried about Catherine. "It's not healthy to be spending so much time alone."

"But I don't have all that much spare time to break into these 'new circles,' " Catherine protested. The truth, they both knew, lay in the fact that she simply lacked the self-confidence to make the effort.

Catherine found spending money a catharsis, but it was one that, like most, had a cost that went beyond financial. The cost, of course, was guilt. Inevitably, the day after a depression-lifting shopping binge, she would remorsefully return all but the few necessary items. She hadn't much need for expensive clothes anyway, because except when she was being paid handsomely for it, she rarely wore them.

Appearances in fashion layouts in *Glamour* and *Mademoiselle* added impetus to a burgeoning career that already kept her busy eight to twelve hours a day. In the autumn months she began to have less time for rounds between her busy schedule of shootings and go-sees for specific jobs, but she managed to squeeze in a few visits, promising herself never to lose contact with that most basic fact of modeling life. It was, after all, the foundation of the pyramid upon which a model's career was built, and a weakening of that foundation would eventually weaken the entire structure.

For Catherine, the most relaxing hours were those she spent reading before bedtime, comfortably hollowed into her soft mattress and propped lazily against the headboard by half a dozen puffy, down pillows. Inevitably, as the evening hours waned, she would almost guiltily set aside Hemingway or Updike or Sinclair Lewis and reach for the tiny vial of powder in the drawer of her bedside table. After greedily sniffing every last grain of two small, wispy lines, and with her head still expanding and contracting in a dizzying rush, she would pick up her volume of short stories by Anaïs Nin or thumb to a particularly juicy passage in Judith Krantz or Shirley Conran that she'd previously marked and already read ragged, and carefully read again every deliciously erotic word. It was then that, enshrouded in the euphoria of the drug, she would drop her forgotten book to the floor and quietly snap off the light.

A fashion shooting for a Bloomingdale's catalogue prevented Catherine from attending Peggy's Friday evening rehearsal dinner and almost made her late for the 6:00 P.M. Saturday ceremony. As the maid of honor, she was breathtaking in her clinging, low-cut, navy blue satin gown.

The wedding ceremony and reception were held in the Temple Beth Sholom in Huntington, Long Island, and when Catherine entered the synagogue, she immediately realized that Peggy's father, a jolly and agreeably rotund man of about sixty, whom she had met several times in the city, had put one over on the rube from Iowa.

"Your father's a ragpicker?" Catherine said sarcastically when she had a moment alone with her friend.

Peggy shrugged. "It's his little joke. He's in the garment business."

"And I pictured him behind a horse-drawn cart on the Lower East Side," Catherine admitted sheepishly.

"That's really about the size of it," said Joe Markle, who came up behind her and draped his arm around her shoulder paternally. "We take old rags and turn them into new rags."

Following the traditional Jewish ceremony came a reception that was nothing short of a bacchanal. There was a buffet with sumptuous hors d'oeuvres, at which Catherine, starved after having had nothing to eat all day, ate and drank altogether too much, not realizing there was to be a full-course, sit-down meal, an open bar, and dancing to a twelve-piece orchestra to follow. Eventually she slowed her pace while managing to remain pleasantly high throughout most of the evening. A jubilantly proud father was sending his cherished princess out into the world in style.

But as impressive as the party was, nothing was as impressive as the best man, a childhood friend of Peggy's new husband. He was several inches taller than Catherine and had a deep suntan highlighting gold, sun-bleached hair that hung well over his collar. His face was neither handsome nor homely and was dominated by a large nose and small close-set blue eyes that darted about constantly, as though he was afraid some small detail of the proceedings might escape his notice. Although he was only twenty-five, the skin at the corners of his eyes crinkled into deep furrows from a life of year-long overexposure to the sun. His lean, muscular body was fitted snugly into an impeccably tailored tuxedo. He was athletic looking, alert, quick, and graceful. He was Webster Greaves, the fifth-ranked professional tennis player in the world. And a semi-inebriated Catherine Ward couldn't take her eyes off him.

Most of what Catherine knew of Webster Greaves she had read in the sports pages of the *New York Times*, though from time to time his life managed to overflow onto the front page. In seven years on the tennis circuit, though he'd never made it above a brief stint as number two in the world, Webster Greaves had rarely been ranked out of the top ten. He earned a six-figure income in prize money and ten times that in endorsements, but though tennis had put him *in* the news, it was his hedonistic lifestyle that *kept* him there. He was a native New

Yorker and natural athlete who had made the transition to big-money corporation—which he now was—as smoothly as he wound into his masterful bullet of a serve. He had about him a challengingly mysterious air that dared you to ferret out his innermost secrets; and in fact ever since he had first burst unannounced onto the tennis scene, every newspaper and magazine in the country had at one time or another tried unsuccessfully to do just that.

Webster Greaves was a notorious playboy and bon vivant, a fixture at Studio 54; and if indeed "where there's smoke there's fire," he was also a heavy recreational user of drugs, specifically cocaine. In the most recent of his brushes with the law, all of which had previously ranged from nitpicking to minor, he had narrowly escaped indictment on a variety of drug-related charges—ranging from possession to sale—involving twenty-five thousand dollars worth of cocaine found in his car after an arrest for speeding (though to close friends he boasted, "I've never sold drugs. I give it away! Christ, I *snack* on twenty-five grand").

Catherine should have guessed by his reputation alone that Webster Greaves had requested to be seated next to her at dinner. Mystery sat beside her . . . male sexuality . . . the chance for involvement without commitment, and she had to force herself to resist his enticing physical magnetism, a magnetism she suddenly realized she'd never before felt toward a man. She ate very little at dinner and, under the festive circumstances, overdrank acceptably, hoping she would need the bravado.

Webster Greaves was predictably glib and self-centered, and when—after the time-honored father-daughter first dance—he invited Catherine onto the floor, he held her a bit more closely than normally would have made her comfortable, and only the alcohol pulsing through her system staved off her embarrassment at his adolescent attempts to draw attention to himself—to them.

Webster Greaves made it clear from the start that he had laid unassailable claim to Catherine Ward, and any interest the handful of other single men in attendance might have had in her quickly wilted when they saw how outmatched they were. Webster Greaves was a star, a celebrity, the kind of man a woman like that would want.

Catherine did not find Webster Greaves particularly likable. He had an ego as expansive as his tennis itinerary and an abrasive self-confidence that, with her peripheral knowledge of sports, Catherine associated with the Yankees, Muhammad Ali, and other perennial winners. It was the attitude she guessed an athlete had to have to be

149

successful, but which was so intensely offensive it made her root against them. Though she already knew he would have his chance to score with her tonight in bed, it was only because *she* wanted it that way—and because she continued to drink enough champagne to maintain a pleasant buzz and stave off her native inhibitions. She had a feeling that Webster Greaves would *never* score with her *out* of bed.

"It's getting kind of close in here," he commented predictably as he held her tightly in a waltz. "Want to split?"

"Love to."

Even his goodbyes were ostentatious, and his mechanical adherence to his press image almost made it easier for Catherine to think of him as a tool, like her vibrator, to be manipulated for her pleasure.

In his Rolls Corniche—of which he owned three, this one burgundy—they sped along the Long Island Expressway and into the city in relative silence. Without an enraptured audience, talk was difficult for Webster Greaves. In any case, real conversation he found impossible. He was most comfortable performing—whether for a crowd of thousands or a crowd of one.

At On Stage, Webster pulled the Rolls up to the curb and walked around to take Catherine's arm as the doorman helped her out of the automobile. As Webster thanked him with a curt nod and a shake of his head, he discreetly slipped the uniformed man a bill, eliciting a litany of *thank you*'s.

"We'll just be a short time, Frank. Keep an eye on her, will you?"

"Certainly, Mr. Greaves. Certainly. Take your time," the doorman said, still bowing diffidently as Webster led Catherine into the nightclub. The show of obeisance clearly inflated Webster's already abundant ego.

An extremely tall blond man stood just inside the door with his back to them, but Catherine barely noticed him, so intent was she on surveying the boisterous, dimly-lit club. A thick cloud of smoke hung just above head level, like fog over an Iowa cornfield on an early autumn morning. A new-wave band blasted from the stage and shadowy forms gyrated across the small dance floor. The flashing colored lights glittered off the mirror-topped tables around the room, and the body heat inside was almost oppressive despite the coolness of the evening.

"Mr. Greaves." Catherine heard the tall man greet her escort with the stiff formality of an employee.

"Mark," Webster replied.

"Mark!" she echoed when she looked up and saw him.

"Umm." Mark hesitated, pointing his finger as though scolding himself as he squinted into his memory. "Cathy," he said finally.

150

"You two know each other?" Webster asked. "I thought you'd never been here before, Cathy?"

"I haven't. Mark and I did a job together a while back. In the Bahamas," Catherine explained. Then she turned back to Mark. "What are you doing here?"

"Working," he answered apologetically. "I'm the bouncer. It keeps me busy between jobs." He had to yell to be heard over the music. "I'm too big to get much print work, so most of the jobs I land are television." He turned his attention back to Webster Greaves. "There's a table back in the corner, Mr. Greaves."

"Gee, I thought he did well enough modeling not to have to moonlight," Catherine remarked when she and Webster had made their way through the crowd to the empty table.

"He does," Webster answered, eyeing her with the impatient smirk of one in the know. "He also makes more here in a month dealing drugs than he does modeling all year."

On Stage's Manhattan pseudosophisticates were above fawning over a celebrity jock, so Catherine and Webster made it to the table with only an occasional greeting from someone Webster barely knew but who no doubt considered the tennis star "a close personal friend."

After three drinks and conversation strained both by the noise and a predictably inarticulate Webster Greaves, it was Catherine who suggested they leave. "Let's find someplace quieter," she said, standing tipsily.

Webster took her arm to steady her and led her through the crowd to the door where Mark still towered, scanning the sea of bobbing heads for signs of overexuberance. "Early night, Mr. Greaves?"

"Big tournament coming up. Got to get my rest." Catherine noticed that Webster slipped a tip unobtrusively into Mark's breast pocket. Her only thought was of fresh air.

Mark nodded thanks and exchanged smiles with Catherine. "Good night."

"Where to?" Webster asked, wringing his hands in anticipation before starting up the Rolls. "Regine's? Studio 54?" Webster Greaves was a man who thrived on being seen, on being a star.

"I'm already plied with alcohol," Catherine slurred playfully, sliding across the front seat to his side. *God, what am I doing?* she thought. But the answer was clear in the marvelously excruciating ache that made it almost painfully exciting to hold her thighs together. Suddenly, for the first time in her life, *she* was the huntress, *she* was the user, and she knew she would have her way with this hollow jock. "Anyway," she went on, "I thought you had to get to bed?"

"Bed can wait," he answered.

Catherine, suddenly the seductress, slowly stroked his rippling thigh from the knee upward. "But I can't," she whispered.

Catherine nestled into the luxurious silver sheets, with the deliriously erotic feel of the cool silk against her hot skin. One large pillow was propped under her head. She remembered little of the drive except for the harsh, bright city lights that had tracked them through the night and the two lines of coke they'd shared, one at the beginning and one at the end. She lay back in the enormous circular bed for what seemed an eternity, looking up at her reflection in the mirrored ceiling. Finally the bathroom door opened, and as Webster strode purposefully toward her in the dim light, she watched impatiently, mesmerized by the hypnotic sway of the purple head of his long, flaccid penis.

"Another hit?" he asked, sitting on the edge of the bed. *Another hit? Another drink? Another set?* must be the extent of his vocabulary, she thought. Right now she couldn't wait until he added *Another fuck?* to his repertoire.

"Why not?" She sat up, letting the silk sheet fall from her breasts.

He looked at her, smiled wanly, and returned to his absorption in the preparation of the cocaine.

She checked in his lap for a reaction but there was none. What the hell was wrong with her? Never before had she touched one soft and it felt exceedingly strange. "Don't you like me?" As soon as the words were out of her mouth she regretted them. Christ, she sounded like a junior high school virgin.

"It's not you. Sometimes I get preoccupied before a big tournament, that's all. I like you, really."

She took her hand away. Even under the influence of drugs, it was at best awkward trying to carry on a conversation with a strange man's cock in your hand.

She was still sniffing the last of the powder when Webster snapped off the light and crawled into the bed beside her. Sightless in the pitch black of the darkened room, and with her other senses honed as sharp as the razor blade that had cut the white crystals into a fine powder, for Catherine hot was suddenly hotter and cold colder, wet wetter and dry drier. His lips were on hers savagely, his tongue finding hers, and when she stuck her tongue into his mouth he sucked it avidly. The heat of his tightly muscled torso pressed roughly against her. He fumbled clumsily with her breasts, but she could still feel the rubbery lump of him against her abdomen as she unconsciously returned the impotent rotation of his hips. She parted her legs so that his slipped between

152

them, and the feel of the spare, wiry hair against the soft skin of her inner thighs drove her nearly mad with desire.

She moaned something inaudible in her husky, seductive voice and was suddenly flooded with an indescribable aloneness, an aloneness she instinctively knew she would feel when she died. Even when Webster crouched over her and sucked her nipples hard and she felt his still-limp penis drag ticklingly across her thigh, even then it was as though she were alone in her room with this mindless male body and she was torturing herself beyond all reason. Slowly he lowered himself, painting her flat stomach with flourishing strokes of his tongue. "Oh please, yes!" she cried, and Webster took her clitoris lightly between his teeth and flicked it with rapid, expert strokes of his pointed tongue until, racked with spasms of pleasure, she thrust her pelvis against the pressure of his hungry mouth and came in a quivering convulsion more pleasurable than she had imagined possible. It was her first orgasm ever with a man.

She barely had time to catch her breath before he was kneeling over her. "Suck me," he commanded softly, and she obeyed. Then, before he was even hard, every muscle fiber in his body went rigid, and grunting gutturally as though serving for the match, Webster collapsed beside her.

Catherine didn't know how much later it was when she awoke, wondering wistfully if anyone did it "the regular way" anymore. When Webster sat up and lit a candle, its light chased away the darkness the way the joint he passed her chased away the buzz of cocaine and alcohol that still filled her head.

"Maui Wowie," he said. "Picked up a pound in Hawaii last month."

"Mmm." She rolled onto her stomach, propped herself on her elbows, and looked up into Webster's blank face. From where he sat against the headboard, the candlelight cast flickering shadows across his sun-lined face. Catherine held the smoke in her lungs and passed the joint back to him. When she lay her hand gently on his thigh, he twitched as though her fingers were live wires. "Don't you ever relax?"

He inhaled deeply and sighed, took a long, slow draught, and leaned his head back again. "Not often enough, I guess."

She eyed the length of his athletic body, tight and hard except for the rope of flesh curled in the dark thatch of pubic hair in his lap. While the joint floated dreamily between them and the tickle in her crotch once again became an itch, in the back of her mind she wondered about Webster Greaves. Would he tell stories about her in locker rooms around the world to perpetuate his image? Would her indiscretion become public knowledge? Could it hurt her growing but delicate career? What was he thinking about her? That she was just another tennis groupie?

Stop! What the fuck difference did any of that make? There was only one thing that mattered. Catherine's sexual appetite, once rekindled, was a hunger gone gluttonously out of control. When she again looked up at him, Webster's soulful eyes were wandering the superb length of her: the wide shoulders and strong, muscular back of a farmhand, and the plump round bottom he couldn't hope to resist.

Catherine watched his penis crawl, like a sprouting vine, up the thin path of pubic hair that rose to his navel. "Let's do it again," she said, articulating his thoughts, she was sure, as she started to roll anxiously onto her back. But his strong right hand gripped her near shoulder, and with catlike agility he sprang on top of her, wedging his knees between her thighs and forcing her legs apart. He was much quicker than she had imagined, and she released a short gasp of surprise as he swiftly entered her. It was not at all that she was shocked or offended by his desires. He was a physical man; what she wanted from him was a totally physical relationship. She was just surprised, that was all—surprised by his roughness, surprised that this was what he wanted.

"That was good," he managed when he was finished, struggling to whisper the words between steady gulps of air.

Fuck me. Suck me. That was good. Three sentences that were a concise summation of all that their relationship was or ever would be. Sometimes they didn't speak to one another at all. Sometimes she awoke early in the morning and he would already be gone.

On the infrequent times he was in town long enough to take her out to a restaurant, the *paparazzi* besieged them, rudely popping flashbulbs in the middle of dinner or catching her as she stepped out of the Rolls and a gust of swirling New York wind blew her dress up around her ears. Occasionally a photo ran in a local newspaper—usually the *Post*—with a caption such as "Webster Greaves on the town with leggy Cline Model Cathy Ward," or something equally tacky.

"What are you complaining about?" Webster would say. "In your business the ink's going to hurt you?"

"But just look at that awful picture!"

"It's not that bad," he would say patronizingly. "At least they spelled your name right this time."

From that first night together, each time they met, theirs was a purely chemical reaction. Only the tacit understanding that the physical utility of each to the other was mutual kept them together. Never did a meaningful glance pass between them, and the purposeful taking of their lovemaking remained undiluted by a fond touch or a gentle word. They were strangers even in their continued ardor for one another, and except for their physical intimacy, the only thing that separated them from an ancient, uncommunicative married couple was that they had *never* known each other.

Catherine began to associate sex so closely with Webster Greaves that she actually became aroused when she read accounts of his matches in the sports pages. She began to anticipate secretly that he would be upset in the early rounds of a distant tournament, so he might then have a longer time to stop in New York.

After the initial thrill of getting wonderfully, shamelessly laid had worn off, she became for a time mildly offended that Webster showed not the least bit of interest in either her or her career. But then, hadn't she wanted it that way? He was a man and she a woman and they turned each other on. Almost literally the only thing Webster Greaves knew about her was what she looked like; and the *only* thing she knew about him that she couldn't read in the pages of *Tennis* magazine was that he preferred fucking her up the ass to straight sex.

It was just before Christmas when Peggy Markle Symonds eyed Catherine worriedly from across the kitchen table in the apartment they had once shared. Catherine looked tired, the luminescence drained from her beautiful skin.

"You look like hell, Catherine," Peggy said in her usual blunt style.

"Thanks. It's nice to see you, too."

"No, seriously, Catherine, you're not trying to keep up with that playboy, Webster, are you? The whole world knows he's into sex and drugs and not necessarily in that order. It's ruined his career. Don't let it do the same to yours."

"I'm all right, mother."

"I'd just hate to see you get hurt, girl, that's all."

"I won't, Peggy," Catherine said defensively. "I can read a newspaper, too."

"Hey, listen," Peggy said brightly, sensing her friend's irritation and quickly changing the subject, "what are you doing for the holiday?"

Catherine shrugged. The question hadn't even occurred to her. "Nothing, I guess. I've got to work the day before and the day after Christmas, so I guess I won't get a chance to go home."

"How about coming out to Long Island with Phil and me? The

155

folks would love to have you. Hanukah, Christmas—we Jews celebrate them all. It'd be nice to have a *shiksa* around."

"Thanks, but I don't think I'll have the time."

"Well, if you change your mind, it's an open invitation."

"So how about you? Married life seems to be agreeing with you."

"Well, I don't get it as much as when I was single," Peggy said with a sigh. "But I guess quality *is* better than quantity."

Webster Greaves was a loud, abrasive prima donna, who despite offending nearly everyone he met, was still the recipient of their fawning admiration. Even in private his crude desires might have repelled Catherine were it not for the calculated mindlessness of their affair, the anything-that-feels-good-goes bargain they had tacitly struck at the beginning. Now, after two and a half months, their relationship was becoming increasingly difficult for her to dig out of.

He had given Catherine a key to his plush Park Avenue condominium, and he always called ahead to let her know when he would be arriving. And always she would be there waiting, as she imagined others waited in other cities. But she didn't care.

Through the fall of 1981, Catherine averaged twenty-five to thirty hours a week of bookings, most in studios around the city. So when Webster invited her to go with him to the Australian Open in early December, she was forced by her schedule—however reluctantly—to decline. She was disappointed but not devastated. Her career came first. In some respects she was relieved: a week with Webster Greaves might have killed her.

Though she found herself wanting to, she didn't telephone him after the first day of the tournament, when she heard on the six o'clock news that he'd won his first-round match against Johann Kriek. What would she have said? And anyway, who knew what time it was Down Under? Nor did she call him the next night, after he'd upset Jimmy Connors in the second round. And she didn't call him two days later when he lost to Ivan Lendl. What she did was immerse herself totally in her work until he arrived back in town on Friday—which she only learned from Warner Wolf in a taped interview on Channel 2's 11 O'Clock Sports Report. Then she impulsively packed her overnight bag and called a cab. Maybe she was a crazy romantic, but possibly— just possibly—she was capable of giving Webster Greaves more than good head.

In the taxi she had plenty of time to second-guess herself, but no matter how long she thought about it, it was still something she suddenly felt she owed him—and maybe even herself. It crossed her mind more than once during that endless crosstown ride that Webster might have another woman there with him to ease the pain of his defeat. She simply convinced herself it didn't matter. He would probably tell the other woman to leave. But if he didn't, well, that was all right, too. What counted was the effort, the effort to raise their relationship above the wordless, selfish, drugged-out screw-athon it had been from the start. Maybe each of them was only waiting for the other's first move. Maybe he had been hurt by love and his abrasiveness was merely a defensive veneer. It wasn't that she cared for him, either, she told herself, though not without considerable guilt. It was that she had such a growing need to be cared *for*.

When she stepped out of the cab in front of Webster's apartment building, the temperature that greeted her seemed to be twenty degrees lower than when she had left her own place ten minutes before. Even so, she braved the cold to duck into a neighborhood liquor store for a liter of Dom Perignon.

The doorman recognized her immediately. He seemed a bit flustered by her appearance so close to midnight.

"Is Mr. Greaves expecting you, Miss?"

"Yes," she lied, producing the bottle of champagne.

"Uh, I'm not sure he's in."

"I have a key. I can let myself in," she said, sweeping past him before the dumbfounded man could explain that Webster Greaves was indeed at home—but not alone. Oh, what the hell, it wasn't his problem. The broad had a key, didn't she? And if the rumors around the building were true, she most surely *would* surprise him.

Catherine placed her travel bag and the bottle of champagne on the hall carpet and jiggled the new key lightly in the lock. Once inside she tossed off the navy blue Fila jacket Webster had given her, which she had miscalculated would be heavy enough for the December night. Then she turned on the living room light and went to the kitchen to put the champagne in the empty refrigerator.

Back in the living room she picked up her bag and walked down the narrow corridor to the master bedroom, feeling the security of the thick, plush carpet beneath her feet. She couldn't wait to change into her sexiest nightgown and slip between the smooth satin sheets with a glass of chilled champagne . . . and wait. She was taking a chance, she knew, but what was life if you didn't take a few chances? She had opened the bedroom door and flipped the light switch before the muted sounds registered.

There on the center of the circular, silk-sheeted bed was Webster

Greaves—with another *man*! A man who, Catherine guessed when he looked up at her in surprise, was not yet out of his teens. As a glazed-eyed Webster stared blindly into Catherine's ashen face, she staggered back through the open door and across the corridor, thumping the back of her skull painfully against the far wall and shaking her head to edge herself back into the black reality of . . .

"You didn't tell me you were married!" she heard the young boy shout.

"Jesus," she gasped inaudibly as she back-pedaled down the corridor, her bag still over her shoulder. Then she sprinted headlong to the apartment door and lunged out into the hallway, her jacket lying forgotten on the living room couch.

It all made sense now, she thought as she rode the elevator to the lobby. Why he could never get it up with the lights on. Why he always wanted her *that* way. Webster Greaves, playboy of the western world, was a faggot—and she was just his beard, the affirmation of his cocksman image.

When she stepped out of the elevator and into the lobby, she slung her bag over her shoulder, calmly removed the two keys from her key chain, and handed them to the nonplussed doorman.

"Would you please give these to Mr. Greaves for me?" she asked, as she walked without breaking stride through the door he held open for her. Then she turned and said with false bravado, "By the way, you were wrong: Mr. Greaves *is* in—all the way in."

Out on the street the winter wind whipped her face raw as she strode north along Park Avenue. But she didn't feel the cold, just the heat of the wet streaks that ran down over her cheeks. But they weren't tears. No, damn it all, they weren't tears. It was only the wind.

9

During the nine months she lived alone in Boston, finishing up her final year at Harvard Law and cramming for the bar exam, Aimée turned down every sexual advance—male and female—including a presistent one made by Todd Thornton, who had first called her at her office at the *Law Review*.

Initially her work kept her so busy that she rarely had time to be lonely. She and Lynell visited one another every several weeks—in New York, Boston, or Pine Orchard, but never in Marblehead. "For the life of me, I don't know what you see in him," her mother always said, obviously echoing her father's sentiments.

"You used to think he was charming."

"Charming indeed, but charm has a way of tarnishing with age— and irresponsibility. How old is Lynell now? Thirty? Thirty-one? Isn't it about time he got a job?"

Aimée's mother and father conspired to remove Lynell Alan from their daughter's affections by inviting a variety of Boston's most eligible bachelors to Sunday dinners. It was a conspiracy that backfired completely, providing if anything a catalyst to Aimée's continued rebellion. Her father's show of interest had come years too late. But as the train wove through Pine Orchard on one of Aimée's infrequent trips to visit Lynell, and she gazed out the window at acre upon acre of rich Conn-Tree soil, Aimée wondered when Lynell would finally realize there was nothing wrong with this life, with inheriting a position, if he made something of it for himself, for them.

Ironically one of her parents' later conspiracies involved Todd Thornton, and after a surprisingly pleasant Sunday afternoon, Aimée consented to share an occasional casual dinner with him, at first only because she realized how desperately lonely she had become, but eventually because of how thoroughly she enjoyed Todd's company. They began to develop the comfortable, unpressured friendship they had never seemed to have time for when they were lovers. But the fact that they were not lovers left Todd with no small amount of frustration.

"You've got to be a masochist to be in love with that guy," he snapped, when once again she refused to sleep with him. "Anyway, we've slept together before, and he's not even here. What's the difference?"

"I'm sorry, Todd. That's just the way it is."

And that was the way it remained. Only once did her resolve bend, when a booking forced Lynell to cancel his visit and she faced a week of Easter vacation alone. But it didn't break, and she was all the happier when Lynell phoned unexpectedly the following day.

"Let's go to Martha's Vineyard for a few days. I need to get away."

"Can you afford it, Lynell?"

"I have some bookings coming up, and I've convinced the old man to give me an advance. Anyway, I won't have rent over my head for a while. I moved out on Dan and Tommy this morning."

"Good!"

They were able to rent a small, picturesque, secluded eighteenth-century colonial home, on a cliff in West Tisbury, at off-season rates. It was a weathered-shingle, two-bedroom summer cottage, warm and cozy, with fieldstone fireplaces in both the living room and master bedroom, and a mammoth pillared porch surrounding it on three sides. "It's been for sale for over two years," the realtor lamented. "If the owner would just come down a few thousand on the price . . ." Lynell simply adored the house, and for a week he was his old, carefree self. L.C. (who, to Lynell's disappointment, had had to remain in Boston with Aimée) came with them and, if possible, enjoyed the week even more than they did, stalking through the dense shrubbery, menacing dozens of animal species she had until then not even known existed.

Lynell treated Aimée as though she were a queen, waiting on her hand and foot and making exquisite love to her day and night. In the evenings they bundled up warmly and sat on the front porch overlooking the angry Atlantic. Time seemed almost to have stopped for them. As the week drew sadly to a close, something became clearer than ever

160

to Aimée: she wanted a life with this man if it was to be—the same comfortable, secure life they had enjoyed for this short time. But something else was clear, too: she would not waste her whole life waiting for him.

And if Lynell insisted, over her protests, on giving her ten percent of his modeling fees, and if that ten percent ever amounted to anything, she now knew what she would do with it—*exactly*.

Aimée had left it to Lynell to find them an apartment, and she tried not to allow her face to register her disappointment when she saw it for the first time.

"You get a lot less for your money in New York City than in Boston," he explained, anticipating her reaction to the small, third-floor walk-up. Its beige wall-to-wall carpet showed so many stains that on first glance they appeared to form some intricate, yet unrecognizable pattern. "I think it'a a map of New Jersey," Lynell said, watching Aimée stare forlornly as L.C. slinked between her ankles and herself tried to warm up to her new environment.

Instead of the quaint cobblestone streets of Lewisburg Square, the seventeenth-century homes of Back Bay, and the clean, expansive Boston Common to stroll through on a Sunday afternoon, there were the gray, unimaginative asphalt of Park Avenue, the sooty storefronts of the Lower East Side, and the filthy, decaying, and dangerous Central Park. It would have been so much easier to have stayed in Boston—in the same, spacious Commonwealth Avenue apartment that had cost less for Aimée alone than half the outrageous rent on this dump on Lexington Avenue. And it wasn't as though she'd had no offers. Almost every prestigious law firm in Boston had joined the race for her services—though as much, she knew, for the satisfaction of scooping her from her father's firm of Adams, Hudson, Green, Harris, and Adams, P.C. (whose conspicuous absence from the race kept the pursuit from being unanimous) as for her Phi Beta Kappa key, editorship of the Harvard *Law Review*, three-year number one ranking in her class, and her sex.

So why had she come to New York when she could literally have gone anywhere in the world? The reason was very complicated. She could try to convince herself it was the $45,000 a year Morton & Stearns would be paying her, compared to the $35,000 top offer she'd gotten in Boston, but that wasn't it. Forty-five thousand dollars was obviously worth less in Manhattan than $35,000 was in Boston, she thought, as she surveyed the dormitory-sized room that suddenly re-

161

minded her of the one she'd left behind at Harvard well over a year before.

She could tell herself it was the opportunity to practice with what was reputedly the premier contracts law firm in the world. Still, Wilhyte & Charles in Boston, though smaller, was every bit as good, she knew. But those arguments paled next to the single reason that had flesh and blood, and that now, from across their tiny living room, stopped in midsentence of a mock real-estate broker's apartment salespitch, and looked at her in the way he had that chased from her mind all but her insatiable hunger for him.

Lynell, for his part, had thought that with Aimée's arrival things would even out for him. But he was wrong. No matter how hard he tried, things just weren't going as planned.

"You can't wait around for something to happen to you, Lynell," Aimée said one evening, in response to his chronic ill-temper. "You've got to go out and make it happen for yourself."

"That's easy for you to say."

He tried to convince himself his black moods were simply a product of his own lack of career progress and bore no relation to Aimée's concomitant success in her prestigious and stable career. But that was impossible. Envy was an insidious disease, and there was no denying it was beginning to infect their relationship.

During the growingly frequent nights when they went to bed in taut silence, he was haunted by thoughts of a woman sacrificing to be with him, a woman who even now begged silently for his attention.

On his increasingly depressing rounds, Lynell began to suck up his courage and stop at some of the more high-gloss agencies. At Zoli they told him flatly he was definitely not a fashion model.

"Your eyes are too far apart," the interviewer told him. "And they'd still be too far apart even if you got your nose fixed."

Well, if taking it was part of life as a model, he'd take it.

But when he returned two months later, the same funny-looking little man who controlled his destiny said, "I remember this book, don't I? Sure, your eyes are still too far apart and your nose is still broken." He never went back to Zoli.

Three different representatives at Wilhelmina told him on respective visits that fall that he was too commercial, too old, and too tall. That each time at their Thursday-morning open interviews he'd had to

162

wait three hours for a two minute put-down only further eroded his self-esteem.

Elite was both less personal and more encouraging, but the result was the same. There, an effeminately striking young man collected the portfolios of each of the twenty-five to thirty aspirants, who'd had to mail in photographs and self-addressed, stamped envelopes just for the chance to wait in the office. Lynell was one of two—the other was a woman—whose portfolios they selected to keep for the day, to show to the "higher-ups." And again the anticipation was for naught.

"They were impressed," the pretty, young man told him on his return late that afternoon. "But they're looking for a proven money-maker."

Ford wouldn't even open his book, which was bad enough, but as he turned away, already defeated, the receptionist felt obliged to deliver the *coup de grace.* "You're a little *older* than most of the men we're interested in."

"Thanks for the vote of confidence," he said sarcastically. "I needed that." And maybe he did. Maybe it was exactly what he needed to smarten up—to let this stupid and increasingly humiliating dream die before his dignity did.

At Cline Models, which had in recent years passed Ford as the most prestigious and successful modeling agency in the world, he was literally awestruck. Each time, the attractive, salt-and-pepper-haired woman greeted him with the familiar words he'd come to expect. "I'm sorry, but we're not taking on any new men at this time."

But on each successive visit she smiled more broadly and looked at him a split second longer—or was it his imagination? That was one thing about constant, unremitting rejection—one didn't need much of a positive response to be encouraged.

Christmas of 1981 was a lonely season for Lynell, even among the gathered Alan clan. As with many couples who have not made that final commitment to one another, Lynell and Aimée both felt an underlying responsibility to be with their own family for the holiday.

In Pine Orchard Lynell drank too much, trying to forget that, at thirty-three, his sister (who had lived next door to their parents with her young family since the deaths of Grandmother and Grandfather Alan within a week of one another the previous year) was a nurse, who had married a doctor and had a five-year-old son; while he, fast approaching thirty-two, was unemployed, insolvent, and unable to make a decision concerning just about anything meaningful in his life.

* * *

In Marblehead, Aimée accompanied Todd Thornton, now a new law associate at Ropes & Gray in Boston, to the first of an interminable round of seasonal cocktail parties that featured imported champagne and beluga caviar and a guest list she had memorized by her eighth Christmas.

Through the evening, Todd wrestled with her will and she with her conscience. Her conscience won, but the margin of victory was narrowing. She owed that much to Lynell, from whom she hoped soon to get some kind of commitment or even the pledge of a future commitment; Lynell, whom she was beginning to wish was more responsible, more farsighted, more acceptable, and—though, indeed, Lynell was handsomer and brighter—more like Todd Thornton.

In Manhattan Christmas Eve was bitter cold. At seven that evening, Catherine Ward had returned to her apartment, which was unembellished with seasonal decorations, and tried to think of it as just another hectic working-day. The day's booking had kept her mind off the holiday, yet now she almost wished she had accepted Peggy's invitation to join her and her family on Long Island. But Christmas was for family, and she'd only have been an intruder. So she had called home. She would catch a plane for Iowa tomorrow, though she'd barely have time enough to stay the night. But she had to get home to regenerate, to face the one thing that could remind her that life was worth living— the embrace of what family she had left. She poured herself a glass of chablis and opened the small package Webster had sent from his condo in Boca Raton, though she had promised herself she would return it still sealed. She briefly admired the gorgeous diamond earrings in the mirror before replacing them in the tiny box. She would have to remember to mail them back the day after Christmas.

At eight she stood naked on the tiny fire-escape platform outside her window, with only a pair of slipper-socks to protect her feet from the stinging cold of iron. A glass of chablis was in her hand, the first snort of cocaine was in her nostrils, and the question she'd been asking herself for weeks was drifting around her head like the sparkling granular snowflakes.

"Oh, no, I'd never jump," she answered herself out loud. "Too showy."

By nine o'clock she was peacefully drugged into oblivion.

164

10

By January 1982, Lynell Alan had been in New York City for a year, and Aimée Harris and a still-disoriented L.C. for three months. The first few weeks of the new year gave him no promise at all that in 1982 his career would fare any better than it had in 1981, a year in which he had hustled and glad-handed his way to barely eighteen thousand dollars in modeling fees. Subtracting the Munson Agency's fifteen percent and his other expenses, in Manhattan he was far below subsistence level. The jobs had almost completely dried up, and he wouldn't last much longer on the few hundred dollars he had managed to save. If something didn't happen—and soon—he'd have to get a "real" job. Accounting? A giant step backward. Waiting tables? He didn't have the temperament. Conn-Tree? He didn't even want to think about it.

He was terribly disappointed in the Munson Agency. Every booking he managed to land he had gotten directly, through his own undignified persistence, and with no help at all from Gretchen. Still, the ironic part was that though agents didn't seem to do anything for anyone, a model had to have one to get work. It was just the way the system operated.

"Who's your agent?" was the first question at every stop along his interminable rounds. Occasionally he still went to other agencies to make inquiries, but he quickly became discouraged.

"Times are tough," he was told at one. "The economy is so bad that

165

only the 'biggies' are working, the Jeff Aquilons and the Jack Scalias. You're lucky to have an agent at all."

He envied Aimée her new job with Morton & Stearns, a job she seemed to enjoy so much, a job with a future. But she had worked for it. She hadn't quite adjusted to New York City yet, but he knew that would come. At least she was a success in her young career.

"What are you doing today?" Aimée asked as she kissed him good-bye at the door one brisk winter morning.

"I think I'll go over and get kicked out of Cline Models again," he answered fatalistically.

"Great attitude. The attitude of a star."

So on this Monday, January 18, he stood in Cline's opulent offices, fully expecting this visit to end exactly the way his first three had: in failure. The offices were bustling with activity, following the usual holiday season lull, with telephones ringing and models, both male and female, coming and going in a steady stream, picking up appointment slips and dropping off vouchers, most seemingly unaware of how intimidatingly beautiful they were.

Unlike the Munson Agency's reception area, where one entire wall was a mirror, here there wasn't a mirror in the room. It was as though if accepted as a Cline model, you must *know* you looked gorgeous at all times. He noticed, too, that here no one checked out the new arrival. Not a single man seemed to worry that Lynell Alan might be here to take work away from him. In fact, not one of the models of either sex so much as glanced in his direction. And why should they? They were the cream of the crop. All of them—male and female— were young, smooth-skinned, blue-eyed blondes, with square jaws and angular features. Lynell suddenly wished there was a mirror so he could check to make sure his hair was in place.

"Do you have an appointment, sir?" the woman asked when she looked up during a brief respite from the telephones. No model she— nor, he was certain, had she ever been one—but a cheerfully plump middle-aged woman who greeted both employees and visitors with equal enthusiasm, while balancing two telephone lines like a pro. This was not at all like Munson, where out-of-work models chronically picked up a few bucks answering telephones between the quitting of another of Gretchen's disgruntled assistants and the hiring of another.

"No, I'm sorry, I don't. I was just passing by and . . ."

"Just a sec. I don't think we're hiring any new people, but that's not my area. I'll check for you." She punched a button on her console to stop a ring and picked up the receiver. "Cline Models. One moment, please." Then she punched another button and called over her shoulder, where an extremely attractive, fortyish woman with fantastic legs was leafing through what looked to be the agency headsheet. "LeeAnn?" The woman balancing telephones looked back at him and asked quickly, almost as an afterthought, "You *are* a model?"

Lynell nodded self-consciously. "Yes."

"LeeAnn, this gentleman is here about openings for men. Do you have time to look at his book?"

"Oh, Thelma, I'm really backed up at the moment," LeeAnn Schneider answered. Then she looked up and gave a faint smile of recognition. "Oh, it's you." She kept looking at him, even longer than the last time. The other woman went back to her telephones. "You *are* persistent," LeeAnn Schneider said as she led him into her small office just off the reception area.

"Yes."

LeeAnn Schneider was a stunning woman: tall and slim, with a cameo complexion and fine, delicate features. She was dressed casually in a tan corduroy skirt, and a royal-blue cashmere sweater that accentuated her high, small breasts and her pale gray eyes. Flecks of silver glinting from her short-cropped black hair were the only signs of age—until he was closer. Up close, her face was drawn and the large, oval, gray eyes were sad. She offered him a chair opposite hers with a wave of her hand. When she sat and crossed her legs, he hoped she didn't notice that his glance slipped quickly between her thighs.

She swiveled her chair absently and began studying his portfolio for the fourth time, though there were, he pointed out, several new tearsheets she hadn't yet seen. Why did he always do this? he wondered as he studied the impossibly high angle of her near breast and the way the soft fabric of her loose-fitting sweater attached itself to its perfectly rounded contours as though to repudiate any notion that small couldn't be sexier than large.

She looked up from his book and his eyes met hers. "Yes," she said, tapping an acetate-enclosed eight-by-ten photograph with her open palm, "I think we can use you."

"Excuse me?" he asked, thinking for a moment he had misunderstood.

"I said, 'I think we can use you.' This shot is terrific." She tapped the eight-by-ten again. It was a picture taken the previous Fourth of July by an amateur who thought she was an artist. In the shot he wore a bathing suit and was leaning on one elbow. A young woman was draped over his right shoulder. He had had to skip his planned trip to

Boston to attend Aimée's Wimbledon breakfast-party, because Gretchen thought he needed to update his book. But that wasted day at Compo Beach in Westport, Connecticut, had finally paid off.

"You look very European in this one. Is your hair this curly naturally?"

"Yes, but it straightens easily."

"I like it better curly. It's more you."

"So do I, but my present agent thinks curly hair is out."

"Nonsense. Curly hair like this is never out," she said. "Your present agent is"—she found and removed a copy of his composite that was tucked inside the front flap of his portfolio—"oh, Kevin Munson. Or, should I say Gretchen?" She seemed to jog herself out of a brief reflection. "Anyway, Lyn, I know Munson requires models to sign exclusives. When is yours up?"

He grinned with self-satisfaction and winked. "Last week."

"And they didn't ask you to renew?" she asked suspiciously.

"They did, but I've managed to put off going in for about two weeks. Knowing Gretchen is going to be there makes it easy."

LeeAnn tried to suppress a smile. Obviously she knew the much-loved Gretchen. "When can you start with us?"

"How does now sound?"

LeeAnn liked him. He could tell. "You don't have any bookings coming up with them?"

He shook his head.

She returned his book as she stood. "We'll see if we can do you more justice. If you can manage without your book someday soon, I'd like to select some shots for a new comp. We don't like those eight-by-ten foldouts Munson uses. They're too big. Clients throw them out because they don't fit in their files with the standard five-by-eights. Anyway, those," she said, indicating the Munson composite she had removed from his portfolio, "aren't the particular shots I would have selected. Also, I'd like to get you on the headsheet that comes out in April."

He took a last, appreciative look at those fine, long legs and stood, accepting his portfolio from her. "Great, Ms. Schneider. That's great."

"Please, call me LeeAnn."

"Thank you, LeeAnn. What's the cost of being included on the headsheet?"

"Two hundred fifty dollars. But you don't pay directly. Since you're an experienced model, we'll deduct the fee from your first booking—along with our twenty percent commission."

Now *there* was the way to run a business. He had only one more

168

question. "I don't mean to rush things, but when do I sign my contract?"

"There is no contract. At Cline Models we work with a model for as long as the relationship is mutually satisfactory. If you don't like what we are doing for you, you may leave us at any time. We don't feel comfortable tying people down. If someone isn't happy with us and feels that he or she can do better elsewhere, then we give them our blessings. On the other hand, if we feel you aren't producing for us—you show up late for bookings, won't go on rounds or go-sees, or otherwise aren't performing—we will let you know that, too. No obligations on either side but to do our best. It's a policy that's always worked well for us."

"Fine."

She escorted him to the door and they shook hands. "Keep in close touch, Lyn."

"You can count on that."

"Oh, and by the way. Will you drop off a stack of those comps, too, when you have a chance? At least it will give us something until we get the new ones."

"Sure thing. Thanks again." He could barely contain his excitement until he reached the street. Then he threw his fist into the air and let out a primal scream that could be heard for blocks. But as he began walking west on Fifty-ninth Street, he was suddenly struck by the stark emptiness of his paperless contract. Somehow it was like going to a wedding without getting to kiss the bride. Maybe when he went back tomorrow they would ask, "Lynell Who? There must be some mistake. Why, your eyes are too far apart—and even if they weren't, your nose would still be broken." God, maybe it had been a mistake. Maybe he'd never get a job among all of those chisel-featured men. The fire of anxiety raged through him: another new agency, more weeks of trying to hold on to clients who had hired him through Munson, of trying to get his face known and remembered. Well, at least LeeAnn would be a pleasant change: a head booker who was personable and attractive. She seemed to like him and that couldn't hurt either, and she'd certainly be a lot easier to keep in touch with than Gretchen. He didn't care if he never saw Gretchen Saczynski again in his life.

In spite of his reservations, at least his foot was finally in the door and that was cause enough for celebrating. Four tries at Cline; another four at Ford; two at Zoli, before they'd delivered the ultimate put-down; half a dozen at Wilhelmina, where they had been only the slightest bit more encouraging; and five at Elite, culminating in an "almost." Yes, this was cause to celebrate. He splurged on two pounds of filet mignon and a bottle of Dom Perignon for dinner, then extended his usual seven-mile run to ten in anticipation of the feast.

"It's vintage 1979," he joked to Aimée as he uncorked the champagne over a candlelight dinner. "That was a good year," he added, his voice softening as he looked into her eyes. "It was the year I met you."

Aimée smiled as she touched her glass to his. "That's fantastic, Lynell, just fantastic. Things are finally beginning to break for you."

"Who knows?" he asked skeptically. "It's a tough business. But at least now I've got a shot with the best. That's what I've been trying to get for the past year."

"I guess now is as good a time as any to tell you some news of my own," Aimée interjected hesitantly. "Actually it hasn't really been news for a couple of months."

Lynell eyed her suspiciously over the rim of his wineglass. "So, what's this news that isn't really news?"

"Cline Models is a client of mine."

From her first day on the job at Morton & Stearns, Aimée Harris had created a stir. It was not that the twenty-odd attorneys in the mid-size Wall Street firm didn't know what to expect. They had each met her on her recruiting visit to their offices and had, if not actually spoken with her, at least seen her.

"Christ, Saul," one senior partner remarked at the post-interview confab, "if I didn't know better I'd say the child wasn't out of high school."

"And," another put in, "even in that business suit, she looks as though she'd be more comfortable on a surfboard than in a boardroom."

Even long after she had been hired, the latter gentleman, though well past sixty, could never quite look at her without envisioning her in a bikini—which put him at a distinct disadvantage when attempting to argue a point with her, whether it was the wording of a contract clause or the choice of restaurants for lunch with a client.

No, it wasn't that they didn't know what to expect. She was like the season's first tropical storm—the one meteorologists, as is their quaint custom, give a cute "A" name, such as Aimée. They knew she was coming, but still, somehow, they just weren't quite ready for her.

It was 1981, and the staid old law firm was already a decade behind the times. Not only was Aimée Harris the first woman ever to have graced their letterhead in over seventy years, but she was also one of

170

the first two Gentiles. It wasn't so much that the firm intentionally invoked a policy against women and non-Jews as it was that most of the top candidates at law schools such as Harvard, Yale, Columbia, Virginia, and the few others at which they recruited seemed consistently to be Jewish and, until recently when women had begun attending law school in greater numbers, men. At any rate, Morton & Stearns had always prided themselves on keeping pace with the world around them, especially the legal world, and in 1981 keeping pace meant hiring a woman.

Saul Stearns, Jr., whose father, along with Jason Morton of that now extinct line of Mortons, had founded the firm in 1905, would have preferred the first woman to have been Jewish; however, the only viable candidate was a pasty-faced and patently unattractive girl who was only third in her class at Columbia. Aimée Harris was, quite simply, the best candidate he had met, male or female, Jew or Gentile. Oddly, the second best was another WASP, a young man who had been ranked first in his class at UVA. Morton & Stearns hired them both.

John Hayes shared his third-ever elevator ride to the suites of Morton & Stearns with a tiny auburn-haired nymphet—perhaps the only sight that could have taken his mind off how impossibly nervous he was to be struggling with his first assignment at one of the city's most prestigious law firms. "I see you're headed to thirty-eight, too."

"Yes," she answered. "I work there. Actually, I'm about to work there. Today is my first day."

"Oh, really?" The fact that there would be someone greener than he at the firm buoyed his confidence. "It's my third. John Hayes," he said, extending his hand.

"Aimée Harris."

John Hayes was of medium height and mildly attractive, with small blue eyes and sandy hair that was already thinning, leaving a vast expanse of barren forehead between his bushy eyebrows and the memory of a hairline. Along with a thick, dark brown moustache, it lent his smooth-skinned young face an artificially mature look. He was thin but slightly heavy-waisted, as though his leanness was not a result of exercise but of a rather casual monitoring of his diet. Physically he was the prototype of the eager, studious, young attorney, and Aimée resented him for it immediately. "Gee," he said as the elevator came to rest on the thirty-eighth floor, "maybe you're the secretary they've been promising me." He was almost visibly licking his chops.

Aimée had taken one step out of the elevator and stopped dead in her tracks. She looked back over her shoulder and fixed him with a surly stare. "Maybe."

What a bitch, John Hayes thought as he watched her walk away. Fantastic ass, though. "Good luck with the new job, Aimée. I'll be seeing you."

She ignored him.

At ten-thirty A.M. Saul Stearns led Aimée Harris into John Hayes's small office and introduced them.

Hayes stood and greeted her again with a formal bow of his head. "Yes, sir, we've met. On the elevator on the way up this morning."

"Oh, fine. Aimée is here to help you with the Robards matter."

"I told you we might be working together, Aimée," Hayes said pompously.

"You did at that."

"Ah yes, well," Stearns stammered. There was some understanding—or perhaps misunderstanding—passing between his two new employees and he was uncomfortable not knowing what it was. He could only guess that Hayes had come on to her and she'd put him in his place. Oh, well, let them work out their personal differences, and right away. It now figured to have been an even better decision than he had imagined, putting them on the same case at the outset. "Attorney Harris has a great deal of experience in contract law per se, and specifically that of the personal service genre, so you'll be reporting directly to her on this case, John. Any trouble with that?"

John Hayes's jaw was only slightly slack. "Ah . . . no, sir."

"Good. I want a preliminary evaluation on my desk by Monday morning."

When Stearns had left the office, Aimée turned to Hayes, mimicking his earlier look of smug superiority. "Anything you'd like typed, sir?" It was bitchy, sure, but she couldn't resist.

The only word John Hayes could think of to describe his condition from the moment he first saw Aimée Harris on that elevator was an antiquated one he'd heard his father use when he was a boy back at Whitehead, the family plantation on New Point Comfort, across the Pamunkey from Williamsburg, on the shores of Chesapeake Bay. He was smitten. Though their relationship, as it developed, was purely professional, he wished it was more. She was bright, knowledgeable . . . and sexy as hell.

Occasionally he invited her to lunch, which was appropriately unthreatening, and by Thanksgiving had just about worked up the courage to ask her to dinner—or at least so he told himself—when her boyfriend showed up at the office for the first time. The guy was a college-jock type, big and smooth and annoyingly comfortable with his body, the type who was always picked first by the guys for backyard ballgames and by the girls for everything else. But the worst thing about him was that when the three of them went to lunch with Stearns's secretary, another woman Hayes would have given his right arm to have, the guy pretended not to notice that she spent the entire hour mooning over him—as though he were so used to that kind of attention it no longer made an impression on him. The afternoon's single consolation was that Aimée Harris was so small and serious, and Lynell Alan so big and undirected—a model, just imagine—that the pair was obviously totally mismatched. Unfortunately John Hayes was the only one who seemed to realize that fact. Aimée Harris was clearly crazy about the guy.

"Well, what did you think?" she asked.

As he looked across his desk at Aimée Harris, at the lapel of her white satin blouse that fell away from the soft swell of her breast, at the shadowy hint of nipple through the shiny fabric, John Hayes imagined for the first time that sex might just have the capability of being satisfying and guiltless. He suddenly crossed his ankles and clamped his thighs against his most magnificent erection in recent memory.

"Are you all right, John?"

"Hmm?" His voice was weak and scratchy.

"You look a little green."

"No, I'm okay. A touch of indigestion."

"So, what did you think of Lynell?"

"A match made in heaven."

"No, seriously."

"Seriously? He seems a nice enough guy. Tense, though."

"Tense? Lynell?" She laughed. "Are we talking about the same guy?"

"Do you think he's happy being a model?"

Aimée didn't like the way he say "model." It was the same demeaning way her mother and father said the word. "Yes. Well, most of the time. He works hard. He just needs a break. It'll come."

"It better come pretty soon."

"What do you mean?"

Hayes pulled in his horns a bit. He didn't want to be too obvious. "Only that there isn't much security in his profession," he explained innocently, "or longevity. And he's getting toward the upper end of the desirable age-bracket, I would think." He paused and waved off his words with a fanning of his hand. "Don't mind me. I'm just

173

projecting. Because I couldn't live that way, I guess I think no one else could, either. Anyway, to answer your question, Lynell seems a very nice man. Now, I have to get back to work on this Fenster deal. Would you excuse me?"

"Oh, sure. Well, I'm glad you and Lynell were finally able to meet one another."

"My pleasure, Aimée. Have him stop in again when he isn't busy." John Hayes's eyes watched the pensive look that clouded her pretty face, then his gaze contentedly fell to her cute little rump as she spun and silently left his office.

That night, long after their candlelight dinner and 1979 Dom Perignon were history, Lynell carefully unwrapped himself from Aimée's naked warmth, swung his legs off the bed, and quietly padded across the cold hardwood floor to the closet. There he probed the darkness with his frigid toes until he found his sheepskin slippers. Then he pulled on a red plaid shirt long enough to double as a nightshirt. On the other side of the darkness, Aimée stretched and purred contentedly.

Lynell walked from the bedroom, closing the door behind him and feeling his way through the lightless living room to the kitchen. His stomach was restless, and though in his business one had to be a disciplined eater, he opened the refrigerator and poked through the evening's leftovers, looking for an interesting snack. Along with his daily exercise routine and running, in order to keep his weight under 170 pounds he normally stuck to a strict diet—of sorts: a cup of black coffee for breakfast and nothing at all until dinner, at which he consumed everything in sight.

"Christ, no wonder your weight stays down," Aimée had remarked. "A cup of black coffee on an empty stomach? That's like being on speed all day!"

"I can't help it," he had explained. "I have absolutely no willpower. Once I start eating I just can't stop. My only hope is to put it off as long into the day as possible."

Now he foraged as frantically as a bear in spring, until he found his nectar: the chocolate mousse Aimée had whipped up for dessert. The mousse was in tall, slim parfait glasses, and he pulled out two and placed them on the kitchen table, topping each with a huge gob of whipped cream. L.C. appeared in the wedge of light that fell across the kitchen floor, and meowed plaintively. Lynell bent and picked her up, petting her until her tiny body hummed contentedly. "You hungry, too?" he asked in his best baby-voice. "You like mousse?" He held her near the dessert, but after a brief sniff she lost interest. "Ah, you thought I said mouse. Well, let's see what else we can find." Giving her a last hug, he put the cat back on the floor and poured her a small bowl of milk. "There you go, sweetheart. That better?"

"What are you two up to at this hour of the night?" Aimée asked through a sleepy yawn. When she snapped on the small fluorescent light over the sink, an eerie gray penumbra filled the kitchen, like a scene from a black-and-white movie. She looked from the floor, where L.C.'s lapping was the only sound that broke the midnight stillness, to where Lynell sat with his spoon poised over the first of the two mousses. He looked as though he'd been caught with another woman. "You didn't tell me Cline Models wants you to double for the Goodyear blimp."

Lynell put down his spoon and watched her lean over the sink to pour herself a glass of water. What was it about this woman that instantaneously re-routed the blood through his veins? She had slipped into his Dress Campbell cotton flannel bathrobe and had it drawn snugly around her and tied tightly at the sash so it covered her from throat to ankle. It was half a dozen sizes too large for her, and there was no way to discern where her hips ended and its bulk began. Still, when she turned toward him and smiled to find him watching her, he could think of nothing but being in bed with her again. They were so different, Aimée and he: she with her mainstream career and social aspirations, and he with his search for something he couldn't even name. Perhaps it was true, after all, that opposites do attract. Yet he couldn't help wondering if the chemical reaction between them wasn't acidic, eating through the sharing, understanding, and need that were the basic foundation of a relationship. "I was hungry," he said remorsefully.

She put her glass on the counter and walked around the table, stopping to bend down to pet L.C. When she sat across Lynell's lap, she wrapped her arms around him and leaned close, feeling him rigid beneath her. "I'm less fattening," she whispered, her breath warm in his ear. His breathing had quickened, and when she stood, the tail of his shirt fell away from his lap. In silence she gathered the robe until the hem was in her hands, then straddled his chair and slowly lowered herself until her already wet vagina enveloped the tip of his penis. She raised and lowered herself, covering then releasing just the head until its tight skin became so sensitive Lynell twitched involuntarily at her touch. After each time she rose over him again, she lowered herself farther by millimeters, inching torturously down, down, down, spreading

175

her legs until her groin popped like the cracking of knuckles and he was completely inside her. Hips swiveling gently, they ground into each other rhythmically until they were at the brink, then held each other motionless for minutes, prolonging the delicious ecstasy until they could prolong it no more.

"So what's the matter?" Aimée asked when they were snugly back in their bed. Sleep was impossible with Lynell's nervous tossing and turning.

"The matter?"

"You only get snacks in the middle of the night when you're nervous. And now you can't get to sleep. So what's the matter?"

He rolled onto his back, gazed up at the ceiling, inhaled deeply, and sighed. "Aimée, I'm scared shitless!"

"What are you scared of?" She had a fleeting thought of John Hayes. "The way you've been carrying on, with lunch today and our celebration dinner tonight, I thought you were overjoyed at finally being taken by Cline."

"I am," he answered assuredly. Then a long silence rang out through the darkness. "I am," he repeated softly.

"Then what's the problem? You should be on top of the world. It's not every model who gets a chance like this."

"That's the problem."

She waited silently for his explanation. It took him several minutes to collect his thoughts.

"You see, if I don't make it now, it's my fault. Before, I could always blame it on Gretchen and the agency. Now I can't blame it on the agency anymore. Either I make it or I flop. Me. Not the agency. Not anyone else. And I feel so naked without that piece of paper. Christ, you're a lawyer. I shouldn't have to tell you about verbal contracts."

"Yes, but for you it's a two-sided coin. If they don't produce, you can go to another agency."

"Hah! If they don't produce, *I'm* not producing. And if I can't produce with them, I can't produce with anyone. Don't you understand, Aimée? I'm thirty-one years old. If I can't make it now, I'm finished as a model. And what's going to happen to me then? That's what's worrying me."

"But, Lynell, you're giving it your best shot. And if you don't make it at least you have something to fall back on. You have your education. You have your family's business. You know how much your father still wants you. Anyway, didn't that photographer just call you tonight about that Halston job?"

"Oh, yeah, Dudley. But I've worked with him at Munson. He

176

doesn't care about agencies, just that I'm always available on short notice."

She sighed, sensing his disappointment. Maybe she *didn't* understand. What was beginning to worry her was not what would happen if he *didn't* make it, but what would happen if he *did*.

11

Catherine Ward had been in bed since ten o'clock. At midnight she was still lying awake. She fumbled in the darkness for a match and lit the stub of a hand-rolled joint she found wedged into a notch in the lip of the ashtray. Praying it would now succeed in bringing sleep where it had earlier failed, she inhaled deeply and held the thick smoke in her lungs.

Unlike Lynell Alan, her new year had begun with the burst of energy from which stars are created. In the first six weeks of the year, not counting travel days, she hadn't had a single day off. There were spring catalogues for Bloomingdale's and Macy's, another print campaign for Playtex, and new ones for Camel cigarettes and Arpège perfume. And it wasn't all glitter and glamour, the way they portrayed models in the television movies, with flitty photographers gushing orgasmically, "Oh yes, babe, beautiful, that's it!" while they smiled and swirled and the wind machine tantalized their glossy hair. No, it was tedious, tiring, and—except for the money—remarkably unrewarding work. Once she'd seen herself in a few magazine advertisements, up on a billboard, or on television, the novelty wore off and it was just another day at the office. Work meant arriving at the studio at 9:00 A.M.—which she was having increasing difficulty doing—and then, more often than not, drinking coffee and reading a book until they were ready for her at 10:30 or 11:00 or noon. It meant being pinned and stuffed and taped and stapled like a rag doll. It meant standing for a Polaroid, then holding that position until the photographer had developed the picture and, along with the art director, dissected it and decided what was wrong with it. It meant an hour for lunch and returning in the afternoon for "safeties." It meant waiting for one of the other models who was late or sick—or facing their ire after they'd waited for her; or waiting for a replacement for someone who had been booked somewhere else by mistake. Of course, it also meant $1,500 to $2,000 a day. She wasn't complaining. She was just beginning to realize that modeling, like everything else in life, wasn't all she had imagined it would be.

Modeling had first occurred to Catherine only as a means of escaping Iowa. Lying awake in her bed, she now recalled how easily it had all started: the taking of Manhattan, 1–2–3. And except for an occasional pothole, the road had been that smooth. She had been unbelievably fortunate in her career—almost too fortunate. These days she couldn't even go on vacation. Take this week, for example, which she had set aside for a well-needed rest and had booked out over a month ago: already Mike Dudley had called in desperate need of her. Nobody else; it had to be her. Then LeeAnn had phoned about some new shampoo product that wanted to use her in a television commercial.

"No interview? No audition? No reading? The job is mine? Just like that?"

"Cathy," LeeAnn explained, "you're becoming a hot property. A few more successful spots and you'll be in the Christa Blair and Cherry Taylor category. You'll be a celebrity. It might be a bit premature right now, but I'm all ready to call you girls 'The Three C's.'"

Now as she puffed smoke rings silently into the darkness and watched her toes wriggling beneath the covers in the far-off shadows at the foot of her bed, Catherine looked into her hand mirror, feeling the incipient satisfaction of one who has miraculously managed to transform what she had once considered a liability into an asset. Maybe Webster Greaves had been right, that sleazy faggot. The exposure she'd gotten being seen with him certainly hadn't hurt her career. But it had hurt nonetheless.

The pain returned now, tempered by the passing of the weeks since she'd last seen him. "That bastard," she hissed out loud. "That rotten bastard." He had been the only thing in this city she'd had to hang on to. But like Marianne Johnson before him, from this vantage point Webster Greaves seemed only to have been another minor detour. Webster Greaves, Matt Vine, Marianne Johnson, Bobby Stillwell. As she thought back over the years, she wondered if it would ever end. Would there *ever* be someone she could trust? Or would there always be lust, greed, and perversion lurking in the wings? Well, it didn't

179

matter now. She had discovered the formula: go out and do your job, come back to the apartment, have dinner and call home. Then, if it wasn't too late, maybe watch a little TV or read a good book before going to bed—alone. It had worked fine before, and it worked just as well now. To hell with people. They just used you up and then cut you loose.

If only she could get to sleep. If only she could quell the jangling of her nerves. If only there was something that would wash away this terrible loneliness. Lately she had felt a growing sense of isolation, which was laughable considering she lived in a city of over eight million people. And cocaine no longer chased away the ghost as it once had, but only held it at bay for a few short moments, moments in which she felt good, happy, and relaxed, and on top of the world again. No, no longer could cocaine chase away the ghost. It had become the ghost.

How on earth had she let herself get like this? Where once she had sniffed it to feel good, now she only sniffed it not to feel bad. She was forever chasing the elusive high. Nothing felt good to her. Not sex. Not food. It was New York. It was this goddamned city. Iowa was the place to be—out in the open where you could spread your wings without bumping into some pervert or bum or worse, where you could breathe genuine, all-American, fresh air. Iowa—her roots, the precious remnants of her family.

The ghost was still there and only one thing would satisfy its hunger. The palms of her hands were moist and her nose twitched. Even as she reached into the bedside drawer and removed the small vial, she once again promised herself it would be the last time. No more after this. It would be easy. Easier than calling Mark, because especially since his telephone call earlier this evening, asking her to meet him at the Waldorf tomorrow afternoon for a drink, she suspected he was building up an account and would eventually be after something in addition to the money in return. A lead on a go-see? A good word at an audition? And easier than calling Molly, because that meant an obligation, too, and right now she just wasn't ready for that. Nobody did something for nothing, especially in this town, and in this business. And this time she wouldn't ask where and when the next party was, either, or subtly hint around to find out who was holding. No, this was it; this was the end of it.

Seconds after she had sucked the last grains up into her nose, it suddenly occurred to her that her life wasn't so bad. She was thin and beautiful—didn't everyone always tell her she was beautiful? Christ, didn't she earn her living being beautiful? And now she was well on her way to becoming very, very wealthy. Anyone who dropped a thousand dollars a month on a frivolous habit had to be pretty well-heeled. Though she was now too busy to visit home as often as she liked, she was able to send two thousand dollars a month, and that certainly wasn't hay. Shit, if she'd stayed back in Iowa she'd still be milking cows in a drafty barn or waiting on customers in the five and dime. And now she was almost a celebrity. On the brink of fame and fortune. *The Three C's.* It did have a nice ring to it, didn't it? Catherine Ward, the celebrity model. If only she felt like a celebrity.

When she awoke the next morning, Catherine instinctively reached for the still-open drawer of her bedside table. "Oh, shit!" she groaned when she realized that what she was looking for was no longer there. Her temples throbbed and she felt as though she hadn't slept for a month. Nausea swept through her, and she clutched her mouth desperately with her right hand, knowing that if she couldn't suppress the vomit she would never make it to the bathroom in time. After the nausea had passed, she managed to roll over and check the digital clock. Damn, it was already nine and she was due at Mike Dudley's studio at ten. Or was Dudley's tomorrow? A few days off and she didn't know what day of the week it was. Well, better safe than sorry.

She reached for the telephone and dialed Mike's number, taking deep breaths and croaking out a few *hello*'s as it rang, trying to clear away the last of the sleep. When Jayne Dudley answered, Catherine spoke in the most convincing imitation she could muster of a woman who has been up and bustling about since dawn. "Hello, Jayne. This is Catherine Ward."

"Catherine, dear. Is there any problem? I almost expected to see you walking through the door about now."

"No, no. No problem at all. I was just wondering how long Mike is expecting this to take. This *was* supposed to be my vacation week, you know. I was thinking about doing a little shopping later on." There was no point admitting she had forgotten all about today or at least had wished it back to tomorrow.

"It's down for a couple of hours, three at the outside. You'll have all afternoon."

"Okay, see you in a little bit."

Catherine dragged herself out of bed, shuffled to the window, and drew the shade on another, bleak winter day. The frigid wood stung her bare feet. The cold was the only thing that reminded her she was alive. As she turned and began padding toward the bathroom, she saw the dark stain on her pillow and was gripped with a fear that was, for an instant, so debilitating she was sure she would let loose her bladder.

When she had collected her emotions, she calmly stripped off the pillowcase, took it to the bathroom, rinsed it thoroughly in cold water, and left it to soak. After she had showered and dressed, she wrung it out and draped it over a towel rack.

She blew into Mike Dudley's studio at ten minutes past ten, all apologies and excuses. "I thought I'd left plenty of time, but the traffic was horrendous . . ."

"No problem. Mike and the young man are already upstairs, but I think they've got a few shots they can work on without you. Here, let me get you your dress," Jayne said as she led Catherine into the tiny dressing room. "It's this pale green number." She took it from the rack, held it up in front of herself, and did a feathery pirouette. "Sexy, no? It'll look dynamite on *you.*"

Catherine had already slipped out of her dress and hung it on the rack. She unhooked her bra, and unconsciously stooped her shoulders and hunched them forward until the straps slid down over her arms. "I hope Mike wants braless. I didn't bring a strapless bra."

"Braless all the way, kid. Cheap thrills for the boys upstairs." Milt Myles, cosmetologist and unabashed homosexual, had flitted inconspicuously into the dressing room to apply her makeup. When Catherine fumbled to rehook her bra and readjust herself into its cups, he seemed to be genuinely insulted.

"No offense, but I don't find your chest the least bit interesting. Now," he said, tilting his head back, gazing upward, and tapping his powder brush against his chin as though that would allow him to see through the ceiling, "if you were that fellow upstairs . . ." He broke from his trance, looked back at Catherine, and put one hand on his hip impatiently. "Shall I leave?"

"No, I'm all set."

"Well, good. We're just going to do a little touch-up," he explained, as he seated her in front of the mirror and began brushing on skin-toned powder. "Oooh, not getting enough sleep, dearie?" he asked cattily.

Jayne looked from one to the other and shook her head. "I'll leave you two girls alone," she said as she turned and walked toward the door. "Don't be too long. They're waiting upstairs."

Though the dress was undeniably smashing, it was designed for summer, and Catherine tried to rub some warmth back into her bare arms and shoulders as she climbed the steep stairs to the studio loft. At the top she paused and tried to catch her breath. The man with Mike looked familiar, but she was unable to place him. Even though he politely looked her straight in the eye, she couldn't help feeling naked.

It was as enjoyable a job as she could remember. Milt Myles soon departed, taking his cheeky disposition "uptown." Lynell Alan was warm and attractive and unthreatening, and Mike and Jayne Dudley were, well, Mike and Jayne Dudley. Mike, as usual, ran behind schedule, so Jayne ordered sandwiches delivered and the four of them swapped light, uninhibited conversation over lunch.

Lynell Alan didn't come on to her, the way most men did. Nor did he speak to her condescendingly, as though she were just another blonde air-head. He spoke thoughtfully and listened contemplatively. When she recounted her horror story of near-sunstroke in the Bahamas, which she was now able to do with a touch of humor, he didn't just laugh in the right places but reacted with the considerate smiles and sympathetic sighs of one who has been there. But what impressed her most was that *he* was totally unimpressed—by everything about her except what she had to say. Few men had ever ignored the way she looked—even fags. And one thing was very certain—Lynell Alan was no fag.

By the time Catherine left Mike Dudley's studio in midafternoon, she was hurting. It wasn't a physical hurt. The headache and nausea of earlier in the day were gone. She wasn't tired or infused with that heavy-headed marijuana hangover she had had earlier. But she was hurting nonetheless. The jitters had returned, and she had to think of something to do to ward off the grim melancholy that had suddenly engulfed her. She wasn't due at the Waldorf until five—almost two hours—and as she walked north with the cold, blustery wind in her face, she wondered if the hours would ever pass.

Everything was all right until she had time on her hands. She was beginning to regret having tried to take this week off. It really hadn't worked out the way she'd planned anyway, what with this thing with Mike today and the shampoo job tomorrow. Well, it was still her vacation even if there were only a few more hours of it.

She hailed a cab and gave the young driver the address of Tavern on the Green. She had already had half a sandwich and a handful of potato chips, but what she could really use was a drink. It was between shifts and the restaurant was half empty, the way she liked it. The maitre d' greeted her by name. "Your usual table?"

"That would be nice, André."

"And will Mr. Bennett be joining you today?"

"No, not today." As he helped her with her chair, she thought of how curious it was that pseudohighbrows always preceded questions with "and."

"And will you be having a cocktail, Miss Ward?"

"Bourbon and water, please." Every time she'd been here before, she had been with Martin, but she had seen little of him in the past few months—since she had begun seeing Webster. Martin hadn't cared much for Webster. She had thought it was a question of his being uncomfortable with the tennis player's brash, macho style, but the more she thought about it now, the more she wondered if lovable little Martin hadn't sensed something in Webster that was beyond her intuitive capabilities. Perhaps he'd thought he had been replaced. It was true that Martin was busy and frustratingly difficult to get in touch with but even so, she should be more persistent.

The first drink settled her jittery nerves, and by the middle of the second, much of her melancholy had evaporated. Still, the time dragged and at 4:15 she signaled André again.

"And would you care for another?"

"Thank you, no. Just the check, please."

She decided to start walking to the Waldorf just to pass the time. If she got too cold she could always hail a cab, and the exercise would do her good.

There was nothing redeeming about February in New York, even along Fifth Avenue. It was cold and drab and dingy, and the remains of the last snowstorm sat huddled in filthy little piles where they had been swept like unwanted refugees into the no-man's-land between storefronts. When she walked into the Waldorf at just after five, she went directly to the Astor Suite and asked for the table in the farthest corner. The cold had sliced off a bit of the edge, and even before she was seated she had ordered another drink. It was fifteen minutes before the drink arrived, and another twenty before he did.

"Sorry I'm late." As he sat he combed his yellow hair off his forehead nonchalantly with his fingers, and the few women in the room went back to their vegetables julienne and their whiskey sours.

Catherine shrugged as if to say, What can you do? It showed less than annoyance but not quite forgiveness.

Mark Collins was what Catherine's mother used to call a real hunk. He was all blond hair, blue eyes, and muscles in exactly the right places. "I love this place," he said after he'd ordered. "Like the fellow says, 'You don't get jostled at the Waldorf.' "

"You don't get served the same day, either." She already knew he was after something, but as yet she didn't know what. So they would sit and spar politely over cocktails. Then he would get to the point. She did know she wasn't going to fall for the killing good-looks or the glib cocktail-conversation ploy.

And she knew, too, that whatever it was he wanted she would probably give him.

Catherine let Mark order a third drink alone. She had already had enough to make her pleasantly relaxed. There was never the slightest question as to what she wanted from him. This time the ball was in his court, and there was not the least bit of pressure on her to initiate conversation or, for that matter, even to keep one going. She had ordered a small tossed salad, and methodically pushed it around her plate with her fork whenever the lull in the conversation threatened to intimidate her into taking the offensive. The background noise in the small but elegantly appointed dining room had risen significantly as it approached the dinner hour, and perhaps for him that made the relative silence between them more tolerable.

"You're working a lot," he said finally.

She shrugged modestly. "Lucky. You?"

He shrugged. "Some."

Under normal circumstances she would have taken over. But this was a rare opportunity—an opportunity to watch him squirm a little, to be in control—and she wasn't about to let it pass. For some time, whenever she had needed a few grams of cocaine she had called Molly Falk. But it was never just drugs with Molly, and Catherine wasn't so sure she wanted that part of it anymore; well, on second thought she guessed she did, but only when *she* wanted it. After her breakup with Webster, she had decided to take a big chance and call Mark. It was across from the Metropolitan Museum of Art that they had made their first exchange—and each subsequent one until today. Today, for some still-unstated reason, he had invited her to share a drink at the Waldorf. Unstated, but she had her suspicions.

"It's actually about work that I wanted to see you," he began hesitantly. He could see she still wasn't going to offer much, so he forged ahead, albeit reluctantly. "LeeAnn telephoned me yesterday."

Catherine, who was resting one elbow on the table and her chin in her hand, pursed her lips and shrugged.

"It seems I'm in line for a television commercial that's potentially pretty big." He paused before continuing, but if she already understood what he was driving at, she gave no indication. "It's over at Roberts & Young with Billie Devlin. LeeAnn seemed to think they'd already selected you for the female part." Catherine's sudden comprehension was obvious, but Mark pressed on, afraid now that she might comment before he had a chance to explain completely. "Now, I

185

wouldn't ever ask you to do anything sleazy or underhanded. You know, ah, I just, ah, thought, you know, that you might just, ah, mention that we've worked together before. You know, that we worked well together and you felt comfortable with me and we're ..." His voice trailed off as he searched for the appropriate word to define their relationship. "Friends," he added hesitantly. "And, after all, what are friends for? You know: I help you, you help me."

By now Catherine was mustering a reply, but Mark forged ahead with his last convincing argument.

"We certainly did work well together in the Bahamas, didn't we? So, what could a good word hurt? And, actually, by helping me you'd be helping yourself, because if we click again who knows how far we can go with this thing." Mark Collins's gaze dropped humbly to his lap, then rose once again to meet hers. "I need a break, Cathy, and this could be it."

It was now obvious to her that he needed her as she had never needed him. They both knew that small-time pushers were a dime a dozen. Sure, he was convenient and reliable, but there was always another party, another name. "All you're asking me to do is what I would have done anyway," she said flatly.

"That's right!" he said cheerfully. He sounded immensely relieved. "You know I'd do exactly the same thing for you if our positions were reversed. Any friend would."

"Yes. Any friend." She knew she was in no position to pass judgment, but where before it wouldn't have mattered a single bit who played opposite her, Mark or anyone else, she suddenly realized that his overture had worked to cross-purposes because now she hoped he wouldn't get the job. There was something sleazy about him, as though he would prostitute himself without compunction to get what he wanted. She wondered how often he had—literally—as she gazed across the table at his remarkably chiseled features. But then again, she asked herself, who was she to pass judgment? She would be surprised if he didn't get the job, regardless of anything she did or didn't do. "I'm flattered that you think anything I might do would have an influence on anyone."

"Maybe it will, maybe it won't. I'm just covering all the bases. I mean, I can act circles around most models and I *know* I'm good looking enough."

His ego had apparently escaped intact, and Catherine smiled at his quick reversion to form. "You'll probably get the job and I'll get canned."

"You're already in."

"No. I may be their first choice if I can do the job effectively. But they certainly have no commitment to me."

"I'll get it," he offered when the waiter arrived with the bill.

"Thanks, but I'll pay my half," she said, not wanting to be beholden to him for even a few dollars. Out on Fiftieth Street he reached into his overcoat pocket and she into her purse, and they silently exchanged five grams of cocaine and $750, as had become their custom.

On the way back to her apartment, Catherine sat in the backseat of the cab and wiped a film of cold sweat from her forehead. Then she held her purse tightly against her lap with both hands. This was the last time. Definitely the last time.

At about the time Catherine Ward was meeting Mark Collins at the Waldorf, Lynell Alan was morosely dressing himself in a narrow changing-room that ran along the far wall of Franco Canero's Fifth Avenue penthouse studio, feeling very tired and very, very used. He had just finished the last go-see Gretchen would ever send him on, and he had the gut feeling the bitch had known all along the kind of experience he had been in for. Well, it was his own goddamn fault for being so stupid and naive to think Gretchen would actually do him a favor.

Lynell had known Franco Canero was gay the moment he heard his voice over the intercom. "You're late, darling. Come straight up," Canero had said petulantly before buzzing him in.

"How long can it *take* to walk ten blocks, for heaven's sake?" Canero continued with equal petulance, as though Lynell's sixteen-story elevator ride had not intervened.

It was fourteen blocks and fuck you, you flaming faggot, Lynell wanted to say. "Sorry, I've been at a shooting all day, and Gretchen said you'd be here until five. I didn't realize there was a rush." This was the part he hated: the false deference, the obsequiousness, and he tried not to infect his apology with too much sarcasm.

"No harm done, I suppose." Canero was middle-aged and short, with pock-marked olive skin and sparse dyed-black hair. His only remarkable physical characteristic was an anorexic thinness. He wore a burgundy cashmere sweater and a pair of designer jeans trimmed with white piping. When he turned and minced toward a low leather couch against the opposite wall, Lynell noticed the "Beer Can" trademark on the back pocket and decided he would remember that name. He wouldn't be caught in a pair of those for $250 a *minute*.

Halfway across the bare parquet floor, Canero looked over his shoulder, pursed his lips in exasperation, and crooked his index finger mechanically several times as though Lynell should have anticipated and followed.

Christ, why do I do it? Why don't I quit? Lynell asked himself as he followed the "Beer Can" trademark to the couch. Some photographers would toss you out on your ass for presuming you had been invited in. In that moment Lynell wondered again just what lengths he would go to get a job, any job, to prove to Cline Models that he was a hot property.

Canero sat on the boniest rear end Lynell had ever seen and patted the cushion next to him. As he sat, Lynell planned how far he'd kick the condescending bastard's skinny little ass when he told him to "roll over" or "fetch"—or worse.

"You *have* a book," Canero said, holding out his palm like a waiter about to accept a tray.

Lynell unzipped his canvas shoulder bag and handed the photographer his portfolio. "I've just left Munson and joined Cline," Lynell offered hesitantly.

Canero seemed unimpressed. "And Gretchen sent you over?" he mused. "Interesting."

Canero opened the black leather case to Lynell's head shot, an eight-by-ten full-face macho look, and reached nonchalantly for a half-eaten sandwich on the table beside him. Lynell couldn't watch.

As Canero thumbed rapidly through the 25 to 30 eight-by-tens and print job tearsheets, *hmm*ing occasionally through a mouthful of what Lynell's olfactory sense told him was pastrami, the model's eyes wandered around the L-shaped room.

The part of the room they sat in more than made up for the lack of forestation along the streets and avenues of Manhattan. All manner of trees, vines, and plants sat, hung, and climbed around them. However, Lynell sensed the density of the plantlife wasn't entirely decorative. The rubber plant beside him partially hid a large water stain, and a closer inspection of the room revealed walls that were cracked, peeling, and badly in need of paint. Beyond the flora the studio had the forlorn appearance of a Tennessee Williams garden struggling to conceal a more prosperous past.

The functional area around the corner of the L was clogged with photographic equipment, props, cue cards, and familiar consumer products. The dressing room/lavatory jutted into and ran along the studio's far wall. The dressing room wall was covered by a variety of backdrop curtains that could be raised and lowered for the desired background color.

"Can I get you a cup of coffee?" she asked before Lynell saw her or even where she had come from.

"Oh, no thanks," he answered quickly, before Canero could say he wouldn't be staying that long. "I've already had plenty today."

"I'm Ginny. I help out around the studio. Sort of a Ginny of all trades."

"Hi. Lynell Alan." Ginny went back through the swinging door, and between swings Lynell caught a glimpse of a fully-equipped kitchen.

Ginny was homely and dumpy, but her tits could have won prizes. He immediately loathed his automatic sexual categorization of people, but it was a fact of life—particularly in this business. She did seem pleasant enough.

"Some marvelous shots," Canero said. He handed the portfolio back to Lynell, who surreptitiously wiped the cover against his jeans to remove a spot of mustard. "Would you strip to your underwear, please?"

"What?" Lynell didn't know why he was surprised. "I don't do underwear or nudes." As soon as the words were out of his mouth he wished he had waited one more sentence.

"Don't flatter yourself. I don't do nudes, either. You're going to be wearing a dreamy, tight-fitting jumpsuit," he said matter-of-factly, "and I have to see the body."

Lynell stood and reluctantly stripped to his underwear: pale blue bikinis. He suddenly wished they were boxer shorts. It didn't bother him that Ginny had returned to the room. He felt more immodest in front of Canero.

"You'll do. The suit's on a hanger in the dressing room. And no underwear, please. We don't want a visible panty-line, do we?"

"You're shooting now?"

"Why not? You're here now."

The suit was skin tight and the thought of wearing someone else's clothes without underwear was repellent, but like overbearing photographers and rejection, it was sometimes part of the business. Lynell was both surprised and relieved they shot for only fifteen minutes. He still might get in his run before dark.

When Lynell Alan returned to the dressing room to change back into his street clothes, Franco Canero loaded film into his camera for the first time since early in the day. Then he raised the black back-

189

ground curtain on the two-way mirror and watched as the model stepped out of the jumpsuit. During the next five minutes Canero would take the pictures he was really after—to add to his private collection.

A new Cline model had potential, and he was fortunate to have gotten one. The way the economy was going, the legitimate agents were cutting more models than they were taking on. This Lynell Alan wasn't the pretty-boy type by any means. He was more exotic, more distinctive looking.

"You think he's worth it, Franco?" Ginny had asked bluntly, pouring him a cup of coffee in the kitchen after Lynell had adjourned to the dressing room to change into the jumpsuit for the "testing."

"Indeed I do. He has a certain . . . *je ne sais quoi*," Canero answered, squinting pensively as though trying to see into the future. And though of course there would be no black-and-white confirmation, during the brief shooting that followed the man had shown a versatility and grace that had done nothing to dispel Franco Canero's artistic judgment. "And, besides," Canero added with a shrug, "what's one lousy roll of film?"

She was unabashedly naked when she came out of the bathroom. Lynell held his Levi's defensively in front of himself. "Excuse me, Ginny, I didn't know you were in here."

"That's okay," she said, walking toward where he stood blocking her way to the door of the narrow room. "I'm not proud. Franco's taking some shots of me in a few minutes."

"Great." He stepped to the side to let her pass, nodding nervously and still holding his pants in front of himself. Apparently Canero did do nudes, though why he would do Ginny he wasn't quite sure. Lynell wondered if he had misjudged Canero. Maybe the man was into large breasts. Perhaps a man's choice of adjectives wasn't indicative of sexual preference after all.

Just as he thought she would pass, Ginny reached behind him and squeezed. "How about a quick hand job?"

He was taken aback. "Why?" he blurted. As she pushed her breasts against him he began to rise in spite of himself. It was an advance he might have expected from Canero.

"Why not? You locked it?" she asked with a nod toward the door, abruptly grabbing his pants and tossing them on the bench that ran along the wall.

He began to backpedal, but there wasn't much room. He was staring at her chest, the only part of her anatomy he found even remotely attractive. She was not a woman he would have been particularly interested in under ordinary circumstances, but as she took him in her hand, he realized there was only so much a man could resist.

But he couldn't risk it. "Canero might find out," he said, taking her firmly by the shoulders, not wanting his rejection to offend her. "And I don't want to lose the chance to get a job."

"Ah, but I can *get* you a job with Mr. Canero." Then she turned her head in the direction of the studio. "Franco, I'll be a few minutes. The zipper on the jumpsuit is stuck," she yelled, never letting go of Lynell Alan's stiffening penis.

"Take your time, sweets. I'll be a while setting up," Canero called back from the studio.

Ginny looked into Lynell's now-vacant eyes. "Sorry it can't be more, but we don't have *that* much time." Both her hands were on him now, and he returned her strokes, mildly surprised at the flabbiness of her breasts.

"I'd better get some tissues," she whispered, backing away carefully. "Don't you move." She turned and walked slowly back to the bathroom, and he didn't care about the ripples in her thighs, only wanted her to come back. He didn't move but stood there alone and saw his reflection in the mirror, looking dumbly back. He felt more naked than naked in his arousal, an arousal that was a patent reminder of a warning his father had given him long ago: "Son, a stiff prick has no conscience."

Canero began shooting when the man was alone, making occasional light stirrings to maintain the deception. He didn't want Ginny in the pictures. God, he couldn't imagine what a man would see in that cow. But at least she did the job right. The guy couldn't have been in a better spot if there had been a X marked on the floor. He didn't even have to change the camera angle. And all for a lousy twenty bucks.

When Ginny returned to the model's side, Canero stopped shooting. In the time it took him to pull the royal-blue background curtain down over the mirror, the man's cock had disappeared again into the disgusting slut's pudgy little hands.

Ginny left the dressing room first, and when Lynell had dressed and come into the studio, he saw Canero taking shots of the nude, overweight young woman and he was flushed with embarrassment and guilt: that Canero might know . . . at the vague feeling of having been used again. But if Canero knew, he showed no sign.

191

"Thanks." Canero waved without looking up from his lens.

"I hope they come out. When do you think they'll be ready?"

"Call me next week. But don't get your hopes up. It wasn't all that I had expected."

As he closed the door behind him, Lynell Alan wondered how the photographer could already know.

Five minutes after leaving Canero's studio, Lynell was on the street and headed back to his apartment. To say he was confused would have been to underestimate his emotions. To say he was feeling guilty would have been to underestimate his conscience. For it was the first time since Aimée had moved to New York that he had been unfaithful to her. At that moment he was sure it would be the last. As he was sure it would be the last time he would compromise his morals—for a job or anything else.

Then for the second time since leaving the shooting at Mike Dudley's studio earlier in the afternoon, he changed his mind about going back to the apartment. In his attitude, at least, Lynell Alan faced a turning point in his career. When he had left the Dudleys' studio, he could easily have justified calling it a day, and probably would have when he had been with Munson—a few short days ago. But after dropping by Aimée's office to make a date for dinner, he had stopped in at the agency and reminded LeeAnn of his existence. Then, the fateful call to Gretchen. The fucking bitch had had the last laugh after all. He'd *never* be that naive again. Now it was almost five, but damn it, he had promised himself he was going to do it right this time. So he stopped at another row of pay phones, these just outside Canero's building at Madison Avenue. He had to try three before he found one that wasn't out of order, then had to wait several minutes in the sub-zero windchill while an older woman who had slipped in before him completed her call. The page that Cline Models would have been on had been torn out of the directory, so he first had to call information. When he finally reached LeeAnn, his fingers were numb and he immediately had mixed emotions about his decision to call.

"Oh, Lynell, this is terrific. I'm so glad you called. Where are you?"

"At a pay phone at . . . um . . ." He looked up at the street sign. "At the corner of Madison Avenue and Fortieth Street."

"Good. You're only about a mile or so from Bloomingdale's. They want you there immediately. Go to the third floor and see Harriet Wrigley. If you can run that far, run. Got it?"

"Got it," he said, hanging up and setting the stopwatch on his Casio to zero.

It was twenty-one blocks—nineteen long and two short—and he was in Harriet Wrigley's office in five minutes, fourteen seconds, and change. And he wasn't even out of breath.

There are among models three distinct echelons: that vast majority who subsidize their losing efforts with other, more reliable employment. Those few—usually recent-past members of the former group—who scratch out a living, albeit modest, on modeling alone. And finally, that third, elite handful who, more often than not, have leapt the first two classes from neophyte to star simply by virtue of being "discovered"—one day a clerk in a department store, next day a Calvin Klein billboard; one day a pizza chef, next day the Chaz Man.

Conversation on jobs often flows freely between members of the first two groups, who are often booked for the same low-budget, low-visibility jobs. All are acutely aware of the others' positions in the modeling world, because they have either just worked their way out of, or are trying desperately to work their way into, the others'. But between members of both groups and the elite, there is a heavy door—locked on one side by awe and envy, and on the other by either a total lack of understanding and respect or by the wish to forget—which, on the rare occasions they do share a booking, preempts any contact beyond, and sometimes including, the basic amenities.

Lynell Alan changed quickly into his street clothes and fluffed his curly hair with his fingers, feeling the intimidating presence of Jason Wexler and Craig Burton, two men who had graced the pages of virtually every Bloomingdale's catalogue put out in the past three years, and unquestionably *the* two biggest male models in the city—which meant the world. It was a job Lynell had been grateful to land, even though it was as a last-minute replacement for someone else, and it reinforced his conviction that Cline Models would be his last big chance. It also made him feel better about finally having relented and called Gretchen to announce his defection. It hadn't mattered that he owed her nothing. He owed it to himself to be strictly aboveboard.

Well, he had worked five hours today, and that was more hours—and at a higher hourly rate—than he had ever worked at Munson in a single day. And if he just kept plugging, if every time he was about to give up or quit early for the day, he just thought of Gretchen Saczynsky—who knew? Maybe he had a chance, even with these heavy-

193

weights. His ears perked up when he heard the now-familiar name.

"Jason, you ever work with Cathy Ward?"

"Sure, a couple of times."

"What's the story on her?" Burton asked as offhandedly as he could manage.

"Pretty nice kid, but I hear she's a coke head."

Craig Burton shrugged, and Lynell Alan went about his business in suddenly confused disappointment, as invisible to the two men as though he were another Bill Blass spring-weight suit hanging on the rack along the wall.

"There's a lot of that going around," Burton continued. "That's not what I meant."

"Forget it, man." Wexler had been shot down by Catherine Ward twice in the fall and had seen her on two subsequent occasions with other men. His ego was still reeling.

"Why? Has she got a boyfriend?"

"You know Martin Bennett?"

"The writer."

"Yeah, well he's as queer as a three-dollar bill. And Webster Greaves?"

"The tennis player. Of course. I mean, I know *of* him."

"I live in the same apartment building he does, and rumor has it that although he loves to be seen with the girls, he occasionally gives lessons to the young boys on the tour—backhand lessons, if you know what I mean."

"And Cathy Ward goes out with them?"

Wexler shrugged fatalistically. "She's a fag hag."

12

Albert Cline had been back in New York for three days and he already missed the bright California sunshine. He stood and walked to his office window. Below him the lights of Manhattan twinkled like the reflections of a million stars in a huge undulating black river. But there were no stars shining on this cold, bleak evening, and he wasn't looking down at the lights. He was looking at the transparent reflection of a tall, balding, and rather unattractive man who was twenty pounds overweight and pushing fifty harder than most men of forty-nine.

Albert Cline was a product of the Brooklyn slums who by fourteen had dropped out of school and by eighteen had banked his first $25,000 pimping neighborhood black girls. By the late fifties his growing business had been "absorbed" by a powerful local crime-syndicate. He was offered three choices: "Close up shop, come to work for us, or make your next investment a burial plot."

In 1959 he set his sister up in what he fully expected to be a hobby: Cline Models, Inc. And for the first few years it had been exactly that: a hobby, albeit an expensive one. Albert was half-owner in name only, having by then graduated from pimping and leg-breaking to the distribution of pornographic films. But Mary had proven to be both a shrewd and ruthless businesswoman, and by 1967 her business, too, had come under the scrutiny of the local bosses.

"We want her to use our accountant, Al," Rocco DeMarco told him. "We've got a lot of extra cash floating around. That way we could

195

clean it up some, if you get my meaning. Your sis don't even have to know."

In return he'd been promoted again, been given a small piece of the narcotics action, a piece that had grown over the years, until now he moved almost five kilos of cocaine a month. And he never had to touch the stuff. Models were perfect movers: the travel and the exposure, added to the final ingredient—greed—made for a perfect mixture.

Mary had been pleased when her brother quit his job in the import-export business in 1968 to take over the financial end of the business, and she was amazed that along with the help of their new accountant, Albert's guidance had seen the business grow many times over. Even in poor economic times when other agencies floundered, Cline Models flourished. Last year they had opened a Los Angeles branch and, with Albert more or less at the helm, had gotten more and more actively involved in television and films.

"We haven't done all that badly in twenty-five years in the business, have we, Albert?" Mary asked her brother as she watched him looking out over the Manhattan skyline.

"No," he answered, "not bad at all."

Albert and Mary Cline were on top of the world—and enjoying the view.

Albert Cline sidestepped to his left so he could see the reflections of the two women seated behind him: a still-attractive former mistress, whose glowing beauty had dimmed to an elegant memory, and his possessive sister, whose unremarkable looks had, if anything, improved with the years.

LeeAnn Schneider had had a brief flirtation with stardom fifteen years before, and *he* had made her, a brainless beauty whose gratitude had been boundless, until his sister had found out—homely, brilliant, ruthless Mary. He had offered to dump LeeAnn on the spot, but that hadn't been enough for Mary. He'd had to break LeeAnn—call in favors to insure that the only bookings she would ever see were the ones no other model wanted: passing out perfume samples in Bloomingdale's for thirty-five dollars a day, or a new brand of cigarettes on a street corner in subzero temperatures. And he'd had to watch her do every man in town, on the promise of jobs that never came. And when she had come back begging, it was Mary who gave her a job: a menial job so he could watch her crawl every day—big star brought crashing back to earth. And it wasn't that Mary thought he cared about LeeAnn. There had been other women. It was more Mary's built-in reminder of what she was capable of doing to anyone encroaching on her territory. Her brother. Her possession. But LeeAnn could follow orders, had learned this side of the business and had worked her way up to become a good booker and a reliable aide. Mary now even allowed her to make an occasional inconsequential decision.

From their hazy images in the glass, he could barely tell which one had been the gorgeous, sexy young model. Yes, personally he would rather have brains—you had a better chance of holding onto them. With looks, time was the great equalizer. Though Mary had never looked like much, the agency had come a long way, thanks in no small part to her brains. And as for the other thing, he could still turn up an occasional twenty-year-old who volunteered, even begged, to do "anything" for a chance (especially since he had begun overseeing the new Los Angeles operation and didn't have his sister breathing jealously down his neck twenty-four hours a day—at least not twelve months a year). But he rarely solicited favors anymore, and that was more the nature of the business than waning desire on his part. He and Mary had strived to earn a respected spot atop the modeling business, and any more than an occasional, discreet dalliance could compromise that position.

"Mary, right now what I need more than anything else is a nice dry martini." He did not turn from the window.

"Al," she scolded, as though admonishing an obese child for begging for another cookie, "we've got to finish this."

"I know." He looked at his watch. "But it's already seven o'clock. Does it have to be tonight?"

"I promised Billie Devlin we'd have a man for their new shampoo this week, and by God, we're going to deliver the best possible man— the perfect man. She puts a lot of trust in our judgment. I'm *not* going to lose this account."

"This new . . . ah . . . what is it?" he asked, groping for the name as he turned to face them.

"Now Shampoo."

"This Now Shampoo. I still don't see what's the matter with Wexler or Burton. They're not big enough for her? Christ, they're the two biggest in the business. And what about that pretty-boy Collins? Why'd you send him over there if you didn't think they'd use him?"

"I told you: Wexler is too macho and Burton is too preppy. And I've got other plans for our Mr. Collins. Besides, they want a new face, a new *kind* of face—a face that will be identified with Now Shampoo. They want a warm face, sensitive, intelligent—a man with some charisma, some charm, and brains. They're going to push the hell out of this product, which means pushing the hell out of the guy. There's got to be something there, something substantial *behind* the look, so when

197

he gets in front of a television camera, the audience will see and hear that he *is* more than just another pretty face."

"Oh, sweet Jesus, we've got to find a brain surgeon among this group?" He walked to his desk and patted the top of the pile of composites that represented every one of the fifty men in the agency. "There's probably not a sum total of three brains in the whole stack."

"Al! Now you know that's not fair. Some of those men are very bright."

"Yeah, sorry, I know." That was a sensitive issue with his sister, so he tiptoed delicately away from it. "But none of them suits *you.* Christ, any one of ten of them would be great. Just pick one. All I know is: it's late, I'm thirsty, I'm hungry, and we don't have any new faces we haven't looked at a dozen times in the last three days. And shit, Mary, we have tomorrow yet."

"But, Al, tomorrow is Friday," she answered, her voice rising with impatience, "and the choice is going to be just as difficult then. And I want someone from this agency *there* tomorrow. I won't have another agency steal this account. It's too big: print, TV—the whole package could be worth twenty-five, fifty thousand a year for us, maybe more if the guy works out. And if we don't have the right face, a fresh, new face, they'll call Wilhelmina or Ford or Munson or . . ."

"But, we don't *have* any new faces. We just have these."

"Excuse me," LeeAnn Schneider broke in for the first time, hesitantly. "We do have a new man. The agency took him on a couple of weeks ago when you were out at the Los Angeles office."

"Yeah, we didn't find anything out there either." Albert Cline looked across at LeeAnn. "Well, why the hell isn't he in with the rest of them?" he snapped, motioning toward the composites as though the fifty men were there in a corral.

"I'm sorry, Mr. Cline, but we didn't have any of his new comps until today. He just dropped them off this afternoon."

"Well, why isn't he in here now?" Cline persisted, rapping his index finger on the top of his desk.

"I probably shouldn't have even mentioned it. I'm sure he's not what they're looking for." She was beginning to tread on dangerous ground, presuming to make a decision like that. Taking him on in the first place was one thing. Even Mary Cline recognized her eye for talent. But that he was right for a big job . . . She changed her tack. "What I mean is, I guess I sort of forgot him because there are so many better-looking men right here." Anticipating Albert Cline's next offensive, she forged ahead, truly sorry now that she had ever acknowledged Lynell Alan's existence. "Of course, we wouldn't have taken

198

him on if he didn't have a marketable 'look.' He's only been in half a dozen times, and he *is* very nice." She concentrated on evoking a mental picture of him. "And his looks *do* sort of grow on you."

"Great," Albert Cline lamented, "now we've got one who *grows* on you." He shook his head. "I'm not looking at one more picture until I get something to eat—and drink." He turned to face his sister. "We'll have a few martinis, Mary, and you'll change your mind. They'll all look great."

"LeeAnn." Mary Cline looked absently into space, rolling the phrase through her mind: *he grows on you.* She hoped this man would be the right one, though she doubted it very strongly. And if he wasn't, she would still have the enjoyment of shoving it back into LeeAnn's face, showing once again how stupid and presumptuous the little slut was. (*"I'm sure he's not what they're looking for."* *Is that what she had said? Just follow orders and spread your legs around town. Stick to things you* know. *But don't* think.) "Get his picture and card, would you?" Her tone was as supercilious as she could manage.

"Just *one* more," she said to her brother, when the younger woman had left. "Then we'll go have something to eat."

Mary Cline looked at the head shot thoughtfully: nice looking—not great, but pleasant; beautiful teeth, straight hair, thirtyish. There were two other tearsheet shots on the reverse side. He wore his hair curly in one, straight in the other. If she had had a son, she would have wanted him to look like that: the eyes, the curls. He was definitely attractive, and almost the perfect size: 40-long suit; 32-inch waist—not that it mattered for a shampoo ad, but it certainly would if he was to go anywhere with the agency. She flipped it back to the front side and continued her silent appraisal. Then she glanced down at the name printed across the bottom: LYNELL ALAN. Her brother walked across the room and stood behind her. Poor Albert, always so impatient. He had a genuine knack for turning money into more money, so she let him handle their investments, keep raising their station from wealthy to super-wealthy. This was her end of the business. This was what *she* did best.

"Jesus," he said, tapping his index finger against the face smiling up at him from the front of the composite, "he looks like he's got a broken nose."

"I like his nose. I like the way he looks." Mary Cline was nodding pensively. "Not blatantly sexy, but sensual, soft—nice lips." She thought of Jason Wexler. "Is he from New Jersey?" she asked LeeAnn.

"Gee, I don't know, Ms. Cline," LeeAnn answered earnestly, having missed the sarcasm. "I think he's from Connecticut."

"Well, besides his statistics, what *do* we know about him?"

LeeAnn looked to the five-by-seven card in her lap. "Nothing, really. His address and phone number."

Albert Cline was reading his Mary's mind. Anticipation was part of the reason he stayed on top in business and in favor with his obsessively jealous sister. "Have him here in an hour."

"What if I can't get hold of him?"

"Then he shouldn't be in the business. If you can't get hold of him . . . dump him. Now, we're going to grab a bite to eat down at the corner deli. Join us after you've reached him."

"No thanks, Mr. Cline. I'm not really too hungry." She was famished but still felt uncomfortable in the presence of this odd, vaguely incestuous sister/brother relationship, even after all these years. Mary Cline had a way of treating her like hired help on *and* off the job.

"Suit yourself. See you back here at"—he checked his watch— "8:15."

The first time LeeAnn called Lynell Alan's apartment she let the telephone ring twelve times before hanging up. Then she dialed his answering service.

"No. The last time he called in, at 5:03, he was still at his apartment. Maybe he stepped out for a minute."

She left a message—urgent. Then she phoned his apartment again, and again hung up only after the twelfth unanswered ring.

She waited fifteen minutes, thumbing absently through the stack of composites, then dialed again. Eight rings, nine—no answer. The poor schnook would miss out on what could be the biggest break of his career. Ten rings, eleven (and the Clines *would* dump him—flat). Twelve rings. The guy was finished with Cline Models, practically before he started. He probably *wasn't* right for the job anyway. Shaking her head and sighing her disappointment for him, she hung up the phone on Lynell Alan's career.

At 7:15 Lynell Alan was in his third-floor walk-up, lying naked on his bed in the darkness, resting from his evening run, listening to Jackson Browne on his Sony Walkman. He knew the "7" setting was too loud, but though he didn't exactly know why—except that recently his moods seemed to run in cycles and he recognized this as the beginning of an up cycle—he felt good tonight. And you had to play J.B. on "7."

When the cassette's last cut, "The Pretender," was over, his ears were still ringing faintly. When he stood in the shower a few minutes later, he interrupted his own rendition of "The Pretender" to listen. But then it always sounded like the phone was ringing when you were in the shower. He began singing again, sure it wasn't the phone, or, if it was, that it couldn't be important enough to run soaking from the shower to answer.

At 7:45 he stood in the hallway, turning the third key in the third of the locks Aimée had insisted on for security, when he heard the phone ring from the other side of the door. He hesitated for a moment, then finished turning the key. "Fuck it. It couldn't be *that* important," he said quietly to himself as he started down the dimly lit stairs, "and with my luck they'd hang up by the time I got all of Aimée's locks unlocked."

When he reached the second-floor landing he could still hear the faint ringing from his apartment. He stopped and listened, counting six more rings. He looked up the narrow stairway, down at the floor at his feet, up the stairway again. Shit, it could be Aimée calling to tell him she couldn't get away or that something else had come up. Heaving a deep sigh in anticipation of the bad news, he climbed dejectedly back up the stairs.

He placed three calls in rapid succession. His mood began to spiral downward as he dialed the first number. No answer at Aimée's office. He called his answering service on the chance she would have left a message. Anxiety replaced depression as he responded to LeeAnn's "urgent" message, left almost half an hour before.

LeeAnn picked up halfway through the first ring. "I've been trying to get you for over half an hour. Don't you tell your service where you're going to be?" she yelled impatiently. "Frankly, I'd given up on you."

"Sorry, I went out for a few minutes. I just got back." It wasn't exactly a lie. Her anger, coupled with her urgency, doubled his anxiety. *Jesus, Canero found out about Ginny and she's only seventeen and they're having me arrested, or at the very least Cline Models is dumping me.* "My service said it was urgent?" What would he tell Aimée?

"Yes, it is. It's now ten minutes before eight. You've got precisely twenty-five minutes to get over here."

"To the agency?"

"Yes, to the agency."

"Ah . . . ," he thought about Aimée. What would he do about their dinner date? "Well . . ." If LeeAnn was calling to say they were drop-

201

ping him, let her do it on the phone. He didn't need to go all the way over there for that. "Ah . . ." He gazed up at the ceiling as though the answer would be written there among the cobwebs.

"Ah well, nothing. Albert and Mary Cline *want* you here at 8:15 sharp."

"They want to see *me?*"

"Yes, they want to see *you.*"

He was reaching the edge of despair. "Are they going to tell me something I want to hear?"

"I don't know. Just be here." And she hung up.

The weather report had forecast temperatures in the teens tonight, but he decided a brisk walk would do him good. He could make it to the agency easily in twenty-five minutes and it would clear his head. He didn't have money to waste on a cab, and he certainly didn't want to arrive in ten minutes and have to sweat out a fifteen-minute wait once he was there. The damp chill had kept most New Yorkers inside tonight. There was not much traffic and even fewer pedestrians.

Rumor had it that not many of their models ever even met one of the Clines, let alone both of them. He couldn't figure why they wanted to see *him.* He thought about the best possibility first—a job—but quickly dismissed it. That's what bookers were for. The owners of the agency didn't tell you about a lousy job. Maybe the rumors were wrong and they wanted to meet their new man. But why on such short notice? Why at night? And why "urgent"? Which inevitably brought him back to the worst possibility: Ginny. She'd told Canero and he had told the agency. Christ, he'd be blackballed from the business— how hypocritical. The biggest part of the business was sex: selling sex.

He couldn't imagine that too many men—straight ones, anyway— would have turned down Ginny's blatant advances. Not that that was an excuse. And even though he had disappointed himself by having engaged in sexual diversion around business for the first time, he could almost have lived with that. What he couldn't live with was that it might have been more; he might actually have done it for the chance at a job. And this thing with Ginny, this . . . what would you call it? . . . *nothing*, really . . . had made him feel soiled, dirty, guilty from the start, as though everyone would find out about it, as though Aimée would find out about it. Well, maybe his instincts had been right. Too bad he hadn't followed them.

The blast of a horn sent him scrambling back onto the curb at Forty-second Street. His anxiety wasn't keeping him warm but it made him forget the cold. The "WALK" sign stopped the two-way crosstown traffic, and he plunged across the street and continued up Lexington Avenue.

He wondered how many guys had blown that little Canero fag for a job. Then he recalled a day-booking last winter at a Country Club in Connecticut—summer clothes in a winter scene to create the illusion the clothes were cooling, refreshing. He had left the city early to be sure to be on time—Conrail was so unreliable in winter—then had taken a cab and he was there almost an hour early. The clubhouse was deserted. He tried the front and side doors, found them locked, and had about given up when he noticed the door to the men's locker room and lounge. "Eureka!"

It was almost as cold inside the locker room as it was outside, so he continued walking briskly toward the lounge. It might be warmer, might even have a fireplace he could throw some wood into. When he opened the door, his heart leaped into his throat, his, "Excuse me," a prepubescent croak.

"Get outta here. You're early," the fat man yelled from the couch without missing a beat.

"Sorry," Lynell croaked again, backing out quietly, eyes magnetized on chubby hands that held the long, black, silky hair tightly against the head in his lap, held it like a vise, pounding the head up and down viciously, as though it wasn't attached to the body kneeling in front of him.

Safely behind the door again, he sat on the freezing porch in a state of shock and confusion. He felt like he'd been hit by a truck.

When three other models, a photographer, and his assistant arrived for the shooting, Lynell was still numb, but this time from the cold. The overweight advertising agent appeared and introduced himself, as though seeing him for the first time. The girl—and she *was* a girl, probably no more than sixteen or seventeen—averted her eyes when they were introduced. The fat man had appeared amused by that.

Later in the morning as they stood together in front of a snowbank, thinking summer, she looked up at him shyly as the photographer changed film. "It's $650 for the day," she shrugged, as though that made it all right. Well, maybe for her it did.

"I try not to pass judgment," he answered. He didn't tell her he was getting $750 *without* blowing anyone. But then, he'd gotten the job through the photographer. God, it must be tough to be a woman in this business.

He had gotten to know her over lunch. She seemed like a nice kid. Just needed the money, needed the job. All day he fought the unbear-

203

able urge to report the bastard, but to whom? His agency? That would involve the girl and maybe they'd fire *her*. That was more likely than their firing the almighty advertising agency. Shit, they'd probably both deny it and *he'd* get canned. He had decided to keep his mouth shut.

He couldn't believe they were going to dump him over Ginny. No, it just didn't make sense. Anyway, it would be Ginny's word against his. She certainly couldn't prove anything.

He stood glumly at the corner of Fifty-ninth Street and Lexington Avenue and looked up at the brooding steel and glass skyscraper, feeling oddly like a small boy about to face the principal.

Mary Cline was reading his card. "How old are you, Mr. Alan?"

"Doesn't it say on my card?" he asked, wincing. He wasn't being flip, he simply couldn't remember what he had written. Usually he said twenty-six, but recently he had gone to twenty-seven and even twenty-eight, thinking that twenty-six might be stretching his credibility too thin.

"Your card says twenty-seven. You could be twenty-seven, but I think not. Everyone—especially in this business—lies about their age. So . . . how old are you really?"

"I'm thirty-one." He almost choked on it. Maybe they thought he was too old. But there were successful models older than he. Not many, but . . .

"And how long have you been a model?"

She was being too pleasant. Was this the good cop/tough cop routine he saw in all the movies? She'd soften him up, and big brother Al, standing quietly but menacingly behind her, would jump in and lower the boom. ("So, *you like sex on the job with underage girls?*") "I'm sorry," Lynell said, putting his hand to his face and closing his eyes for a moment. *Keep your composure,* he told himself. *They're going to tell you either that they're happy to have you aboard, or that there has been a big mistake and they're cutting you from the squad. And what's the difference? Maybe it's time to get out anyway. They'll just make the decision easier.* He looked up, took a deep breath, and relaxed. "Let's start over. I'm thirty-one years old and . . . I forgot what the next question was, but I *do* remember that I knew the answer." He smiled broadly, displaying sparkling, pearl-white teeth that would have been perfect except for a slightly crooked and minutely chipped incisor (of which he was overly self-conscious).

This time it was LeeAnn Schneider, sitting inconspicuously across the room, who winced.

But Mary Cline returned his smile, mildly amused by his subtle admission of nerves and drawn by his winsomeness. "I asked you how long you've been in the business, Lynell. May I call you Lynell?"

"Yes, please do." He decided to answer her questions truthfully. It would be easier than trying to supply answers he thought they would want, and possibly digging himself into a hole. "Just over a year, here in New York. But before that I worked at it some in Boston for a couple of years—part time."

"You began rather late. Have you made a good living?"

He paused for a beat. "No, not really." That hurt, but why lie? It would be easy enough for them to check. "To be honest, it's been kind of a struggle for me. I think I have my own kind of look, and I figure it must be marketable because I keep landing with better and better agencies—and I'm not just saying this, because I'm sure your ego doesn't need my opinion—until now I'm with the best.

"Maybe I can anticipate your next question. I know what my problem is: I'm not aggressive enough. I'm not on the street all day promoting myself. I've only been with you for a few weeks, and already I've done more of that than I'm accustomed to. But I'll get used to it. I *am* reliable. I *would* keep appointments, if maybe the agency would help me get them. I still think I can make myself a successful model."

"And what if you can't?"

"I'll give it another six months to a year, and if things aren't looking up by then, I'll try to get back into business."

"How often have you said that before, Lynell?"

He nodded silent agreement. Obviously she knew the marginal model's rationale for giving it one more shot—always one more shot.

So this was how his career would end. Mary Cline would give him his walking papers. A strange, almost eerie calm pervaded him, as though he were watching the scene through someone else's eyes. He was finished for sure and he would accept it gracefully.

"You said *back* into business? What kind of business were you in?"

"I spent five years in Boston as an accountant."

"You must have some education?"

"Dartmouth College and Dartmouth's Amos Tuck Business School."

"Hmm. Why did you leave a field that employed your impressive education for one that doesn't?"

"I quit before I was bored to death. I decided I'd always have my education but I wouldn't always have my looks—such as they are."

"You married?" The tough cop took over challengingly.

"No." Before he could ask why it mattered . . .

"Girlfriend?"

"No, I'm not gay." Lynell grinned, pleased that his blunt response had knocked Albert Cline momentarily off balance. He had *some* pride left, and if he was going down, at least he would go down swinging. The look that passed between the men said more effectively than words that the battle lines had been drawn.

"Oh, man." Lynell slapped himself lightly on the cheek. "I *had* a girlfriend." He had antagonized Albert Cline enough and employed the man's reference though Aimée would have strangled him if he referred to her as his "girlfriend" in her presence. "I'm sorry to interrupt, but I was supposed to meet her for dinner at eight," he said as he glanced quickly down at his watch. It was 8:30. "In my rush to get over here I forgot to cancel. May I use your phone to make a quick call?"

"Certainly," Mary Cline answered with a smile. She pointed to the door. "Why don't you use the phone at the reception desk? It'll give you some privacy. Take your time. We've got a few things to discuss."

At 9:45 Lynell Alan left the offices of Cline Models with a smile on his face and Mary Cline's business card in his hand. On the obverse of the card were scrawled a name and address:

Belinda Devlin
Roberts & Young Advertising
816 Madison Ave. (at 68th St.), 14th floor
226-7239
10:30 A.M.—sport coat and tie

When he reached the street he hailed a cab.

Albert Cline had developed an immediate dislike for Lynell Alan. The guy had that smug self-assurance of education. Christ, he had almost *challenged* them to drop him, like he had better things to do. "I still think the guy should get his nose fixed if he wants to work more."

"Albert, the young man is absolutely right: if he had his nose fixed he'd look like every other man in the business."

"And, by the way, he ain't that young."

"But he's the age they want."

"You really think Billie will like him." It was more statement than question.

"I think she'll love him—he's perfect for the campaign. I think it's fate lending us a last-minute helping hand. Don't you, LeeAnn?" She

206

turned to face the younger woman as if she *cared* about her opinion, knowing she would say "Yes" if she thought it was called for, and "No" if she thought that was called for.

She said, "Yes."

Albert Cline was shaking his head slowly. His instinct told him this would come to a bad end.

"Trust me, Albert. The man is charming and bright. He's a handsome man, he's got beautiful curly hair, and he's not *so* perfect that other men won't identify with him. And women—they're the shoppers, the buyers—women are going to love him. The only problem they're going to have is deciding whether they'd like to jump his bones or cook him a pot of chicken soup." She shrugged her shoulders and delivered her summation: "Albert, he's *very* appealing."

It was quarter of eight when Aimée Harris walked into the China Pavilion. "I'm waiting for a friend. We have a reservation for two at eight: Alan."

"Yes, Alan. Eight o'clock."

She smiled. Aran. Eight o'crock. "I'll wait for him in the bar."

"Certainly."

She hoped Lynell would arrive soon. She had had to skip lunch and was famished. The first vodka and tonic made her lightheaded, but she felt good and ordered a second. The ornate, dimly-lit barroom, with its burgundy velveteen-covered stools and plush carpeting, was a seedy, overdecorated adjunct to the restaurant, which itself had the brightly-lit tile-and-formica austerity of a family establishment.

She finished her second vodka and tonic and checked her watch, a slim, delicate, gold Seiko Lynell had given her on her twenty-fifth birthday, though she had known he couldn't afford it. It was 8:15. She'd give him fifteen more minutes. Damn, was he going to stand her up? She wouldn't do that to anyone, let alone someone she was supposed to care for. Well, maybe he was just running late.

A middle-aged businessman-type in a gray suit took the barstool next to her. A few minutes elapsed before the inevitable, "Can I buy you a drink?"

"I'm waiting for someone." She smiled. The alcohol pulsed warmly through her.

"Sure," he said, as though unconvinced and slightly hurt.

"Really." She nodded affirmation, tempted to add that if he were Paul Newman—which he patently was not—she'd still be waiting for someone.

"Well, how about a drink while you wait?"

He seemed harmless enough. She capitulated. "Okay." She had fifteen minutes to kill. "Vodka and tonic," she cued him as the bartender arrived. In the middle of her drink she wondered how she would escape if Lynell didn't show.

David Welles looked over his martini appraisingly. "You remind me of my daughter," he said, though Aimée doubted he looked at his daughter the way he was looking at her. He ordered another round, which carried her through the ensuing monologue (complete with snapshots). She felt the heat of his stare and absently tacked the open neck of her blouse closed with her fingers.

It was close to nine o'clock when she finished her fourth drink. Her face felt flushed and was beginning to numb. The bastard wasn't going to show up. It was time to leave. *He could at least have called me. Damn, I don't know if he's worth all this.*

"Well, David Welles," she said with mock formality, climbing down from the stool tentatively and holding out her hand. Then she laughed giddily. "*Well*, David *Welles*," she repeated animatedly. "Looks like I've been stood up, so I'd better be going . . . while I'm still able to." The vodka had washed down her anxiety over an exit line.

He took her hand firmly, held it. "Do you have to leave? We could have dinner . . . and a nightcap. . . ." The sentence hung like an unfinished painting.

"No. Really. Thanks, David, but I can't."

"Okay." He nodded slowly. "But if you should change your mind," he continued, with an expression that said he knew she wouldn't, "I'll be here for a couple more hours. It's close to my hotel."

"I don't think I will, but thanks."

God damn Lynell anyway. She inhaled deep gulps of the crisp night air as she stood out on the curb waving her arm. *Never a cab when you need one.* Poor, pathetic David Welles. She should go back in there, have dinner with him, go back to his hotel room, and give him the time of his life. Yes, she had seen the resemblance to his daughter in size and coloring, though she was prettier than Marsha Welles could ever hope to be. Yes, she could take Mr. David Welles to the place he wanted to go—finish his sentence the way he would tonight in his dreams.

The cab screeched up to the corner and the driver threw open the back door. She reached for it, hesitated, looked back over her shoulder at the China Pavilion, and thought again of David Welles. There was a time when she would have done it without so much as a second thought. Maybe she would do it now if David Welles were just a *little* more appealing. But then he wouldn't need her so badly.

"Hey, lady, is you in or is you out?"

Her eyes held the cabbie's for a long moment. "Seven forty-seven Fifth Avenue, please."

John Hayes couldn't believe his good fortune. He listened as the muffled footsteps approached determinedly yet unsteadily along the long, carpeted corridor. It was only when they were close enough for him to hear the unmistakably highheeled gait and the light jingling of delicate jewelry that he knew it was a woman. It was only when she stormed mutely past his open door with her eyes trained resolutely on the floor that he knew it was Aimée Harris.

He waited a few judicious minutes before walking down the hallway and knocking hesitantly on her door.

"Come in." She was still pacing the office.

"What are you doing back here?"

"I've got nowhere else to go."

"Ever consider home?"

She stopped pacing and looked up for the first time. "The world hates a smart ass."

"Geez, sorry. It just seemed so obvious, I was surprised you hadn't thought of it yourself."

It was obvious she had had a few drinks. She tried to hang her coat over the back of a chair but missed and left it in a pile on the floor.

John picked it up and lay it across the seat. "What's the matter?"

"Would you believe that prick stood me up? We had a date for dinner and he simply didn't show."

"Who, Lynell? Well, maybe there's a good excuse." Hayes knew the psychology of the moment called for him to defend, though not too rigorously, the absent man's honor.

"There's always a good excuse," she answered sarcastically. She strode truculently around her desk and plopped into her leather swivel chair, but enough off-center that it slid out from under her and rolled to the wall. For a moment she seemed to hang there, curiously suspended in midair. Then a surprised look crossed her face and she slammed her coccyx against the unforgiving floor with a teeth-rattling thud.

Hayes sprinted around the desk to where Aimée sat staring up at him with a pained expression. Even in her undignified posture she was adorable. "Are you hurt?" he asked with genuine concern.

She curled her lip disgustedly. "Only my pride."

He reached down, grasped her under the armpits, and, with very little assistance, helped her to her feet. When she was standing there in front of him, her face so close to his he could smell the light, sweet scent of her, overlaced with alcohol, he wanted desperately to hold her. When she looked up, their eyes held briefly and all his male instincts told him to kiss her. "How did you get that tiny star-shaped scar between your eyes?" he asked as he let go of her and stepped away.

She raised her eyebrows and rubbed her index finger lightly over the scar as though trying to erase it. "My brother hit me with a baseball when I was a little girl. These are the seams."

"It's cute." It was the first personal thing he had ever said to her besides "you look nice today," and even that, which he could have honestly said every single day, he tried to keep to discreet intervals.

John Hayes would have done anything to stay. He wanted to look at her, to touch her, to smell her the way he did now, the intimate aroma of her body one had to be this close to experience. It was, he knew, the way she must smell after sex—not like anything else but only like her; wonderfully, excitingly like her. "Would you like to go out and get a bite to eat?"

"Thanks, John, but I'm not really very hungry right now. Anyway, I do have a bit of work I could catch up on."

She was surprised at how disappointed he looked. In almost five months, they had shared little besides a sandwich at Agle Bagel and the problem of how to most concisely word a non-compete clause in a personal-service contract. Still, there was something subtly adoring in the way he looked at her and something more than professional courtesy or respect in the way he deferred to her judgment on legal matters. It couldn't be that he was attracted to her, she thought. Not a man as serious and professional as John Hayes. And yet if her judgment hadn't been still slightly clouded by spirits, she would have sworn he had come *that* close to kissing her a moment ago, and she to letting him. "Maybe another time," he said, shrugging bashfully as he reached the door.

"Maybe." There was no reason for Aimée to get carried away. Not with life as confusing as it already was. Let her lover stand her up for dinner. Let a strange man old enough to be her father try to pick her up in a cocktail lounge. Let a co-worker attempt a subtle seduction in her own office—if that was what had just happened. Let the whole world lose its sanity all around her. She, at least, would maintain hers.

*　*　*

210

"Where you been, counselor?" He was propped against a backrest, with his long, bare legs stretched out in front of him. The sash of his midthigh kimono bathrobe was tied loosely. The apartment was dark, the only light coming from the fireplace, an orange glow that danced eerily across his shadowy face. A joint winked from his lips like the eye of a cat, its tail a smoke ring that curled contentedly around one hand while the other stroked L.C. lovingly as she slept beside him.

"I might ask you the same question," she answered indignantly, slamming the door and sliding the deadbolt noisily as L.C. scurried for cover. "I went back to the office and worked on my case," she huffed, "*after* I got stood up." She threw her coat on the couch and stood in front of him truculently, waiting for his explanation.

He told her about the interview with the Clines, and when his languid recitation reached the part where he called the China Pavilion, he apologized. "I'm sorry. I should have known that fucker wouldn't get you the message. He could hardly speak English."

At the office she had done fifteen minutes' work in three hours, during which the muscles of her shoulders and neck had tightened into ropes. Now her shoulders slumped as the tension drained from her. She knelt between his outstretched legs, took the joint from his lips, and kissed him—a long, amorous, sensual kiss—then inhaled a deep draught of the acrid-smelling drug.

Aroused, he pulled her to him, fondled her.

"Oh, Lynell, I've had a long day. I've got to take a shower and wash my hair. Shouldn't you be in bed anyway if you have a big go-see tomorrow?"

"Jesus Christ," he slurred, "if I'd stopped living for every 'big go-see' I might as well have shot myself long ago. And it wouldn't have been suicide. It would have been euthanasia. A 'big go-see' is like potential: it don't mean nothin'. When I'm counting my money is when I'll put stock in *any* go-see, big or small. Hey, you taking my joint?" He watched in disbelief as she stood and crossed to the bathroom.

"Right now I need it more than you do. You're wasted. All you'll be good for tomorrow is the 'after' shot of Muhammad Ali's latest victim."

The rush of the shower through the open bathroom door was a siren beckoning him with the promise of the rubbing together of soapy, frictionless bodies, of washing each other beyond clean, of mouths on water-sweet bodies, of the purification of every imaginable act of love, of lust. The Siren beckoned, and he surely would have sailed to crash upon the rocks, but he lay paralyzed, a second half-consumed joint dangling from his parched lips.

The sounds of the shower mingled with thoughts of Carl ... Carl who? Curious that he should think of him now, after all this time. But then, he'd rather not remember. Carl Howard. Marblehead. The North Shore Summer Theater. There it was—Carl Howard: actor, horseman, and incongruous rapist of Don Quixote's Dulcinea. Disjointed thoughts raced through his mind, degenerate thoughts of a dozen horsemen gang-raping Dulcinea, of the horsemen gang-raping Aimée while he looked helplessly on ... the horsemen gang-raping *him.* He watched himself rise under his kimono in spite of himself.

"What are *you* thinking about?" She sat beside him, smelling faintly of Herbal Essence.

He awakened and felt her, soft through an Irish-knit sweater, hard through a pair of just-washed Levi's. "You," he said from a thick haze.

"Hungry?" she asked, spinning the top off a jar of peanut butter. A loaf of bread and a knife were on the floor beside her.

"Very," he answered, not seeing the peanut butter and bread, grabbing a fistful of her damp hair, pulling her head toward him, and opening his mouth to kiss her.

"It's all we have," she laughed, as she stuck a peanut butter-laden finger into his mouth.

"Umm." His tongue tugged gently at her finger, suggestively. "Peter Pan."

He dipped his finger into the jar and brought it to her lips. She rolled her tongue languorously around it, between the fingers and over the palm of his hand, slowly up his arm, licking, kissing, across his chest and down along his stomach, teasingly around his navel. Then, with aching deliberation, she opened his sash, took him in her mouth, made the same gentle suction sounds he'd made with her finger, raised her head. "Umm, it *is* Peter Pan."

"Take off your clothes."

She stood, took a log from the small stack by the fireplace, added it to the dying flames, and turned to face him. Crossing her arms in front of her, she took the opposite hems of the sweater and slowly raised her arms above her head, breasts shimmering crimson in the rising fire.

The force of the sexual electricity that connected them was so violent he began to tremble involuntarily as she unbuttoned, then slowly unzipped the tight Levi's, bending low to work them down over her hips, along her legs; her breasts hung freely, seductively. Slowly she straightened, smoothing her hands up over her legs, up over the gentle rise of her.

He could almost see the bright yellow firelight illuminating the backs of her shapely legs as she stood facing him, hands on hips, feet a shoulder's breadth apart, torso silhouetted by flames that licked the smooth-shiny skin inside her thighs.

She came to him then, knelt before him again, roused by their perpetual fire.

13

An eye for talent, that was Mary Cline's forte, although it had precious little to do with talent—anyone else's, that is, but her own. Her own talent for picking a face, a body, out of a crowd—a face that was not only beautiful or exotic or spectacular, but absolutely riveting; and a body that was sensual but not overpowering. An eye for talent: it was what had kept Mary Cline in business for almost twenty-five years.

But an eye for talent wasn't all there was to it, not by a long shot. There were plenty of others who had that knack for picking the stars: Zoli, Wilhelmina, Eileen Ford—even that brash relative newcomer, John Casablancas, over at Elite—that knack for plucking them off the streets, where she'd found Cherry Taylor, or off the beaches of California, where she'd found Christa Blair, or out of a pizza delivery truck, where she'd found a pimply-faced-but-can't-miss Jason Wexler; or out of the water-polo wars of a Malibu college, like Craig Burton—out-of-the-way places where most of the great ones seemed to come from.

Sometimes, though, the most difficult ones to find were the Catherine Wards—and maybe even the Lynell Alans—who walked right in off the street and fell into your lap. But Mary Cline had the knack; oh my, did she have the knack. But she had more than that, much, much more. She had an ear for it, too, a nose for it, a taste for it, a *lust* for it. It was what had brought her to the top—and kept her there.

Not that she was always right. She'd made mistakes, plenty of them, and she'd make mistakes again. That was one of the only certainties in this uncertain business. There were the kids who didn't have the guts or the determination or the brash self-confidence needed to steel themselves against the inevitable, crushing rejection. Even the best, the crème de la crème, faced rejection, faced it every day of their working lives, rejection from a dozen people down the line: from their booker to their agent to a photographer to a client to all the middlemen in between the model and the final product. And there were the ones who didn't have the innate knowledge, not a hope or a dream but nothing short of an unshakable conviction, that they were *the best*—that when they strutted their stuff, be it down a strobe-lit runway or in a cold dank studio, all eyes were on them. And finally there were the ones without the aggressive, almost-but-not-quite-to-the-point-of-abrasive assertiveness of a born winner.

Models? They were all good looking, all spectacularly attractive in some unique way that could one day make them a hit. Mary Cline picked them that way. All her models bore a distinctive trademark, something that made them outstanding, that had the potential to make them famous—sometimes almost literally overnight—if *she* determined that they had it.

She thought of Maggie Austin's dramatic cheekbones, Barbara Sheridan's bushy eyebrows, Catherine Ward's incredible dimples, and Christa Blair's body, though it could just as well be almond eyes or pouty lips or baby's skin. But that wasn't the talent that made them distinctive to Mary Cline. To her the talent that would see them through, that would give them "legs"—endurance in this sizzlingly competitive business—was something intangible, something subtle, something you couldn't see on the surface like you could see skin and hair and teeth and eyes. Guts! How much hair did they have on their balls? as Albert so disgustingly, but aptly, put it. Beauty, brains, and balls. In her field it was an unbeatable combination. You couldn't succeed without all three.

Of course, the fly in the ointment was that a fairly heavy investment of time and energy and reputation—all of which added up to dollars and cents—had to be made in beauty and brains before it could be determined if the balls measured up. It was there Mary Cline stood head and shoulders above the rest, and even so, she'd had her monumental failures. She'd made dozens of women and even a handful of men into household names, but the ones who stood out in her own mind were the failures, the ones she'd invested in, promoted, and stuck her neck out for, and whose balls had shriveled up as quickly and as surely as Johnny "Wad" Holmes's during a dip off the shivering Maine coast.

Mary Cline shook her head and thought pointedly of Joan Price.

Raisins. What Mary Cline had hoped for were watermelons. What she'd gotten were raisins. Not that Joanie hadn't been big, really big. But what she *could have* been? Mary shuddered to think. What she could have been was the first true international celebrity model/actress, a multimillion-dollar personal corporation for a decade, maybe longer.

Mary had seen Joanie in Germany recently, when she and her brother had stayed at the austere little Bavarian country inn Joanie and her husband ran by themselves, and even well into her forties Joanie looked spectacular. Even now Mary was daydreaming . . . if she lost fifteen pounds . . . But it was only a dream, because Joanie had lost her nerve. And in this business, without your nerve you had nothing. Without your nerve you had your credits—your tearsheets and video-tapes—and you had a starburst of activity as Mary Cline cut her losses by booking you and overbooking you, exposing you and overexposing you, using you and overusing you, until she'd used you up, until you had about you only the residual glow of a fading star. And overnight you were gone, dead as a model. Funny thing was, you'd been working so much you were usually the last one to know.

But I'm fair, Mary thought as she dialed. "If I do say so myself," she said out loud, "I *am* fair." She always gave them a shot—a fair shot, to show her that either they had or didn't have it.

The phone was ringing now, and she settled back into the deep leather cushions of her high-backed swivel chair, imbued with its warm security. And she would give Catherine Ward a shot, too—a fair shot—because she'd put a lot of time and energy into that girl, as well as a huge chunk of her reputation. She'd billed Catherine Ward against the competition: prettier than Cheryl, sexier than Christie. She'd promoted her—to every client who would ever have a call for a model even remotely her type, and then some. It was more of an in-vestment than she had ever made in a model before; before she was *sure*, that is. But then there was more competition today than ever be-fore. And Catherine Ward was more woman than she'd ever had her hands on before, had more potential. Of course, potential was an ex-tremely dangerous commodity. But, hell, where would you be without taking chances? Nowhere.

"Good morning, Billie. Well? What do you think?"

"What *can* I think? She's spectacular," Billie said in that level, solic-itous, I-knew-she-would-be-because-you-told-me-so tone. "My only res-ervation is that she's *so* spectacular that maybe no one will remember what the hell it is we're selling. I mean, the man and his shampoo are supposed to be the center of attention, but she . . ."

216

"Oh, come now, Billie, you don't really believe that, do you?" It was a question to which Mary Cline wanted no answer, so she gave Billie Devlin no time to answer it. "Your shampoo will be unforgettable because Catherine Ward is so unforgettable, dear. You mark my words." She paused as though realizing for the first time that what she was assuming just might not, incredibly, be a *fait accompli.* "You *are* going to use her, of course." The inflection was purposely left vague but carried an unmistakable suggestion that to interpret it in the interrogatory might potentially lead to disaster. Cline Models had several models under exclusive contracts with Roberts & Young Advertising, for which Billie Devlin was one of the newer account executives, having recently been hired away from Benton & Bowles, and though each contract was mutually advantageous, Billie Devlin was unquestionably the new kid on the block. As a twenty-five-year veteran of the wars, Mary Cline trusted to instinct that the young woman on the other end of the line would take care not to rock the corporate boat so early in her career. Mary could almost smell the young woman's sweat in the heartbeat it took her to respond.

"Of . . . of course," Billie Devlin answered. "I only had that single reservation."

"And a good point, at that," Mary Cline agreed. She'd gotten her way. Now it was time for placation. She had plenty of enemies; she certainly didn't need another. "Of course, I'm sure your thoughts are that Mark Collins *with* Catherine might be overkill. I guess I should have considered that when I sent him over. They *are* more or less the same type; and quite stunningly so, as you so accurately pointed out: blond, blue-eyed body-beautifuls both."

"Yes, well . . ."

And now for the coup de grace, Mary thought, as she availed herself of Billie Devlin's halting protest, if indeed that was what it was going to be, and cut her off as neatly as though she'd never opened her mouth. "Which is exactly why I'm sending you another man this morning. I figured you for a quick study, Billie," Mary continued with a hint of maternal pride, "so I decided to send you a man with an entirely different look. Just last night over dinner at Lutèce," she went on, quite certain the snotty little bitch couldn't call her on that one, "I said to my brother, 'Albert,' I said, 'that new man, Lynell Alan, would be just right for Roberts & Young's shampoo campaign.' Right in the middle of our consummé it came to me. 'What Billie Devlin needs is the perfect adjunct to Catherine Ward's exquisite beauty. What Billie Devlin needs is Lynell Alan's soft, sensual, masculine . . . sort of gracefully athletic maturity.' So, Billie, I've taken the liberty of sending him over to see you this morning. Ten-thirtyish. I think you'll like him. In fact, I think you'll adore him. I think you'll agree that his look is the perfect counterpoint to Catherine's. Of course, I've called Catherine to have her there, too. You'll give me a ring after the test?"

Billie Devlin was overwhelmed. She suspected she was being played like a player piano, but what did she have to lose? Mary Cline was one of the biggest names in high fashion and had been for ten years. At this point Billie couldn't afford to alienate her. And Catherine Ward's was the name most often heard thrown around as potentially the next big celebrity model. It might be a good idea to establish a working relationship with her now. She also guessed she couldn't afford—professionally—to turn her down, even though that had been her first instinct, when everyone else in town would give their eyeteeth to have her.

And Mark Collins? Shit, he was good in bed, and he had an unending supply of the sweetest coke she'd ever done. But business was business. Maybe she'd keep him around to let Mary Cline know she didn't hold *all* the cards, and to keep this Lynell Alan character on his toes—competition brought out the best in all of us—and in case he just couldn't hack it, which was always a possibility when dealing with an unknown, even an unknown being pushed by Mary Cline herself. And last but certainly not least, she'd keep Mark Collins around for his other obvious assets. Textron, Inc., the company that was going to produce Now Shampoo, certainly could afford Collins's booking fee. It was the least they could do for her. "Certainly, Ms. Cline," Billie Devlin answered after a moment's reflection, "I'd be happy to phone you as soon as the session is finished."

Catherine was late. But then she'd been late yesterday, too. Maybe Billie expected it, because she made not the slightest mention of it as Catherine passed through the studio.

Yesterday, Mark Collins. Today, some guy named "Joe." Maybe she was going to get this job—the girl behind the man who used Now Shampoo—but she certainly didn't feel like a girl who would make a man want to use anything, except maybe his last subway token to escape from the witch she saw staring back from the mirror over the dressing table. God, she felt awful. She ran her fingers through her windblown hair and they stuck in a snarl, sending a shock of pain down through her roots. At this moment she wasn't all that sure last night's reconciliation with Webster had been such a great idea.

"But I *need* you," he'd said as he stood at ther door with a bouquet of roses in one hand, a magnum of Roderer Crystal in the other, and an infinitely forlorn look on his face.

"*You* need *me?*" she'd asked sarcastically. "What for? Run out of tennis partners?"

"That's cold."

"What's cold? The truth?"

He didn't answer.

Catherine shook her head, looked up and down the hallway as though afraid someone might overhear her, then grabbed him by the wrist just above the bottle of champagne, pulled him in, and closed the door.

"You can help me," he said, once they were behind closed doors. "You've already helped me."

Catherine heaved a deep sigh of semicapitulation, took the roses, and motioned him to the couch. She went into the kitchen, refrigerated the champagne, and arranged the flowers in a tall crystal vase. Back in the living room she raised the thermostat, which she had lowered moments before Webster's unexpected arrival, in anticipation of bed. Then as an involuntary shiver ran through her, she tied her flannel bathrobe snugly around her waist and sat heavily in the worn chair at right angles to the couch, where Webster now sat wringing his tanned hands nervously.

"Six weeks," she said to break the silence. "It's been six weeks."

"There was the Masters," he said.

"I see you got your ass handed to you," she said viciously. "No pun intended."

The pain was etched into his swarthy face, in the look of abject surrender that turned his crow's feet into sprigs of white. *This must be how he looks after a match with Bjorn Borg* (whom he'd never beaten in fourteen tries), Catherine thought. *And I'm enjoying it!*

"And then there was Southern California," he continued almost in a whisper. "I did better there," he offered, when no acerbic comment was forthcoming. "Quarterfinals. But I couldn't concentrate. Some unranked guy . . . from India, I think."

Catherine sighed heavily again.

"And I . . . ," he ventured tentatively. "I thought you needed time."

"Yeah, like the remainder of my natural life." She was being cruel, she knew. But in spite of it, Webster Greaves hammered away at her with an arsenal as relentless as his trademark forehand.

"It's not a way of life for me," he was saying. "I'm definitely not gay. *You* certainly know that."

She thought immediately of his penchant for aberrant sex, and it was as though he were reading her mind.

"I mean, just because I enjoy ... You are a very provocative woman."

She wasn't hooked yet, but she'd gotten a whiff of the bait.

"So if I go 'bi' once in a while ... just for a change of pace. Tell me *you* never have."

And the hook was set. Of course she couldn't tell him, in all honesty, that she never had, because he knew about her sometimes-relationship with Molly Falk. She had told him herself in an unusually tender moment when she had needed to get it off her chest. It had even seemed to stimulate him—and here he was using it against her.

He pursed his lips and nodded as if to say *I thought so,* when, of course, he *knew* so. Leaning back into the couch, he crossed his right ankle over his left knee and warmed to his task. The true professional competitor, he moved in for the kill. "As I understood it, we had no commitment to each other. I certainly never intimated that I expected you to be faithful to me. I mean, we're both out of town so often; and realistically, we haven't reached that point in our relationship yet. But if we ever did ..."

Now that she was listening to the words—now they had begun to make sense to her—Catherine looked intently at Webster Greaves. It wasn't as a check of his sincerity that she scanned his features; nor was it for a crack in the veneer. No, everything he'd said made absolute sense. He had even stopped short of pointing out that she'd had no business barging into his apartment uninvited and unannounced, or that it was he who had every reason to have been outraged and offended. No, she was simply looking at him and wondering if their casual affair would now simply resume as before, or would this confrontation mark a giant step in the growth of their relationship?

Webster was leaning back, his arms now stretched out laterally across the back of the couch. He wore a white, pinpoint Oxford shirt and a dark brown tie under a meticulously pressed beige cotton suit with its sleeves pushed as far up his forearms as his bulging Popeye muscles would allow. He hadn't worn an overcoat. *Good old Webster,* Catherine thought, *never quite sure of the climate in this week's tour-stop.*

His wavy hair was neatly cropped across the front and at the sides but fell down over his collar in a mass of yellow ringlets. Even the thick, coarse hair on his forearms sparkled golden against his ever-bronze skin. He was the very picture of the stalking lion on the hunt; and she, Catherine knew, was the prey. His right arm, slowly so as not

220

to startle his victim into flight, fell to the cushion beside him, patted it gently.

The time for decision had arrived. "I need you," he said again, as he had when he'd first appeared at her door.

And the really sick thing was, as she realized two hours later with a snort of dope up her nose and Webster Greaves up her ass: she needed him, too.

Not all of the people Mary Cline managed appreciated the way she managed them, but you can't please everyone, she reasoned. Not every model, not even every Cline model, could be a star, after all. Naturally there was a direct correlation between the number of bookings a model landed and his or her level of satisfaction, so only the "stars" were *really* happy. It was a fact of life and Mary Cline had long ago accepted that. She didn't care about popularity—only about success. If they thought they could do better elsewhere, let them go. But they rarely did. Everyone knew there was only one direction for an ex-Cline model to go. So models seldom finished with *her*; she finished with *them*. When she sensed—or got a rare earful of—their dissatisfaction, she would get out of them what she could and then cut them loose. Hey, it was a tough business.

If the truth be known, which it wasn't by Mary Cline, almost none of her models appreciated her—male or female, hard-working or as yet hardly-working; only the very green and very promising did, the ones she took under her considerable wing and whose careers, and often personal lives, she watched over and guided like a mother hen. The rest, to be brutally frank, spent the better part of their working hours wishing she'd be hit by a taxi. Because the rest worked like slaves, catching cabs to here and jets to there, posing from sunrise to sunset, living out of suitcases, sleeping as best they could in strange hotel beds, catching a few winks in a frayed and sagging director's chair, and taking some of these to sleep and some of those to wake up. The money, without a doubt, was fantastic, but you often crammed fifteen years of living into two—and looked it. And then you were through. Just like that. No more calls, no more jobs, no more glitter, no more glamour, no more parties, no more fawning gofers, no more attentive celebrities, and unless you had a great deal more foresight than most—no more money.

Yes, they prayed she'd be hit by a taxi, some so intensely that they feared, when seeing her approach along a busy Manhattan sidewalk, that they'd reach out as she passed and push her underneath the next passing hack themselves. But they only smiled obsequiously and nodded good morning to the woman who controlled their very lives with an iron grip, who was making them and at any moment could—and one day would—break them.

For his part, Albert Cline's sole function at Cline Models was simply to turn money into more money. Mary not only didn't seem to mind feeding her brother's once lusty but long since waning appetite for firm young flesh, she actually seemed to encourage it—along with discretion—as long as he stuck to a strict diet of her agency castoffs. It gave her one more thing to hold over a nonproductive girl's head before she lopped it off. It was a perfect arrangement. Everybody was happy. Everybody that mattered, that is.

And who mattered? Mary and Albert Cline mattered. Sister and brother and no one else. They helped each other. They complemented each other. They needed each other. And in some real way—bizarre, perhaps, but real nonetheless—they loved each other, more perhaps than most husbands and wives. Sex, her brother could get anywhere; unqualified love, he could get only from her. And they both knew it. They were wealthy beyond their most extravagant desires and powerful beyond their own dreams. They maintained a stranglehold on two hundred of Manhattan's most beautiful—and about a dozen of its highest-earning—young men and women, not to mention countless numbers of photographers, ad agents, and other underlings around the fashion world, who worked—or didn't work—at their whim.

Since opening Cline Models West in Los Angeles six months ago, they were already giving Nina Blanchard a run for her money—the old witch. Another six months and they'd be number one out there, too. Trouble was, it was kind of difficult for Mary to keep an eye on her brother when he was in Los Angeles and she in New York, so recently she'd been trailing him from coast to coast and continent to continent—New York, L.A., Paris, Milan—like some jet-setting bloodhound. It wasn't so much that she *cared* who he was boffing. She just didn't want, and their reputation couldn't afford, another LeeAnn Schneider.

She should perhaps be kinder to LeeAnn these days, more appreciative, Mary Cline thought as LeeAnn strode briskly past her open office door. But then LeeAnn was paid *damn* well for what she did. In fact she was overpaid, which was why Willy and Zoli and Eileen Ford and Nina Blanchard hadn't been able to hire her away: they couldn't afford her. And make no mistake, that was the only reason the ungrateful slut hadn't switched agencies. She certainly wasn't even remotely familiar with the word "loyalty."

Occasionally in the years since his affair with LeeAnn, Albert had shown a spark of interest in a budding star, and at those times Mary raised LeeAnn's profile markedly. Albert had always seemed to get the message. She trusted he would get the message this time, too. Her brother wasn't a stupid man. Only this time, the object of his less-than-subtle interest was a time bomb; and a time bomb, if you didn't maintain complete and utter control, was liable to explode in your face. And in a business whose stock in trade was faces, the results could be disastrous.

Over a month had passed since Mary Cline had first sensed danger.

New Year's Eve is Amateur Night all over the world: the common folk with their tacky, classless displays of overindulgence being the order of the day. And in New York, the concept of New Year's Eve as Amateur Night is stretched to its ultimate limit.

Young people jam Times Square so that some day they will be able to tell their grandchildren (who will no doubt themselves jam Times Square in fifty years) that they were there to see the famous ball drop. Hours before midnight, inebriated revelers pile out of subways and buses and trains and drink their way downtown, pausing briefly in the bitter cold to retch pathetically into the gutter or to urinate lustily through a steaming subway grating. The common folk. Mary Cline would go to any lengths to avoid them.

On New Year's Eve that meant throwing a party, a party where the rules were made tacitly clear and were strictly adhered to, a party where overindulgence of any kind was unacceptable, a party where imported champagne and caviar and truffles and canapés majestically graced the mahogany center table of the Clines' opulent Park Avenue duplex, a party where a few—perhaps fewer than two hundred—of the really "in" people graced the guest list. And they *all* came—from uptown and from downtown. They came from the West Coast and they came from Europe. A Mary Cline invitation was a command performance. Being invited to a Mary Cline New Year's Eve party was akin to making the *New York Times* best-seller list, carrying with it the tag of outrageous success. And nothing but outrageous success and the whim of the critics—in this case the host and hostess—insured continued inclusion in the Inner Circle. Here this year, gone next year was an invitee's expected fate. But to be here this year was enough.

"As long as Eunice Blair remains behind the editor's desk at *Vogue*, she'll be on the guest list," one veteran of three seasons remarked reverently, a twinge of jealousy sneaking into her tone with the realization that if her own star continued to dim she would perhaps not see next year herself.

"Yes, I believe this is her tenth," noted her companion, the senior casting director at ABC and herself a five-year veteran. "But I don't see Barbara Goffe or Harold Cummings from NBC."

The first woman shrugged fatalistically. "They've had an off year."

"Quite," agreed the second.

In a corner adjacent to the foyer, a trio of gentlemen in the obligatory black tie had managed to ditch their wives long enough for a parley concerning the rumor that NBC would soon be seeking a new program director. "I haven't seen Weinstock tonight," said one.

"I haven't seen him in a week," said another.

A television executive could be sure he was history long before his pink slip arrived simply by eavesdropping on the right cocktail party conversations and finding that he had passed unnoticed from "Fred" to "Weinstock" almost overnight. The smaller birds of prey tend to distance themselves from the quarry when the vultures move in.

"Holy shit, who's that?" breathed the third man, who had been quietly sipping his champagne. It was just after ten o'clock, and Catherine Ward was making her grand entrance, per Mary Cline's instructions, in a breathtaking sequined gown whose neckline plunged to within an inch of her navel, revealing the inner hemispheres of two of the most succulent breasts any of the three men were ever likely to see.

"Oh," explained the first, jolted from his cock-stiffening fantasy, "that's the new 'find.' We had her in for an audition earlier in the year, but Mary was holding her out then."

"Who's the dwarf?" asked the quiet one.

"That's Martin Bennett, the . . . ah . . . writer," the first one explained, bracketing "writer" with a crook of his index fingers.

"Christ, what's a piece like her doing with a dork like him?"

"Maybe she keeps his pencil sharp," said the first with a wink, smiling and nodding as the unlikely couple passed them.

Everyone here serves a purpose, Mary Cline thought smugly as she mingled among the attractive, well-attired crowd. *Everyone has a function*. And that function was either to see or to be seen. Eunice Blair's was to see, Cherry Taylor's to be seen; Richard Avedon's to see, Craig Burton's to be seen; Case Lawson's, she thought, eyeing the first-time guest she anticipated would soon become program director at NBC, to see, and—Mary spun her head toward the affectionate grasp of her shoulder to face perhaps the most beautiful of the beautiful— Catherine Ward's was unquestionably to be seen. For if this party was

224

a showcase, which it outspokenly was, then this was the show of shows.

"Catherine, how good of you to come. And . . . Mr. Bennett, how nice to see you again."

"A pleasure," said Martin Bennett, clicking his heels smartly and bowing with stiff formality as he extended his hand. "I'm honored."

Yes, this season the showcase was for Catherine Ward. Last year's had been for Joey, who frankly hadn't been worth it; the year before had been for Denise, who so far had been. Three years ago it had been for Donna, and four years ago, Michelle—a brilliant few years before a nightmare finale. And three years before that, it had been for Laura. Yes, she remembered them all. But this year's undeniably was for Catherine Ward. "Help yourselves to champagne and caviar," Mary said as she slipped off into the growing crowd. "I have to mingle."

And mingle she did. She spent nearly the next three hours pointing Catherine out, pushing her, promoting her to the most important of the important. Starting with Number One and working her way down the line, she unfortunately ran out of time at around Number Seventy-five because of another cardinal commandment of The Party, perhaps the First Commandment: "Thou shalt have given thy parting thanks to the hostess within an hour of the passing of the old year." It was in that hour Mary sensed something that disturbed her.

Catherine Ward was stoned. Not falling-down stoned, mind you, but glassy-eyed stoned—and not on champagne. She'd been watching, and Catherine had taken only two glasses of champagne and finished neither. No, it wasn't champagne and it wasn't marijuana, either. Mary had been in this business, around kids with money, long enough to be familiar with all the signs, and Catherine didn't have the blood-shot, drowsy look of a pot head, nor had she affected the giddy laugh that verged on paranoia. It wasn't champagne and it wasn't grass. It was something potentially far more deadly—to her career, at least. It was cocaine; and it was then that Mary Cline entertained her first serious doubts.

Mary Cline didn't like drugs, and she didn't like druggies. Everyone knew that. Her models knew it. Albert knew it, too. The ugly thing about drugs was that they could come to control you. Ask Joey, last year's forgotten phenom. But then again, Mary thought with a self-satisfied grin, the single redeeming thing about drugs was that with them, sometimes *she*, Mary Cline, could come to control you—completely. Ask Denise, the radiant star whose own white-hot glow was on the brink of burning her world to a blackened crisp. But even at that, even with control, druggies were too volatile, too much of a risk. But did getting stoned on New Year's Eve make Catherine Ward a druggie? Hardly, Mary thought. Only time would tell. It would pay to keep an eye on the girl.

Mary's grin widened again as she scanned the festive room. And there was Albert—Albert, who could sense an animal in distress from three thousand miles away. He was staring at Catherine Ward, who flirted playfully but innocently with the three ad men who had admired her show-stopping entrance. Albert, whose leer was so hungry that spittle glistened in the corners of his mouth. Albert . . . her brother . . . Albert . . . her soulmate. As her head swung back toward Catherine Ward, the smile left Mary Cline's lips. No matter what happened, she would never let Albert have this one. Never.

New Year's Day had fallen on a Saturday, but Mary Cline was at the office well before 9:00 A.M. *Days like these are the most productive*, she thought as she let herself into the deserted suites on the twenty-third floor. Of course, she had the home telephone number of everyone in New York who meant a good goddamn—and she certainly wasn't above phoning them, even if it was in the middle of the fucking Rose Bowl. But mostly days like these were for thinking, for planning, for keeping yourself—and your business—one giant step ahead of the competition.

She didn't bother turning on the overhead lights as she entered her office but sat behind her desk in the dusky gray winter sunlight that reflected off the East River and filtered in through the wall-length, floor-to-ceiling window behind her. It was good light for thinking.

Absently opening the bottom right-hand drawer of her teak desk, she reached in almost without looking, plucked out a handful of Catherine Ward composites, and fanned the five-by-eight cards across the desk-top, head shots facing up. She leaned over them for a long time, looking not so much *at* them as through them, through them and into the future, beyond today or tomorrow or next week or next month . . . even beyond next year. Then, still locked in her trance, she reached down and, with the long, tapered, crimson-painted nail of the little finger of her right hand, deftly flipped the bottom card so all of them, all but one, turned over in a single row like wafer-thin dominoes. The one, the top card, teetered on its edge for what seemed to Mary an impossible time before falling back face up. Mary smirked. How prophetic, she thought, reaching out with stern deliberation and turning the card herself, punctuating its conformity with an ominous snap of its corner on the desk. There is always one part that resists control—one small part.

"I wonder what part of you resists control, my precious," Mary Cline asked out loud to a smiling Catherine Ward, who lounged at the water's edge in a stunning, royal blue, one piece, French-cut Joubert swimsuit. "I really wonder. And I wonder what will be the key to controlling that smooth, resistant part of you."

With Michelle Evans last year, it had been ego. *I mean, talk about balls! The kid's had outgrown her shorts.* But Mary had pricked them, all right. Michelle had thought Mary was working her too hard, overexposing her—which of course she was. But the nerve of the kid to think she knew the business better than Mary Cline! What could she tell poor, innocent, stupid little Michelle? "I know the shelf life of a model, dearie. Some types are more perishable than others. You've got a year of good use left, two at the outside. I'm using you up now because otherwise you'll rot on the vine." Well, of course she couldn't tell her that, because Michelle's ego wouldn't have accepted it. She wondered who had had to tell Mickey Mantle he was nearing the end. Who would tell Baryshnikov?

So Michelle Evans had walked, walked on Mary Cline. After three years of solid bookings and the promise of a good six months riding the crest, she had walked—walked when there was still a considerable piece of change to be earned because of Cline Models' investment in little Michelle; walked to, of all places, the Ford Agency, The Competition.

Well, Mary Cline just couldn't accept that. Not for a single, solitary minute. So she'd spent an entire day on the telephone. First she had called every last client who had upcoming bookings with Michelle Evans made through Cline Models and canceled them all. "We're just at our wits' end," she told them in a brief monologue she could have taped and simply played back several dozen times. "The girl is never, and I mean *never*, on time. One ad agency, who shall remain nameless, canceled her the other day after she kept them waiting for over two hours. By the time she finally did arrive, the other models had to leave for other bookings. Really, her attitude is appalling. After this latest episode, I'm thinking of letting her go entirely. I'll admit, she *is* good. After all, I discovered her," she said, only half in jest. "But talent can compensate for only so much. And I have my reputation to think of. Frankly, I've put up with it long enough. Let Eileen have her, or Zoli or Willy. Maybe Casablancas thinks he can deal with her. Good luck, I say. Anyway, enough of my problems with Michelle. I have this new girl, a real sweetheart, easy to work with, quite experienced but not overexposed. She's fresh, a relatively new face, a girl who's alive with enthusiasm. I just know you'll *adore* her. Shall I send her over?"

"Oh, you poor dear," they inevitably said with effusive sympathy. They knew how obstreperous top fashion models could be. And with Mary Cline putting the word out on one of her own models, the girl must be impossible. To a man, the clients were so thankful for the money they would save in models' fees, and the time on rescheduled shootings, that they welcomed Mary's suggestion of a new girl with open arms. After all, who knew the flesh market better? "Thank you, Mary, for your candor, and I'd love to see the new girl. No promises, you understand . . ." But in fact, they were so grateful, and Mary so keen a judge of their needs, that they almost always used the girl she sent.

After that initial barrage of calls, Mary had settled back and telephoned to arrange two weeks of lunch dates with ten of the most important and influential fashion people in town: the fashion editors at *Vogue, Mademoiselle,* and *Glamour* for starters; then the art directors at Gray Advertising, Young & Rubicam, Benton & Bowles, and Roberts & Young; and finally, the three most respected and booked photographers in town—Richard Avedon, Francesco Scavullo, and Gene Tillman. Well, there went the diet.

Each of the lunches, of course, centered around some current fashion topic of mutual interest, but at each Mary managed to drop an offhand bomb about Michelle Evans. Eight solid hours of phone calls and two weeks of lunches—not to mention three extra pounds—but it had all been worth it. By the time Mary Cline had washed down the last buttery mouthful of Tavern On The Green's famous mocha mousse pie, she had virtually guaranteed that Michelle Evans would never work another hour.

Mary Cline gathered up the handful of composites and put them back in her side drawer. She hoped it wouldn't come to that with Catherine Ward. But if it did, she had an idea how she might milk, rather than kill, the goose she had already set up to lay the next golden egg.

So here she was, late again, and Catherine wondered, was it something psychological? Some deep, dark secret out of her past that wasn't going to allow her to succeed? Something, like the fear of failure or perhaps even the fear of success, that would haunt her throughout her career? Or was it simply getting wasted just about every night of her life? All right, so it was *every* night of her life. So what? She owed herself that single, small pleasure, and what harm did it do her or anybody else? She could easily afford it, and of course she could quit any time she wanted—*if* she wanted, which she didn't.

Catherine heaved a deep, cathartic sigh as she kicked off her shoes, reached behind her back, and unzipped her navy blue Norma Kamali shift, letting it drop softly off her shoulders and to the floor in a single, graceful movement. Then she stopped short and thought for a moment.

As a rule, she didn't like to do it on the job, but there was no way she was going to make it otherwise today. Besides her throbbing headache, she felt the bloated nausea that accompanied the onset of her period. Wearing only panties and pantyhose, she reached into her purse and removed a small glass vial, popped off the plastic lid, tapped a tiny mound of powder into her palm, and dipped the fingernail of her pinky into the powder. Then she sucked one fingernailful into her left nostril, a second into her right nostril, and replaced the vial in her purse. Three or four brisk snorts and a shake of her head, and her brain had already begun to clear and the nausea to fade.

She rolled off her pantyhose and removed her panties. When she had donned her tiny white string bikini, she took a step back and regarded herself in the dressing table mirror. Not bad, after all, she decided. In fact she looked pretty damn good. She was a little too pale for swimwear, especially white swimwear, but otherwise . . .

She turned half-profile to the left, dropped her chin an inch or two, and with her teeth slightly apart and her mouth closed, sucked in her cheeks enough to accentuate the arc that fell from cheekbone to jawbone, affecting the gaunt look so popular among models. She wet her lips in a half-smile/half-sneer. It was her "look."

"Oh, excuse me." Billie Devlin had entered the tiny dressing room unannounced. "I didn't realize you were already here. The others are just arriving." Billie was glad that she had spoken to LeeAnn about the girl's lateness yesterday; Catherine was on time today. As it was, she was twenty minutes early. Billie casually tossed a single sheet of paper onto the makeup-cluttered dressing table "Here's the script, in case you want to re-familiarize yourself with the lines." *God, what I'd give for that body,* Billie Devlin thought enviously—*or that face.* But to have them both? Christ, it wasn't fair. She wondered what it must be like to be Catherine Ward. *Easy,* Billie thought. *With those looks and half a brain . . . Life must be so incredibly easy for her.* "Can you be ready in ten minutes?"

Catherine nodded.

"I'll have someone give you a holler," Billie said as she spun on her heels and left, closing the door behind her.

Alone again, the flush of embarrassment at having narrowly escaped being caught doing drugs drained from Catherine's pallid face. She busied herself folding her underwear and hanging her dress on a satin clothes-hanger on an empty clothing rack along the side wall. How could she be ten minutes early, she wondered, when she had thought she was forty-five minutes late? She must be living right. Either that or she was even more fucked up this morning than she'd realized.

"I've had two recent complaints about your tardiness, Catherine," Mary Cline had told her just last week. "It's not that difficult to be on time, dear. Not for the money we're being paid. Try setting your alarm an hour earlier. Go to bed an hour earlier. Party less. At two thousand dollars a day, you can't afford *not* to be on time, and clients certainly can't be expected to pay the other models, photographers, and everyone else involved in a shooting to sit on their hands waiting for you. You do a beautiful job, Catherine. Clients are unanimous on that. But if you establish a reputation as being difficult, it will be hard to erase, and you could compromise a brilliant future. If for any reason you feel you can't make it to a particular booking, let me know well in advance and I'll send someone else."

"No. I'm sorry." Mary's final sentence cut with the subtle but unmistakably sharp edge of a crystal clear threat: *Tell me you want off the gravy train, and we'll toss you off—without even slowing down. Because you're just a passenger, kid. Make no mistake. I'm in the driver's seat. You're just along for the ride.*

It was the first hint of hostility Mary Cline had ever displayed toward Catherine, and it had frightened her. She had looked down to see gooseflesh crawling up along her forearms, standing the soft, downy hairs on end. "I'll do my best to see it doesn't happen again."

But that had been just last week, and already LeeAnn had had to call her yesterday; even then Catherine just wasn't able to get out of bed—until she'd had a little pick-me-up. And today? Today she'd just lucked out. LeeAnn must have said 10:30, though Catherine would have sworn she'd said 9:30. It was certainly fortunate she'd misunderstood.

Catherine pinched the bridge of her nose between thumb and forefinger, took a deep breath, exhaled slowly, and walked calmly into the studio, bare feet slapping on the cold linoleum floor. She hoped today's guy was better than Mark. He was beginning to get on her nerves.

*   *   *

It was LeeAnn Schneider who had received Billie Devlin's irate and upsetting telephone call the previous day.

"She kept us waiting for almost an hour, LeeAnn. Out-of-pocket expenses alone—models, photographer, the whole deal—cost us over a thousand dollars. At this rate we won't be able to afford her."

"I'm very sorry, Billie. Catherine has always been so reliable." It wasn't true, of course—not recently, anyway. If Mary found out about this there'd be hell to pay. Jesus Christ, what was the matter with the girl? "I assure you, Billie, it won't happen again."

The second she hung up, LeeAnn buzzed Thelma Preble. "Thelma, would you please come to my office for a moment?"

"The phones are ringing off the hook out here," Thelma Preble said urgently.

"Let Doris and Nancy handle them for a few minutes. I want to speak with you . . . now."

"Sure thing, Boss," Thelma Preble said respectfully, for LeeAnn Schneider *was* the boss. This place could run just fine without me, Thelma thought as she scuttled her squat frame down the thickly carpeted hallway. And it could run without Doris and Nancy and all the other managers and bookers and secretaries. It could even run without Mary and Albert Cline. Mary Cline had the name and the connections and the influence, all right. But the business couldn't *run* without the person whom, in the Clines' absence, they referred to as "Boss." It couldn't *run* without LeeAnn Schneider. Not for a month, not for a week, perhaps not even for a day. It would be utter chaos.

Thelma just wished that LeeAnn knew it, or if she did, that she had the guts to act on it, to break away—to go with Ford or to L.A. with Nina Blanchard, both of whom were constantly after her, and probably for more money—or, better yet, to start her own agency. She could do it. Of that, Thelma hadn't the least doubt. LeeAnn was a keen judge of what look was right for the agency, for the times. She had a sense for the right fit of model to client, and she had a head for money. But most of all, she had something that was sadly lacking in this business. She had compassion. If she ever did leave, Thelma Preble would follow her without a moment's hesitation. But LeeAnn would never leave. There was something that kept her tied here—either insecurity or some misguided sense of loyalty to the Clines, those tyrants.

"Close the door," LeeAnn said as Thelma huffed in. "It's about Catherine Ward," she began dourly.

231

"Problems?" asked Thelma. "She wasn't late again?"

LeeAnn nodded. "I want her to be told an hour early for every in-town booking, morning or afternoon. And I want her to be phoned at her apartment two hours before that. You're busy, so I'll take care of it myself today. There shouldn't be a problem when she's booked out of town because all the client has to do is knock on her door. We'll get her to jobs on time if it kills her—or us."

"What'll we do when she catches on?"

"When she catches on, maybe she'll realize we're doing it for her own—and our own—good. If she doesn't," LeeAnn said with a twin-kle in her eye, "then we'll just have to think of something a little bit more devious, won't we?"

Thelma Preble smiled. "I'll see that it's done, Boss."

"You know I don't like it when you call me that."

"I know."

LeeAnn watched as the stumpy little woman scurried out the door and down the hall toward the insistent jangling of telephones.

14

"Slate!"

"What is this, my sixth try? And you still don't know my name?"
The cameraman fixed him with a surly stare.

"Okay. Sorry. Lynell Alan." He paused, took a deep breath, cocked
his head slightly, and began reading from the off-camera cards. "Listen, I don't pretend to know *everything* that pleases even *one* woman.
They're too complex." Each time he wondered if he was being too animated. "But I do know *one* thing that pleases *every* woman." Or
speaking too slowly. "Clean, soft, *sexy* hair. The kind of hair I get with
. . ." As he reached for the bottle, he swept it neatly from the table
with the back of his hand. Glass and viscous, cream-colored liquid
splattered across the floor. The sound of the bottle cap spinning on the
tile magnified the sudden silence.

"Cut!"

"*Every* woman," he continued with proper pacing, as though the
camera were still rolling, "likes plastic bottles." He looked over his
shoulder at the slim, string bikini-clad blonde who had stopped in her
tracks.

She laughed a tension-breaking laugh. "I'm wearing a path in this
floor."

"And that's about all you're wearing," he countered, tapping the
ash from an invisible cigar.

"Let's call it a day, gang." Billie Devlin swung toward the studio door. "Lynell, could I please speak with you for a minute in my office?"

He turned to the blonde again. "It was nice knowing you, Cathy." His voice carried a level, fatalistic finality.

She nodded as he followed Billie Devlin from the room.

"That was pretty bad, Lyn." The office was modern, with a panoramic view of a sunny winter day in New York.

"You're being kind. It was abysmal."

"I know you can put it together. You're very convincing on camera. We just have to clean up the technical part: picking up the bottle, keeping the label visible. The pacing and facial gestures are natural, and you and Cathy interact beautifully. You're not nervous, are you?"

"No. I should be. I'm sorry. I should have been more prepared. I didn't get a whole lot of sleep last night—a bit of premature celebrating."

"Well, you've got all weekend to recover. Monday morning is a go. I want you to be good, Lyn." She thought of Mary Cline. "I'll be honest with you, though. We're testing another man—a young, scrubbed, collegiate type. We're going to test-market both of you at scale. I've told Cathy she's going to be the prop for both of you. She's experienced and she's good. I'm not trying to put any more pressure on you than there already is. I just want to be fair."

"I appreciate that, Ms. Devlin." He felt vaguely uneasy with the formality. She was no older than he, perhaps a year or two younger.

She must have felt it, too. "Please . . . call me Billie." She stood and extended her hand. "Good luck, Lyn. See you Monday at ten."

Catherine Ward was waiting in the lobby when he stepped from the elevator. He almost didn't recognize her, dressed now as she was for winter. She grimaced as though in pain and shook her head slowly as he approached. "Ever done a TV commercial before?"

"Another critic," he joked. "That Gillette ad I got dinged on last summer was my first audition. This was exactly my second. What did you think?"

"I think I'd better give you some pointers."

"You'd do that for me?"

"No, I'd do that for me."

His look was a question.

"I know I'm not a casting director, but I've been around." Her concentration seemed to lapse for a moment as the association of "been

234

around" and sultry summer nights in Iowa crossed her mind. Then, almost visibly, she shook her head from the reminiscence. "Mark just doesn't have it compared to you. Not on this one."

He was almost afraid to ask. "Mark?"

"The competition? Mid-twenties? Blond? Built? Gorgeous? Mark!"

"Thanks, I needed that. And what, pray tell, makes me so great compared to him?" he asked as they walked into the bustling lunchtime crowd of a brisk sunny afternoon.

"Nothing. You stink. But I happen to think you're the image that'll sell this stuff."

"You do," he stated, without sounding at all convinced.

"Yeah. If you can somehow learn to talk and pick up a bottle at the same time."

"All right, so I don't know what the hell I'm doing and the only reason I wasn't nervous is because I'm too tired to be nervous." He stopped in front of a Burger and Brew Restaurant. "Want to grab a sandwich?"

"Sure."

"So what's in it for you? Either way you work. You got stock in the company?"

"What's in it for me is: the way I've got it figured, I'm *in* with you or Mark, right?"

"Right."

"Well, I also have it figured that I'm *out* with you or Mark, too."

He looked across the table quizzically, as the waiter approached.

"Small chef's salad and tea," she said before he asked.

"Same," Lynell agreed, barely having heard what she had ordered. "Go on."

"They'll decide on you or Mark and then tape the ads for the minor markets. If the shampoo does well there, they'll move into the bigger markets. Then maybe another ad. The more they sell, the longer they'll keep churning out the ads. It could be a career. When they decide to dump the campaign or maybe even Now Shampoo altogether, I'll get dumped, too. They won't keep the same old broad and hire a new guy. They'll make a clean sweep." She shrugged. "They always do."

"Got it all figured," he nodded, unabashedly impressed. As the waiter served them, Lynell noticed the man's eyes jump quickly from Cathy's chest to her face as she thanked him. Sure, he would be impressed with her striking looks. Any man would be. He thought of her in that string bikini—breathtaking. But he had worked with many

235

breathtaking women. At the moment he was far more impressed with her brains.

"Yeah, I've got it all figured. And the way I've got it figured is: I'm going to ride *your* coattails to fame and fortune."

"Glad to be of service. So, Professor Higgins, where do we begin?"

"Well, Eliza . . ."

Oh, yes, this was some woman.

By 7:00 A.M. Monday, he had been up for an hour, had a light breakfast with Aimée, been unable to coax her back to bed before showering, and settled down with the morning paper, a dry towel wrapped around his waist. He was sure the telephone was not for him.

"Hello." He managed to sound put out, not wanting to give the impression that seven was an appropriate time to call.

"Hello, Lyn? This is Billie Devlin. We've had to change our plans a bit."

His heart sank. Who was it who'd said, "It ain't over 'til it's over?" Shit, was it over already? "Oh?"

"Tom Deloria—our photographer?" She identified him, though Lynell had his name and exasperated expression etched in his memory from half a dozen botched takes three days ago. "He decided the studio won't work, so we're going right to the proposed location. We've already called to book you and the other models for three days. Any problem with that?"

"Not as far as I'm concerned."

"Sorry to call you so early, but we're on a 10:00 A.M. flight from La Guardia. Want to catch the last light in Sarasota."

"Super."

"See you at nine-thirty at the Pan Am terminal. I'll have the tickets."

"Do I need to bring anything?"

"Just your toothbrush."

So, he would meet gorgeous Mark. Head-to-head competition. He was surprised at his own excitement over the impending confrontation. One-on-one was rare in this business. The usual cattle call was strictly impersonal, sometimes as many as two dozen men vying for a single job, waiting for someone to look at their books or to tape them delivering a single line, knowing that a few hours later two dozen more would be waiting in the same room, and maybe two dozen more after that. It was difficult for him to feel a sense of "me against you" when the opponent was so overwhelming and impersonal.

But one-on-one was different. It elevated Lynell's level of intensity to a crescendo, leaving a numb tingling in his chest. There was no denying it, no holding it back. Three years in the business—the interminable rounds and go-sees, the unrelenting rejection, the sacrifices, the degradation—and it all came down to this: his "big chance." Adrenaline pumped through his veins. When he heard the shower splash alive behind him, the energy heightened. Without thinking, he stood and crossed the room, unwrapped the towel from his waist as he walked through the open door of the bathroom, and stepped into the shower, his excitement now obvious.

"Lyn," Aimée protested lamely, the truncating of his name and her frown giving way to a wry smile as she looked down at him. "Boy, are you greedy. Who was that on the phone?"

"Billie Devlin. I'm going to Florida for three days—location," he answered, reaching for her, pulling her close.

"Lyn . . . I don't have much time."

"This won't take long."

As the cab pulled up to the curb, Lynell crouched, ready to jump out and run into the lobby to buzz Catherine's apartment. The familiar neighborhood reminded him of the first time he had been here two days ago. "Would you mind terribly if I called you Catherine?" he had asked sheepishly.

"My father called me Catherine." A faraway look had darkened her face, like a cloud crossing the sun.

"But I'll call you Cathy if that's what you like," he had said quickly, feeling like a burglar breaking into dreams.

"No . . . Catherine . . . I'd like that."

His hand was poised on the door latch of the cab, but she was already waiting on the corner. "Sorry I'm late," he said as he slid across the seat and took her bag. He was surprised it was so small for a three-day trip—smaller than his, in which all he carried were his warm-weather running clothes and his shaving kit. Aimée would have brought every suitcase she owned.

"That's okay. I was enjoying the sunshine."

"Yeah, wouldn't you know it," he began, as the cab sped into the flow of traffic. "We're going off to Florida, and it gets sunny and warm in New York. Never fails." He leaned forward and glanced sideways at her. Their eyes met. He was barely conscious that his right profile was his best—that he was, even now in the backseat of a cab careening through midtown Manhattan, "going for his angles," reproducing his "look." Suddenly the artificiality of it embarrassed him and he straightened, smiled genuinely, and patted her denimed knee. "Thanks for the other day."

"Hey, it helped me, too," she said with a wink. "We'll knock 'em dead."

The ride to La Guardia was quiet—not the kind of quiet where they couldn't think of anything to say, but a thoughtful quiet, a quiet of both reflection and anticipation, comfortable and symbiotic.

Saturday she had given him the confidence it would take to do his best. By day's end he was sure he had known Catherine Ward for a long time, and though he knew precious little about her, he experienced an empathy with a distant sorrow in her which he couldn't quite identify.

Her ashen, colorless face had greeted him at the door. "You're early." She pushed the door open for him and stepped back.

"A little. Should I come back later?"

"No. Put on some coffee." She crossed her feet, extended her arms parallel to the floor, and arched her back in a groaning, stretching yawn that was for him somehow a religious experience. A sense of betrayal rose in him as his eyes sought the dark swath through her translucent nightgown, the liquid undulation of her breasts when she snapped herself back from her yawn. Knuckling her eyes, she turned and walked toward her bedroom. He didn't look, though he wanted to, the temptation strangely not rooted in sexual desire but in a vague longing to be closer to her in some indescribable way. She was like a child not yet grown into her body and totally unaware of its awesome power to enthrall.

"Will I be able to find everything?"

"I understand you're a college graduate," she called groggily. "You'll figure it out."

Ten minutes later she shuffled barefoot into the kitchen, wearing Levi's and a black sweatshirt with "IOWA" stenciled in gold across the front. After placing two insulated mugs on the table, along with sugar, cream, and spoons, she sat across from him and rested her forehead in the palm of one hand.

"You feeling all right?" he asked with genuine concern. For a beautiful young woman, she looked terrible.

"I'll live. Just a little headache. To much partying."

They exchanged basic backgrounds over coffee: home towns—Morgan City, Iowa and Pine Orchard, Connecticut; educations—too little

238

and too much; parents—neither living and both living; and other cocktail party conversation. Then he helped her set up her Polaroid home video system.

"It was expensive but it has earned its keep. Besides, my accountant told me it was a write-off."

"Good advice," he agreed. "I used to be an accountant."

"No!"

He nodded slowly. "Would I lie about something as embarrassing as that?"

She laughed. "You just don't look at all like an accountant."

"Thank you."

They practiced their scene for two hours. After a light lunch and a glass of chablis, Catherine went to her bedroom. She reappeared wearing a bikini that Lynell immediately judged to be, if possible, smaller than the one she'd worn the day before at the studio. "Take off your shirt," she ordered as she padded to him.

"You expect me to concentrate with you dressed like that?"

"Monday I'll be dressed like this and you won't be wearing a shirt." She stood on her tiptoes and kissed his cheek lightly, platonically. "Loosen up. You're all tense." She shook his shoulders, started to unbutton his shirt. "You're a nice guy, Lynell—not like the egotistical jerks I work with all the time—and I have faith in you as a professional. Now, let's get into this, let's enjoy it, and let's do it right."

They practiced until, by three o'clock, the tapes showed that his delivery had passed through the point of natural nonchalance and back toward the mechanical. But it *had* been there. Catherine's performance, he noted with grudging respect, was evenly believable.

"I think we've got it," she announced, laughing. "I feel kind of guilty. Poor Mark won't know what hit him. But . . . I'm just protecting my own ass, right?" He watched as she turned and headed toward her room again, and he had to shake his head. The kid really was awesome, even from behind, with legs that were never-ending and skin on the backs of her thighs that was as smooth and shiny as the surface of a pond on a windless day.

"And it's definitely worth protecting," he said kiddingly, raising his eyebrows in unison as his father always did when a pretty girl passed them on the street.

"Men!"

He slipped on his shirt and went into the bathroom. When he came out, he wanted to ask her about the bloody tissues in the wastebasket that hadn't been there at lunchtime, wanted to ask her about the speckles of dried blood on the sink. He recalled the conversation he'd overheard at Bloomingdale's between Craig Burton and Jason Wexler. Concern suddenly flooded over him but was beaten back by the guilt of a discovery he hadn't had the right to make.

As he left her at her door, he took her chin in his hand, touching it as lightly as though appraising a priceless Rodin. It was smooth, hard, and as surprisingly cold as the bust of some long-dead martyr. "Take care of yourself, Catherine. Get some rest. I owe you. And if I can ever return the favor . . ." He let the words trail off.

She nodded absently. "Lynell? On camera? With Mark? I'll give it my best."

"Of course you will." He turned and started down the narrow hallway, stopped, and looked back to where she stood, her eyes still following him. "And Catherine? Thanks."

"I've got it," he said as the cab pulled up at the Pan Am terminal. The meter read $7.75. He handed the cabbie a ten.

When they reached the double doors, she turned to him. "Don't be intimidated by this guy, Lynell. He's beautiful, but he hasn't got what you've got." She clenched her fist for emphasis.

"I know. He hasn't got you." Her confidence swelled in him. When he saw Mark, he needed all that and more.

The name was different, but the face was the same—a few years older, maybe, but very much the same. Lynell Alan saw it across a sea of faces, across a sea of years. As he drifted with the tide of humanity, the distance narrowed by strides between Lynell Alan and the bottom of his life.

"I'm so glad you could make it . . ."

"Lynell," he filled in, when the young man couldn't come up with a name. "I enjoyed the play very much; and you were great," he added sincerely. The small, dimly-lit dressing room was bustling with other bit players, male and female, and it seemed to Lynell that they all stopped their immodest clothing changes, boisterous conversation, and drinking to check out the latest conquest.

The young actor sensed Lynell's anxiety and quickly swiped a liter of wine from the table. "Let's find someplace quieter." Lynell flinched at the touch of the stranger's hand on his elbow as he led him from the crowded room to another so small and dark that Lynell at first thought it was a walk-in closet. "Not much for the headliner, eh?" the young man asked as he lit a candle on the tiny dressing table. "He won't even use it. Changes at his hosts' house down at the shore."

Lynell took a seat at the opposite end of the threadbare couch from the young actor. He had no idea what he was doing there, and a bottle of burgundy and two joints didn't help him decide. When the handsome young man finally slid close to him and placed his hand gently on Lynell's thigh, the specter of an adolescent boy years ago appeared before him, wiping away the recent memory of his two abysmal failures with women.

"Remember what I said when we met today on the beach," the young man said. " 'Don't knock it until you try it.' "

"I can't." Lynell, suddenly frightened, stood so abruptly he knocked over the small table, sending his glass of wine splashing into the young man's lap. "Oh, I'm sorry," Lynell said, taking several swipes at the stain on the young man's thigh before pulling his hand away as though he had been scalded.

The young man laughed.

"I'm sorry," he said. "I just can't." And he left in confusion.

But that had been three years ago and this was now, and Lynell composed himself as he stepped up to greet the embodiment of his demon, a demon that still haunted his dreams.

"Good morning, Lyn, Cathy."

"Hi, Billie."

"Cathy, you know Mark, of course."

"Of course," Mark answered quickly for both of them. Lynell was unable to identify the look that passed between the beautiful pair.

"Mark, this is Lyn Alan. Lyn, Mark Collins."

They shook hands and their eyes met, and Lynell Alan couldn't decide if he was more hurt or more relieved that the young man didn't remember him. Carl Howard, Mark Collins—Lynell would have known him if it had been a hundred years ago.

"Sorry we had to do this all together," Billie Devlin was saying, "but . . . expenses."

"Sure," said Mark Collins/Carl Howard.

"No problem," Lynell Alan nodded, and the competitive spirit redoubled in him. He didn't have the still-perfect body, which actually never had been *perfect*. He didn't have that straight, golden, wind-blown-without-wind hair, or the perfectly chiseled features and thin, straight nose. But Lynell Alan's soft features were augmented by something intangible from within. He played to the crowd that gathered daily around the shooting, at first and last light, on Longboat Key's endless white sand. And he played to Catherine Ward. With each take he was aware only of her, of the growing knowledge that he loved her—was not *in love* with her, didn't suppress a deep sexual passion for her. It was different from that, more than that: he cared for her, was grateful for what she had done for him, for his self-confidence. He did not *want* her, only wanted *for* her. He saw the fragile spirit that danced in her eyes, wanted to help her, to be her friend, to lower the curtain of suspicion, to help her lift even the smallest burdens of her life, and perhaps the biggest. She was as delicately exquisite as a butterfly. But he sensed that, like the butterfly, that perfection of form and detail masked some violent metamorphosis that had only covered its ugly past with a beautiful veneer. Its freedom was its beauty, and to try to capture it would be to destroy it.

The afternoon sun had returned the color to Catherine's cheeks, and she was stunning even before the ninety-minute makeup job. She was perfection with him and she was wonderful with Mark, too. But with Mark it was a technical perfection—perfection the chemistry between her and Lynell rose above.

"Listen," Lynell said to the lens as he waded into the warm Gulf waters that gently lapped the beach, soaking the cuffs of his slacks, "I don't pretend to know *everything* that pleases even *one* woman." His eyes then drifted slowly, languorously, to a beautiful, bikini-clad young woman, who returned his stare as she walked toward him, ten feet above the water line. His eyes continued to follow her, over his shoulder, as she walked past him. Then he looked back at the lens. But for him it wasn't there. He was speaking confidentially, personally, to John Hayes, who, of all the men Lynell knew, most needed the advice. "But I *do* know *one* thing that pleases *every* woman . . ."

The woman, a stranger, had backtracked and quietly walked up behind him, reaching around to press his chest with an open palm, running her other hand through his curls as she clung passionately to him. "Clean, soft, *sexy* hair," she purred, her exquisite face in view above his shoulder.

Still facing the lens, he turned his head to his left shoulder. (His right profile was his best angle, so Billie had placed Catherine to his left. With Mark, he'd noticed, they had tried each side, as both his profiles were perfect.) His heart raced as Catherine's lips brushed his cheek. "The kind of hair I get with Now Shampoo," he offered, looking again at John Hayes.

"With Now Shampoo," she cooed, "I'd follow him *anywhere*."

If he'd been wearing a shirt, Catherine's "anywhere" would have steamed out every wrinkle.

He grinned at John Hayes and shrugged lightly as though he couldn't believe his own fantastic luck. Living the illusion, he *was* the illusion. He was charm. He was charisma.

"Cut! Beautiful!" Polite applause sprang from the crowd that reappeared with the cool sand under his feet and the orange sun sizzling into the Gulf horizon: the surroundings that reappeared with reality.

They shot again Wednesday morning, not willing to waste the good light, though Billie Devlin was secure in the knowledge that she already had what she wanted. Early in the afternoon, finishing a lazy, five-mile run on the beach (abbreviated in a concession to the unaccustomed heat), Lynell smiled to himself through another flashback as he strolled toward an introspective Mark Collins, sitting alone on a Colony Beach & Tennis Resort beach towel.

"Excuse me."

"Oh, hi." It was miraculous how someone who was so obviously feeling badly could look so good.

" 'Man of La Mancha,' North Shore Summer Theater, 1979."

Mark paused, frowned, shook his beautiful head, hair like corn silk dancing on the wind. Then he laughed softly. "I thought maybe you'd forgotten. The name change and all," he added, betraying no discernible emotion.

"I *have* forgotten. It's just taken a long time. But I *have* forgotten."

Mark Collins broke the long, uneasy silence. "You really blew me away, man. Jesus, you and Cathy looked like you were going to climb inside each other. Everybody on the whole goddamn beach had their tongues hanging out. It even turned *me* on."

"Thanks. Catherine's very good. I thought it went pretty well. But you and she were just as good," Lynell offered magnanimously.

"Yeah, but you two were the money."

"Well, we're comfortable together, I guess. I've worked with Catherine before. Anyway, who knows, a TV audience could very well like yours better." He stood and clapped the younger man's shoulder, warm and smooth, and when Mark looked up at him, the incredible good looks caught his breath and he wished that somehow they could be friends. But the unrelenting competition would probably preclude that. He patted Mark's shoulder. "Take it easy."

"Yeah," Mark nodded. "Thanks."

* * *

243

Billie Devlin arranged a table for herself and the three models at dinner. "I want to discuss use of the commercial prints, residuals, and future tapings—if the client likes either or both final prints."

The familiarity Mark shared with both women made Lynell uneasy, and he had the growingly anxious feeling that he was about to be cut out again.

"Oh, I'm sorry, Lynell," Catherine apologized when he saw her to her room. "I guess it's just because we've all worked together before."

"I feel like a jealous little boy," he said abashedly.

She reached up and kissed his cheek fondly. "You are."

Billie Devlin knew what the two tapes would show. Her experienced eye rolled the finished print across her eyelids, and Lynell Alan, chin tilted slightly downward, right profile a shade toward camera, smiled winningly into the lens as a warm Gulf breeze riffled through his soft curls.

"This can't change anything," she said before the rush came on her. "It'll be the client's decision in the end." Then she finished sucking the fine white powder into her nostril, pinched the bridge of her nose, and pulled upward, clearing the passages with several short sniffles.

"No sweat," Mark Collins said as he lowered himself over her. By the time he got back to New York he'd have made eight thousand dollars on this shooting, plus another six thousand (tax free) on the coke he'd deliver to Billie for her cronies. Not a bad week's work. And he had a callback on that off-Broadway audition next week. He couldn't care less about Now Shampoo, he convinced himself.

He eased into her slowly, the way she liked it. This was the part of the service he could do without. She was thick-waisted, heavy-hipped, and unappealing, but it was a tacit part of the deal by now. He thought again of Lynell Alan and reached to snap off the bedside lamp. "Don't give it another thought," he said. "The best man will win."

The tingle was on her and Billie Devlin moaned involuntarily. Mark Collins had maybe the best toot in town, and without a doubt the best body. "I'm not so sure of that," she whispered.

Carl Howard made every effort to keep his two careers separate. Three years ago he had decided to adopt the name "Mark Collins" for use exclusively in modeling. He thought of himself first and foremost as an actor and considered nothing else as demeaning as having compromised himself to "do some modeling" to keep the wolves away from the door between acting jobs. In fact, though financially rewarding beyond his dreams, modeling had brought more wolves *to* his door than it had kept away. And the money had been so easy it had in many ways seduced him from his true passion. He had no feeling for modeling, other than for fat paychecks, and he often wondered if he would have "been somewhere" as an actor were it not for the seduction of that easy money.

He also lamented that he was simply a high-priced whore—just using his face *and* his body to make money. Maybe it would have been better to have been poor and happy and proud of his craft. But it was almost too late for that.

He used to enjoy both sexes but had grown to enjoy neither. And it had nothing to do with morals or scruples. When at eighteen he'd had to perform fellatio on the casting director to land his first professional acting role ("Your first taste of the theater," the fat old queen had quipped when it was over), he had done it because he had known that if he didn't someone else would, and all he had to do was get *that role* and he'd be on his way to stardom. And when he'd had to service the leading lady, a fading has-been as old as his grandmother, in order to keep the part, he'd accepted that, too, because living that part, even for his three minutes on stage, made it all worthwhile.

Then he'd been hired for his first big modeling job through the same "willingness," and it had been demeaning because all he had gotten in return was money. And even though he was continually passed over in acting auditions, often with the rationale that he was "too handsome to be taken seriously as an actor," he still focused his energy on acting, attending workshops, reading for anyone who would listen, and accepting bit parts in underbudgeted productions, often sacrificing high-paying modeling jobs for a chance at his big break, a break that never came.

Sex, too, like modeling, was nothing to him now—simply a means to an end. He had once prided himself on being able to get it up for any*one*, and any*time*, but now he agonized that it might never again have any real meaning or enjoyment for him, as it once had—that it might never again be exciting and pleasurable for him, as it once was.

And then there had come the "moving" of drugs—as he liked to think of it—and now he feared that life itself might never again be as exciting and pleasurable for him as it had once been. All he needed now was enough money to get out. Then a role, just a small one to show what he could do, and he'd have his life back.

* * *

245

In the morning Lynell called Aimée at her office from his room at the Colony Beach & Tennis Resort. "It was fantastic," he said enthusiastically. "I was fantastic."

"I'm so happy for you, Lynell."

"I'll be home by eight."

At nine they sat down to a candlelight dinner, and Lynell wrote her a postdated check for eight hundred dollars, which represented twenty percent of his four-day earnings (which he was overwhelmed to receive a mere three weeks later).

"I don't even want ten percent and now you give me twenty," Aimée protested.

"The agency gets twenty percent and you've done more for me than they have."

She shook her head slowly in resignation.

"Anyway, it'll all go to the same place, and you're much better with money than I am."

"That's for sure!" But she was thinking, *It'll all go to the same place.*

The following Monday, Lynell and Catherine—with Mark conspicuously absent—sat before a studio monitor with Billie Devlin and two business suits named Wiecker and Thompson: the former, president of Roberts & Young Advertising; the latter, head of the cosmetics division of Textron, Inc., which owned Now Shampoo. The small group was tensely viewing the twelfth consecutive running of the final edition of the past week's performance. Lynell proudly admitted to himself that he wouldn't have changed it by a single frame. And Catherine, in silent confirmation, squeezed his hand where it anxiously gripped the armrest between them.

"It will be some time before we test-market the product," one of the business suits announced when the lights in the small studio snapped on. "But you've all done a class-A job."

Lynell Alan was back at Arthur Young & Company, and who was he kidding if he doubted that executives would always run his life— and not necessarily these executives but executives above them and more above those and . . .

"Just sit tight on this thing for a while. I'd think twice before doing any other shampoo commercials. As a matter of fact, I'd get approval for anything cosmetic. The potential is definitely there. If this thing works out, we have tentative plans for follow-up productions in San Francisco and Honolulu . . . for starters. But don't get your hopes up," the business suit went on. "You know the program, kids. First we've got to see how it plays in Peoria."

If Lynell had some inner conviction that Now Shampoo would launch him to instant fame, he was to be crushingly disappointed. In the months that followed, it seemed he worked, if anything, less rather than more than he had before the Now shooting. On his dutiful rounds the majority of potential clients still turned him away rudely, and he began to doubt whether the commercial would ever make the New York market, and wonder whether it might be pulled completely before he made more than small change on residuals from the minor markets or, indeed, whether he'd ever actually see a bottle of Now Shampoo on a drugstore shelf.

On the infrequent days when Catherine was in town and not working, she was kind enough to accompany him on rounds. "You can never make too many contacts in this business," she said, but he knew and deeply appreciated that she did it mainly for him. For his part, Lynell's punctuality kept Catherine on time and, coincidentally— since he was unaware of the problem—in Mary Cline's good graces.

On those days he was up with Aimée at seven and at Catherine's door by eight. While she showered, put on her makeup, and got dressed, Lynell brewed the coffee and virtually committed the *New York Times* sports section to memory. When Catherine was ready, as often as not with Lynell encouraging her with an occasional time check, they planned their day over a cup of coffee—her first of half a dozen she would have throughout the morning, his third and last, after a cup with Aimée and another with the sports section.

"I should get you one of those automatic coffee-makers," he said one morning. "You know, the ones you set up and program the time the night before, so the coffee's all made when you get up?"

"What do I need one of them for?" Catherine asked with a shrug. "When I have you."

Catherine rarely had an entire day without a booking, and eventually even on those days when she had one, Lynell would arrive at her apartment early and accompany her to the studio to begin his inevitable litany of rejections there. "One place is as good as another to start the day," he explained, but in fact they had both come to enjoy their morning ritual.

Lynell might not have worked at all that spring and summer of 1982 had it not been for Catherine. As it was, people who had turned him away without a look invited him in when he was with Catherine Ward, and he saw what it was to be in demand, how unbelievable it was to be in such demand that she could pick and choose. And it seemed that every client who could afford her wanted *her* to choose *them*. And if they paid far more attention to her—in spite of her attempts to divert that attention to him ("This is my friend, Lynell Alan. He's also with Cline. Take a look through this fantastic book.")—at least they looked, no matter how quickly, and even though it was only as a favor to her, at least they looked.

"Close" wasn't just a word for Lynell, it was a condition. It was a condition that kept him always on the edge: on the edge of a career, on the edge of self-respect, on the edge of friendship, on the edge of love. There always seemed to be something missing and it was missing from every part of his life. And if it was this business that dragged him through a painful wringer, then it dragged Aimée along with him.

He was down. He was way down. He had celebrated his thirty-second birthday a week ago, the 22nd of May, and here he was, nearly broke, schlepping through the rain with neither a job nor the hope of one, a seven-and-a-half-hour day of total rejection behind him, smiling wanly as he geared himself for one last stop, though why he bothered he wasn't quite sure. The name of the photographer he was looking for slipped his mind when "Benton & Bowles" jumped off the building directory and caught his eye. *Why not?* he asked himself, and he rode the elevator to the first of the three floors occupied by the advertising agency.

"I'm a model from Cline," he informed the receptionist, trying to make it sound as though it wasn't the twentieth time that day he'd made the announcement. "Can you direct me to the person who hires models?"

"That would be Mrs. Fine. She's up in the studio on the tenth floor."

First the Benton & Bowles sign that practically spoke to him as he scanned the directory, and now the empty studio waiting room with the tired-looking young woman bustling through. "Mrs. Fine will be right with you. They're in the middle of a test shooting. Scripts are on the table."

And he was up. He was way up. It was just a feeling he had. Call it fate. Call it intuition: that certain larger-than-life something that suddenly falls ominously across your path, like your own shadow on a winter afternoon.

He nervously snatched a script from the low table, tossed his portfolio into a chair, and began pacing, reading, memorizing. It was a short, 30-second spot. He was a quick study. Perfect: the young father. He was even dressed for the part, in khaki slacks and a plaid sport shirt. And he was ready. This time he was ready.

He set the script back on the table and delivered the lines from memory. " 'Morning, honey," he said brightly, lightly kissing the air that was her cheek. "Ooh," he cooed animatedly, looking down into the bassinet where his tiny son gurgled happily. At the same time he draped an arm possessively around Aimée's shoulder. "Johnson & Johnson's Baby Powder. Boy, little fella, you lucked into the right family," he continued with just the right pacing. "Your grandma used Johnson & Johnson's Baby Powder on your aunt and me when we were little babies." He reached down and tickled the infant playfully. "And she was the best mommy in the whole world." Then he looked up at Aimée in her Lantz nightgown and smiled adoringly. "Second best."

"Name?"

He was in another place, another time, lost in a happier life, a life it seemed would only be his in his imagination. "Lynell Alan."

Roberta Fine scanned her clipboard. "I don't have you listed."

"I'm from Cline," he blurted, hoping she'd be impressed.

"We don't have anyone booked from Cline," she said with an abrupt shake of her head. Roberta Fine, an unremarkable looking woman, was dressed casually and was, he guessed, younger than he.

It was fate, a soda fountain at Schwab's Drugstore, and he forged ahead undaunted, knowing this was his time, his place, his future. "I know the script cold. Just give me a chance."

Roberta Fine checked her watch. "It's 5:08. We can't afford the overtime."

He hated to do it, to lower himself, but it wasn't begging because she was going to relent, and that would make it so that it wasn't undignified and the word came out softly—slipped out, really. "Please." He looked her directly in the eye. "Just give me a chance."

She looked at him then and his eyes held hers for a long moment and he felt her softening, felt his belief in himself infecting her, and he knew he had her when she inhaled a deep breath and sighed. "Sorry," she said flatly, and when she walked out he stood alone in almost giddy disbelief at her callous rejection and it took several minutes for reality to overcome him, but when it did, he was down, unbelievably down, irretrievably down.

A depression-induced eating binge followed. It ended, after two weeks and ten pounds, when LeeAnn sent him to a print go-see for a new Jesse Jeans advertising campaign and he didn't get the job or even a chance to get the job, because no matter how he tugged and squeezed, he couldn't zip the standard size 32's over his bloated waist and behind. Then he punished himself with a series of ten- and fif-teen-mile runs and one meal a day of raw vegetables until he'd lost the ten pounds and a little more.

Whenever Catherine was back in town she called to take Lynell on rounds, and Aimée became so sick of hearing her name she could have screamed. "She gets you when you're up. I get you when you're down!"

But as jealous as Aimée was becoming of Catherine and the other beautiful young women Lynell worked with, it was at least matched by his growing envy of her career.

It seemed to Lynell that Aimée talked about nothing but her job, and it rankled him to hear about it because her success only served to remind him of his own growing sense of failure. "Mr. Stearns said the merger contract I drew up for The Talmadge Group was the cleanest he'd ever seen."

"Great," he acknowledged unenthusiastically from behind *A Tale of Two Cities.* Increasingly they ate dinner quietly in front of the tele-vision, and though on most nights they still made love, more and more it was mechanical missionary-position fare and he knew in his heart that she, too, sometimes faked it.

And Aimée also felt it slipping away. "Why" was floating around in the back of her brain, but unlike her inanimate contracts, she was un-able to connect its myriad parts into a simple, neat package.

Dozens of dinners on TV trays ran into one another in a dizzying swirl of pastel watercolors, like twenty-five years in a comfortable mar-riage. But one stood out. It was the day JFK was shot, only closer. It was the night they landed on the moon, only in color. It was 9:15 P.M. on a Friday, during a summer rerun of "Dallas." It was mesmerizing.

"I'd follow him *anywhere,*" the commercial finished, and Lynell broke from his hypnosis and yelled. "All *right!*" and kissed Aimée and ran to the telephone to call Catherine. "Did you see it? Channel 2. Just now. Just *now,*" he laughed, and a wrenching knot was being tied in Aimée's stomach and unconsciously she squeezed L.C. too hard and the cat squealed and jumped to the floor and Aimée wished they were back in Boston, he with her career and she with their baby.

The telephone didn't stop ringing for two days: his parents, his sis-ter, and friends—some of whom he hadn't heard from in years—all called to congratulate him. Within two weeks, even though they were in the midst of the usually slow summer season, Lynell's bookings had already tripled. People began double-taking when he passed them on the street. The commercial was taking off and it seemed *everyone* had seen it. Textron, Inc., the manufacturers of Now Shampoo, booked them for two more commercials in what was to become a series. The first was to be shot in San Francisco, the second in Hawaii with Diamond Head as a backdrop. He was ecstatic, though he couldn't help but wonder how long this flirtation with success would last.

It bothered Catherine's conscience not even the tiniest bit that she had, for reasons that weren't entirely clear to her, neither helped Mark Collins nor put in a good word for him, and in fact had effectively undermined his efforts to land the Now account. Not that she was presumptuous enough to think she had gotten Lynell the job. He had gotten it because his look was right for the product. All she had done was help him polish his technique and become familiar with the lines, with her. It had been a business decision, she told herself, and that was all. But although it didn't bother her conscience, it nagged at her nonetheless.

Perhaps it was that Lynell Alan was beginning to look as though he had every possibility of turning out to be as sleazy as she knew Mark Collins to be. It certainly had nothing whatever to do with the commercial's patent lack of success so far in its brief life. She was becoming ever more popular and heavily booked and had no need at all for Now Shampoo to insure the appreciation in the value of her own personal stock. Porsche and *Sports Illustrated* had already done that.

First Ken Rossini—who had previously brought Ferrari back into the American consciousness with a then-unknown model named Tom Selleck—macho, dominating, sexist Ken Rossini had reckoned that what Porsche needed to increase American sales of its top-of-the-line Carrera sports car was a woman in the driver's seat.

Then, after five years as the main attraction in *Sports Illustrated*'s controversial annual swimsuit issue, Cheryl Tiegs had gotten uppity in a well-publicized demand to be guaranteed an appearance on the cover of the issue before she would agree to the booking. *SI*, having declined for so-called artistic reasons, had hired Catherine to take her place. To Catherine's own amazed delight, she was not only used in more photographs than either the high-powered Carol Ault or the budding celebrity Christie Brinkley—a statistic of great importance to models and the only one taking precedence over how they actually look—but one of her shots was on the cover! The exposure—both literally and figuratively—was worth the spate of irate letters to the editor in the issues that followed, letters that impugned *Sports Illustrated*'s journalistic in-

251

tegrity only slightly more than they did Catherine's morality: "I discovered the March third issue of *Sports Illustrated* under my son's bed, where he had hidden it like any common girlie magazine. If I'd wanted him to be exposed to such filth, I'd have bought him a subscription to *Playboy* for his thirteenth birthday. . . ."

"Since when are half-naked women considered 'sports'?"

"Again the pigs who run *Sports Illustrated* have chosen to denigrate women. When will you put the female *athlete*, not the female *anatomy*, on your cover?"

"You and Miss Ward should be ashamed! I hereby cancel my subscription. . . ."

The staff at *SI* not only was unintimidated by the attacks, they actually seemed to enjoy basking warmly in the limelight of the withering criticism, preferring to print a vast majority of unfavorable letters, flaunting the if-you-don't-approve-then-we-don't-need-you attitude reserved only for the healthiest and most self-assured of publications. Indeed when she read the letters to Lynell on their flight to San Francisco, he informed Catherine, a non–sports-enthusiast, that he and many other of the *SI* faithful anticipated the vitriolic letters almost more than the photographs that spawned them.

Of course, *SI* did print a few positive letters as well, such as the one that said, "The vision of Catherine Ward wading into the ocean in a striped, French-cut bikini should be enough to keep me warm throughout the rest of the unending New England winter—but in case it's not, will you please print just one more shot of her?" Which request the magazine had obliged with a small photo out-take following the letter in the editorial section.

Another stated, "I've permanently marked the Seychelles islands on my wall map."

But after all the prior flap over what the issue would be without its star, the one Catherine cherished most asked simply, "Cheryl Who?"

The apparent inevitability of her professional success aside, it was in San Francisco that her doubts about her initial assessment of Lynell Alan's character first surfaced. Not that she deemed herself in any sense an appropriate judge of others' morality. But she knew what she liked—and didn't like. And she didn't like being made to feel like the middle-aged mother of a wayward teenage boy.

Rarely did a day pass at a location shooting when women didn't stray about the outskirts of a set—men, too, for that matter. There was something gloriously exciting, almost hypnotic, about the hum of a rolling camera that invited rubber-necking as surely as a fender-bender on a busy freeway. But there were always visitors who were there for more than a look, and male or female, by now she knew them the way she knew her cues, the way she knew her lines; indeed, the way she knew her own style.

There is a special technique to being a groupie, which requires a subtle distinction between aggressiveness and abrasiveness, and the two teenage girls who clung to their San Francisco troupe like abalone to a rock had honed it to an art. Lynell Alan, in his defense, didn't have a chance. Also, though it was a far weaker excuse, he *was* a man. So when, following the third long day of shooting, after having on successive days flattered his ego with a request for his autograph and doused his thirst with a soft drink during a break, the girls brazenly followed him back to the hotel, it shouldn't have surprised Catherine that he disappeared into his room with the alluring pair. That he subsequently pounded out a resounding and tuneful duet on their flexible and willing young bones, which neither the television nor the radio in her adjoining room was able to out-fortissimo, at first produced in her only mild disappointment. But eventually it became the source of boiling indignation, not to mention drug-aided sexual excitement which even a long, cold shower couldn't wash away.

"Did my television keep you awake last night?" she asked sweetly when he joined her for breakfast at the hotel coffee shop early the following morning.

"No, didn't even hear it," he answered, stretching his arms over his head and stifling a gaping yawn.

"Well," she continued hesitantly, "was my radio too loud?"

"No problem."

"My shower running didn't keep you awake, did it?"

Suddenly, understanding dawned and he snapped his head up from his grapefruit and looked at her guiltily. "Oh, shit, I'm sorry. I kept you awake. . . ."

"Bingo!" She bolted to her feet, catapulting her chair noisily to the floor. In the deathly silence that followed, Catherine slowly began to comprehend the degree of her overreaction, and quietly sat as the soft clinking of utensils built around them again like a cocoon.

"I'm sorry," Lynell whispered. "I . . . I . . . didn't realize . . ."

Catherine shrugged away the apology. "No, it's my fault. And that wasn't really what kept me awake. It's just that . . ." She looked at him across the table and shook her head slowly. "Lynell, they were so obvious. I just hate it when men fall all over women who are that obvious. It makes the rest of us feel as though that's all you're after, as though that's all there is."

"I guess I'm just not used to the attention," he said. "I haven't been getting much of it at home recently. Then again, I haven't been giving much, either," he added remorsefully. "I'm not really like that at all."

Catherine didn't bother to pretend she believed him. What would be the point? There had never been much of a chance that as a human being Lynell Alan would prove to be measurably superior to any of the other men who had systematically ransacked her life. There was only slightly less chance of it now.

Over the final days of the shoot, he seemed to be trying to make it up to her by being charming. But even his unflagging attentiveness and pleasant companionship were mere baby steps toward his redemption alongside his polite but determined avoidance of the relentless pair of teenagers.

"Maybe you really *aren't* like that," she remarked out of the blue as they strolled through a sun-drenched Ghirardelli Square on their final day in the Bay City. She was that close to forgiving him.

"Like what?" he asked through a mouthful of sourdough bread.

Still, she almost couldn't help but like him.

15

In Manhattan heads don't turn—not for princes and not for kings. New Yorkers don't gawk up at "jumpers" and they only glance down at a wino long enough to sidestep with practiced nonchalance the grizzled body stretched soddenly across the littered sidewalk. They are as unimpressed by striking beauty as they are by gruesome ugliness. They disdain exhibitionism in any form.

Catherine Ward, who was anything but an exhibitionist, turned left off Lexington Avenue onto Fifty-ninth Street and glided her shiny new Porche up against the long expanse of empty curb in front of No. 150. Before getting out of the scarlet convertible, she sat back in the rich, tan leather bucket seats, letting them briefly swallow her in their crinkling security. As she looked up at the sparkling steel-and-glass skyscraper looming over her, she sighed deeply, trying to steady her runaway heartbeat. In this summer of 1982, though she was not yet twenty years old, depending upon which magazine you read—*Vogue*, *Harper's Bazaar* or *Glamour*—she was, though perhaps not yet of the celebrity status of Christie Brinkley or Cheryl Tiegs, either the first, second, or third most in-demand fashion model in New York, able to command fees in excess of two thousand dollars a day. When she stepped from the automobile, heads turned.

With a quick twist of her left wrist, Catherine checked her gold, diamond-studded, wafer-thin Omega watch, another gift from an appreciative client, and realized she was fifteen minutes late. She hesitated only a fraction of a second on the curb beneath the "TOW ZONE" sign, remembering the comment her insurance agent had made when explaining the ridiculously high premiums on her new automobile: "The average life expectancy of a new Carrera unattended on the streets of New York is approximately twelve minutes." Catherine shook her head in disgust, then picked her way carefully through the midday pedestrian traffic toward the massive glass double doors ahead of her. It had taken her less than a month, the time since the company had virtually given her the show-room model, to realize how impractical an automobile—especially one like this—was in New York City. It had already cost her $1,500 to insure, $300 to garage for a month, and $50 in parking tickets. Let them tow it away—or better yet steal it. She tossed back her head regally and pushed her way into the lobby.

Catherine's white cotton dress highlighted a smooth, golden tan acquired on the recent Now Shampoo television commercial shooting in Hawaii. The dress was the perfect weight for a bright, sunny, comfortably warm mid-May afternoon. Once inside the sterile, overly–air-conditioned building, she was glad she had remembered to bring a sweater. She slipped into it without breaking stride, pulling the red wool cardigan protectively over her broad, bare shoulders. The cavernous lobby clattered noisily with dozens of the busy leather footsteps of corporate types, while the sneakered feet of a messenger boy squished their muffled urgency among the scattered giant rubber trees and ferns that only seemed to magnify the barrenness of the open enclave.

The messenger boy, in the overtly conspicuous style of youth, ogled her long, slim body from sandal-top to throat, barely bothering to take notice of the exquisitely chiseled face that towered over his own. The corporate types, anesthetized as they were to the comings and goings of the beautiful people from the twenty-third floor, still tried for a passing glance at her. A few—the young ones who were still able to dream—tried unsuccessfully to catch her eye as she hurried past them toward the long banks of elevators. Usually she acknowledged them with a smile or a nod, these vaguely familiar faces with whom the only intimacy she shared was this sterile building. But today she was too preoccupied to notice them at all.

Catherine's meteoric rise through the ranks of her profession had become almost legend along the grapevine of the fashion world. She was the all-American girl, and as breathtakingly beautiful as she was in person, the source of her incredible income was the way that beauty was reproduced, even magnified, in photographs and on videotape.

She pushed the heat-activated "UP" button and clenched her fist in nervous anticipation. When the elevator arrived, a middle-aged businessman held the door and Catherine stood aside for the unloading passengers. Their attentive stares made her suddenly self-conscious, and she pulled her sweater over her breasts, knowing without looking that her nipples had peaked against the light cotton fabric. Several people had gathered behind her, and she was glad, when the businessman ushered her into the elevator with an embarrassingly ceremonious wave of his hand, that she would be at the rear of the cab, beyond the scrutiny of the rest of the passengers. Once the cab began to rise, Catherine felt a rush of nausea in the pit of her stomach, and each time the elevator stopped, her stomach continued to rise sickeningly, until by the twenty-third floor she could barely draw a complete breath. A midwesterner to the core, she was sure she would never get used to the claustrophobic confines of those tiny cubicles.

On the twenty-third floor she hurried toward the massive oak door with CLINE MODELS written across it in raised gilt lettering. Behind the door was the world of illusion—the world she had sought so obsessively, the world that had made her and of which she would never quite feel a part. She paused with her hand on the huge handle, taking a deep breath, trying to steady her rapid breathing, which was all she could hear in the empty hallway. Her throat was parched and sore, and she quickly abandoned the thought of swallowing, grasped the handle tightly, pulled the heavy door open, and went in.

As she crossed the burgundy-carpeted reception area, her purposeful stride belied her growing anxiety, which had raised her body temperature so that she no longer needed her cardigan. Two men and four women, whom she caught with casual indifference in her peripheral vision, sat on the black leather couches that flanked the large but comfortably appointed room. These were the hopefuls, waiting tensely, their portfolios held across their laps in tightly clasped hands. The hopefuls, who knew only of the glamour, the excitement, the travel, and the money, and who knew nothing of the other side, the side with which she had become so intimate.

Catherine slipped her sweater over her arm as she walked. The young women were defeated. This was the competition and, pretty as they were, each was suddenly embarrassed by the nerve that had brought them here, to the most famous modeling agency in the world. Even the young men were intimidated by Catherine's stunning, statuesque beauty, for if these were the impeccable features required of the women, then certainly the men must measure up.

Though bursting with anxiety, Catherine crossed the room with the obvious familiarity of one who belonged, and six pair of eyes regarded her intently, enviously.

She nodded perfunctorily as she passed Thelma Preble at reception and proceeded directly to the high, oak-topped counter behind which several secretaries busily arranged last-minute interviewing schedules for the afternoon. She waited impatiently to be buzzed in through the gate at one end of the counter, returning the *hello's* and acknowledging the congratulations when someone finally looked up. Once inside she headed straight for the private corner-office at the end of the hallway, where Mary Cline would already have begun without her. At the door she heard the muffled voices from within, and again the anxiety welled inside her. Though the voices were indistinguishable, she knew that besides Mary, Lynell Alan would probably already be there—in spite of the fact that they had just gotten in a few hours ago, after an overnight stop in San Francisco on the return flight from Hawaii—and Aimée Harris. Catherine smiled tentatively when she anticipated this first-time meeting with Aimée Harris. She had heard so much from Lynell about the feisty little lawyer that she felt as though she already knew her. She knew, too, as everyone at the agency did by now, that Aimée and Lynell were lovers long before either had ever become directly involved with Mary Cline. Speculation over who had ridden whose coattails into the agency had long since ebbed with the realization that each was an invaluable asset. She raised her hand slowly to knock.

"You'd better get in there pronto. You're late." LeeAnn Schneider had come upon her suddenly, and Catherine jumped back skittishly from the door. "Sorry," LeeAnn said, placing her hand soothingly on Catherine's bare shoulder. "I didn't mean to startle you."

"That's okay. Is Mary upset?" Catherine asked.

"When isn't Mary upset? Let's put it this way. I've seen her happier." LeeAnn looked understandingly at Catherine. "Don't worry, Cathy, she'll get over it."

This was an important meeting, and Catherine was seized by another pang of anxiety. She bit her thumbnail nervously. "Who's in there with her, LeeAnn?"

"Just Aimée Harris. Lynell's late, too. I don't think anyone from the shampoo company is coming. They just sent the contract over with a messenger—signed, sealed, and delivered. It's all up to us. I'm really happy for you and Lynell." LeeAnn smiled again and continued down the hallway with a simple grace that gave no hint of the pressures she labored under.

Catherine clicked her thumbnail noisily between her teeth. God, she didn't want to go in there—she *couldn't* go in there. At least Lynell was late, too. That would make it easier. But why the Christ did she have to be late today of all days? They were waiting for her and Lynell to go over the contract. She had had to sign things before—agency contracts, waivers, vouchers—but never an exclusive contract to represent a product. Exclusives were rare and extremely lucrative, and to land one was a monumental coup. But she wasn't at all sure she was ready. It was all happening too damn fast. She should be eager and excited about the opportunity, but she wasn't. She was scared to death.

Funny how for years you wanted something so badly you'd do anything for it—even some things you weren't especially proud of—and then when it happened . . . you just weren't so sure. All the hard work and sacrifice and swallowed pride, and you just weren't so sure any more. She spun on her heels and retreated down the long, plushly-carpeted hallway. When she was halfway to the reception area, LeeAnn reappeared from the Xerox room. "Cathy, where are you going?" she asked as though the young woman had taken leave of her senses.

Catherine smiled sheepishly. "I'm so nervous I have to go to the bathroom."

LeeAnn chuckled and shook her head in wonder. "Well, you'd better make it quick, girl, or you'll be out of a job—Lynell, too," she said, checking her watch.

"LeeAnn, would you be a doll and tell them I'm here? I'll only be a minute."

Before LeeAnn could answer, Catherine had slipped into the ladies' room, snapped the lock, and leaned breathlessly against the heavy metal door. After inhaling deeply several times to calm herself, she placed her small white clutch-bag on the washbasin and hung her sweater on the hook inside the door. With both hands on the edge of the sink, she leaned close to the mirror and saw the dark shadows beneath her eyes that even Revlon and the deceivingly healthy glow of a Hawaiian suntan couldn't hide. She swiped the back of her hand across her face and felt the film of perspiration on her skin. Another "break of a lifetime" for a simple midwestern girl. *Welcome to the major leagues, Catherine Ward! But do you have the balls for them?*

Aimée Harris had been in the Cline Agency offices all afternoon, and was enjoying both the professional challenge and the growing and unmanufactured drama of the interpersonal relationships that electrified the air—some of which included her. Aimée was well aware that

259

her relationship with Lynell Alan was common knowledge, and she was also well aware of the growing rumors around the agency connecting Lynell and Catherine Ward.

Though Aimée had lived in New York City for over one and a half years and had become as acclimated to life in that metropolis as she ever would—which was not quite totally—she remained as steadfastly Boston Brahmin as the Cabots and the Lowells. The r-less Harvard accent alerted anyone who might otherwise mistake her origins. Her eyes flicked from side to side with ceaseless urgency, as though she were subconsciously aware of her position of trust and remained ever vigilant against anyone who would try to usurp it. But behind the serene face and impudent figure of a cheerleader was the quicksilver brain of an unsurpassed contracts attorney, backed by the confidence of an education at the finest schools and an apprenticeship at one of Manhattan's most prestigious law firms. Even the crop of fine, auburn hair that hung lankly over her shoulders, Mary Cline thought with smug satisfaction, was a natural artifice that, like the rest of her adolescent appearance, was capable of lulling an unsuspecting adversary into dangerously underestimating her considerable professional capabilities.

Mary Cline was pleased that Saul Stearns had assigned young Aimée Harris to her account. But she refused to allow that pleasure to show either on her face or in her brusque, condescending manner. She had the greatest respect for this young woman, but it was enough that she knew that herself.

"Aimée, dear, how many times do we have to go through this? By now I should say I am almost as familiar with the wording of the contract as you are. And it's not as though I've never seen one of its type before. Indeed, I'm quite sure I've seen more of them than you will in your professional lifetime."

Aimée Harris had gone over the proposed contract between Textron, Inc., the manufacturers of Now Shampoo, and Cline Models with Mary at least a half-dozen times before today, and though Mary admired the woman's tenacity and thoroughness, she was beginning to question her efficiency. "And after all, we're signing the contract this afternoon. Isn't the time for second thoughts a trifle late?"

"It's never too late for second thoughts. Not until the signatures have dried on the parchment. And you *should* be as familiar with the contract terms as I am. And so should your models," she added, nodding pointedly toward their two empty chairs. "It's your business. After they're signed I just walk away." Aimée had a professional self-confidence that bordered on arrogance, and though it grated on some people, she figured she'd earned it. No, she re-earned it every time she drew up a contract proposal or studied one drawn up by someone else. She earned it with the tireless dedication she put into poring over and over contracts until she knew every paragraph, every nuance, every possible pitfall as intimately as she knew her own body.

"How, Aimée, my dear, can you remain so enthusiastic about something we've discussed *ad infinitum, ad nauseam?*"

Aimée looked up from the papers that lay on the desk between them, and her eyes locked challengingly with Mary Cline's. "Ms. Cline, getting it right is never boring. It's what you pay me for."

Mary sighed audibly. "You're right, of course," she said. "But it's not the contract terms that are worrying me at this point. It's what we can anticipate from this thing down the road. It doesn't pay to become too identifiable with a single product."

"That's not my area of expertise, Ms. Cline," Aimée said with her evenly professional tone.

And that was the way the afternoon had gone, anxiety grating on Mary Cline's brittle nerves, alertness humming in Aimée Harris's nimble brain, and the static of wariness and respect clicking unrelentingly between them.

"Lynell Alan is on his way down to your office, Ms. Cline," the receptionist announced over the intercom.

"That's what you said about Catherine Ward five minutes ago," Mary snapped back. "So where the hell is she?"

There was a light rap on the door and Lynell Alan walked in, looking nothing short of spectacular in a neatly pressed pair of pale blue chinos and a white, pinpoint Oxford shirt that contrasted his deep Hawaiian suntan. "Sorry I'm late, but we were on a plane all morning. I just had to stop at the apartment and shower."

Aimée Harris's aplomb faced its first genuine test of the afternoon. Mary Cline searched the restless eyes for a sign of weakness, but they were seemingly unaffected.

Lynell swapped kisses on the cheek with each of them, though with patently more affection toward Aimée, whom he also hugged tenderly, and Mary wondered how much substance there was to the rumors or, if there was any, how far it lagged behind the facts.

"Well, hello stranger," Aimée greeted him, and Mary Cline quickly surmised that the young lawyer hadn't seen Lynell since his return this morning from the shootings in San Francisco and Hawaii. Maybe they were true, the rumors that were beginning to connect him with Catherine Ward, though somehow Mary doubted it. And if Aimée Harris believed them, Mary thought with renewed appreciation for her, the young woman never let it crack her cool, professional veneer. But

261

though she remained as crisp and unwrinkled as her ivory-toned linen suit, Lynell was beginning to look decidedly uncomfortable.

Mary cleared her throat to break the uneasy silence. "I'd better go check on Catherine," she said, slipping past them to the door. "I'll be back in a few minutes."

When they were alone, Lynell went to Aimée, knelt by her chair, and kissed her again. "I've missed you."

"I've missed you, too," she said.

They both felt the strain of the growing unfamiliarity that wedged between them, but when Mary Cline returned to the room, they abruptly reverted to the business at hand and, with something besides the volatility of their own personal relationship to occupy them, much of the discomfort, for the moment at least, melted away.

LeeAnn Schneider knocked on the door to Mary Cline's office and then waited an appropriate interval before entering. LeeAnn, as always, was nattily attired, today in a crisp khaki suit over a madras plaid blouse. Though she was at the office six days a week in this bustling spring season, her olive skin had already taken on a darker hue than most people's would in an entire summer on the beach. Her salt-and-pepper hair was cropped short, and at forty-one, she was still a strikingly handsome woman.

"LeeAnn, I'm glad you stopped in. Would you track down Catherine Ward for me? Thelma said she arrived five minutes ago, but I couldn't find her out in the hallway."

Mary hadn't even given LeeAnn a chance to say hello to Lynell and Aimée Harris.

"She'll be right along. She's in the ladies' room." LeeAnn loathed Mary Cline, but fortunately the woman spent the majority of her time wining and dining clients, not in the office. Mary still held a grudge about the affair LeeAnn had had with her brother over fifteen years ago. But in spite of their differences, Mary had given her a chance to make it in this end of the businsss, and for that, at least, LeeAnn was grateful. It was for that reason alone that she continued to spurn offers from other agencies, offers of more money and more responsibility, not to mention more dignity.

Lynell Alan stood politely and greeted LeeAnn with a warm, genuine smile. "I missed you when I came in, LeeAnn. How have you been?"

"Not as good as you have."

Lynell smiled that modest *aw shucks* smile of his, and LeeAnn thought she might melt into the floor. It was no wonder that in his few months at the agency he had already begun to make a name for himself. *Who says nice guys finish last?* she thought. It was Mary Cline who had, unbeknownst even to Lynell himself, within the past few days begun the skillful and strategic negotiations that—if they worked—had the potential to skyrocket him to the very pinnacle of male modeling. But LeeAnn nonetheless swelled with pride that it had been she who had first seen him and eventually signed him on with Cline Models. Okay, so she had turned him away three times, but everyone else in New York had turned him away the fourth time, too— and soon they would all be slitting their wrists: Ford, Elite, Wilhelmina, Zoli, all of them. Lynell Alan had the type of face that you became more and more comfortable with the more you saw it. As she had explained to Mary and Albert Cline months ago, he grew on you. The look wasn't flashy, but charismatic. It was the kind of look that would stand up—that would keep him working for a long, long time. He was going to have what they called in the business "legs."

"Fine," LeeAnn answered with a grin and a slow, pensive nod. "I'm doing just fine."

"Good, I haven't seen too much of you recently."

"Only the scramblers see me." She felt Mary Cline's stare searing through her. "Hello, Ms. Harris," she said with a quick nod. Then she turned to Mary. "I'm on my way. I'll have her down here in a minute." Before she could get out the door, Albert Cline stepped in with a quizzical look on his face. "Ladies' room," LeeAnn said as she eased past him. "I'm on my way to get her." Albert's presence added an almost visible tension to the room, and LeeAnn was glad to let the door close behind her.

"I hope that one doesn't give us any trouble," Albert commented.

Lynell came quickly to Catherine's defense. "She's fine. She's probably just tired. I know I am. It was a long week and she works awfully hard."

"Yeah, I hope you're right, smart guy," Albert snapped. Then he turned again to his sister. "We've invested a lot of money in that broad."

Aimée Harris went rigid in her seat, her eyes cold with revulsion. Dealing with Mary Cline was one thing. She was a tough businesswoman—opinionated, dictatorial, and demanding, maybe—but Aimée respected her. Mary Cline had earned her spot on top of the fashion modeling world with a combination of shrewd business acumen and an uncanny anticipation of trends, of which Lynell was only the most recent example. Hers was an incredibly competitive business,

263

and Aimée gave the neat, little woman credit for the nerve it had taken to claw her way to the top.

Albert Cline, on the other hand, was a crass, tasteless thug whom his sister had dragged kicking and screaming into respectability. He was a bully without an ounce of compassion. She didn't know him well, but then again, she already knew him better than she cared to.

"Let me know if you have any trouble, Mary," Albert said tersely as he backed out into the hallway. Albert Cline would be listening at the door, Aimée thought, afraid he might be left out of the action. The man was as transparent as glass.

While LeeAnn was assuring Mary of her presence—in their suite of offices at least—Catherine was in the ladies' room running cold water through her fingers and patting them lightly against her face. Her temples throbbed painfully, and she pressed her index fingers between her cheekbones and her nose, trying to counteract the pressure that had built up to a dull, almost constant ache. Reaching down for the spool of toilet paper, she gave it a sharp yank and a yard of it unraveled annoyingly on the floor. When she tried to gather it, the flimsy paper disintegrated in her wet hands, and she threw a fist to her mouth and bit her knuckle in frustration. Catherine Ward knew then she wouldn't make it. No, she had known before that, really, as she had known all the other times—she would never leave her demon behind. It had taken her over irreversibly. It told her when to eat and it told her when to sleep, both of which, sadly, it told her to do less and less often these days. It told her when to be up and it told her when to be down. It told her when to be beautiful and it told her when to be grotesque. It was inside her, beating in her heart, pulsing in her brain. It *was* Catherine Ward. It had taken hold of her and it wouldn't let go. Not now. Not ever.

As resolutely as though the decision was hers alone and she was reaching it for the first time, she snatched up her small bag from the edge of the sink and began rummaging impatiently through it. Keys, a hairbrush, and a tube of lipstick clattered to the floor, but she ignored them and continued to rifle her bag as though possessed. And she *was* possessed—possessed by the fine white powder she now held up in front of her. Her breathing quickened in anticipation as she shook the powder to the bottom of the tiny plastic bag. With a final deep sigh she tried to exorcise the devil. But there was nothing else that could ease her deepening depression and the gnawing fear accompanying it.

Lynell, Mary, and Aimée were alone again for only a few minutes before Catherine flounced into the office without a knock. The three of them looked up simultaneously, and Catherine thought that Lynell, at least, looked happy to see her. "Hello, everybody. Sorry I'm late," she said, beaming. "Couldn't fine a place to park my new car."

Lynell stood and smiled, but Catherine ignored the gesture. Women always seemed to assume she was trying to steal their men. Well, she would put any speculation about that to rest immediately. She walked straight to Aimée, extending her hand formally. "It's a pleasure finally to meet you, Aimée. It may be a cliché, but I do feel as though I already know you. Lynell never stops talking about you." Then she stepped back and sat on the couch with a sigh, throwing her bag and sweater on the cushion beside her. She gave them all another cheery smile. "Did I miss anything?"

Catherine Ward hit Aimée Harris like a kick in the stomach. She was nothing less than the most unbelievably gorgeous woman Aimée had ever laid eyes on, and she hoped no one had heard the wind suddenly knocked out of her. The woman herself seemed almost oblivious to the attention, as though she was as inured to stares as a grossly fat woman.

Catherine Ward was a wealthy and beautiful woman who seemed totally unimpressed by wealth and beauty. She steered the conversation immediately toward Aimée Harris, and it became apparent that what she *was* demonstrably impressed by was Aimée herself: her obvious intelligence, her top-grade education, her outstanding career, and her undeniable self-confidence, and Aimée found herself, however grudgingly, liking Catherine.

"You look too pretty to be a lawyer," Catherine said as Aimée led them through the complex contract clauses.

"Thank you. And you look too pretty to be true."

"God, I wish I was a lawyer," Catherine continued, ignoring the compliment.

"Why? You'll make more on this contract doing nothing than I will working all year."

Catherine shrugged modestly.

The contract Lynell and Catherine signed that afternoon was an exclusive to represent Now Shampoo. They were each to be paid a $1,500 a month retainer, plus $2,000 per shooting day and royalties at SAG scale. The major conditions were proscriptions against working for another shampoo or hair product or having their faces appear together for any product at all during the life of the contract without the written approval of Textron, Inc.

"It's a big sacrifice, Lynell," Catherine said levelly. "How much money have we made working together outside of Now? Seven, eight hundred dollars?"

"Oh, at least," he answered, quickly snatching the pen from her hand and signing the four copies. And after three years of scratching to make ends meet, with the stroke of a pen Lynell Alan was finally earning a decent living.

Within a month Lynell, Aimée, and L.C.—he excitedly and they reluctantly—moved from their one-bedroom, third-floor walkup into a sprawling two-bedroom apartment in a hundred-year-old brownstone overlooking Gramercy Park on the Lower East Side. And for the first time he could remember, he was really happy.

16

"I know, baby, I know," Aimée said over her shoulder. "I know you don't like these things, but you've got to go. The Clines have invested a lot of time and money in you. Actually, I'm surprised the law firm didn't ask me to go, too. After all, the Clines are a big client of ours. And it's not every day someone celebrates twenty-five years in business. Maybe they figured I'd be going with you anyway. Come on, Lynell, be a sport. It could be fun."

"I doubt it," he said dourly.

She stood over the sink, rinsing three days accumulation of breakfast dishes. "I'm the one who should be begging off. All those gorgeous women? Christ, most of the *men* you work with are prettier than I am."

He walked up behind her and pressed himself against her. "But you'd be the sexiest one there," he said. "I could think of something better to do," he added, reaching around her and inside the lapels of her bathrobe, cupping her breasts and squeezing them firmly.

"Ow! You're hurting me," she snapped as she squirmed out of his arms. But he knew she meant, "You're annoying me."

"Jesus, all right. I get the message." He backed several steps into the middle of the kitchen, then spun and stalked away.

Weeks of trying had been fruitless. The mere fact that they were trying so hard seemed in itself to signal failure. There was no spontaneity anymore. Even their lovemaking was predictable, almost perfunctory.

Being out of town as much as he had been recently would, he knew, put a strain on even the strongest relationship. But that wasn't the cause of their problems, it only served to magnify them. Of one thing he was sure: Aimée was growing impatient. All meaningful conversation seemed inevitably to lead her in one way or another to the same conclusion she had reached that morning, when they lay side by side and she answered for the thousandth time his frustrated question, "What's the matter?"

"I'm not sure how much longer I can take this, Lynell. I know what I want, and until you do, you'll never be able to make me or anyone else happy—because you won't be happy yourself."

"I know what I want. I want to be a successful model."

"Do you?"

"What's that supposed to mean?"

"Only that you don't seem to be willing to do the things that it takes to become one."

"Like going to their parties?"

"Like going to their parties—rubbing elbows with the people who can make you."

"Or break you."

"Come on, Lynell, have some self-confidence. You can be charming as hell—when you want to be. And I've been going to parties with the big muckity-mucks since I was old enough to stop wetting myself. Together we'll knock 'em dead."

"Yeah," he said, unconvinced.

"Look, you're doing all right so far. Things have started to break for you. And what the hell is a successful model, anyway? I want to be a successful lawyer, too, but I don't expect to wake up some morning and read a headline in the *Times:* 'Today Marks Aimée Harris's Ascension to the Ranks of Successful Attorneys.' Will you know when you're successful? And what will you do when and if that happens? Will you finally get on with the rest of your life? I'm not sure I can wait that long."

The relationship was dying before his eyes and he could think of nothing that would save it but time—and he sensed there was precious little of that remaining for them. But he needed time: time to be sure of his career, time to be sure of himself, time to be sure that if he married Aimée they wouldn't end up on the same garbage heap as a million other marriages. Time to be sure. But would there ever be enough time for him to be sure? He honestly didn't know.

She was kneeling behind him now, kneading the muscles in his shoulders. "I'm sorry, Lynell. I want what you want. I'm just not always sure what that is."

"We'll go," he said, relenting.

"It'll be fun," she promised. "You'll see." She kissed the nape of his neck and he felt the warmth of her breath on his cool skin. She smoothed her hands down over his back. "Your skin is so soft." Then she reached around him and ran her fingers teasingly through the hair on his chest, without touching his skin. "I'd follow him *anywhere*," she mimicked, batting her eyes coyly.

Then she leaned around him and kissed his throat, his chin, and then her mouth was over his. As he lay back he slid her robe from her shoulders and heard the snaps popping as she pulled the flap away from him. She writhed against him sensually, but when he moved to enter her she wriggled away. "No," she said. "Let me make love to you."

Their hands were on each other's bodies and she was kissing his chest. Her tongue was on his nipples, in and out of his navel. When he reached below her waist, she elbowed his hand away. She kissed his lips again, then looked into his eyes for a long moment, running her tongue languorously over his lips.

"Do you want to come in my mouth?" she asked, lowering herself over him. It was a rhetorical question.

He hated these "anybody-who-was-anybody" gatherings and avoided them whenever possible, though he knew they could help him advance in his career. He had resented them when he was a "nobody," and he couldn't help but resent them almost more now that he was on the periphery of becoming a "somebody."

The cab eased to the curb through the crowd that spilled onto the street in front of On Stage. Lynell had often said that On Stage was a place he wouldn't go to on a bet. On a given night, throngs would stand in line for hours waiting for a chance to be offered admittance. The club had an air of self-importance and controversy. It was a headliner, a superstar. Not only had it survived a "cocaine on tap" scandal, it had thrived on it. Like the forbidden fruit, its expensive, out-of-reach-of-the-common-man image made it all the more seductive to the social-climbing multitudes. Ryan O'Neal and Farrah Fawcett didn't wait in line. Warren Beatty didn't wait in line. Reggie Jackson didn't wait in line. On Stage was a capricious and lustful siren, beckoning to those who would enter her, with a sensuous, pulsating beat and the promise of mystery and glamour and hedonistic delights only she could keep.

Lynell stepped from the cab, resplendent in his new tuxedo, and he wished Janet Shupe could see him now. It was a $750 suit he'd bought through a client for $400, especially for the occasion. The tailor had paid scrupulous attention to its impeccable fit. "On what side do you carry your personals?" he had asked. Lynell had at first naively thought the man meant his credit cards.

Lynell hooked an index finger inside the tight collar of his ruffled white dress shirt and tugged at it nervously. If he hadn't suddenly become the center of attention he would have reached into his pants and adjusted himself. The crotch was extremely uncomfortable despite the tailor's ministrations.

He held the door as Aimée bent through, and for a heartbeat he knew her breasts would fall out of the low-cut red silk dress, but somehow the spaghetti straps held. At the door he showed their invitation and they were ushered inside, even as several other couples were turned away with a terse "Private party tonight." Lynell was at the same time embarrassed and inflated by the preferential treatment. Aimée appeared totally blasé, as though she expected nothing less.

Inside, the primordial backbeat of a live rock band pounded deafeningly in their ears, and the dusky darkness was pierced by a rhythmic strobe light that danced jerky silhouettes across the floor. Two acutely discernible smoke aromas hung heavily on the air and mingled with the acrid scent of human sweat.

"Is that Laura Xenon?" Aimée asked incredulously as Lynell bent to hear her over the pounding beat.

He looked up at the stage. Christ, it *was* Laura Xenon, belting out one of her new hits. Her enormous, sequined breasts swayed in time with the music. Lynell could hardly believe his eyes. He was so close to the biggest female rock star in the world he could see the rivulet of sweat that glistened down her cleavage.

Lynell took Aimée's hand, and they weaved through the writhing crowd to where the honored and slightly incongruous-looking brother-sister duo sat at a table in the raised section of the room surrounding the dance floor. His reason for coming was to be seen, to show his appreciation, and he would get that chore over with first.

As they waited in line by the Clines' table to get close enough to congratulate them, Lynell greeted several people without attempting to formally introduce Aimée, instead simply nodding in her direction. In the overwhelming cacophony, formality was impossible.

When they were finally received, he kissed Mary Cline on the cheek

270

and spoke directly into her ear. "Of course you know Aimée. We both wanted to extend our heartiest congratulations, Mary. Here's to twenty-five more successful years. And thanks for everything." He was on the air again and wondered if his delivery had been too matter-of-fact.

Aimée shook Mary's hand, then Albert's. Mary beckoned Lynell closer. "She looks charming, as usual, Lynell. Call me in the morning, will you please—at home." Albert's eyes never left Aimée's chest.

Lynell nodded and let the flow of the crowd carry them to the bar. He and Aimée each downed a glass of champagne before attempting progress toward the dance floor. Lynell was already perspiring from the intense body heat.

He estimated the crowd at three hundred, average age twenty-five, and it had a musky sexuality that was electric. When he took Aimée in his arms, her bare back and shoulders were hot and dewy. He pressed against her almost instinctively, but she recoiled and he couldn't hear over the thrusting backbeat but could see the words forming on her lips. "Later," she complained, "it's too hot." Then she shrugged apologetically.

The dancing spontaneously evolved into foot-stomping and clapping. Men cheered and women gasped as Laura Xenon screamed into the microphone, her flashing, skin-tone, skin-tight dress sparkling in the lights and droplets of sweat flying from her face into the appreciative crowd. As the song reached a crescendo, she straddled the microphone stand and gripped it tightly between her legs, drawing it back and forth rhythmically, urgently, suggestively. When the song ended, the ovation began—and it was deafening. The strobe light was cut and Lynell watched the stage through a murky haze of smoke.

"Don't go away now," Laura Xenon breathed into the mike with her raspy baritone. "We're gonna take a short break and go get a little wired up, and when we come back," she said, hefting her breasts proudly, "I might even show you my tits." She then made her exit to cheers and catcalls and wild applause that took up the cadence of the exaggerated sway of her hips, and Lynell would have bet that every person in that room—male or female, straight or gay—would have given their last dime to have her.

The crowd seemed almost relieved at the prospect of an intermission in which to collect themselves. "Christ, she's something else, isn't she?" Lynell said, laughing at his understatement over the crackling hum of conversation.

They had to hold their ground against the surging crowd as it pressed toward the bar. Lynell would have enjoyed another glass of champagne, of anything. His mouth was dry and cottony. But when he saw the horde around the bar, he decided that for the time being he would have to live with it.

He introduced Aimée to Peter McGee, a young, freckle-faced, Howdy Doody-type Lynell had worked with when they were both back at the Munson Agency. "Hey, Lynell, I'm happy as hell for you. Shit, I'm beginning to see you everywhere, man. You've come a long way from thirty-five dollars an hour, passing out free tennis balls at the Head booth at the U.S. Open."

"Luck, Peter, my boy. Pure luck."

"I know," McGee laughed, "and gimme some of that," he added, rubbing Lynell's sleeve vigorously. "What do you think?" he asked, flashing a smile as he motioned over his shoulder with his thumb at the empty stage.

"Amazing," they said in unison. Lynell looked over at Aimée. She seemed bored.

"Want some of this?" McGee asked, pulling a joint from the inside pocket of his dinner jacket.

Lynell looked pointedly over the smaller man's shoulder.

"Sis and Big Brother have exited for the evening," McGee said through his Howdy Doody smile.

"Thanks." Lynell took the hand-rolled joint with a smug grin.

"Nice to meet you," McGee said, offering Aimée his hand. He started to leave, then stopped abruptly. "Oh, I saw your partner downstairs. Cathy Ward," McGee prompted. "The most gorgeous creature I ever laid eyes on," he began, slowly shaking his head. Then he looked directly at Aimée and shrugged, "and she's gay."

Of course Lynell was aware of the rumors—about both Catherine and her on-again off-again "boyfriend," Webster Greaves, who was at present making headlines in Milan at the Italian Open. But for some reason hearing McGee say it made him flush. He was ashamed to think it might be because he was embarrassed for her.

Lynell watched McGee as he bounced off, glad-handing his way across the dance floor. He was certainly going to make the most of this evening, Lynell thought. God, if Peter McGee didn't make it, it wouldn't be for lack of trying. He must know every client in the room.

"Huh?" Lynell asked, turning his head toward Aimée at the sound of her voice intruding on his thoughts.

"I said, 'Is she really?' Or did you just put him up to that?"

"Is who really what?" he asked disinterestedly, though he knew exactly what she meant.

"Is your 'partner' really gay?"

"That's what they say."

"And what do you say?" Aimée asked, curling her lip challengingly.

"I say I don't know. And I also say it's none of my business."

During the intermission they were greeted by the Dudleys, who seemed uncomfortable and out of place, he looking nonplussed in a double-breasted tuxedo that smelled faintly of mothballs and which Lynell would have bet he'd been married in, and she looking lovely but as aimless as a bird watcher from the Audubon Society.

"Great fun, eh, Mike?" Lynell asked sarcastically.

"Yeah, and I owe it all to you and Cathy."

"I bet you'd rather be at the Mets game."

"Offhand I can't think of anyplace I *wouldn't* rather be."

After leaving the Dudleys, Lynell saw Gretchen Saczynski, now rumored to be half-owner of the Munson Agency. As he approached her, Gretchen, who obviously still bore a grudge over his defection, appeared loaded for bear. Even in the dim light, he could see she still wore too much mauve blusher, and to her left . . .

"My God. Janet, is that really you?"

"Yes, my dear Lyn, in the flesh." Janet Shupe reached up to kiss him on the cheek, simultaneously rubbing the material of his lapel between thumb and forefinger. "You're looking more gorgeous than ever," she said proudly, an artist gazing again on an early painting she had always known would become a masterpiece. "Though I judge you've made a sartorial move up in the world. Not to mention your career," she added as she surveyed the surroundings appreciatively.

"Thanks to you," he said, squeezing her hand.

"Nonsense. Thanks to yourself." Then she turned to Aimée and smiled. "Miss Boston."

"Oh, dear, you simply must meet Richard," said Gretchen, putting an abrupt end to the reunion.

"Wonderful to see you, Lyn," Janet said as Gretchen led her away. "Continued good luck."

"Is the old warhorse trying to woo you back?" LeeAnn Schneider slipped her hand under his arm possessively. She was breathtaking in a plain, clinging, pale green Bill Blass gown, though even on her salary, with her practical business sense he doubted it would be an original. Lynell suddenly felt very pretentious in his Halston tuxedo. "I told Ms. Cline we shouldn't invite the competition," LeeAnn continued. "I hear that Gretchen has them Number Two and Trying Harder over there, now that she owns the place."

"So the rumors are true?" Lynell asked.

"The rumors are always true. Good evening, Aimée. Enjoying the show?"

"Yes. Laura Xenon isn't bad, either."

"The way your man is going," LeeAnn offered conspiratorially, patting Lynell's forearm affectionately, "we'll all be able to retire soon. Love the ad, Lyn."

Lynell grinned bashfully.

"Oh, hello Jacques. Hang on a sec," LeeAnn called to a distinguished-looking middle-aged man with thick silver hair offset by a deep, luxurious tan. "Well, back to work," she whispered to the couple with a parting wink as she whisked away across the floor.

"That's the guy I pay $150 a shot for a lousy haircut—fifteen minutes," Lynell said out of the corner of his mouth as he saluted Jacques with a tip-of-the-hat gesture. "What a goldmine. I think he does everybody at the agency."

"I'm sure," Aimée began with a smirk as she watched LeeAnn join a trio of attractive young women who were already gushing over Jacques, "but can he cut hair?"

The lights dimmed and the applause rose, and Laura Xenon reappeared, resuscitating the crowd en masse, as though it occupied a single body.

It was only in the shadowy light, when all eyes were back on stage, that Lynell asked Aimée for a match. Even then he took a deep drag as surreptitiously as possible and held the smoke in his lungs as he passed it to Aimée.

Already beginning to feel light-headed, he looked back up toward the stage where Laura Xenon was doing a muddled intro to the band's upcoming set. So drugged out she could barely stand up, she had changed into a sexy, tight-fitting red dress that magnified the proportions of her Rubenesque body, a dress which, on a smaller woman could have been described as slinky. It was a dress so low-cut and form-fitting her breasts exploded over the décolletage. It was Aimée's dress, he realized. His head snapped toward the woman at his side, and she seemed to have shrunk in the presence of the larger-than-life rock star.

Several couples danced, but most simply watched as Laura Xenon ground out "My Body Beautiful," a ten-minute self-celebration that was another of her recent smash hits.

Aimée again declined Lynell's invitation to dance and they finished the joint without even attempting conversation. Lynell's head was swimming, his eyes following the bob of those incredible breasts, and he prayed that Laura Xenon would keep her earlier promise to show them. In his narcotic-heightened excitement he felt himself inching down the leg of his tailored pants.

When the singer turned to face the band during the pounding instrumental bars, when she stood with her back to the crowd, leaned her elbows on the piano, and ground those voluptuous hips, his mind was on stage with her, lifting the hem of red silk; raising it above the surprisingly slim calves and thick, tight thighs, the heavy round behind; thrusting himself roughly into her; and the throng cheered and he clutched her heavy waist and watched her hips as they kept on pounding to the beat, pounding, pounding, and she spun around and the thought left him just in time and she finished the final verse to another tumultuous ovation.

"Want to go downstairs and join Catherine?" he half-yelled to Aimée between songs. "I've still got a few people I should say hello to."

"No, no. You tend to business and don't worry about me. Anyway, my ego's suffering enough just being here. Catherine would be overkill." But it was obvious she wasn't suffering one bit. He could almost feel the glee as her gaze scanned the room, lighting on personality after personality—sports stars, movie stars, television stars, stars from every entertainment medium.

"Well, can you take care of yourself for a little while?"

"Sure. Go ahead. Have fun," she said absently, touching his arm lightly to acknowledge his existence but never taking her eyes off Christie Brinkley, who could have eaten peanuts off the top of her new boyfriend Billy Joel's head as they waltzed by.

"Try not to miss me too much," he said. "I'll be back as soon as I can." But even his sarcasm went unnoticed.

"Take your time."

Christ, what the hell is the attraction? he wondered, as he left her alone on the dance floor. But as he scanned the crowded room once again, he knew. It was the beautiful people. Whether it was physical appearance or wealth or power that made them that way, it was the beautiful people, her people, like the politicos and pedigreed socialites she'd grown up with back in Boston.

He moodily pushed his way through the revelers, most of whom looked as though they were fresh from the set of a catalogue shoot for "After Six," and made his way toward the less crowded end of the bar, where Franco Canero and Mark Collins were in close conversation. Seeing Canero again stung him with an old anger and guilt.

"Hi, Mark, Mr. Canero." Lynell nodded to each man.

"Lynell." Mark greeted him flatly, then turned from Canero and edged his way down toward the crowd at the middle of the bar.

"Excuse me, Mr. Canero, I didn't mean to interrupt."

"Not to worry. We had nothing more to say to each other. And call me Franco. I'm not *that* old."

"Sure. Nice to see your again, Franco. By the way, I never got a chance to call you about those tests shots we did a while back. Were they any good?"

"A couple were passable," Canero said thoughtfully, while circling the rim of his glass with the tip of his finger. "Nothing you could use, I'm afraid."

Lynell really didn't give a damn about the pictures anymore. "My bad side?" he joked.

"You could say so."

When Lynell caught the barmaid's eye he raised two fingers, then excused himself and maneuvered along the bar to Mark's side. "So, how's it going?"

"It's going." Mark's face was tanned, angular, expressionless, as though straining to hide something. Lynell wondered if it had been the sun that had bleached the man's hair almost white.

"Working much?" Lynell asked, even though Mark seemed preoccupied.

"I'm working now."

"Tell me about it," Lynell agreed.

"Incredible," Mark sighed, and Lynell followed the man's eyes toward the stage. He wouldn't have thought the man would be that interested in Laura Xenon.

Between them and the stage Aimée stood in Laura Xenon's dress, and Lynell watched them both, so different and yet both so basically sensual: Laura Xenon—pounding, screaming, sweating sex; and Aimée Harris—quiet, demure, and emanating a magnetic animal sexuality that could be released only with the proper key.

The tug on his sleeve drew his attention. "Your champagne." The barmaid smiled adoringly. "It's still an open bar," she added when Lynell reached into his pocket. She had that meet-me-in-the-alley-after-work look on her face that he had seen more and more in recent days.

Mark's attention was still riveted to the stage, and Lynell didn't bother to speak to him as he left the bar.

"You're a godsend," Aimée sighed when he handed her the drink. "By the way, look who I found." She pointed enthusiastically and

276

Lynell almost dropped his own drink when he saw the tall, handsome black man beside her.

"Hey, man, good to see you."

"You, too, Dan," Lynell said.

"Good things happening to you, my man," Dan said, bobbing like O.J. Simpson in a Hertz commercial.

"How's . . ." He was going to say Tommy until he saw the new young man by his side, a young man who was, if anything, prettier . . . and whiter . . . than Tommy. "How's Gretchen?"

"Still a bitch. But I'm not complaining. Business is booming. Hey, later, man. Good to see you," Dan repeated, as he turned and bobbed off through the crowd, waving, his little friend heeling as obediently as an Irish setter.

Aimée grinned wryly at Lynell.

"Nice-looking boyfriend," Lynell said.

"Yeah, but can he take a punch?"

Aimée pulled Lynell down by the neck, kissed him lightly, and smiled. Then she put her lips to his ear. "Lynell, you're here to work the room, so go get 'em. And take your time. I'm enjoying the act—and I look better in the dress."

He smiled, grateful for the encouragement, and left her again.

She should have gone with him, she thought through a mild haze, to meet some more of his business associates and say hello to Catherine, though it was ego-shattering to be in the same room with a woman like her. Gay or not, men still hoped.

She could never understand what it was that bothered Lynell so much about all of this, and all the attention that went with it. It was painful to see what he went through, trying to mix in this group—this group that was judged and accepted on looks alone—when all he had to do was let it happen.

She smelled the marijuana smoke, strained through the glittering strobes at the beautiful, empty faces, recognizable faces, and the perfect bodies hung with designer originals, and superimposed on the tabloid were Boston cotillions where the music was soft and the lights were low and people had something to say—real people, the right people, *her* people. This was fun, exciting, but was it real? Or was it just a fling? And what about her relationship with Lynell?

They were different people from different places, with different backgrounds and different goals. Perhaps too different. Lynell seemed to have begun his rebellion at thirty, when hers had begun at thirteen. Maybe hers was over. There was only one problem: She loved him. But perhaps it was true, after all, what Mother had said to her as she had agonized over whether or not to follow Lynell to New York. "The one you love most isn't always the best one for you."

The man at the bar was still staring at her. God, he was gorgeous, and tall—taller than Lynell. He was tanned, with straight, white-blond hair; sharp, perfect features; and dimples even when he didn't smile. And if he ever did smile, he would, of course, have perfect teeth.

In the dim, smoky light, he probably wouldn't notice her staring at him. But then he must be used to women staring. Watching him, Aimée felt a faint sense of recognition. She had probably seen him in magazine advertisements or on television. Recently people had begun to look at Lynell with that same don't-I-know-you-from-somewhere stare.

First things first, Mark Collins thought as he drained his glass of champagne. He'd taken care of business for tonight, and even if Al Cline had paid off every cop in the city, it was time to get as far away from this fucking joint as possible. He had to think. Franco Canero's subtle innuendos kept coming back to him. He stepped from the bar and made his way toward the door, glad-handing with the amateurs who tugged on their drinks and sucked on their hand-rolled cigarettes. The real pros were downstairs.

It was only then that he saw her again, standing alone, arms folded across her chest, magnificent breasts spilling over the crimson neckline of her low-cut gown. His cock remembered her three heartbeats before his brain did.

"May I have this dance?"

It was a dog-eat-dog business, and so what if this was his girl? It was almost better that she was. Maybe it was time he was knocked down a peg. The last woman Mark had *had* was that two-faced, squeaky-clean bitch, Billie Devlin. He couldn't remember the last time he'd *wanted* a woman. Christ, or a man either, for that matter.

For him Devlin had been strictly business. For her? The vengeance of a scorned lover? An ego boost to assuage the hurt of a cheating husband? Plain and simple horniness? He didn't know and he didn't care. All that mattered were those magic words: "This job can be yours, Mark." Those magic words that meant sack-time. She wasn't so bad for a woman her age. All she'd wanted was straight sex. He'd had worse—much worse. And then Alan had shown up at the airport. She hadn't even had the nerve to tell him they were testing someone else, too. And he'd still had the confidence he would win the job anyway—until he'd seen Alan and that dyke bitch on the beach in Florida. What a performance. Had again. No job. No big break. No big money. But what the hell: four days' work was four days' work, and eight thousand dollars was eight thousand dollars; and the coke deal . . . Not bad. Not bad at all.

No, he couldn't remember the *last* time he had wanted a woman. But he'd take this one, he thought as he unconsciously drew her tightly against him.

She pulled away and smiled up at him, interrupting his vengeful daydream. "You're going to crush me," she laughed, over Laura Xenon.

Yes, he'd take this one for sure.

Franco Canero stood alone at the end of the bar. Only a few of the old faces were still around: the Clines, of course—though he almost didn't count *them*. They were in the secure end of the business, the business end of the business. It was the photographers and the models who came and went. He watched as Max Shapiro tried to put a move on a girl young enough to be his granddaughter. The only reason Shapiro was still in the business was because of the Clines. All the Jews stuck together. It was a lousy, goddamned world. His work made Shapiro's look like it was done with a frigging Polaroid One-Step, and he couldn't *beg* a job these days.

Then there was Mike Bradley: old models never die, they just wreck their livers. Too bad—the guy used to be good. But he'd turned into a hopeless drunk. It must take a pound of makeup just to hide the roadmap on his nose.

And LeeAnn Schneider. Now *there* was a classy woman. Of course she was past her peak by now, but she was still a real class act.

Canero drained another glass of champagne and tried to catch the barmaid's eye. He smiled as he remembered his arrival from Milan in the midsixties to instant success in New York. He had always been a good photographer, but in Milan he was one of a million. In New York he was one *in* a million. Provincials loved a foreign accent. But now they were into American photographers. Even foreign models were passé. Everything had to be red-blooded and all-American.

"Miss, got anything stronger than this panther piss?" he snapped when he finally had the barmaid's attention. So the economy was tight; he was going to get tighter.

"Excuse me a moment, sir. I'll be right with you," she said, hurrying away down the bar to where Mark Collins stood brooding. The horny little bitch was taking care of *him* first.

Lynell Alan had moved away from the bar and rejoined his girl-friend. Seeing him again made Canero angry. He was angry at all these new faces. He longed for the days when he'd made money so fast he hadn't had time to spend it all . . . the days when he and lecherous Al Cline swapped aspirants—young girls for young boys . . . the days when Mary had had to stay in the background because men ran the business, and ran it the way they wanted to—with their hard-ons mostly. Today they were a bunch of pussies.

Most of the young faces didn't merely ignore him, they avoided him as though he had something communicable. Oh, he had something, all right—age, and it was virulent. But he'd outlasted hundreds of them, and with a bit of luck—and timing—he'd outlast these.

The barmaid returned and he ordered a martini, dry. Lord only knew what he'd get. The brainless little slut could hardly take her eyes off Collins and Alan. Canero chuckled to himself. If she only knew that one was a fag and the other a jerk-off.

He sipped his martini as he gazed down to the center of the bar, to the privileged place that used to be his by right. He could hear them still. "Oh, Franco, I'd *love* to test for you": young women who thought they were so damned irresistible, and young men who some-times were. But only the best for Franco Canero. Only the best. He could hear them still, and he would hear them again. Then there'd be no more second-rate hour and half-day shootings; no more amateur models to test; and no more groveling to get invitations to parties so he could stand in Siberia with the peons. But he'd have to get a break soon if he was going to keep his studio running. Maybe he could hold on for another year or two if he cut back, moved into a smaller space. But *that* he would not do. He drained his martini and ordered another. He thought of Mark Collins, and of Lynell Alan, and smiled. Timing was everything.

The music filtered downstairs at a more tolerable level. This was a different crowd, and Lynell eased over the jammed stairway step by step, greeting the nameless well-wishers he'd met on jobs, at go-sees, at cattle calls. These were the cattle and he wouldn't delude himself into thinking he was any different. He'd only been temporarily moved up toward the front of the herd. But with a few more wrinkles, or when curly hair was out, or when people got tired of looking at him, or simply when the winds of fortune changed, he'd be back in the pack. And that day was as near as his next gray hair or his next few pounds, as near as the striking, swarthy, curly-haired, and noticeably younger man who shared the upper landing with him and a dozen others packed shoulder to shoulder. It was as near as tomorrow. ("Call me tomorrow," Mary Cline had said not half an hour ago.) It was around the corner. He expected it. The time on top would be short—if he ever made it there. But could he deal with it if it was tomorrow? Answer: yes—because he would have to. In more than four years, the modeling business had taken a lot out of him. Now he had weeks, months, at most a year or two to take some of it back.

He stayed in the shadows, leaned out over the railing, and watched the world fifteen feet below. It was a phony, ass-kissing, fast-paced, and heartbreaking world that chewed people up and spit them out. Glamorous, everyone said. You had to be on the outside to think this business was any more glamorous than being a doctor or a dentist or a plumber or a ditch-digger. For every gorgeous, silken-skinned chest whose heartbeat you checked, a hundred were old and wrinkled. For every pink-gummed, perfect-toothed mouth, a hundred were diseased and rotting. For every beautiful location-shooting with svelte, sexy women, there were a hundred rejections and humiliations . . . a hundred sweaty, stinking studios . . . a hundred times to wonder about tomorrow.

Jenny Wilder, another in a long line of new, young Cline discoveries, was on the other side of the floor by the coatroom working Peter Elliot, the photographer from *Photo House*—working him hard.

Catherine was in the middle of the room, with two other women and a man, and he guiltily wondered if one of the women—or both—were her lovers.

Catherine unabashedly snorted a patch of white powder from her pinky and passed the vial to the woman on her left, a chestnut thoroughbred with sensuously swollen lips and large almond eyes that caught his as she tilted her head back. Her eyes never left his as she pressed an index finger against one nostril as though she were Mary Poppins about to take flight. She ran her tongue languorously and invitingly over those puffy lips, and Lynell suddenly wished he was here alone tonight.

When he smiled, the woman turned and spoke to Catherine. When Catherine saw him on the landing above, she laughed and waved cheerfully. As Lynell made his way slowly toward them, threading his way down the staircase, Catherine spoke to the woman and he realized from her look of surprise that she had not recognized him out of context—had not recognized him as her friend's "partner," as Peter McGee had referred to her—had perhaps made some lewd or suggestive remark about him.

Lynell and Catherine embraced heartily as comrades would embrace, and she introduced him around. Forgetting his rule about names, Molly Falk was the only one he heard.

Lynell declined the offer of the vial from the man, a small, plain, behind-the-scenes type. He was mildly disappointed in himself, at how quickly he dismissed the man as someone who couldn't help him. When he turned to Catherine and Molly, he knew they were lovers. It was not an overt demonstration of affection that told him, but simply the quiet familiarity that passed between them. But when Molly addressed him in a smooth, low, detached voice, her jade eyes still disconcerted him by their unabashedly sexual appraisal.

"So, you're the man dear Catherine would 'follow anywhere,' " she said, continuing the visual stripping.

"It does seem unlikely, doesn't it?" he joked, hoping to hide his discomfiture.

"Not at all," she answered, quickly putting him back on the defensive. "It seems fortunate for Catherine, I would say."

"Thank you," he said sheepishly, turning to Catherine. "I hear you've been busy without me."

"Mmm." She nodded absently. She seemed not to have noticed his exchange with Molly. Perhaps they weren't lovers, after all. The behind-the-scenes type and his wife had faded back into the crowd, leaving Lynell with two coked-out beauties he had no difficulty—but considerable guilt—imagining in bed together.

When he turned to acknowledge a tap on the shoulder, he found Peter Elliot—without Jenny Wilder. "You're doing that towel thing, Lyn, if we can work out a deal with Mary."

"Great, Peter," he said, beaming as sincerely as he could manage, pretending not to feel like a piece of easily replaceable machinery. "You cast the woman yet?" he asked, only to keep the conversation going, not giving a damn who it was unless it was Catherine—and he knew they wouldn't cast them together even if they could, not without running the risk that the market would forget about towels and start trying to place where they'd seen the couple before.

"We're seriously considering Jenny Wilder," he answered with a sly grin. Over Elliot's shoulder, Jenny appeared from the coatroom— where there would be few coats on such a night. "Ever work with her before?"

"Sure, a couple of times," Lynell said as he watched Jenny run a brush through her thick hair. "She's very good," he added, catching her eye.

Peter Elliot leaned closer to Lynell but made no effort to keep his stage whisper from being overheard by the group next to them. "Very good *head*, anyway," Elliot said with a self-satisfied grin. "Later," he sighed, turning to make his way to the stairs. He'd gotten his easy sex from a woman who, if she hadn't wanted something from him, hadn't wanted it desperately, wouldn't have given him the time of day. He had impressed a few people with his conquest, and now it was time to catch the late train home to the wife and kids in Westchester County—the bastard.

Jenny squared her shoulders and returned Lynell's smile with a brazen self-confidence more appropriate for a woman who had just struck a major business deal than for one who had just performed fellatio on a virtual stranger in a dusty nightclub coatroom with a hundred people milling around outside. But then it *was* a business deal, wasn't it? And a major one for her. She joined another group of revelers. A transfer of assets. A job he'd wanted for a job she'd wanted. Mutual satisfaction. But it was a buyer's market and Lynell hoped she'd at least get the job. As he watched Peter Elliot maneuver his bulk up the staircase, he wondered how many others had been promised the same job.

"Sorry," he said when Catherine shook his arm to get his attention.

"Would you like to escort Molly and me home?"

"Aimée is with me. She's upstairs. Otherwise I'd love to."

"Bring her along." Molly pulled back her chestnut mane and held it off her neck. The smooth skin on her shoulders was tanned nut-brown, and Lynell could almost see the steam rising from her sleek neck, like from a priceless racehorse after a dawn workout. "The more the merrier."

"Yes. Do bring her," Catherine said, hooking his arm possessively.

What could it hurt? Though it was still early, he'd had enough of this place. He'd make no more meaningful contacts in this drugged-out zoo. And it just might work out perfectly to bring Aimée with Catherine and Molly—maybe put to rest once and for all any lingering ideas she might have about him and Catherine.

They pushed their way up the staircase into the rising heat, into Laura Xenon's rising volume. He suddenly remembered Laura's promise. One enormous breast had fallen exposed from her tight red dress. She made no effort to cover herself but shook the breast vigorously until the song ended, obviously proud of its awe-inspiring defiance of gravity. Then she hoisted the strap absently and re-covered herself as she down-shifted into a song with a slower beat.

Lynell saw Aimée dancing with a man he didn't immediately recognize in the smoky darkness. He stood head-and-shoulders over her, his straight, perspiration-dampened hair pressed back over his ears and close against his head. The beat of the song was slow and sensuous and he held her close, and it gave Lynell an unsettling sense of *déjà vu*.

Catherine stood on her toes and leaned to Lynell's ear. "Is that Aimée with Mark?" she asked.

He nodded pensively as he watched his last fragile link with sanity waltz away across the floor.

"She's having a good time. Leave her alone," Catherine said. "She's safe with Mark." Molly was on his other arm as Catherine led him through the crowd to the door. "It's only ten o'clock," she said when they were on the sidewalk. "You can drop us, have a drink, and still be back by eleven. She'll never miss you."

And it was *that* that Lynell Alan was suddenly afraid of.

"Evenin', folks." The huge uniformed doorman greeted them pleasantly. His craggy, pockmarked face betrayed no hint of curiosity as he ushered the attractive, formally-attired young trio into the lobby.

"He must really be confused now," Catherine chuckled.

If the huge doorman was confused, Lynell thought, he wasn't alone. Across the slowly rising elevator the two women stood shoulder to shoulder. He marveled at how Catherine could have escaped the suffocating heat of the nightclub still looking perfect: clean and scrubbed and with that crisp, all-American glow that sold those untold millions of dollars' worth of products.

And brown-skinned, tousled, small-breasted Molly, with those sparkling emerald eyes that looked into him disconcertingly, as though she could divine all the answers to him without asking the questions.

Though no words had been spoken, the electricity was tangible. "You're not a model," he said to Molly. "Too dark a tan," he continued, in case his meaning had been lost. "You're certainly pretty enough."

"Thank you," she said, as the elevator stopped at Catherine's floor. "I'm an artist." Before turning to step off, she winked flirtatiously. "You'll have to come over and see my etchings sometime."

Though ill at ease, Lynell couldn't resist a surreptitious peek at Molly's sleek, brown legs as she strode into the corridor and the slits along the sides of her dress parted to the hip. Christ, were they lovers or weren't they?

"Molly's a makeup artist," Catherine explained as he followed them

284

along the narrow hallway. "We met in Nassau with *GQ*." Catherine seemed either not to have noticed or not to have been concerned about Molly's flirtation.

"Won't you have that drink with us?" Molly asked as Lynell hesitated outside the apartment.

He suddenly felt like an intruder. "Aimée will be looking for me." He had never before felt uncomfortable with Catherine, but now it was as though she were testing his trustworthiness by tempting him to steal her most prized and desirable possession.

"Just one short one," Catherine invited.

"No, really. Thanks, but I can't. Another time."

"Sure," Catherine said as she and Molly stepped inside. "Call me?"

"Of course."

"Another time, then," Molly said seductively as she slowly closed the door.

On the return trip to On Stage, Lynell was unable to sort out his confusion, was unable to keep his mind from violating Catherine's and Molly's privacy, as he imagined them pressed against each other in a passionate lovers' embrace. Surprisingly, he found himself feeling vaguely . . . jealous? But why? And of whom?

Inside the apartment Molly spun and playfully pinned Catherine's shoulders against the door. "I thought you said decent men weren't interested in you?"

"He's not," Catherine answered seriously, making no effort to resist the light pressure of the smaller woman's hands against her bare skin. "He's interested in you. And anyway, he's not my type."

"Not your type? Then who in Christ's name *is* your type?"

Catherine looked into the multifaceted jade eyes and shrugged.

"For heaven's sake, what's wrong with him?"

"Nothing's wrong with him. He's a nice guy. But if you need reasons: For one thing he's practically married, and for another he cheats on the woman."

"That sounds like a 'bad news/good news' joke." Molly sighed and began kneading the taut muscles in Catherine's broad shoulders. Then she kissed her fondly on the cheek. "Well, we're just going to have to find you a man one of these days, Catherine, my dear. There are a lot of good men out there—brave men, honest and true," she said with mock seriousness. "And if Lynell Alan isn't one of them, well then, there are certainly plenty of others." Catherine leaned her head back against the door, relaxing for the first time in the entire evening. Molly kissed her throat gently and went on talking about men in general and occasionally one man in particular.

But Catherine was barely listening. She was wondering what she would feel if Molly Falk ever slept with Lynell Alan, an event Molly would surely gloat over. The possibilities were infinite. Would she lose a lover or gain a friend? Or would she lose a lover and gain two friends? Or gain a friend and keep a lover who had another lover?

"You're not taking me seriously," Molly protested good-humoredly. "I'm trying to have a serious conversation with you about men, but you're not even listening."

"How can we have a serious conversation about men with your hand up my dress?"

It was only as the cab pulled up in front of On Stage that Lynell began to get edgy about Aimée. On the trip uptown he'd been preoccupied by vivid imaginings of what might have happened between Catherine, Molly, and himself. But he had evaded that question fifteen minutes ago in the hallway because of—because of what? Loyalty to the woman he lived with? Or a responsibility to another woman whose sensibilities he imagined had all-too-often been neglected?

Mike Bradley passed him in the doorway. He was a suave, fiftyish man with thick, dark hair and graying temples. He had come from Australia in the sixties and become the first big male model—at least big by the standards of a then-microcosmic industry. Twenty years ago he had worked constantly and made, and spent, money hand over fist, until one day the clients had stopped calling for him. And twenty years later he was still hanging on. "It was too easy," Mike had once lamented to Lynell over cocktails after a fashion show. "It's always too easy for the ones who make it, and too hard for the ones who don't."

"I didn't expect to see you back here, leaving with those two," Mike slurred.

"Well, here I am," Lynell answered with mock cheer. "The night is young."

Bradley, as though on alcoholic impulse, grasped Lynell by the biceps and led him into a harshly-lit alcove outside the front door. Lynell had a sudden, terrifying glimpse of himself in fifteen years: fleshy and burned out, a deeply lined forehead and crow's feet etched in the corners of the eyes from too many phony and long-lost smiles. It was as though he were looking in a mirror, and no amount of pancake makeup would hide the darkened eye-pouches or the distant hurt in the pale blue eyes. There was an urgency in Bradley's voice as he whispered conspiratorially, "Let me give you some advice, kid. You can tell me to fuck off if I'm out of line." But he knew Lynell wouldn't stop him. "You know, the surest and fastest way to the bottom is from the top. Ten years from now? Ten years from now? You'll be awake and this will all be like a dream. The handshakes? The backslapping? The jobs? The trips? The money? The booze, drugs? The women? The men if you want them? All one great big wet dream. I had my time once—five or six years. And if it wasn't for my fucking tearsheets, I wouldn't have any memories at all. Use it, kid. It's not for the squeamish," he said fiercely. "It's not for the one-woman man. You're not a human being, Lyn. You're a fucking illusion. Clients want the illusion. Women want the illusion. Take everything—every last dime they're willing to pay for it now, because they won't pay for it for long. And save it—the money. Save the money and you'll save the good times. Then when they throw you out, you'll be able to tell them to go fuck themselves and you won't have to hang around scrounging a living."

Bradley suddenly released Lynell's arm and steadied himself against the nearest wall. Lynell wanted to say something but couldn't find the words.

"You're on your way up, kid, so you gotta give 'em what they want, *when* they want it, and the *way* they want it," Bradley said, continuing to back away. "But make 'em pay. Make 'em all pay while you can still get your price." Then Mike Bradley turned and disappeared alone down First Avenue.

"Jesus," Lynell whispered to himself. His heart was pounding out of control and cold sweat had popped out on his forehead. He was thirty-two years old, with a nearly empty bank account and a shaky future, and he had never in his life felt so alone.

The crowd had not diminished appreciably and Laura Xenon still had them roused to climax point. But Lynell barely noticed her as his eyes swept the floor for Aimée.

As he rode the cab back to the apartment, he thought of the earlier eye-contact with the barmaid, the immediate service she'd given with a smile that offered much more. He thought of two young girls in San Francisco, and of Molly Falk's small breasts, tight nipples embossed on her evening gown. He had to get firmer control over his life—over his libido.

He was relieved to find Aimée alone, still in her red dress, sitting on the couch with her legs folded under her.

"I looked for you," he said. "How did you get home?"

"I looked for you, too. A cab."

"I took Catherine and a friend home."

"Who says chivalry is dead?"

"We wanted you to come with us, but you looked like you were enjoying Mark's company."

"He was nice."

"He's supposed to be a fag."

"That's odd. He didn't seem to be."

"You looked as though you two had met before."

"Never laid eyes on him," she said with no intention of lying.

"You're becoming an extremely popular young man." With that Mary Cline hung up the telephone. Of course Lynell Alan couldn't see the grin that spread across her face or the dollar signs that were superimposed on her image of him.

"Well, what was so important that it required a phone call to 'Herself' on a Saturday morning?" Aimée asked as he scratched his illegible shorthand in his appointment book.

"My schedule."

"Isn't that LeeAnn's job?"

"Yes, usually. But it seems I'm getting to be 'an extremely popular young man.' 'Herself' has taken something of a personal interest in the kid."

"Lynell, I don't mean to be a killjoy, but you're thirty-two years old. Sure, you're on the rise, and God knows, I'm happy as hell for you, but even if you reach the crest, this wave of popularity can't last all that long."

"I know that, better than you think."

"So what are you going to do?"

"Ride the wave, Aimée. Ride the wave."

"And what happens when it reaches shore?"

"Maybe I'll have enough money so it won't matter."

"It will always matter. Where is all this taking you, Lynell?"

He turned to her and shrugged sheepishly. "To Milano."

"As in Italy?"

He nodded.

She was stunned. When she looked back at him, her eyes were shining with tears. She had stopped stuffing clothes into her small satchel. For the first time in her life, she could think of absolutely nothing to say. "Does this mean we're not going to Connecticut for the weekend?"

Saturday morning was a blistering one in Manhattan, with the sun searing brightly through the gray haze of pollution. The mass Labor Day Weekend exodus had begun Friday afternoon, thinning the Saturday traffic appreciably. It was not a day for walking, so Lynell hailed a cab, tossed their two small bags into the backseat, and slid the picnic basket carrying L.C. gingerly in after them. Aimée was still in shock but had recovered enough to insist they bring the cat.

"How long will you be gone?"

"Probably only a few months. Mary says I have a European look and I'll be able to build up a good portfolio over there while the agency promotes me over here."

"You've got to do something about that cat. We'll kill each other here alone. Anyway, I'm too busy to worry about her. And what will I do with her when *I'm* out of town?"

By the time they arrived at Grand Central Station, they were both damp with perspiration. "Holy shit, we'll catch pneumonia," Lynell complained as they stepped aboard the 10:00 A.M. Conrail train to New Haven. "It can't be sixty degrees in here."

Lynell's parents picked them up at Union Station and they reached Pine Orchard at just after noon. The air at the shore was twenty degrees cooler and noticeably less humid than in the city, and the cloudless sky was a deep, crisp, royal blue. Lynell felt renewed as the foursome sat sipping lemonade on the front porch overlooking the water, with Cedar Island in the distance across South Harbor.

"Wasn't it nice of you to bring little L.C.," Liz Alan purred, stroking the contented cat as it lay curled in its own wicker rocking-chair, enjoying the cool ocean breeze.

"Ah . . . about L.C., Mom. I was hoping you wouldn't mind if she stays a while," Lynell ventured. "You see . . ." But before he could explain, Aimée was gone, walking slowly down the beach, alone.

Aimée was assigned the guest room. They never slept together at his parents' house. The subject had never been specifically discussed; it was simply an arrangement they all seemed comfortable with. When he stepped into the guest room, preceded by a light tapping on the door, Lynell caught only the briefest glimpse of Aimée's bathing suit as she slipped a brightly striped beach-dress over her head. He winked playfully. "New suit?"

"I picked it up at Bloomie's the other day."

"Good choice."

The east end of Cedar Island was inhabited during the summer months, but the west end was deserted, and it was there that Lynell steered his father's small outboard. Childhood memories flooded back to him as a young boy water-skied past them.

At the island Lynell anchored the boat securely in the shallow water, but deep enough that he was sure the falling tide would not strand them. Then they crossed to a small half-moon cove on the south side, where the sky was so clear they could see the hills of Greenport, Long Island, twelve miles across the Sound.

The afternoon was a complete and utter escape for both of them, and neither spoke of Milan. Not a soul approached the entire day, either by land or by sea. During midafternoon Lynell left the cove for a long, lazy, and nostalgic stroll along the beach. When he returned over an hour later, they went for a swim in the clear, briny water.

Aimée was one of very few women who could wear a white crocheted string bikini, and Lynell watched her as she lay on her back, straps hanging to her sides to avoid tan lines. She was as enticing in the unrelenting sunshine as a cold drink, and he spread his palm on her hot, sweat-beaded stomach. She smiled, and he leaned over her and gently kissed her throat.

The top of her bathing suit was salt-water damp as he peeled it down. Her breast was cold and salty on his lips, and he tugged at the nipple like a child.

Suddenly he jumped up from the blanket and scanned the empty beach. "Let's go skinny-dipping!" he yelled.

Aimée sat up, momentarily startled, and watched as he dropped his bathing trunks, his erection springing unabashedly in front of him. Then he kicked the trunks away and ran splashing into the water. Aimée stood, raising the top of her bikini, and walked to the high-water mark, shaking her head. "You're nuts. Somebody will see us," she protested, but they both knew she only needed a little coaxing.

"Come on, live a little. There's no one around. It feels great," he called, and he swam off with his white bottom flashing above the water line.

Aimée waded tentatively into the water waist-deep before unhooking her bra and flinging it backhanded to the water's edge. When she turned and bent to remove the bottom, Lynell stared hypnotically at the cleft whiteness and knew he had been there before; something in the memory distressed him. Before he had time to discover what it was, Aimée swam to his side.

He loved the feel of her body against his, its warmth a sensual contrast to the tingling coolness of the water around them. God, he wanted her here and now, in the great out-of-doors, with the awesomely erotic possibility that someone was watching them. The thought made him ache as he watched Aimée's breasts floating on the water between them, while under the surface he moved to slip his icy stiffness into her warmth.

"Lynell, we can't," she said, and before his dream came true, she broke from him and backstroked away.

"Why the hell not, Aimée?" he snapped.

She looked nervously out to sea, where a dozen sailboats ran on the distant wind, and up the beach, where two small boys played in the sand in front of a far-off aqua cottage. "Someone might come," she told him.

"Yeah," he sighed, "but for sure it's not going to be me."

Three days later at JFK Airport, the Northwest Orient 747 lifted off into a cool mist that clung to the runway like the last breath of summer. Lynell fingered the zipper on the portfolio he held possessively across his lap. He was as apprehensive as he had ever been in his life, as he headed into an uncertain future—alone. Was it worth the sacrifice? Was Europe the right place for him, now that a few things were beginning to break for him at home? Was he making a mistake in trusting that Mary Cline knew what she was doing? He sighed and ordered the first of the many cocktails that would fuel his resolve across the Atlantic. The answer, of course, was that he had no choice. He had to believe Mary Cline knew the best way to manage his career. And if she was wrong? He had come to New York City with nothing. The worst that could happen was that he'd leave the same way.

17

Catherine Ward arrived at the studio almost an hour after she'd been told to report, but no one complained. Of course she still wasn't positive that Thelma Preble had been instructed to tell her to be there earlier than the actual starting time. She had her suspicions, but she had yet to confirm them.

She hated to admit it, but she missed Lynell and his punctuality. He had been gone for over three months and she hadn't heard from him at all, so she supposed the feeling wasn't mutual. But that didn't seem to matter. She missed him dreadfully. Funny, it had never occurred to her she would. When he was here, there just didn't seem to be all that much to their relationship: work, rounds (which she actually looked forward to when she was with him), an occasional lunch, and even a movie or two when Aimée was out of town. No big deal. But now that he wasn't here, it was almost as though someone had taken away her morning coffee. His friendship was something she had, somewhere along the line, begun to take for granted, to depend on. Catherine chuckled to herself. Lynell would be insulted by the analogy, but he was as comfortable as the little mutt she had grown up with, the only pet she had ever had. No sparks flying, mind you. Just comfortable and warm and easy, like it used to be with her father, long, long ago.

"Catherine, would you kindly read the script the way it's written?" the director snapped impatiently. "A very good copywriter was paid an exorbitant amount of money to write it."

"I'm sorry, I'm sorry. My mind was wandering. Let's do it again."

"Okay, Fortune's, take seven."

She read the lines from the teleprompter once again, trying to concentrate harder this time. She hated these low-budget, corner-cutting, that-was-good-enough productions that, no matter how hard you tried, you could never hope to raise above mediocrity.

"A little more life, please, Catherine," the director broke in wearily. "It's a restaurant, not a funeral parlor. People should *want* to go there after they see the ad. Christ, Molly, fix her up, will you? Take the sheen off her face and put more color in her cheeks. Jesus, she looks like hell."

Catherine whirled, threw down the sequined clutch bag she held as a prop, and screamed. "Fuck you, Adam!" She had reached the end of her rope. "I don't need this shit!" And she stormed off the set, leaving her stunned "dinner partner" and a crew of a dozen standing astonished in her wake.

"That bitch is more trouble than she's worth, Adam," the photographer said. "She pulled the same stunt two weeks ago when I worked with her on a Pepsi ad. She's killing herself, man. She's strung out all the time."

Adam Metz turned to Molly Falk with a beleaguered look. "Molly, you two are friends. Go see if you can get her back here, will you please?"

Molly raised her eyebrows and shook her head with a sigh. "I'll try."

"And do fix her makeup while you're in there," Metz added, as though to reassert his authority, as Molly sighed again and walked resolutely toward Catherine's dressing room. Metz then turned back to the tuxedo-clad model, the photographer, and the all-male crew and shrugged fatalistically. "We're stuck. She's all we've got. Unless one of you guys wants to play Paul's date in drag."

"Pepsi dumped her," the photographer added, apparently proposing an alternate solution. "Flat."

"Yes, well, this isn't Pepsi," Adam Metz answered angrily, as though the trappings of the low-budget production didn't dramatically demonstrate that. "This is just a local businessman who laid out practically his last dime for"—he looked around the set to confirm they were no longer in mixed company—"that cunt, and we certainly can't afford to go over budget. We're just going to have to live with her for a couple of hours more."

The photographer sighed heavily. "Great."

Catherine Ward was angry with herself. Why the hell did she do these things? But then why did people pick on her all the time? She

293

was just trying to do her best. The only reason she ad-libbed her line was because it sounded better to her that way, more natural, more like what a person would really say.

The bottom line was that nobody liked her and she couldn't imagine why, unless it was that they were all jealous of her success. No, on second thought it wasn't true nobody liked her. Lynell liked her. Molly and Mary Cline liked her, too. No, Molly and Mary Cline needed her, used her . . . and, of course, she used them. But they didn't like her. Not really.

And what about Webster Greaves? That gutless wonder. She should have abandoned him when she'd had the chance. She shook her head in abject defeat. Scandal. That was all she needed. To be dragged into a major scandal.

She had no idea how the young reporter who had shown up at her door last night had gotten her address. But then he didn't work for the *New York Post* for nothing.

I'm a rape victim, she thought immediately when she threw open her door in answer to his knock and found to her shock that it wasn't Webster.

"I'm a newspaper reporter," he said, holding his palms up to cut off her scream. "From the *Post.*"

"How did you get past the doorman?" she asked, not believing him. She was wearing—almost wearing was perhaps a better description—a sheer, lacy peignoir, unbuttoned to her breasts.

He smiled, held up his right hand, and rubbed the inside of his index finger vigorously with his thumb.

"So, what do you want?" She'd deal with the doorman soon enough.

"I'm here to get your reaction. May I come in?"

"No. My reaction to what?"

"The lawsuit."

"What lawsuit? Nobody's suing me. You've been misinformed. Now, if you'll just . . ."

"Not you," he said, closing in, "Webster Greaves."

"Webster? Webster and I are just friends. I stay out of his business. If some racquet or clothing company is suing him for breach of contract, he's got lawyers. Why come to me?"

"It's not a racquet or clothing company, Miss. It's a jilted lover."

He was searching her face for a reaction, but even as exhausted and surprised as she was, she tried not to show one. She thought she was doing quite well until he said, "a man named Thomas Barkley. Know him?"

He had to help her to the couch, and by the time he had rummaged through her cabinets and poured them each a stiff scotch, the ruthless, predatory smirk had melted from his face. He appeared actually to feel sympathy for her, a sentiment that no doubt would mark him for extinction if ever made known at the paper. "It seems our Mr. Barkley has taken Marilyn Barnett's lead," he began. "He must believe that if Miss Barnett can go after Billie Jean King's money, then he can go after Webster Greaves's."

"They lived together?" Catherine asked, her voice thin and frail.

The reporter nodded. "In Greaves's Boca condo." He spared her asking the next question. "For almost four years." Then he spent the next twenty minutes filling her in on the details.

Catherine was silent, but through it all her mind was racing, reliving their nights together. Lies. Everything Webster Greaves had ever told her was a lie.

"It's going to be a real mess," the young man finished. The kid was so vulnerable, he thought. *Christ, she looks like suicide material.* He was losing the heart for this assignment. When Catherine Ward looked up at him, a tear was slowly trickling down her face. He had to touch her. Even awakened from her bed, tousled and distraught, she possessed an astounding physical beauty. After all the full-page magazine ads, all the billboards, and all the smiling TV commercials, here she was, suddenly so real, so very, very real. So he stood and walked to her, placing his hand gently on her neck and smoothing her hair back over her shoulders. "I'll tell them I was aggressive as hell, but you had no comment." And he turned quickly and left without another word—before he lost it completely.

She had sat up all night waiting for the telephone to ring, but it never did. And it never would, because Webster Greaves was a coward. He would never have the nerve to tell her himself.

No, none of them cared. Not Mary Cline, not Molly Falk, and certainly not Webster Greaves. Lynell was the only one, and she missed him desperately—especially now, right now, today. And even when he was here in New York, it wasn't as though she had the need—or even the desire—to see him every day. Just knowing she'd see him soon was enough . . . enough to keep her in line and on time, to keep her fairly straight . . . to keep making her want him to like her, to respect her, to be proud of her.

She fell heavily into the chair in front of the mirror and dropped her head into her hands. "I hate this," she whispered under her breath, shaking her head resolutely as she thought of him. "I hate needing anyone this much. Especially *him,*" she said out loud.

"Especially who?" Molly asked.

Catherine jerked her head up to find Molly leaning against the closed dressing room door. "Oh, no one," Catherine answered, flustered. "Nothing. I was just talking to myself."

Molly crossed the tiny room in three steps and pulled up a chair alongside Catherine's. "You okay?"

Catherine, practically shivering with anxiety, nodded.

"Well, you don't look okay. Here, try a few of these," Molly said, reaching into her handbag for a small unmarked amber bottle from which she poured a handful of red and white capsules.

"What are they?" Catherine asked as she carefully plucked three from Molly's open palm.

"Trust me," Molly answered, "they'll calm your nerves." What Molly Falk saw before her was alarming. What she saw before her was a girl who was literally killing herself, and she hated to be contributing to it by offering her these downers. But her job was on the line, and right now that job was to get Catherine Ward back out there on the set; if this was what she had to do to accomplish it, well, so be it. Catherine was a big girl. It was her own responsibility to take care of herself. Molly Falk was looking out for Number One. But Molly wasn't totally devoid of feeling, and the way Catherine looked, as she tossed back her head and chased the three pills with several noisy gulps of water, frightened Molly. So what was the worst thing that could happen? she asked herself. Well, the girl could o.d. and drop dead right here and now. And then what would Molly do?

Molly herself did a modest amount of drugs: grass, cocaine, uppers, downers, 'ludes, speed, even an occasional jolt of "The Big H," but she felt confident she could handle it. Sure, once in a while she worried about herself a little, but then she would cut back or even go cold turkey for a month or two. It was a sort of built-in thermostat that kept her from going overboard. But Catherine clearly had no such thermostat. She did drugs with Molly; she did drugs with Webster Greaves; and, Molly knew, she did drugs when she sat at home alone. That last was the most worrisome of all. Catherine Ward was in deep trouble.

"Catherine," Molly offered tentatively, "you've got to start exercising a little moderation."

But the advice had come a few minutes too late. As Catherine turned back toward her, Molly was panic-stricken. What little color there had been in Catherine's face had drained from it as suddenly as though the plug had been pulled on her blood supply. Sweat beaded her smooth forehead and a few strands of blonde hair were matted

296

against her temples. An almost comically quizzical expression crossed her face, and as she gasped for breath, her eyes fluttered for a split second before rolling back in her head, leaving her eyeballs as blank as a comic-strip Annie. As Catherine's mouth fell open, Molly lunged for her but not quickly enough, and Catherine teetered to her right, her chair suspended tantalizingly close but just out of Molly's reach, before crashing to the linoleum floor.

Molly rose to her feet and stood in shocked silence, watching the viscous scarlet ooze into the fine yellow hair, onto the green and white speckled tiles. And then she screamed.

It was perhaps the first conscious, calculated decision he'd made concerning his career since changing his name, and Mark Collins proudly recalled the precise instant he'd made it. It had come to him at the Clines' Twenty-fifth Anniversary party, within five seconds after Lynell Alan had left him alone at the bar. It had come to him so suddenly, in fact, that for some time afterward he had been unable to retrace the thought process that had brought him there. Yet it was so incredibly obvious, he was almost embarrassed it had never occurred to him before.

He couldn't count the number of acting jobs—both legitimate theater and television and motion picture bit parts—he'd been refused because of his looks. "But what about Selleck," he would say, as he had for a movie role two days before the party, "or Redford."

"There's a big difference between handsome and pretty," had come the reply.

Even in modeling he found his striking features worked against him, limiting his repertoire to swimwear (thanks to his body), and catalogues where college-age men and women were the target market, which seriously curtailed his job possibilities—and income. And then, of course, there was his size—6'4" and 200 pounds—which would keep him out of most clothing ads, and they represented about seventy-five percent of print work.

Here was Lynell Alan, a prime example of a nice-looking but far from perfect man who was beginning to take the fashion industry by storm. What was it about this man? he asked himself. This pleasant-looking man with a crooked nose and a chipped tooth? Why was he working so damned much? Why was he landing the big jobs, the exclusive contracts? Why was it that Mary Cline had decided to push *him* instead of Mark Collins? To send *him* to Europe instead of Mark

Collins—indeed, instead of anyone. He was so . . . unspectacular. It was like taking a glamorous profession and rubbing off the veneer of glamour. It was almost like turning over the rock. Like . . .

And that was when it hit him. Lynell Alan was the virtual embodiment of the profession. Like modeling itself, he had a visible flaw. Visible only on the closest inspection, to be sure, but visible nonetheless—to those on the inside, anyway, to those who saw it up close, without the makeup and the fancy clothes. And it was *that* which separated Lynell Alan from the rest. The buying public could identify with him.

But what could Mark do? Disfigure himself? Certainly not, he thought, and then something Jacques Martins, his hairdresser, had said in passing months ago, clicked in his brain. "Hair makes a statement," Jacques had said. "It's the only way, short of cosmetic surgery or dieting, that a person really has to change the way he looks."

Hair. Not the hair on his head, which had surely gotten him as many jobs as his "pretty" face had lost him. Hair on his *face*. Good God, what an inspiration! And it was one all his instincts told him would work. He could hardly contain his excitement.

The morning after the Clines' party, though it was a Sunday, he phoned a young photographer friend of his who owed him a favor. On the following Thursday morning, he rented a car and they drove out to the tip of Long Island, to a scenic spit of land in Amagansett overlooking Block Island Sound to the north and the Atlantic Ocean to the south, and she shot rolls and rolls of film of Mark and his scruffy five-day growth. He wore faded Levi's and a plaid shirt, faded Levi's and no shirt, cut-off Levi's—he'd sat right there in the meadow with his Swiss Army knife and hacked off the legs just above the knee—a red bandana around his neck, around his forehead. They even flagged down a passing mother and child wandering the beach below, and borrowed the young boy for a shot sitting astride Mark's shoulders in front of a barbed-wire fence separating the meadow from a cliff that fell into the turbulent Atlantic Ocean in the background.

A month later they returned for retakes, with Mark now sporting a sandy, neatly-trimmed, full beard. But the whiskers easily won the day. Three- or four-days' growth softened the severely angular planes of his face, gave Mark Collins the tough edge of a chipped tooth, the masculine sensuality of a broken nose, the believable sensitivity of the boy next door. It removed him from the pedestal of physical perfection. It made him real. It was a novelty in the traditionally clean-cut profession, an idea whose time had come, and because Mark Collins had been its creator, as much as it was copied in the early days, that "look" would never really be identified with anyone else but him. The name "Mark Collins" became as generic to the whiskered look as "Coke" is to soda pop.

As things began to go his way more and more, Mark took another calculated gamble with his career. He stopped wasting his time chasing elusive acting jobs. Instead he concentrated on modeling, on making and renewing the contacts that would be necessary if he was truly to have an impact. He would use modeling, use it for all it was worth, use it to make a living, use it to make a name for himself, maybe even use it as the back door to an acting career, as so many other models had in recent years—Lauren Hutton, Jaclyn Smith, Cheryl Ladd, Tom Selleck, and Jack Scalia, to name a few.

It was the right decision. Mark Collins took off. He took off so stunningly, in fact, that it surprised him. It surprised everyone. It even surprised Mary Cline.

Murphy's Law. That was what Mary Cline was thinking about as she broke the connection and then redialed. *It never fails.* Murphy should have been canonized—or sentenced to eternal torture in the fires of hell, she couldn't quite decide which. Here she was with what were unquestionably the three top female models in the business and the two top males (along with two more who were well on their way: Lynell Alan, by virtue of a stroke of genius, and Mark Collins, by virtue of a stroke of luck), and all of a sudden it was beginning to unravel a bit. Wouldn't it happen now, just when Textron, Inc. was planning to go all out with the Now Shampoo campaign and when dozens of other products were starting to put out feelers about Lynell, interest spawned by and dependent upon the continued promotion of Textron. Just when her plans were solidifying, it looked as though they were going to have to be changed. Whenever anything *can* go wrong . . .

"Hello," the now-familiar voice answered.

"I thought I told you to keep her in line," Mary snapped. No introduction was necessary, no social amenities.

"I'm sorry, Ms. Cline. I did my best."

"Well, obviously that wasn't good enough."

Molly Falk had been bird-dogging Catherine Ward for Mary Cline since a week after Lynell Alan had left for Europe and Catherine had started showing up late for appointments again. That there was a connection between Lynell's departure and Catherine's renewed tardiness was as simple for Mary to figure as adding two and two to get four:

Lynell was businesslike and punctual, almost to a fault. Catherine respected him for that as well as for his brains and obvious charm, which she would no doubt readily admit. But Mary saw something else that Catherine would perhaps not so readily admit and, in fact, might not have even recognized herself. Mary Cline knew that Catherine Ward more than respected Lynell Alan, more than admired him—she adored him. And whether Catherine knew it or not, she had fallen apart when he had left town.

"Ms. Cline, it won't happen again," Molly Falk promised pleadingly.

"You're damn right it won't happen again," Mary agreed. "Because if it does, you'll be out of work—completely." Then she slammed down the receiver.

"Exhaustion" was the official diagnosis released to the press, which, given Catherine's schedule, was believable enough. But when the girl killed herself, which at this point seemed inevitable, Mary Cline wanted it to be on her own time. "Exhaustion" was one thing—"death by overdose" was quite another. At Catherine's level of public exposure, it would be a black mark on the modeling profession in general, a profession Mary had spent her career working to give credibility. But more importantly, it would be a black mark on Cline Models specifically, a black mark which would take years to erase—and *that* Mary wouldn't stand for.

"Shit!" she suddenly swore out loud, pounding her fist on her desk. Another investment gone sour. It was like looking in the stock quotations under "Ward" and finding that your shares weren't appreciating as rapidly as your projections had indicated they would. "Shit," Mary said, softly this time, nodding her head contemplatively. It was getting time to diversify this section of her portfolio. Now was when her real artistry came into play, the time for anticipating when the price would turn from modest gain into decline, the time to put on the squeeze. *Not to panic*, she thought calmly. *Not to panic. Panickers go belly-up.* Anyone could make a quick buck by selling high. Now was the time to play the market, *her* market, to demonstrate once again why it was she who occupied the top spot. Not Eileen Ford. Not Zoli or Wilhelmina. And not John Casablancas. She. Mary Cline. A smile crept across her face. The challenge was there; she would accept it. She already had her first move planned—to bring Lynell Alan back home.

Some people mark the passing of the years by summers, with memories of soft, warm August nights drifting peacefully into dew-dampened mornings and lazy, sunny afternoons. Lynell Alan was such a person, Aimée Harris thought, a carefree soul who recited endless tales of lifeguarding and water-skiing and roasting hot dogs with the family over a charcoal fire dug into a pit on the front-yard beach. It seemed appropriate to her that her own life marched by in a succession of winters, and, more specifically, Christmases. Christmas was the most depressing season of any year, and this one, she considered as she rolled over in this now-familiar bed, promised to be worse than most.

She recalled wistfully that first Christmas she and Lynell had spent together. She thought, too, of that first Boston cotillion, and wondered how differently things might have turned out if she had never dragged him there that night, if she'd never convinced him to go to Montage Models or sent his photographs to New York agents. She imagined Lynell would not have lasted much longer as an accountant in any event . . . that they would have lived out that year and the next in Boston, while she finished at Harvard Law School . . . that then he'd have asked her to marry him and they'd have moved to Connecticut, where he'd be a successful executive in his family's business and she a successful New Haven attorney. And their biggest problem this season would have been when she should quit her job so they could start a family, rather than whose bed the other was waking up in. There would be black-tie parties at the Pine Orchard Yacht and Country Club, and they would entertain Connecticut society in the third beachfront home his father had recently purchased and which was still vacant and waiting for them on its majestic perch overlooking Long Island Sound.

But Aimée Harris was not the type to waste her time looking back. She had to look ahead, to plan. In the months since Lynell had left for Europe, her lifestyle had slipped into a hedonistic eddy that had dragged her relentlessly down to the bottom. And that was where she was now, she thought as he rolled on top of her once more, flat on the bottom.

"Good morning," she said when he had finished.

"Very good," he agreed as he stretched and yawned and brushed his whiskered face against hers teasingly.

"Ouch," she protested, pulling away.

Neither spoke for what seemed to Aimée a very long time.

"He's coming home," she said, finally.

"I know."

"How did you know?"

"It's time," he answered simply. There was another long silence. "What are you going to do?"

"Go on as though this never happened," she answered matter-of-factly.

"Can you?"

"We'll see."

"And what about me?" he asked.

"What *about* you?" she said, frowning slightly as though that was the absolute last question to be considered. "So you've slept with me. Wasn't that the whole point? Sleeping with me? We both got back at him just a little, didn't we? Me for his deserting me and you for . . . for what? For beating you out of a few commercials? Or just for being there? Anyway, we killed two birds with one stone, so to speak."

"It's more than that, Aimée," Mark Collins protested, "and you know it."

"Is it?" she asked, her voice tinged with sarcasm. "Or is it just another way for you to get one up on him? I know what you bastards are like. You'd drive over your own dog if he was standing in the fastest lane to the top."

Mark sat up and swung his legs over the side of the bed. "Aren't we self-righteous? And you're any different? Or him?"

"*He* is."

"Then why the fuck are you here with me?"

"I don't know why," she said finally. "Loneliness, I guess—maybe revenge."

"Bullshit. You know why," he said bitterly. "You know damn well why. You're here with me because you enjoy life in the fast lane. You enjoy going to all the fancy parties he won't take you to. You don't do drugs yourself—a little grass, maybe—but you like the idea of being around people who do: the wealthy, young up-and-comers, the models and doctors and executives, and the jocks and the jock-groupies who hang around them. So how are you going to go back to being a hum-drum lawyer, sitting on the sofa watching TV every night, and arguing about whose turn it is to wash the dishes? And another thing," he said, turning to look into her eyes, "you're right about him being different. He's different because he doesn't have the killer instinct—and that's why he'll never make it in this business, Aimée. You know it, and I know it. There'll be some hills—like now—and some valleys, but basically he'll just grunt along in the wings. If he'd gone into that precious family business you're always talking about, he couldn't have taken playing second fiddle to his old man. But you can't take playing second fiddle to anyone. You're here with me," he said, pressing his index finger almost painfully into the middle of her naked chest, "because you enjoy being with Number One. It makes *you* Number One." He stood up, walked into the bathroom, and slammed the door behind him.

Alone, Aimée felt a tear slip down her cheek, warm against her suddenly cool skin. He was right, she thought sadly: Lynell would probably never make it in the way she wanted him to, in the way she needed him to. He wasn't aggressive enough, hungry enough, didn't want it enough to do the things you had to do, the things she was discovering she liked to do, to make it. No, Mark was absolutely right: Lynell would never make it in this competitive world—not without her. She got out of bed and dressed quickly.

Mark stepped from the bathroom wearing his green velvet robe just as she was fastening the top button of her dress. "You're going to do it, aren't you?"

She nodded and left in silence.

Aimée had been seeing Mark since shortly after Lynell had left for Milan. It was an accident, really, their getting together again after On Stage, an accident in that she didn't contrive to meet him. It was certainly no accident that he was at the party.

She'd decided to go because, well, because there was nothing else to do—and frankly because she was still monumentally pissed off that Lynell, number one, had left so precipitously, and number two, had made no attempt to try to soften the blow.

Lynell had asked her to open his mail in case anything important arrived—such as checks, which she agreed to deposit, and bills, which she agreed to pay. Peter McGee's invitation arrived the first week, and she went, invitation in hand because although he had added on the card, "and of course your lovely friend is welcome," she wasn't at all sure he would remember her from On Stage, through the haze of his glad-handing, since they had never really been introduced. But of course McGee did remember her, because that was his business, and he welcomed her warmly, introducing her around as "Lynell's attorney friend."

And there was Mark Collins, standing out among the many other models, male and female, in a pale blue cotton sweater and a pair of pleated beige slacks, looking, with his three-day growth of beard, more the jock than Webster Greaves, who was cornered in animated conversation with Catherine Ward, or than the burly young blonde Aimée recognized as one of her firm's clients and who was, more notably, the reigning quarterback of the New York Giants.

303

Gorgeous Mark Collins, who himself had the long, lean muscular build of a defensive back, intercepted the young quarterback's latest pass, virtually cross-body blocking him in order to reach Aimée first, where even Mark's modest familiarity with her prevented further interference.

Mark Collins, along with being brighter than she had expected, was possessed of a kind of rogue-like charm she found magnetically charismatic. He had an easy conversational manner and an unforced sense of humor, but he wore his conceit as proudly as he wore his dashing outfit, though it wasn't nearly as flattering. Even when they were alone or he had his back to the party and couldn't actually see every woman present gawking at him, Aimée could tell he was always aware of the attention they were paying him. Even so, she thought him very attractive in a rough-edged sort of way—and there was no denying he was intensely sexy.

So she had left with him—well, not actually with him, because these were, if not his friends, Lynell's co-workers and competitors, and though she was upset and lonely she didn't want to embarrass Lynell. Mark left first, and she had waited what seemed a discreet interval, in which she had again had to fend off the horny young quarterback, before meeting Mark downstairs in the lobby. Afterward they had gone for a few drinks and returned to his apartment, and even though she hadn't at that point quite decided what would happen, when he had reminded her in highly flattering terms of a time years ago in a backyard swimming pool, when he had been a bit player at the North Shore Summer Theater and she a law student on vacation, it hadn't seemed such a big deal and in fact had seemed somehow to complete the cycle. And it *was* something to do. But she had felt sleazy sneaking around behind Lynell's back, even if that back was five thousand miles away. So since she enjoyed seeing Mark, instead of stopping they just didn't sneak around anymore. They were regularly seen together at parties, disguising the relationship as just one between "two close friends," and she even wrote Lynell how terrific it was of Mark to invite her to tag along for an occasional evening on the town—which was certainly no lie.

But in the months that followed, something happened for which she was totally unprepared. Where with Lynell she had teetered on the edge, she now fell completely and utterly victim to the seduction—not to the patent seduction of Mark Collins and his fierce good looks, but to the insidious seduction of the lifestyle itself.

Now as she hailed a cab on the sidewalk in front of Mark's building, she once again calculated how she could hold on to that lifestyle. And again all of her calculations led her back to the same age-old plan. But could she do it? Could she actually pull it off? It was so under-handed—and yet so simple.

After having promised to be home by Christmas, Lynell had called last night to announce he'd been held over for two weeks by Ferrari—no doubt with Mary Cline's enthusiastic approval, but not with hers. Yes, this was going to be another tough Christmas season. Maybe a flight up to Boston for a few days would ease the depression.

Aimée was keenly aware, even if Mary Cline wasn't, that Lynell was facing a crisis in his career—at least emotionally. He needed more than opportunity and financial and promotional backing; he needed encouragement. For despite his brains and obvious good looks, perhaps only she knew how terribly—and to outsiders, irrationally—insecure an awkward, ugly-duckling childhood had left him. Yes, he needed the kind of encouragement only she was close enough to give him (if she could manage to keep Catherine Ward at bay). But at this stage of her life, she couldn't afford to keep taking chances on an investment that wouldn't pay off. After all, she'd encouraged him to come this far and look where it had gotten her.

Her arm was tired from flailing in vain for yet another off-duty cab that sped past her. To hell with them. She decided to start walking. As she walked slowly south along York Avenue, she realized that, at twenty-five, she was now prepared to take a gamble on her future, but only on an investment that had the opportunity for a high return—*for her.*

As she stood on the corner of Sixty-ninth Street and York Avenue on the Upper East Side of Manhattan, waiting for the light to change, she reached into the bottom of her purse and felt around for the round dispenser of birth control pills. Removing it, she turned the plastic over in her palm several times, then casually scaled it into a nearby trash basket. When the light changed, she smiled and continued walking south.

Book 2

18

As the crowded cable car struggled to crest the steep incline of Nob Hill, a stunning blonde bounded down in a crimson dress, revealing a shapely leg through a midthigh slit as the car tilted and hurtled down the other side of the precipitous slope. She danced up behind the attractive, tuxedo-clad man whose curly brown hair tousled in the car's wake. Then reaching around to clutch his chest with one spread palm and running the other hand through his hair, she purred, "With Now Shampoo, I'd follow him *any*where."

The man—at once devoted son and gentle lover—after an appreciative sidelong glance over his shoulder at the woman, turned to gaze out from behind the television screen and shrugged modestly, as though oblivious to his enormous sex appeal. There was little doubt that his dark, seething good looks could cross generations to melt a heart.

"Jesus Christ, I see him more on that fucking thing than I do in person," Aimée Harris hissed to no one, pointing an accusing finger at the television set. Just out of the shower and brushing her damp hair back over her shoulders, she slammed the on/off button with the palm of her hand. It had been like this for the better—or worse—part of a year, ever since Europe. Even after he'd returned, it seemed he was away more than he was home. She wasn't even sure where the bastard was right now: London, Mexico, or any one of half a dozen other places. "I'd follow him *any*where," she mimicked. "I'll bet a year's salary he's fucking her eyeballs out. You can just see it going on between them—and he ain't *that* good an actor." She sat dejectedly on the couch, stroking her hair. "Shit!"

Well, it was Friday, her old high school friend, Libby Robbins, was in town on business and had invited her to an interesting-sounding party and she had no idea when that bastard Lynell would be back and she was goddamned if she was going to spend one more night at home alone.

"I think I've got pneumonia." He plunked himself on the soft couch, the deep cushions embracing him like an old friend.

"How about some brandy, you poor thing?"

"Perfect. Man, I'm still shivering. It was cold as hell out there, Catherine."

"Lynell, you know what you always say about models who complain—they ought to try working for a living. We just earned about ten thousand dollars each on this trip, and the way things are going we might very well end up with ten times that much in residuals. For a week-and-a-half's work." She propped open the swinging door that led to the kitchen, so she wouldn't have to shout to be heard. "So, it was breezy out in front of Ms. Liberty. At least it's September. You don't know what cold is until you've been out there in a bikini in February. In a blue one I looked naked."

"Sounds like 'Can you top this?' " he said wryly. "Anyway, I don't know why they had to do it today. Christ, we just got back. You'd think it could've waited until Monday."

"Time is money." She handed him one of the two snifters and sat beside him. "And time-and-a-half is more money." They swished the liquor gently around the bottom of the glasses, and she clinked hers against his. "Here's to clean, soft, *sexy* hair," she purred, mockingly.

He smiled. "And cigarettes from Marlboro Country."

"And sundresses."

He winked. "And tuxedos." He began to chuckle.

"And cosmetics." The laughter was infectious.

"And sports equipment."

"And . . . underwear."

"And . . . credit cards." He paused, stopped laughing, swiveled on the couch, and looked pointedly into her large, sad, blue eyes. "Catherine . . ." As she held her glass up to his he wanted to say more, but what he said was enough. "Here's to us."

She nodded thoughtfully. "Yes. Here's to us."

Numero Uno di Milano had been Lynell's European agent under a fee-splitting arrangement with Cline Models, and Lynell would have learned to speak Italian if he had had the time either between jobs or before he left Italy for Israel.

"They'll adore your look in Europe, Lynell," Mary had promised him. "And the experience will be invaluable."

Europe *was* wonderful for him. Though because of the language barrier he felt incredibly stupid ("I was illiterate for four months. It was a humbling experience."), it was also because of the language that he learned to emote, to let his expressions describe his feelings, both on and off the job.

It was his first time in Europe, and in his travels he marveled at St. Peter's and Gibraltar and the Alps and the Eiffel Tower and all the typical tourist attractions. France was his favorite because he was at least semiconversant in his Ivy League French. He was even able to make a faint stab at humor when a Parisian model named Claire Duseau took him to the Louvre. "I'd only seen pictures of them in books before," he explained in halting French as he admired the myriad famous paintings. Then he made a tiny square by connecting the tips of his thumbs and index fingers. "I thought they were all this big."

Though the language and customs were different, the work was pretty much the same: ninety percent waiting and ten percent doing. He read literally dozens of books that fall and winter, gravitating mostly to the classics in a conscientious effort to stave off what he feared would have been irreversible atrophy. On most shootings, at least one or two people spoke English, and any spoken lines were written phonetically for him in the script as well as on the cue cards. The long hours allowed less opportunity for reflection and loneliness, and he made an effort to polish his pidgin French during his spare time. But there was precious little of that, as he was sent about western Europe from job to job and country to country like a state-of-the-art hobo.

In September it was Ferrari and Gucci in Italy, in October Sabra Liqueur in Israel and Beck's Beer in Germany, in November men's fashions in Spain, and in December bikini briefs in Paris, for which the clothing company paid millions to buy advertising space and paid him exactly $850: $350 for the two-hour shooting and a $500 bonus when the shot of him lying back on one elbow clad only in the scanty briefs became so popular it was circulated through western Europe on hundreds of billboards. It was so phenomonally successful it reputedly caused a dozen traffic accidents at one busy Paris intersection in less than a month.

"Boulet made millions on that campaign," Lynell later lamented, "and I made nothing. They ripped me off." But the effect on his career was immeasurable: In Europe, at least, it made him famous.

But the life stunk. He lived out of a suitcase and was never really settled. There was scarcely enough time to eat or get enough sleep to look human, let alone tour the sights for which all the places he visited were famous. And he made no friends, with the brief and sole exception of Claire, an attractive, eighteen-year-old tomboy with short-cropped sandy hair and soft brown eyes, whose mature face seemed almost incongruous atop her boyish figure. Though there was very little of substance they could say to one another, there was an undeniable personal chemistry that attracted them to each other from the first morning they met on a print job for Cartier. They shared lunch at Tour d'Argent and dinner at Taillevent that first day, and when the shooting was finished the following morning, Claire offered to take him on a guided tour of the City of Lights.

"You are in Paris long?" Claire asked as they strolled along the Champs Elysée. They only corrected one another for major breaches of grammar and syntax, and only then until it became cumbersome.

"*Trois ou quatre ans.*"

"Three or four years? A very big time."

"*Trois ou quatre semaines.*"

"Ah, weeks. A very small time. Where do you sleep?"

"*A l'hotel de Rochefort en la rue Sainte Famille,*" he attempted.

"For three or four years to live in a hotel," she said, repeating his error with a frown, as though he had been sentenced to a prison term. Then she looked up at him and her face brightened. "Would you like to sleep with me?" she asked ingenuously.

He winked playfully.

She frowned.

It took him less than fifteen seconds to explain the American colloquialism with the use of a few simple gestures.

Claire frowned again. Then the two of them laughed until they thought a curious *gendarme* might have them arrested.

When Lynell left Paris to return to Milan in late December, he and Claire parted ungrudgingly on the same basis that they had lived for a month—as friends—and again Lynell wondered if those might not be the most successful terms on which to have a relationship with a woman.

Lynell's one planned visit to the States and Aimée's to the Continent had both had to be canceled because of business, either his or hers. He had written her twice a week since his arrival in Europe and telephoned once a week, but by Christmas it had been almost four months since he had seen her. The night before his anticipated homecoming, he had to telephone to postpone what would have been their first holiday together. "It's a terrible disappointment to me, too, Aimée," he said over the crackling wire. "But Ferrari wants me back for a TV commercial and . . ."

"I know. It's a big opportunity. I understand." But he knew she didn't—knew she couldn't.

When he finally did return to the United States in mid-January of 1983, he left behind a face that was spread across Europe in the pages of magazines and newspapers, on the sides of buildings and buses and trains, on billboards and television. Mary Cline had been right: the Europeans adored him, even though most of the adoration came after he had left the Continent.

But he arrived in New York to two startling revelations: the first was that Mark Collins, who *hadn't* been sent to Europe for "seasoning," had come virtually out of nowhere with his five-o'clock-shadow look to become the number one male model in New York, while people here—most notably, clients—still barely knew Lynell Alan existed. The second was that from May of 1982 through March of 1983 he had earned slightly in excess of $175,000, and after having paid the first installment of his estimated income taxes for 1983, he had exactly $3,000 in the bank.

"You'd better find a good accountant," Aimée said, only half in jest. "I've got more of your money than you have."

The specter of Mike Bradley began to haunt him, and within a week Arthur Young & Company's New York office had him on a strict allowance. "Funny how things come full circle," he explained to the young accountant handling his newly formed personal corporation.

Arthur Young & Company was an immediate help in stabilizing his financial situation. His career, despite a slow start after his return to America that had made him more than a bit apprehensive, needed no help at all. The Now advertisements were tremendously successful, and he and Catherine were working on those—both print and television—as well as on other accounts: she on Revlon, Colgate, and Chevrolet; he on Ralph Lauren, Marlboro Cigarettes (which, as one who totally abhorred smoking, he did only because he convinced himself it would be hypocritical to start setting standards only because he could afford them), and Gillette (yes, they *had* hired him this time). People were even beginning to recognize him from his work. . . .

313

Following a brief second honeymoon after his return from Europe, his relationship with Aimée began once again to suffer the effects of neglect brought on by the combination of their busy schedules and his indecision. Even L.C., returned from her comfortable life on the Connecticut shore, stalked about moodily, as though waiting impatiently for something to happen.

He rubbed a thumb and forefinger gently over his eyes as he stood and yawned. "I'm exhausted. Brandy's catching up with me. Mind if I use your phone?" he asked. "I've got to call Aimée."

"Of course not. Why don't you use the one in the kitchen? My bedroom's a disaster area. Flip on the tube, will you?" she called as he crossed the small living room.

He pulled on the switch without breaking stride. Then, hearing the familiar words, he turned and backpedaled the few steps. "My God, here we are again," he said as he watched Catherine jump from the slowly moving cable car.

Catherine sat forward intently. Lynell stood back appraisingly. They both fell silent for the ensuing thirty seconds. "Not bad," she said when the advertisement was interrupted by the regular programming. That was how she always thought of it when the commercial was hers.

"Not bad at all," he agreed.

"I still get kind of excited whenever I see myself like that. It's sort of unreal—like seeing someone else. You know?"

"Yes. When I'm alone I can really get into it. But I get embarrassed when I'm with other people. I think it embarrasses my old man, too. My mother is kind of proud, though. You got big plans for tonight?" he asked as he rounded the corner into the kitchen and lifted the receiver from the red wall-phone.

"I look like I've got big plans, don't I? Yeah. The New York Giants and I are having a little get-together later on: a *ménage à quarante*."

He peeked around the corner with an impish grin. "Rumor has it the Rockettes are more your type."

"Very funny." She flung a small, round, embroidered pillow that rattled the teapot on top of the stove after glancing harmlessly off the side of his head.

"No answer," he said when he returned to the living room. "Maybe she went to Boston. When I called her the other day from Honolulu, she said she might visit her folks this weekend." He couldn't hide his disappointment. Aimée had seem distracted recently, preoccupied, and Lynell found himself wondering—but not asking—about her social life in his absence. He never even considered telling her about Claire Duseau. She wouldn't have understood. No, on second thought, she wouldn't have believed him. He dropped the pillow absently in a chair, unzipped his small nylon travel bag, and began fumbling through it.

"If it weren't for all of your running paraphernalia, you wouldn't bring anything at all on these trips." Catherine stood and went into her bedroom.

"You don't mind if I just relax a tad? I'll be out of your way in a few minutes."

"No hurry," she called. "If you're comfortable you can just stay right here tonight. I've got an extra bedroom that's just collecting dust."

"Thanks, but I'd better get going. I don't want to impose."

"Suit yourself, but it's no imposition."

"Well, I'll just mellow out some for the road," he mumbled through a jaw-aching yawn.

By the time she returned to the living room, dressed in a baggy gray sweatsuit, he had already kicked off his shoes and reclined on the couch. "Lynell?" she ventured sheepishly as she sat in a chair across from him and looked pensively into her lap. "I may be speaking out of turn, but I would hate to see you get hurt." She waited, but he made no move to stop her. So she dropped the bomb. "Lynell? If you don't start paying a lot more attention to Aimée, I think you're going to lose her. I'm sorry," she said, looking up sadly, "but I'm only saying this because you're my friend and maybe I see something you don't see. Lynell?" She clicked her tongue in exasperation. Her first major attempt at real conversation had been met with heavy breathing that was just this side of a snore.

Aimée had always been a woman of quick decisions—and quicker action. That was what made being an attorney so frustrating for her sometimes. The wheels of justice turned slowly, and no amount of procedural or technical grease could speed them to her satisfaction.

The Yellow Cab lurched away from the curb at her order. "Seventy-second and York, it is," the young black driver repeated.

She sat back and smiled, anticipating the night ahead. Snap decisions almost always turned out to be good ones. Spur of the moment, that was the way to live. She had thrown on an ankle-length peasant skirt; a white, scoop-neck jersey; a burgundy shawl her mother had knit for her; a pair of sandals, no stockings or pantyhose for a change; and

315

no bra. Standing at the curb to hail the cab, the cool breeze blew up along her legs and between them, and made her feel sixteen again. The pleasant September evening was perhaps too brisk for her attire and she would certainly be underdressed for a New York party, but it didn't matter. She felt wonderful.

"Mind if I smoke?" she asked, only because of the unconventional brand she was about to select.

The cabbie leaned back, turning profile so he could catch her in his periphery without taking his eyes off the road. "Lady, until Seventy-second and York, you *own* this hack."

She lit the joint, forced all of the air from her lungs, and inhaled the smoke so deeply she checked her bare toes, half expecting smoke to be curling up between them. Then she leaned back and looked up through the rear window at the cloudless sky. "Ah, autumn," she said quietly to herself. Stars filled the sky, and when the cab crossed Thirty-fourth Street, she caught the orange ball of the moon rising between skyscrapers over the East River.

She took another deep draught and leaned forward, passing the joint through the aperture that separated the front and back seats.

"You a gypsy, girl? You read my mind," the cabbie said with that New York cool she loved so much.

"What's your name?" she asked when he passed it back.

"James. James Brown."

The dark shadows inside the cab made it difficult to tell, but she judged him to be about her age. "Come on, you can do better than that. All black men are named James Brown," she said good-naturedly. "It's the Afro-American equivalent of John Smith." She passed the joint back, noticing the cab had slowed appreciably.

"Hey, really, no shit. I thought of changing it once—to Rashad Ahmad, but I could never remember it. It's embarrassing to have to pull out a piece of paper and read your name every time somebody asks. And what's your name, gypsy?"

"God, does my outfit look *that* bad?"

"Just different," he answered, looking in the rearview mirror. "On you, mama, it looks *fine*." He drew out "fine" with obvious appreciation.

"Thanks." She made a point of not giving her name though she already liked James Brown. She felt the smoke curling pleasantly around in her brain, and time stood still. James Brown could have spoken to her during the next few minutes, but the first words she heard marked the end of the ride.

"Seventy-second and York."

The meter read $3.25. She handed him a five. "Keep the change, James Brown." She handed him what remained of the joint. "And keep this, too."

"Thanks. Get me through another shift." He smiled broadly through perfect teeth.

He was cute, nice, and though it was against her better judgment— to hell with judgment. "There's a little party up in 12A. Come on up and join us if you don't get off work too late." Without turning to face the apartment building, she jerked her thumb over her shoulder like a hitchhiker.

He grimaced. "Bunch of uptown white folk?"

She spread her arms invitingly, tilted her head, and grinned fetchingly. "And me," she shrugged.

He was still looking after her as the doorman ushered her into the building.

"Aimée Harris." She held out her hand to the well-groomed, thirtyish man who answered the door at apartment 12A.

"All right, Aimée, you came!" Libby Robbins had appeared from nowhere, and dragged her childhood friend into the apartment past the speechless host. "Decided to ding Mom and Dad, eh? Super choice." Libby handed her a joint, lit it for her, and led her to the bar. Then she poured Folinari Soave into two plastic cups and handed one to Aimée.

There were about two dozen people in varying states of inebriation milling around a large, modern, and no doubt expensive apartment. "Early in the evening for this many New Yorkers to be gathering on any night, let alone a Friday," Aimée offered with exaggerated haughtiness, lifting her nose and extending her pinky from her cup as she sipped.

"Most of them have been here for a couple of hours already. Doctors and nurses, mostly. They're all nuts. They think it's party time whenever they're off duty." She grabbed Aimée again and led her down the hallway, past the bathroom, and into a large bedroom. Two men stood at the foot of the bed. A squat green cannister with "NITROUS OXIDE" stenciled in black block letters across the front sat on a low table behind them. Libby took a small red balloon from a cellophane package on the table and fitted its neck carefully over the valve at the bottom of the bottle. "Remember this shit?"

"How could I forget?"

"Paul? The guy who met you at the door? He's a dentist," Libby explained as she turned the handle, slowly filling the expanding toy.

"Wasn't the guy in Marblehead a neurologist or something?"

"Randy?"

"That, too."

Libby unleashed her infectious laugh, then put her lips over the balloon's neck and sucked half the gas out in one gulp. Without removing her lips from the balloon, she exhaled back into it, then inhaled and exhaled in rapid succession several more times. "Wow, what a rush." She handed Aimée the empty balloon.

Aimée filled the balloon again and took the gas into her lungs, held it for as long as she could, breathed back into the balloon, inhaled, and exhaled again. Her head expanded like the balloon, then contracted and expanded again. She almost blacked out, then felt a numbing sensation, a tingling like the leading edge of an erotic dream that rippled out from her pelvis, up and down along her torso and limbs, as though her entire body were being inflated and then rapidly deflated.

People came and went in a hazy montage, filling their balloons, joking in the hallway, and returning to dance to the punk sounds that reverberated through the apartment. But Aimée and Libby barely noticed. They were two childhood friends caught up in old times, between sucks on colorful balloons that lent a carnival air to their reunion.

"Do you think that Randy bastard's wife ever found out? I'd hate to think so. She was so nice."

"What?" Libby readjusted to the subject through a fog. "Oh, you mean that while she was passed out dead drunk upstairs, her loving new husband was doping up and balling her baby-sitter and best friend? In her own TV room?" She began to laugh. "On the very floor where her kids would be watching cartoons a few hours later? He's divorced and remarried now. 'Course that doesn't stop him from dropping by my apartment on his way home from the hospital from time to time. Sexy fucker."

"This rush should last longer."

"Then it wouldn't be a rush," Libby laughed. "It'd be paralysis."

By ten o'clock the party was in full swing, and Aimée wasn't sure if it was the booze or the drugs or seeing her wild, crazy, totally irresponsible friend that made her feel wild and crazy and totally irresponsible again. The wine was wonderful and warming. The grass was colorful and relaxing. The gas was sensual and arousing. She felt free and alive and sexy. Men watched her and danced with her, and during one rare ballad, a man danced with one hand inside her jersey and the stiffness in his groin pressed against her and she didn't care. She was with Libby again, wild and free, and she wanted to turn on the entire room. She was tipsy, stoned, excited, and she suddenly wondered how long he had been squeezing her crotch through the fabric of her skirt. She was too wasted and horny to care. If he wasn't doing it, God, she might be doing it herself.

She looked around the room at an odd assortment of hedonistic New Yorkers, oblivious to all but their own pleasure, most dressed sloppily now even if they hadn't arrived that way, all in drug- or alcohol-induced euphoria or both, unseeing, unhearing, uncaring, only feeling.

It was just after ten when John Hayes arrived, a striking black man ten years younger and half a foot taller at his side. One look at Hayes in his tailored Brooks Brothers, three-piece, charcoal-gray pinstripe suit and the party heaved a collective sigh as though its mother had come to drive it home.

Libby patted Aimée's shoulder. "I couldn't help it. When I was at your office today, the guy was relentless. So I invited him." Then she headed toward the door to greet him. "Don't worry, Aimée I'll keep him out of your hair."

Aimée, who had stiffened self-consciously and pulled back from the stranger at her side, rippled her fingers toward Hayes, who waved back. The black man with him was the object of much attention, due certainly to his good looks. It was only when he, too, waved back that Aimée realized she knew him.

"James Brown," she called with unfeigned delight. "You came." She extricated herself from the lustful grip of her growingly perturbed companion and offered a terse explanation. "I'm sorry, but I invited that guy. I can't just leave him there not knowing anyone. See you later, huh?"

"Hey, gypsy." James took the hand she held out to him. She offered her cheek as naturally as though greeting a friend of as many years as they had been friends minutes.

She took him on a refreshment tour of the party ("This bedroom is bigger than my whole apartment.") and introduced him to Libby and John Hayes ("We met in the elevator on the way up."), who seemed to be getting along rather well.

The music slowed with the pace of the party, and when they danced, the top of her head barely reached his chest and she felt warm and secure enfolded in his arms. He smelled clean and good.

When they went to the bedroom again, they shared a balloonful of the gas, something that had seemed so unhygienic when she had seen it done earlier but seemed so . . . inconsequential . . . now. And with their lungs full and their heads swimming far away, he held her to him and they kissed as though they had long been lovers.

319

Back in the living room they passed a joint between them and danced as closely as it was possible to dance, and she felt him pressed comfortingly against her and remembered when it had been this way with Lynell. Then she forgot about Lynell—and about John Hayes.

Libby's 1979 Toyota was parked around the corner on the next block. Steadying a drunken and disheveled John Hayes, Libby unlocked the front door and reached through to pop the lock on the rear door. "Never in my life have I seen someone get drunker faster." Then she saw the ticket on the windshield. "Oh, fuck."

Aimée unwrapped herself from James, crossed to the driver's side, and plucked the offending citation from under the windshield wiper. "They'd never chase you to Boston for this." And she tore it ceremoniously down the middle and dropped it into the street.

Libby looked wryly from John Hayes, whom she had just deposited in a heap in the back seat, to a rumpled Aimée standing glassy-eyed in the street. "Well, in case they do, do you happen to know a lawyer in this town who isn't all fucked up?"

In the backseat Hayes was mumbling incoherently as he tried to sit up. "You know," Aimée said seriously, "I think this is the first time I've ever seen him without a tie."

Libby held the keys out to her friend. "Will one of you two drive? I want to make sure loverboy doesn't puke on my seatcovers."

Aimée took the keys and held them up toward James, who held up his hands. "All yours, gypsy. I don't want to drive one more mile today."

Through an excess of caution born of a drug-induced paranoia, Aimée drove slowly and erratically enough to catch virtually every traffic light on Lexington Avenue for fifty blocks. The frustrated but restrained cab driver made only one comment as she parked in front of her apartment building. "I think you just set a record."

"It was a dirty job, but someone had to do it."

"You did fine," Libby said, reaching to pat her shoulder. "Now let's get F. Lee Bailey upstairs."

Aimée was looking absently across the elevator: the single convenience she enjoyed about the new penthouse apartment Lynell had insisted on after signing the Now Shampoo exclusive. Hayes was propped up in the corner between Libby and James. It was when James smiled at her that she first considered the remote possibility that Lynell might have returned to the apartment in her absence. She shuddered, the blood draining from her face.

"You okay?"

She had been looking through him. She saw him again now. "Oh . . . sure, James. I'm fine."

Well, no promises had been made. There might have been a tacit understanding between them—but no promises had been made. Just four revelers returning for a nightcap. It was barely past midnight. Nothing wrong with that. Why should she care, anyway? Lynell came and went as he pleased. He wasn't celibate—of that she was certain. But right now she didn't care about Lynell's feelings. What she cared about was not being embarrassed—not embarrassing James. Up to now she had just wanted to keep feeling young and carefree, to flow into this man's arms without the thought that she hadn't known him a few hours ago, might never know him again after tonight. Even John Hayes's presence hadn't bothered her. But now she was suddenly worried. Where was Lynell? On the mere chance he would be home, she wished that they—all three of them—would disappear and she wouldn't even regret spending another night alone.

The elevator rose and fell as it stopped at her floor, and her stomach rose and fell with it—and kept falling as she led the trio along the wide, brightly lit hallway. "You'll have to pardon the mess," she apologized as she turned the third key and pushed open the door, sighing her relief into the darkness. She switched on the light to the apartment exactly as she had left it and crossed to the bedroom, James and Libby whistling their approval from behind her.

"Holy shit!" Libby was unable to conceal her amazement. The living room was enormous, with a mirrored wall reflecting the view out over Gramercy Park so that the breathtaking skyline was visible from anywhere in the room. A sliding glass door at one end of the room led to a spacious fieldstone patio furnished with wicker lawn-chairs, while at the other end there was a large country kitchen on the other side of a swinging door that Aimée apparently left propped open for convenience. "This place is outrageous," Libby went on, as she and James lowered Hayes onto the couch.

Aimée peeked into the bedroom to make absolutely certain they were alone, before pulling the door closed. "Looks like a tornado went through there," she said, ignoring Libby's comment. Aimée wouldn't have denied that she enjoyed the apartment, but thought it far too expensive—as well as ostentatious—and was self-conscious that guests could only see the price tag.

James wandered, slack-jawed, out onto the patio overlooking Gramercy Park. When he returned, closing the sliding door behind him, he asked in a flat monotone that suggested he now feared he might be expected to pay—and dearly—for what he had assumed would be free. "Gypsy, I don't mean to pry—and you can tell me it's none of my business—but what do you *do* that you can live in a place like this?"

"Not *that*," she answered.

"She's a goddamn lawyer," Libby broke in quickly, letting Aimée know she would cover for her. She knew Lynell from their days in Boston—knew from her conversation with Aimée at her office this afternoon that he paid most of the rent, knew that Lynell was out of town much too often these successful days. If Aimée wanted James to know, she could tell him in her own time. "Robs from the rich and keeps it," she added with a laugh. "Got any brandy for the peons?"

When Aimée returned with the brandy, Libby and James had another joint going. Libby sat on the couch where Hayes pawed impotently at her, his lust temporarily winning out over his intoxication. Aimée stood in the middle of the floor, regarding the strange trio, and suddenly knew she couldn't do it—couldn't recapture her misspent youth. In fact, she didn't want to. The brief affair with Mark Collins had taught her a lesson: She had earned too much self-respect to throw it away so carelessly. And there were other things to consider now. Perhaps Lynell would never be ready to marry her. Perhaps it was time to end her painful cyclical life with him. But this was not the way to do it. She set her brandy snifter on the coffee table. "Suddenly I don't feel so well," she said truthfully. "I think I'd better get into bed."

"Anything I can do?" Libby asked with concern.

Aimée smiled wanly. "Just take care of James," she said, smiling at him. "And throw a blanket over John," she added, nodding to where he lay stretched out comatose on the sofa. "Help yourself to the spare bedroom."

At the Gramercy Gardens he pushed "18." The doors slid together and the elevator lurched upward, chain links rattling dimly above and below. It was one of those background noises—like his own breathing—that he rarely noticed in the bustle of daytime. Sounds, like lovers' tender whisperings, that only came out at night.

It was just after one o'clock. Though he'd have walked from Catherine's apartment during the daylight hours, he'd been reluctant to do so this late and had telephoned for a cab.

He was surprised and mildly annoyed that it took only one key to open the door. Here, as at the old apartment, Aimée had insisted on three locks, which had meant changing the two existing ones when they moved in and having a third installed. If it gave her peace of mind, fine—especially since he was away so often. But to go off to Boston for the weekend and leave two of them unlocked? He would try to remember to mention it to her when she returned. A sudden loneliness shivered through him at the thought that she wasn't here.

His hand groped for the light switch but recoiled as though singed when he saw the male form tucked in the fetal position on the couch. From behind the closed bedroom door, sounds, muffled but unmistakable, breached the silence. He reeled back into the hallway and reversed his key in the lock.

As he left the building, he instinctively pushed the source of his pain to the far unconscious reaches of his mind. A cavernous hollow filled his chest as he strode determinedly north in the black moonshadows of the apartment houses lining Lexington Avenue. It was not until he crossed Lex at Thirty-fourth Street, and the setting moon threw his shadow onto the silver-blue pavement before him, that the sounds he had heard moments before became pictures. He stopped, stunned, in the middle of the nearly deserted avenue, then half-walked, half-staggered to the corner, wrapped his arms around the lightpost, placed his cheek against the cold metal and cried.

He was not so much the hypocrite that he cried over being "cheated on." He cried because, though he found commitment impossible with his life always so unsettled, he loved Aimée. He cried because if he had been there, even in spirit, had let her know how much he cared about her and her life, things would still be good between them. He cried because he feared it might be too late for them. And he cried because, as a human being, he was a complete and utter failure.

He rubbed his eyes dry with the backs of his hands and continued north toward Catherine's. This time he *would* walk. Exhausted, he wasn't exactly sure of either the reason he would give for his return or what he would do tomorrow.

The moon lit the cityscape with a rare early-morning brightness that left an afterglow in the wake of the few cars that passed along the avenue, like the phosphorescent tracks of a black and white television after the picture has been turned off—like his life had become: a colorful and ever-brightening fantasy, until darkness fell, leaving only a faint image of a relationship that now perhaps was too dim to ever be turned back on.

He turned east instinctively without noticing the street sign, then north again on Third Avenue like an IRT commuter napping between stops but always waking at his own. No matter how hard he tried he couldn't erase the tape of the closed bedroom door that kept replaying through his brain. But perhaps it was something he *needed* to see.

323

"Hey, mister, you lonely tonight?" The voice was gravelly but unmistakably female.

"No . . . thank you." If you ignored them they went away. She trailed him.

"Anything you want for twenty bucks."

Now he *did* ignore her and stepped up his pace, and she fell farther behind, off the scent. "I'll take you around the world," she called as the distance between them lengthened. "And you'll never even have to leave this block," she added with the waning conviction of one who has let the fish slip the hook.

When he felt safely away, he peered over his shoulder to where the shadows had swallowed her. Then the echo of her footsteps died behind him. The last thing she showed was her pride. "Fuckin' fag!"

Sex. It seemed the world revolved around it. People lived and died for it one minute, then gave it away the next. Intimate and all-important with one partner, it meant no more than a handshake with another. No, the hurt-lover role wouldn't work. The problem was much deeper. The problem was the nagging doubt and insecurity that haunted his life. The problem was what *he* wanted. The problem was *him*.

Exhaustion, emotional more than physical, was beginning to retake him. It was too dangerous to be wandering inattentively through this jungle. He needed to sit down for a few minutes to collect his thoughts. At the corner of Forty-ninth Street, a small flashing neon sign announced "Jackie Shaw's Bar and Grill." Lynell slowed and walked in. It was crowded and rowdy, and he took the first unoccupied seat at the near end of the bar. He spun on his stool and looked out at the reassuring ugliness of asphalt and concrete, half expecting to have been mysteriously transported to a greasy-spoon truck stop in Greenville, South Carolina, where a staccato-voiced Rod Serling would introduce him around: "Submitted for your approval: one Lynell Alan, who has just crossed into . . . the 'Twilight Zone.' "

"Draft," he said when the burly bartender finally glanced his way, and when Lynell looked along the bar at the blue-collar patrons, mostly male and many still in work clothes and baseball caps, he wished he hadn't stopped. The small, dimly lit room was sour with cigarette and cigar smoke, and the neon flashed annoyingly in his peripheral vision. "Baby Love" blasted too loudly from the jukebox in the rear, and he felt the beginnings of a monumental headache.

"Two-fifty," the bartender growled, slamming the heavy mug on the bar.

"Keep it," Lynell said, placing three ones on the mottled black-and-white Formica.

The unshaven man scooped up the bills with a snort. "Thanks. Now I can take that trip to Hawaii."

Lynell ignored the remark. Hell, three dollars was plenty for a beer, half of which had been sloshed on the bar. He glanced quickly along the bar again, but Jackie Shaw's wasn't a napkin joint.

In spite of his gray cashmere overcoat, which he would gladly have traded even-up for the less conspicuous blue "Con Ed" jacket a few stools away, most of the twenty or so patrons had taken little notice of him, with the exception of a heavyset woman standing five yards down the bar. She wore tight slacks and a tighter sweater, and her platinum hair glowed pink with each flash of neon. When she locked eyes with him he quickly looked away. With all of the advertisements he was in now, more and more people were beginning to regard him with faint signs of recognition. Or maybe she was simply admiring his new coat. He unbuttoned it only halfway. He wouldn't be staying long.

"Hey, Mac." The man suddenly on the stool next to him had a short, muscular build; black, deep-set marble eyes; and a long, pointed, rodent-like nose that seemed to be sniffing for trouble. He carried himself with an air of confident power and plunked his beer on the bar noisily when he sat, as though he intended to stay. It was obviously not his first. With his thinning hair and deeply furrowed brow, he looked older but, Lynell guessed, was younger than he. "Lady says she knows you," the man almost hollered over the Four Tops' "Sugar Pie Honey Bunch," a thumb-jerk indicating the platinum blonde at his shoulder.

Lynell looked at her, smiled, and nodded greeting. "I don't think so," he said with a shake of his head. He felt an instinctive pumping in his chest.

"Hey, the lady's never wrong. What's your name?"

"Ah, Lew," he lied.

"Hey, yeah, I'm Tony and this here's Pam. Jackie boy," he yelled down the bar, "bring my friend another Bud."

"Thanks, no," Lynell said, covering his mug with his hand. "I haven't finished this one and I've really got to split."

"Hey, you can't turn down a drink. That ain't friendly," Tony said with a pinched smile, as he drained Lynell's mug and slapped his biceps with an open palm. Lynell's chest pumped harder. "So where do you know Pam from?" His voice held a tinge of jealousy.

The woman smiled again. She was almost pathetically homely, with overbleached hair, crooked gray teeth, and a neck that rose directly to her upper lip, uninterrupted by even the trace of a chin. Lynell shook his head almost in resignation. Though he wouldn't be afraid of this man one-on-one, Tony was an obvious regular, and several of his cronies seemed to be taking a special interest in their conversation. "I was in a television commercial recently," Lynell admitted reluctantly as Jackie delivered his beer. It was a gamble, but he had no choice. Tony was making him extremely nervous. Maybe he'd be impressed enough to get off his case.

"That's it!" Pam squealed. "You're the one the girl follows everywhere."

Lynell shrugged sheepishly.

"Oh, you're one of *those*," Tony lisped, fluttering the fingers of his left hand, then leaning his forearm on the bar again.

"I've really got to be going now. Thanks for the beer, Tony." But before he could step to the floor, Tony had grasped his biceps.

"You can't leave without drinking your beer, faggot." He literally spat the last word.

"Aw, c'mon, honey, leave him alone. He's a nice guy. He's just out to have a good time," Pam whined.

As a lefthander Lynell felt a special kinship with other lefties. They wore their watches on their right wrists. They made gestures with their left hands. They hoisted their beers with their left hands. Some even listed to their left like old unbalanced battleships. Tony did all of those things, and Lynell never took his eyes off the man's left hand where it now lay across the bar.

"I *am* leaving," Lynell said as he shook the man's hand from his shoulder, regretting that there was no way out but to just get out and hope for the best. As he reached for the floor with one foot, his eyes dropped for an instant, then snapped back to Tony's left hand. But it was too late. The first punch deposited Lynell neatly on the floor, and its momentum propelled the squat, muscular man to his feet, poised to continue the attack.

Stunned, Lynell knew the maniac would be on him in an instant and now feared not just for his face, his living, but for his life.

Tony paused and looked down the bar at his friends. "The faggot insulted my woman," he bellowed with mock indignation. Behind him Pam screamed for him to stop, adding fuel to his rising sexual frenzy. When he was finished beating the shit out of this queer, he'd take Pam to the darkest booth, the one way in back, and she'd crawl on her knees under the table and blow him while his blood still thundered with adrenaline. But he quickly lost the thought at the sound of his disabled prey scrambling from the floor.

Lynell felt the fluid leaking from his right eye as he thrust himself to his feet, burning with indignant rage. Using all the power in his driving legs, he planted a stiff forearm in Tony's groin, ripped his hand upward along the crotch until he felt scrotum, and dug his strong fingers into the testicles, twisting simultaneously until they collapsed like Ping-Pong balls and the man doubled over in agony. Through blurring vision, he laced his hands behind the moaning man's head and launched a vicious knee uppercut into his face. He could have killed Tony, he realized as Pam shrieked over the crumpled body. But he'd had no choice. Tony had planned to beat him to a pulp and *enjoy* it. It was him or me, he thought—and it wasn't over.

As Tony's three friends leaped to the aid of their fallen comrade, Lynell snatched a half-empty Bud bottle by the neck and smashed it against the corner of the bar, sending beer and shards of glass flying, and stopping the trio dead in their tracks. Friendship was one thing. Getting cut was quite another.

Quickly checking over his shoulder that the way behind him was clear, Lynell backed the few paces to the door and slipped out, dropping the broken bottle to the pavement as the door slid closed on the Beach Boys: "If some loud bragger tries to put me down . . ."

And then he ran.

"My God, what happened to *you?*"

The three women in his life—best friend, agent, and lover—each greeted him with exactly the same question but with three drastically different emotions. In order, they were concern, outrage, and impatient indulgence.

Catherine was the first to ask the question, while the purple welt still rose under his right eye. Stifling a gasp, she reeled against her door in a panic, and the black silk kimono with gold fire-breathing dragons fell back to where the curve of her slim leg met her hipbone. Above the loose waist-knot, the trough of the silken U carried her flat muscled abdomen, shining like polished ivory, then rose over her lovely breasts. Then Lynell's tired eyes met those of perhaps the most physically perfect female specimen he had ever seen—and one who seemed as unaware of that perfection as a gangling adolescent.

"I'll live," he reassured her. "Can I take you up on that offer of your spare bedroom?"

"Of course. But first let's get some ice on that thing."

Fifteen minutes later he still lay on the couch in the dark quiet of Catherine's apartment, with an ice-pack pressed against his eye and so

327

many unspoken emotions swirling in his brain that he couldn't focus on any of them. He wished he could have talked to Catherine, but the burden was too heavy to shift even a part of it to a friend. He sensed that Catherine had enough troubles of her own. Strange, they were such good friends and yet knew so little about one another. Still, he wished he could have talked to someone, and as he lay there in the darkness, listening to his own heartbeat, battered and bruised both physically and emotionally, he was sure things couldn't possibly get worse. On Monday morning they did.

"My God, what happened to *you?*" Mary Cline demanded, as she stormed behind her desk and sat heavily in the deep leather cushions of her swivel chair.

Lynell walked to the desk slowly, shuffling his feet like a repentant schoolboy. "I'm sorry, Mary, but . . ."

"I've seen my share of shiners," she said through him. Then she stood and leaned across her desk for a closer look. "I'd say that one has just put you out of business for about three weeks."

"Really, Mary, it wasn't my fault. I tried everything I could to get out of there without a fight," he explained, shaking his head at the cruel vagaries of fate. "All I did was stop for a beer," he added finally, more to himself than to her.

"Well, I hope it was a tasty one," she hissed, sitting again and riffling through a small stack of appointment slips before dropping them ostentatiously into the wastebasket. "Because I'm going to estimate it cost you thirty thousand dollars."

And you six, he wanted to say.

"Take a vacation," she said, checking the calendar. "We'll start booking you as of October third. That'll give you three weeks from today."

She never once asked if he was all right.

He left the office with his head bowed and his tail between his legs, and feeling distinctly differently than when he had arrived at Catherine's apartment early Saturday morning: this time he *knew* things would get worse.

Lynell was unsure how many hours he wandered Manhattan's side streets. It was a gray and moody Monday evening when he let himself into the apartment and dropped his duffle bag on the floor. He would make it up to her. That was all he knew. Somehow he would make it up to her.

"Hi, I'm home," he called with forced cheer over Carly Simon, singing mellifluously from the new stereo that sat in the corner opposite the kitchen where he could hear Aimée rummaging in the utensil drawer.

"My God, what happened to *you?*"

And he wished he could tell her. He wanted to, needed to—as maybe he should have told her how he had first seen her those summers ago: to clear the air, so perhaps they could start fresh. But he couldn't. And half an hour later, when in spite of his pain—because no matter how bad it was, it couldn't be as excruciating as her own—Aimée told him what she had waited days to tell him, had waited weeks, months, maybe even years to tell him, he had wanted to explain how empty he felt, how unfulfilled. Because until that moment, he still had hopes for them—fragile hopes, but hopes nonetheless. But he couldn't explain. He just didn't know how.

And as Lynell Alan stood there numbly, Aimée Harris turned to face the future, a future she no longer had with him. "Lynell . . . my life isn't here anymore. I'm going back to Boston."

And he wished he could cry. "But . . ."

"Let me finish. My life never really was here. Your life was in New York, so I came here to be with you. Don't get me wrong. I've learned a lot here—about my career, *and* about myself and what I want, what I *need*. I don't really know what I expected from you when I came here, but I know I haven't gotten it." She shrugged. "Or maybe I have. I've gotten an answer. Not the one I wanted, but maybe the right one. Anyway, you know I've been spending a lot of weekends at home when you're away. See, I don't even think of this as home. I put out a few casual feelers and have gotten a couple of offers. I've decided to accept one of them. It's come time for me to move on."

"But . . . maybe we could get married," he said, knowing before he said it that it was too late.

"A year or two ago I would have agreed. Or the summer I met you. I think I'd have married you the day we met. But it wouldn't work now. Maybe it never would have."

"But . . ." And there was, suddenly, nothing left for him to say. Maybe if he had been ready to leave modeling there would have been; or if, to show his good faith, he had promised to finally accept his father's standing offer. Or if he had known that Aimée was two months pregnant.

329

19

During the brief hiatus necessitated by his black eye, Lynell returned to Pine Orchard to spend some time with his family and, coincidentally, L.C., who had remained, since his departure for Europe, under his mother's care. At first, with little to do besides think of Aimée and what might have been, he missed her badly. He telephoned her several times and left messages she never returned. Once he reached her at her new law office, but she told him she was too busy to talk. When he protested, she hung up on him. It was over, and he had to face that fact. It was just so painful to let go.

When his eye had healed sufficiently for him to return to work, he did so with a vengeance. More and more he saw Mark Collins on go-sees and at auditions, and they even worked the same fashion shows and catalogue jobs from time to time, including the spring edition of *Fashions of the Times*. Somehow the head-to-head competition with Mark spurred him on to work harder and put in more time than ever humping for those "possible" jobs. He tried to convince himself he was too busy to think of Aimée anymore, and perhaps during working hours he was. But in spite of his frantic schedule, something was missing, something big, something important that he either hadn't the time or the vision to identify. It was as though he was marking time, just waiting for that something to happen, though he wasn't exactly sure he would recognize it if it did.

What did happen was that in May Lynell was called back to London to do a television commercial for American Express's European market. "You've become quite famous on the other side of the pond," LeeAnn said in her best British accent. "And Textron has waived your contract restriction so we can send Catherine. American Express wants to do two versions—one with you alone for the European market, and a second with both you and Catherine for possible future use here."

For Lynell, the incredible distance he now felt from Aimée was intensified when he met Catherine at JFK and they hugged affectionately and resumed their conversation as though three weeks had not intervened. Why couldn't it have been this way with Aimée? It was because of the sex, the passion, the commitment and responsibility, and the constant question of the future. It was why good friends remained good friends throughout the years and why lovers never looked back.

He was glad the seed of initial attraction he had felt for Catherine hadn't grown into a sexual relationship, which had been due at least as much to her as to him. She was so young and so beautiful she would never have been interested in him, even if he hadn't been involved with Aimée at the time. Instead their relationship had evolved into a camaraderie that transcended physical bounds. In an intensely competitive business where friends were rare, where backstabbing, jealousy, and the cold veneer of self-confidence were the rule, it was good to have someone who would be there when the glitter faded, and who would understand. A good lover was difficult to find . . . but perhaps not so difficult as a good friend.

In London, business as usual was interrupted only by a drive on a free afternoon to the city of Bath, where the light aroma of sulphur shared the air with freshly baked bread, the architecture of the Roman Empire still exerted its influence, and forty years after World War II, incendiary-blackened building façades shared the boulevards with those that had been and even now were being resurfaced. On their last night in London, Catherine convinced a reluctant Lynell to dine at The Savoy Hotel Restaurant on The Strand. The view from their table was nothing short of spectacular. The evening was clear, and they could easily see across the Thames to the center of the sprawling city and beyond. As the maitre d' led them to their table, perhaps even the precise table Lynell, who always worried about being seated at a bad table, would have selected, a hundred pair of eyes followed.

"Isn't this better than McDonald's?" Catherine asked.

"I'm reserving judgment until we've eaten." After they had ordered

331

a carafe of burgundy, Lynell leaned across the table. "You know why we're getting such great service, don't you?"

"Yes, I do. But I'm wondering if you do."

"Because they recognize you. That's also why they've seated us at the most visible table in the place: so the good patrons can see that a star comes here." In the corner, with two banks of windows reflecting the curious stares around them, Lynell felt as though they were on display.

"Lynell, wake up!" she said, patronizingly patting the back of his hand. "They recognize *you*! I'm nothing over here. And even if they have seen me on television, they wouldn't know me from a hundred, a thousand other women on television who all look the same: blonde hair, blue eyes, tall. *You're* one of a kind. American Express didn't ask for me. And they didn't ask for Jason Wexler, or Craig Burton, or Christie Brinkley . . ."

"She's already doing MasterCard," he broke in.

"Don't interrupt. I'm on a roll. They asked for *you*. And when that ad airs back home . . ."

"*If* that ad airs back home."

"Boy, are you a skeptic."

"A realist."

"Okay, *if* that ad airs back home, people won't just vaguely recognize your face anymore. They'll know your name. They'll know who you are. You'll be really hot stuff then, kid." She looked around at the other diners, most of whom had by now returned to their meals.

"You think?" he asked, looking up with a puzzled smile.

"I *know*."

He straightened his tie nervously. "Are the lights dim enough so they won't notice that I don't look as good in person as I do in pictures and on TV?"

"Don't worry," she answered with a wave of her hand. "The only thing they'll notice is that your fly is open."

His eyes shot to his lap before he realized he'd been had.

"Gotcha!" she said, winking in Lynell's own familiar style.

Textron, Inc. wasn't about to miss a free plug. Even though the American Express ad would never mention Now Shampoo, if it ever did air it would be as good as an ad for that product, with both the presence of their models and the innuendo that the pair knew each other from somewhere, which of course would leave the audience thinking not only of American Express but of Now. So, employing the ever-popular shotgun approach to advertising strategy, Textron immediately sent Catherine and Lynell, along with Billie Devlin and a camera crew, out on the road to cement the image.

When you *are* your own business, you know no weekends and you make no inflexible plans. After a late Saturday return from London, Lynell and Catherine took the first flight Sunday morning to Acapulco via Mexico City with the Now crew—first class, as always.

The trip was a disaster from beginning to end. It began on the runway at JFK as they awaited clearance for takeoff. Suddenly smoke and panic flooded the cabin of the Aero Mexico 727. "Don't they speak English?" Lynell asked, almost as exasperated as he was frightened.

"Easy, big boy." Catherine tried to calm him, patting his white knuckles desperately clasping the armrest between them. "A little patience."

"A little patience? For all we know, the crew has evacuated and left us here to fry. Or worse," he added, ducking instinctively as the nearby departure of a jumbo jet shook the 727 in its wake.

The captain finally announced—in broken English—that the problem was with the air conditioner.

"How does he know what the fuck the air-traffic controller is saying, if that's the best he can do?" Lynell wondered out loud as the aircraft began rolling along the runway with the faint smell of smoke and fear permeating the cabin. "They should have let us get off and take another flight."

With the air conditioner inoperative, the plane quickly became a furnace, and by touchdown in Mexico City four and a half hours later, his shirt was soaked. The delay on the runway at JFK had a ripple effect, causing them to miss their connecting flight in Mexico City, where they waited for five hours in the dank, windowless Rio Rojos Cafe.

At 5:30 Billie Devlin herded them across the terminal to the Aero Mexico departure gate to sit and wait the final half-hour. "Just in case they're on time for once."

It was Catherine who at 5:45 noticed a boarding jetway being slowly driven away from the doorway of a brown and gold Aero Mexico plane on the tarmac. Overcome by a sensation of impending doom, she rushed out of the terminal, approached a uniformed Mexican, and began gesticulating toward the aircraft. "Acapulco? Acapulco?"

"*Si, Acapulco,*" the man answered with a toothless grin, as though delivering the punchline of a 'Gringo' joke.

333

No announcement, no warning, and there was the jetway backing away from the doorway of *their* plane to Acapulco . . . *fifteen minutes early!*

"I expect late," Catherine gasped between breaths, as they boarded the plane on the run, "but early?"

"Why are they in such a rush? The damn thing is practically empty." Billie Devlin was sweating with the exertion though the day was cool and breezy.

Once they were airborne and his respiration had evened, Lynell turned to Catherine and smiled admiringly. "Catherine, I've never seen you so pissed off. I thought you might lie down in front of the plane if they didn't stop and let us on."

"Don't you believe I wouldn't have!" she shot back. Then she softened immediately and patted his hand as it once again gripped the armrest in fear. "Won't you ever get used to flying?"

"Never."

The 727 swept in over Acapulco in the dying light of day, and Lynell saw the isolated airstrip below as the port side of the aircraft dipped gently below the horizon. On the ground a uniformed trio grabbed their bags and equipment like a band of marauding thieves, and when the Now team finally caught up with them, the porters stood at the taxi stand in a neat row, with hands outstretched. As Billie dug for the tip two more men piled their belongings into a caravan of dilapidated taxis, and it seemed to Lynell that Mexicans must be born with one palm up. If the weather hadn't been so agreeable, he'd have thought they'd never left Manhattan.

The Acapulco Princess was one of the most magnificent hotels in the world, and it stood surrounded to the east by a golf course and to the west by an angry stretch of pounding Pacific, out of which erupted a line of mossy cliffs to the north, natural skyscrapers with twin peaks as breathtaking on first viewing as the World Trade Center's awesome spires.

A warm breeze swirled through the open lobby of the pyramidal structure, and tier upon tier of floors rose above them around an immense hollow shaft of open air. "They don't expect rain," Lynell remarked wanly as he gaped up from the reception desk at the blackening sky overhead. But as tired as he was, he was unable to sleep until he had stood on the balcony of his fourteenth-floor room and breathed his fill of the misty salt air.

The trick, for Lynell, was to make each time seem like the first. No matter how many commercials he'd made delivering the same lines . . . no matter how many times on a given day he had made the identical hand gesture, used a facial expression to convey the same emotion . . . no matter how repetitive or tedious, it was his job to make it appear as though it was all happening spontaneously. And if anyone thought that was easy, he had never had to do it.

Not that he was complaining, he thought as he stood out on the terrace of the Calinda el Mirador Hotel, where they had driven the next morning to shoot with the precipitous cliffs of diving fame looming in the background. After all, he could be *working* for a living. But here he was, practically on vacation, a vacation for which, with his contract and depending upon how many times the ad aired in the major markets, he might earn twenty, fifty, or even a hundred thousand dollars—maybe more.

There was a method he used to ward off the tedium of repetition. When he verged on boredom he would remember Arthur Young & Company and *real* boredom, and slide easily back into his character of the moment. Doing it when you were tired . . . doing it when you were sick . . . doing it when you were bored half to death, and still making it seem as though it were happening for the first, idyllic, romantic time—*that* was the challenge.

"Lynell!" His mind was back at a desk in Boston, and his body on a terrace in Acapulco.

"Sorry, Billie."

"We're all tired," she said patiently, "but you should be able to deliver the lines in your sleep by now."

"I was just re-psyching myself."

"Okay, okay, one last time before we lose this great light. With feeling."

He was a weary traveler, and as he strolled from the bar out onto the terrace, the flapping of the pantlegs of his white linen suit in the gentle breeze accentuated his loneliness. At the railing he sighed wistfully. Maybe he shouldn't have taken this vacation. As the sun set he searched the horizon, scanning the darkening cliffs and the Pacific that unfurled at his feet like a crimson carpet welcoming him to nowhere. He turned slowly and leaned against the railing, supporting himself with one hand as the other raised the white fedora to his head.

"Oh, don't, please," she breathed in a voice as deep and diaphanous as the neckline of her white silk gown. The touch of her fingertips momentarily paralyzed his arm, and his clouded eyes found hers. "You'll crumple your hair," she explained with a demure pout.

The finale was a calculated variation on a theme. As he broke from her hypnotic gaze, with a now-familiar expression that marveled at his own good fortune, he reached for the inside breast-pocket of his fastidiously pressed suit. It was advice, pure and simple, on a strategy that had never failed for him. "Now Shampoo," he said, producing the clear plastic bottle, careful to hold it with the label forward, "don't leave home without it."

"With Now Shampoo," Catherine purred, "I'd follow . . ."—she let the sentence drop, turned, and seared the lens with a sensual stare— ". . . *you* anywhere."

Fade to sunset.

"Super!" Billie hissed through clenched teeth, her fist punching the morning air for emphasis. "That's it for this morning. Good work, everybody." There was too much light now for sunrise to pass any longer for sunset. "Back at five."

Where the breaking hours of dawn held the morning audiences to a curious busboy, an early arriving waiter, and an occasional insomniac, the evening shootings were taped before a dinnertime throng of tourists, mostly Americans and Germans, restrained by the ropes the hotel management had placed strategically to cordon off the terrace.

The crew had been shooting in Acapulco for a week and it only came on him the last day. During the afternoon he and Catherine strolled the endless stretch of white sand south of their hotel, wearing Levi's; shapeless, long-sleeved, gray sweatshirts; and wide-brimmed straw hats to protect against the intense tropic sun. The cramps began to seize him about a mile from the hotel, and only subsided when the eternal return trip was over and he was finally back in his room, lying semicomfortably on his bed.

"Shall I tell Billie you can't make it?" Catherine asked when Lynell winced in growing pain as he sat up and swung his legs over the edge of his bed. She sat beside him with the damp facecloth she'd used to daub the perspiration from his feverish brow.

"No, thanks. I'm just a little uncomfortable, but I'll live. The show must go on and all that."

If he hadn't already been ill when they left the Princess, the rollercoaster ride north through the Sierra Madres would surely have done the job. By the time they reached the Calinda El Mirador, there wasn't enough makeup in all Mexico to erase the pasty sheen from Lynell's complexion.

"Did you drink the water?" Billie asked the obvious question.

"Only at the hotel. I can't understand it. I followed all the rules.

336

Christ, the only thing I've eaten all day is a couple of *huevos rancheros* at breakfast."

"At the hotel?"

"No. Catherine and I ate downtown this morning."

"Did you have the eggs, Cathy?"

Catherine shook her head no. She looked so damned healthy it only made Lynell feel that much sicker.

"Well, we just need a few more insurance shots," Billie said apologetically. "Think you'll be all right?"

Lynell nodded. Even speaking required more energy than he could muster.

They had most of what they needed. The final shooting was for background: sunset, cliffs, and the couple on the patio against the russet horizon (for which they all but propped a listless Lynell against the railing).

Back in the lobby of the Calinda, Lynell, dressed in one of the three white linen suits brought for the shooting, felt every bit the weary traveler he had played all week. Billie had been extremely careful with the suits, having her assistant literally press the pants as he stood in his underwear on his spot on the terrace. Several times the young woman had even applied the iron to the pants to freshen the crease while he still wore them.

"Keep the damn suit on," Billie said now as he headed stiffly toward the manager's office, which had served as their makeshift dressing room. "It's yours. Let's just get back to the Princess and pack you off to bed."

"I think he's in for a long night," Billie whispered to Catherine from behind the wheel of the rented VW Rabbit, as she careened south through the mountains with Lynell lying across the backseat doubled up in pain, clutching his stomach with one hand and the top of the rear seat with the other to keep himself from being catapulted onto the floor.

By the time they reached the Princess, there wasn't a single square inch of the suit that wasn't wrinkled. But Lynell was in too much pain to give it a thought. As Catherine helped him onto his bed, he knew he wouldn't even take it off.

"Let me help you," Catherine offered, slipping off his white loafers.

He stretched out on his back on top of the bedspread and pulled the fedora over his face. "Just play taps."

She managed to strip him to his underwear. "A mortician's job is more difficult than I thought."

337

"And you haven't even stuffed me yet."

"Embalmed."

"Whatever," he groaned.

She yanked the covers from underneath him as cleanly as a magician pulling a tablecloth from under a priceless china tea set, and covered him gently to his throat, tucking the blanket tightly around him and brushing his cold, sweat-beaded forehead with the back of her hand. "Want me to sit with you for a while?"

"No. Thanks for your trouble, Catherine. I'll be all right now. Just let me die in peace."

"It's no trouble. I'll be next door if you need me. I hope you feel better."

"Yeah, thanks,"

He slept soundly, well into the night. In fact, he slept better than Catherine, who never risked bringing drugs of any kind out of the country and now lay awake like a doting mother, not daring to sleep lest her ailing child should need her.

It was just after 3:00 A.M. when she first heard movement from his room. She remembered his last words before she had left, "Let me die in peace." She didn't want to intrude on his privacy. But by 4:00 she couldn't stay away any longer. He had to know that she wanted to help.

The rush of cool air from the balcony chilled her bare shoulders, and she reached from the warmth of her cocoon and felt for the flannel nightgown she had dropped by the bedside.

He was like a baby, really: sick, exhausted, and helpless. And it took him a few long moments to answer her light tapping on the door. "Oh, please, Catherine, I don't want you to bother," he croaked. "I'm a mess."

But she *wanted* to bother. "I don't care," she said, and as he returned to his bed, she crossed his darkened room and cracked open the sliding glass door to the balcony to clear the acrid smell of vomit from the air. In the moonglow she crossed the small room and sat on the edge of his bed, tucking her bare feet up underneath her, and stroked his damp hair as she had in so many television commercials. The fresh air began to chill her, so she slipped her feet beneath the covers next to him, feeling the heat radiating from his feverish body. When she sat up against the headboard, he curled fetally toward her, and she held his head against her breast and applied soothing, circular strokes to the small of his back, until the even breathing of sleep came over him and she was suddenly, surprisingly, overcome by a choking emotion that reached so deep into her throat she was unable to swallow. Tears gath-

338

ered in the corners of her eyes and streaked her cheeks. As he wrapped his arm unconsciously around her, she held him as desperately as though he were her own child, and she began to sob softly in the throes of what she pegged as a deep maternal instinct.

When the telephone rang at 6:00 A.M. she was gone, and he barely remembered she had been there at all. Gone, too, were the cramps that had racked him until the early morning hours. But with only a few hours of sleep and a body completely dehydrated, he still suffered from nearly total exhaustion.

"How do you feel?" Catherine asked when he finally emerged from his room.

A weak moan was his only reply.

"If you want to go back to bed, I'll book us on a later flight."

"Thanks, but this is the only one that doesn't go through Mexico City, isn't it?"

"The only one today."

"I'd do anything to avoid Mexico City."

It was Catherine who carried their bags to the taxi stand. It was Catherine he draped his arm around for support on the walk from the terminal to the plane.

"Poor girl," the stewardess consoled her when she lowered him into his seat. "How long is your husband sick?"

"Just last night," Catherine answered as she sat. Lynell immediately lay his head across her lap and fell asleep. As she stroked his soft curls she thought of home.

"I'll take him home, Billie," Catherine said when they landed in New York. "It's on my way."

"Sorry about this, Billie," Lynell managed weakly as Catherine held the cab door for him.

"There's absolutely nothing to apologize for. You two did a wonderful job, as usual. I can't wait to see the edited print. You just get home and get some rest."

The apartment was empty and cold. "How about some tea?" Catherine had just tucked him into bed. He was getting some of his color back but was still very weak. "And toast?"

"Tea would be nice."

As Catherine served his tea, Lynell checked the bedside clock. With the change of planes in New Orleans and the time difference, it was nearly midnight. Catherine was still in her traveling clothes: a pair of khaki slacks and a white LaCoste tennis shirt that were crisp and fresh.

She flushed when his eyes fell briefly to where her nipples stood out against the fabric.

"I wonder if Florence Nightingale was as beautiful as you are," he said in a light, friendly banter that revealed none of the sexual arousal he felt, an arousal he knew was unfair to his friend, rooted as it was as much in his gratitude for her care and his missing of Aimée as it was in Catherine's own physical attractiveness. "Thanks a lot, Catherine."

When Catherine stood and turned toward the door, he tried not to watch the graceful, athletic sway of her hips and looked quickly at the clock again, intent this time on remembering what it said. "You're not leaving at this hour." It didn't have the inflection of a question.

She stopped in her tracks and turned to face him again.

"There's a spare bedroom and there are clean sheets in the bathroom closet. You could be showered and in bed in fifteen minutes. And anyway," he said with a devious grin, "your job isn't over."

Catherine shot him a suspicious frown.

"Not until you fix me breakfast in the morning and make sure I'm fully recovered."

"Breakfast?" She seemed relieved. "How about *huevos rancheros?*"

Later, as she rummaged quietly through her travel bag, Catherine realized there had never been even the slightest question. She *wanted* to stay.

Her shower was—as showers inevitably are for one who has spent the entire day traveling—an almost religious experience. She scrubbed herself thoroughly from head to toe, shampooed her hair, and even found a spare razor and gently whisked away the stubble from her legs and underarms. She stepped from the bathroom a new woman.

When she returned to Lynell's room to borrow a clean nightshirt, she was a little disappointed to find him already asleep. She went to the closet, unwrapped herself from her damp bath towel, and buttoned herself into a red flannel shirt that barely covered her behind. Then she went to his bedside, felt his warm forehead with the back of her hand, and turned out the light.

She made up her bed in a weary trance and gratefully climbed between the crisp, cool sheets. As tired as she was, sleep came easily. Occasionally throughout the night she turned, and in her semiconsciousness only the lower octave of the refrigerator's hum or the unaccustomed firmness of the mattress reminded her she wasn't at home in her own bed. Those differences, and the vivid presence of the man in the next room.

Bacon sizzled in her dreams, its aroma so real it brought a smile of anticipation to her lips. When her eyes blinked open, it took her a moment to reorient herself to her surroundings and to the fact that the aroma *was* real. "Good morning," she said groggily, leaning against the door jamb and running her hand through her tangled hair. "What time is it?"

"It's eleven o'clock, Sleeping Beauty," Lynell answered. "Thought you might like . . ." When his vision of her registered, a beauty standing in a flannel shirt that barely reached below her crotch, he did a double take and spun around. "You want to get attacked?" he remarked, more angrily than he had intended.

"Uh, ah, I'm sorry, I forgot," she stammered as she stumbled from the kitchen. She grabbed a pair of panties and her Levi's and raced to the bathroom, slamming the door behind her. Her big toe caught in the cotton, ripping the panties as she yanked them on. When she was dressed she leaned against the tile wall, out of breath from anxiety. Her recurring nightmare had been evoked by an offhand remark by a friend.

"I'm really sorry, Catherine," he said softly outside the door. "You know I didn't mean anything by it."

She ran her fingers through her hair and opened the door. "I know. I didn't mean to expose myself either."

"You didn't. I overreacted." He lay his arm across her shoulder and led her back to the kitchen. "It's my turn to take care of you for a little while." He held the chair for her. "Sit."

Lynell was wearing a forest green Dartmouth T-shirt with white lettering and a snug-fitting pair of white Marona shorts that revealed to advantage what she decided was a cute, muscular rear end. The whiteness of the shorts accentuated his long, tanned legs. He was broadshouldered and slim-waisted, and his biceps, though not large, were strong and well-defined. When he turned and smiled at her, the corners of her mouth tightened into something that was not quite a smile, and her eyes fell self-consciously to the placemat. "Eggs Benedict," she remarked, obviously impressed, when he placed her brunch in front of her. "You've made a miraculous recovery."

"I had the best medical care known to man."

As they ate quietly she occasionally glanced across the table at him. He was just an ordinary guy—more attractive than most, perhaps, but just an ordinary guy all the same. On the job he blended easily into any group, as he had done with the American Express crew in London. Everyone seemed to like him, though he didn't court their friendship. He simply fit in. He had a natural, unforced charm that put people at ease,

341

so much so that men even appeared not to resent that there was apparently nothing at all he could not do, and do well. In England their American crew had mixed with the English union crew for a game of cricket, and though it was the first time he had so much as seen a game played, Lynell was as natural as though he had been born with a cricket bat in his hand. "A lot like baseball," he'd remarked modestly. And once in Hawaii, he had stepped into a high school boys' pickup basketball game and left them *oohing* and *ahing* at his graceful moves and unselfish pinpoint passes. And there was never a lull in dinner or cocktail conversation. At times Catherine felt a vague twinge of pride in him, in even being with him. Yes, she thought, eyeing him discreetly across the table, he was just an ordinary guy—but so very different from any other man she had ever met.

He looked up from his eggs. "Honestly, Catherine . . . the last couple of days . . . I've never been so sick in my life. I don't know what I would have done without a friend like you."

"Well, you'll never know, will you?"

A confused frown crossed his face.

"Because you'll always have a friend like me."

20

Following their return from traveling, Lynell had seven straight grueling full-day bookings before he had any time off. On three of the jobs—two catalogue shoots for Brooks Brothers and Bloomingdale's, and a print layout for Nike running clothes—he again worked with Mark Collins, who obviously was also a very busy man.

The morning of the eighth day, he and Catherine sat in LeeAnn Schneider's small office, staring anxiously at the after-image on a twenty-four-inch television screen. They had just viewed both rough prints of the American Express advertisement sent to Billie Devlin for approval, which she had then forwarded by messenger to Cline Models.

"What do you think?" LeeAnn asked after a pause so pregnant it could have borne twins.

Lynell shrugged modestly. "Not bad." It was fantastic and he knew it. He had played it perfectly: upbeat but nonchalant. And in the version that would be used in the United States, Catherine had provided an adept assist. It was all he could do to restrain himself from leaping from his chair and slapping Catherine a "high five," the way he would have during his basketball days.

"It's terrific," Catherine said. She turned to Lynell. "And you're not fooling anyone. You know it."

He shrugged again, unable this time to keep the elation from his voice. "It's all right."

"American Express agrees with *you*, Catherine," LeeAnn offered without expression, holding back the punchline. "They're going to air both of them as soon as they have the answer prints."

"All *right!*" Lynell catapulted to his feet, with his fists clenched. He pulled Catherine to her feet and lifted her in a bear hug that left her gasping for air, then took LeeAnn's soft, warm cheeks in his hands and planted a kiss squarely on her lips.

Catherine, still trying to catch her breath, grinned at LeeAnn. "But he thinks it's just 'not bad.' "

"What do you suppose he'd do if he got excited?"

"Well, you can bet I won't try that again," Lynell said, bending toward Catherine and pressing his palm against his lower back to fake an injury.

"Fresh," she said with a smile. "When will the commercial air, LeeAnn?"

"I'm not at all sure. All the marketing analysts and bean-counters are hard at work, I imagine. But I should think they'll have it on as soon as they find a good spot for it."

"Has Mary seen it?" Lynell asked.

"That reminds me. Mary's in Los Angeles on business, but I called her this morning with the news."

"And?" Lynell prompted.

"And she had some news of her own. What are the two of you doing next Wednesday?"

Lynell and Catherine shared a confused look, then turned back to LeeAnn. "Isn't that your department?" Lynell asked finally.

"Are you ready for this?" She looked from one blank face to the other. " 'The Merv Griffin Show' has booked Mary into a slot to be taped next Wednesday in Los Angeles, and . . ." She drew out "and" tantalizingly. "And . . . she wants the two of you with her, along with Mark Collins. He's on location in St. Lucia for the new Club Med, but he'll be there, too."

"You're not serious," Lynell said, stunned.

"Completely."

"What's wrong with Jason Wexler and Craig Burton? They sick?"

"And Cherry Taylor and Christa Blair?" Catherine echoed.

"That's just it: They've been on before, more than once. The people who watch those spots know them already. They want to meet someone new. They want to meet you three." Of course, LeeAnn didn't tell them that they—and particularly Catherine—weren't Mary Cline's first choices. Mary was happy with Mark Collins, but she would have preferred Alexis Stevens, an up-and-comer, to Catherine, who was as

344

hot as she was ever going to be, and maybe Matt Doyle or another young stud, to Lynell. But Textron, Inc., had insisted that if the company were to release Catherine and Lynell from the Now Shampoo contract to do the American Express ad, the models had to be selected for Mary's next talk show appearance.

Catherine stroked her chin pensively and squinted into the future, while Lynell stood in shocked silence.

"Come on, you've seen the spots before. Mary gabs a little bit with Merv about trends in modeling—what's hot and what's not—and then they bring out the cheesecake. They show a few career highlights: a Calvin Klein billboard for Mark: a *GQ* or *Mademoiselle* cover for Catherine; a leather jacket or razor blade shot for Lynell; a Now Shampoo ad of the two of you together. You charm the pants off everyone. And Merv says so long. Nothing to it."

Lynell looked back at Catherine and grimaced. "Holy Christ, wait until my mother hears this. Everyone in Pine Orchard will be watching."

"If she's anything like my Nana," Catherine put in innocently, "the show will get higher ratings than 'Dallas.'"

"Thanks, Catherine. Thanks a lot."

Catherine Ward was disturbingly confused about her relationship with Lynell Alan. She liked him, liked him very much, and enjoyed being with him almost to the exclusion of other people. And she didn't altogether understand it. Sure, he was attractive, bright, and self-assured. But what drew her to him most, she decided, was that he made her laugh. He made her feel like what she had never before had a chance to be—a little girl. And he liked her, too, she could tell, though he didn't exactly encourage her.

Since Aimée had left New York he had phoned her more often, but it was always spur of the moment, as though he were going to "Dream Girls" or the Mets game or the movies anyway and maybe she'd like to come along. So she found herself inviting him to join her in the same nonchalant come-if-you-can-but-it's-no-big-deal manner in return.

Their relationship just wasn't right for *that* kind of interest and probably never would be. He wasn't over Aimée yet, and she wasn't over . . . A shiver went through her when she envisioned a tiny pile of finely cut white powder. And anyway, she thought, brushing away the vision, he consistently gave her the impression he considered himself far too old for anyone her age. So friendship was enough, she told herself. But it was about time it became a *real* friendship. She knew nothing about Lynell Alan, nor he about her. What kind of childhood had he had? What did he expect from his life? What did he think? What did he feel? What made him cry? Perhaps Mexico had been the transition point. Movies and plays and work and laughter were wonderful things, certainly, but friends should get inside one another, know one another, help one another. In Mexico she had freely given a part of herself, and it had felt good.

It was time that Catherine visited Iowa again, and the trip to Los Angeles for "The Merv Griffin Show" would provide the perfect opportunity. They weren't due for the taping until Wednesday. She had a booking on Monday, but she could take a plane to Des Moines Monday night and at least have one day plus at home. As the elevator that carried her and Lynell down from Cline Models emptied into the lobby, a sudden thought struck her. "Are you booked right up until we leave for L.A.?" Catherine asked, her voice as tentative as a schoolgirl's.

"No, only tomorrow. LeeAnn's given me a few days off. I thought maybe I'd take the train out to Connecticut to visit my family."

"Oh," she said, disappointment clear in her voice. "I figured you'd be busy."

"Busy for what?"

"Oh, nothing. I was going to stop in Iowa and visit home, too." She was only vaguely aware that she was shuffling her feet. "I was going to ask you if you'd like to come with me, but . . . ."

"I'd love to."

"What about Connecticut?"

"When are you leaving?"

"Sometime Monday night."

"I'll go to Connecticut over the weekend. Hey, maybe you'd like to come with *me*?"

She slumped her shoulders. "I would, but I have to work this weekend. I'll take a raincheck."

"You've got it."

"Well . . . ," Catherine said tentatively as she backed away, "I'll see you Monday?"

"I'll call you Sunday night."

Catherine had walked halfway to her apartment before she realized she should have shared a cab with him. But what the hell, it was a gorgeous early spring day and the fresh air and exercise would do her good. Besides, she knew she would have had a difficult time trying to make conversation. She hoped he didn't think of this as an invitation home to meet a girl's parents, because it was a friendly gesture and that

346

was all. Still, she felt as though her feet were three inches off the ground, and she was suddenly aware that her arms were swinging jauntily as she walked and she was smiling broadly at everyone she passed. Why? Who cared why? All she knew was that for the first time in a very long while, she felt terrific, really terrific!

Usually when the aircraft began its descent into Des Moines, Catherine's elation would begin its ascent. There was something about home, whether the memories were good or bad, that imbued her with a sense of security, of identity. But with Lynell in the seat beside her, she was suddenly struck dumb by the irregularities in her life and her reservations about his ability to accept them. Perhaps she should have given more thought to this impetuous plan. But it was too late now, she mused with a sigh as the plane touched down on the runway.

"It *is* flat, isn't it?" Lynell remarked as they sped north along Interstate 35, with Catherine at the wheel of the rented Ford. He mistook her silent concentration for the clinging cobwebs of childhood memories.

Constance Ward's was a comfortable, modest, two-story, two-family house, in a row of modest two-story houses lining the crest of a hillside at the edge of town. It was the only one with the porch light still on at this late hour. As they pulled up, Catherine turned off the ignition, sat back, and sighed as though preparing to open a strange door and not knowing if behind it she would find a lion or a lamb.

"Home again, home again, jiggidy-jig," Lynell said with a grin.

"What?"

"My father used to say that whenever we got home from a trip. I don't know what the hell it means."

"Catherine!" Constance Ward greeted her granddaughter brightly at the front door. Lynell stood in the background as the women embraced. Then, as if seeing him for the first time, Constance broke from Catherine, hugged him familiarly, and welcomed him into her home. The slim, attractive woman had skin as smooth and pink and unlined as a baby's, and her smile raised beguiling dimples.

"There isn't much doubt where Catherine gets her looks, Mrs. Ward."

"Oh, you brought me a charmer, Catherine, dear," Constance said, hugging him again. "And please, Lynell, it's Nana."

"Okay . . . Nana."

"Catherine," Constance said, turning to her granddaughter, "I

347

know you two must be tired and hungry, but why don't you go up and check on Heather? She waited up for hours, but she just couldn't make it. She's upstairs in my bed."

Catherine smiled at Lynell, and he returned it with a nod and a grin. Then Catherine reached out and took his hand. "Come see her."

She held Lynell's hand loosely as she led him tiptoeing up over a creaking old staircase lit by a single lamp over the upper landing. She paused once at the lower landing, half staggering to catch the railing.

"Are you all right?" Lynell asked, supporting her with both hands.

"Yes. It's just . . . I get so homesick when I'm away."

"Well, you're home now."

She nodded, and they continued down along the darkening hallway past the bathroom and a little-girl's bedroom decorated in pastels and virtually overflowing with stuffed animals. As they neared the end of the hallway and the half-open door, she gripped his hand tighter.

Catherine stood by the bedside, arms at her sides, staring as though seeing a ghost. There in the dim light of a small bedside lamp was the most delicately beautiful child Lynell Alan had ever seen. As Catherine knelt by the bedside, swept the child's snow-blonde hair from her face, and kissed her plump red cheek, all he was conscious of was the awesome beauty of the small girl and how impossible it must be not to be able to constantly hug her.

Catherine continued to stroke the child's hair tenderly for a few moments, then looked back over her shoulder and smiled wanly. When she stood she took his hand again—desperately, he thought—and they silently left the room. They had reached the top of the stairway before Lynell spoke. "I thought I'd never see a little girl as beautiful as my sister was. But *your* sister . . . ," he continued.

Catherine raised her head slowly, and in the light of the frosted overhead lamp, he saw the sparkle of a tear that slid down her cheek. "Lynell . . . Heather is my daughter."

When she fell against him sobbing and buried her head in his shoulder, he wrapped her gently in his arms. "*Shh, shh.* Easy," he whispered. "It's okay. It's okay. You don't have to tell me anything you don't want to, Catherine."

"But I *do* want to tell you, Lynell. I want to so badly."

By the time Constance Ward reappeared from the kitchen with a pot of tea and a plate of sandwiches and Tollhouse cookies, Catherine had composed herself. But Constance still sensed something was amiss. She placed the refreshments on the coffee table. "It's long past my bedtime, children. You'll excuse me if I say goodnight. Lynell, I hope you don't mind the couch?"

"Not at all."

"It folds out, and I made it up with clean sheets as soon as Catherine told me she was bringing a guest. If you need an extra blanket, there's one in the hall closet. Catherine, why don't you crawl into bed with Heather? She'll be so pleased to find you there in the morning. I'll sleep in her room."

"Fine, Nana," Catherine answered. "Thank you."

Catherine and Lynell both stood and embraced the older woman. When Lynell kissed her cheek, it was as soft and warm as he remembered Grandma Alan's.

"See you in the morning, then," Constance said, and she turned to Catherine with a look at once sad and happy. "I'm so glad you're home, dear."

The sun peeked over the horizon of Catherine Ward's life, and she thought for a moment that she saw it smile again. She had made the first move. She had let Lynell Alan inside her life. Through the night he had listened sympathetically to the tormenting account of her father's death . . . listened in quiet horror to a nightmare of sexual abuse and suicide.

"She knew I would find her, Lynell. She must have hated me so."

"No, Catherine, suicide is a very selfish act. A person in that state of mind is probably not thinking of anything rational, least of all of who will find them and the effect it will have. You can't blame yourself, Catherine. I'm no shrink, but it hardly takes one to see that it was Bobby Stillwell who destroyed your mother's life. Certainly not you."

But the final burden was the most difficult to put down. Day was breaking as she tried haltingly to tell him of the undeserved "reputation" that had followed her to Ames and of her shock and confusion when she had discovered that, at sixteen, she had been left pregnant by Bobby Stillwell. "I actually tried to get an abortion. But it was too late. Imagine: the most important thing in my life, and she wouldn't even be here today if I'd had my way. And then for the first month of her life, I couldn't even hold her. Lynell, I couldn't even hold my own daughter in my arms. And now . . . what kind of mother am I? Traipsing around the world while Nana raises her? I should be here, Lynell. Here with my family, with my little girl."

"Your guilt is misplaced, Catherine. Maybe you were resentful at first because of who Heather's father is. Anyone would have been. But

349

it's obvious you love her very much. And as for the amount of time you spend away from home . . . your motives are the right ones. You're working hard to give Heather more than you had. That's every parent's goal."

"But, Lynell, what she really needs is me."

"And pretty soon you'll be able to come home and give her just that," he said. Then he paused for a long moment before looking into Catherine's sad eyes "Catherine, why didn't you tell me about Heather before?"

"I didn't think you'd understand."

"Oh, Catherine." He shook his head slowly, pushed her hair back off her forehead, and pulled her head to his chest. "Of *course* I understand."

"Every time I come home now, it seems as though Nana is ten years older. She's in her seventies and it's getting difficult for her, I know. I just want to earn enough money to come back and take care of both of them." As she spoke, the imprisoning memories fell away. Each breath opened the door to a new freedom. And Lynell Alan was the key. He sat quietly, listening attentively to every word, consoling her when she needed consolation, encouraging her when she needed encouragement, leaving her alone with her thoughts when she needed solitude. She told him more about her life that night than she had ever confided in anyone, and the revelations did not expose her but embraced her in a warm, plush cloak of caring, of loving. "I've never been back to Morgan City."

"Maybe you should go. It might be good for you. A necessary exorcism. And maybe Heather would like to see where her mother grew up."

"Maybe. But I'm not sure I could."

"Well, it's up to you." He turned to her and added almost in a whisper, "But there must be some fine memories there, too. Those are the ones you should go looking for."

"Lynell . . ." She had told him almost everything—why not the rest? It was humiliating, degrading, but so was much of her past. How does one admit to being a cocaine addict? "Lynell, I need help."

"Of course I'll help you. I'll drive down with you if you want to go."

"Not that kind of help."

When he looked at her, he suddenly understood. He nodded slowly and pressed his lips together in a half-smile of respect. "Of course I'll help you," he repeated. "As much as I possibly can. But the first thing to do is to see a professional."

Neither of them slept that night or the following day. By 6:30 A.M., when Lynell stood to fold out the couch, Heather bounded headlong down the staircase, caroling, "Mommy, Mommy, you're home! Oh, I've missed you, Mommy!"

"And I've missed you, darling," Catherine said, wrapping the tiny child in her arms. "I've missed you so."

And once again Lynell was enchanted. Three generations of Ward females charmed him through a tour of Ames and its environs, and when Heather instinctively gravitated to him, Lynell thought for the first time that this certainly must be what it felt like to have your own child.

"I can do a better one, Lynell. Look!" Heather cried, as she hurtled her young body along the grassy knoll for perhaps her tenth valiant effort at the perfect somersault.

"You don't have to keep watching her, Lynell," Catherine said, grasping his shoulder affectionately as she and her Nana returned to the park bench where he sat mesmerized by the child.

"I know," he answered. But there was not the slightest chance he would have taken his eyes from her.

As the foursome walked along Main Street, Lynell felt Heather's tiny fingers inch timidly into his. When his hand had completely enfolded hers, he looked down into her doll-like face, gripped her hand warmly, and was rewarded with a grin that surely would have melted a father's heart.

After lunch Catherine, Lynell, and Heather drove south toward Morgan City. The whooshing of the utility poles as they sped along the highway was an insistent wind that lashed across the plains, burying all sense of the present under a drift of time.

"Is this your house, Mommy?" As Catherine turned the car off the paved road and onto the long dusty driveway, Heather squirmed in Lynell's lap for a closer look.

"Yes, dear. When I was a little girl like you." She spoke haltingly, braking the car. "I'm surprised, Lynell. It hasn't changed all that much."

"It hasn't been all that long."

The day was, for Catherine, like grasping her memories by the tail and watching as they thrashed about impotently trying to bring her to harm. The farm's elderly owners graciously allowed her to exorcise her demons, and with Lynell and Heather flanking her, she found them surprisingly powerless.

"This was my room," she said somberly, stopping to look in but not

351

to enter. "And this was my mother's." When they stepped over the threshold Catherine fell back against Lynell, and he gently slipped his arm around her shoulder.

Sensing her mother's need, Heather wrapped her arms around Catherine's thigh, then reached out and hooked Lynell's leg with one small hand.

Catherine looked from her daughter to her friend. "Somehow being here isn't as scary as the memory. Nothing is as big. Nothing is as . . . I don't know. Maybe 'overwhelming' is the word."

Before leaving town, they stopped at the Indian River Cemetery and Catherine placed small bouquets of wildflowers on her parents' graves. "This is my Beauty, Daddy," she said, holding Heather tightly in her arms. "I thought it was about time you met her."

Lynell drove the return trip while Heather napped in the back seat and Catherine stared silently out over the fertile plains. She spoke only once, almost an hour after they had left the farm behind for what would be her last time.

"Maybe now I can forget," she said. But even as she spoke she knew she would never forget, knew that only an avalanche of new and wonderful memories could hope to erase the old.

Nana had a sumptuous roast beef dinner waiting on their return. Heather begged to sit beside Lynell at the table, and let go of his hand only when she needed both of her own to clasp together in prayer:

> "Thank you for the food we eat;
> thank you for the birds that sing;
> thank you, God, for everything.
> Amen."

Then she quickly snatched up his hand again.

When it was time for Heather to go off to bed, she pleaded to have Lynell take her. He carried her upstairs on his shoulders, tucked her in, and read from *Charlotte's Web*, which she had heard so often she corrected him when he deviated even the least bit from the text to ad-lib. By the time the spider had woven her first magic web, Heather was sound asleep. " 'Some pig,' " Lynell finished, closing the book and replacing it on the bedside table. Then he brushed the wisps of hair from her cherubic face and kissed her forehead lightly. Perhaps this was love, he thought, as he dragged his tired body down the staircase. Perhaps this was real love. "That's some kid," he managed, as he lay on the couch on the cusp of sleep.

"Yes," Catherine nodded, running her hand through his surprisingly soft and downy curls though she knew he was already asleep, "and you're some guy."

The following morning Catherine and Constance sat sipping their first cup of coffee while Lynell and Heather walked to the corner store for the newspaper. "I can go for one day not knowing how the Red Sox are doing," Lynell explained, "but not two." The apple pancake batter waited on the stove for their return.

"You're in love with him," said Constance, never one to mince words.

"No way," Catherine replied defensively.

"Then Heather is the only one in the family with any sense."

"Heather is starving for a man in her life. Lynell just happened to come along. If it hadn't been him, it would have been someone else."

"I don't think so, Catherine. Heather is much more discriminating than you give her credit for. And even if you're right, the fact is that it *is* Lynell who came along. The kid's crazy about him." As she sipped her coffee, she looked at her granddaughter and lifted one eyebrow knowingly. "And I think you are, too."

"Don't try to complicate my life, Nana. We're friends and that's all. Lynell is a super guy. I like him very much, and I'm happy Heather gets along so well with him. But I hope she doesn't get too attched to him, because he'll break her heart. He's not interested in me romantically. He's not interested in marriage. And he's *certainly* not interested in an instant family."

Nana was still nodding smugly when Lynell ducked in the front door with Heather astride his shoulders, tapping him lightly on the arm with the rolled newspaper. "Watch your head, Annie Oakley," Lynell said as he reached up, swung her around in front of him, and plopped her down on the floor.

Heather ran to her mother excitedly. "Mommy, the lady at the store thought Lynell was my daddy."

Catherine looked up expectantly, but her Nana only stood and quietly walked to the stove. Her expressionless face spoke more eloquently than words.

Leaving was as difficult for Catherine as it had ever been. In a way her Nana was right: There was something about the warmth that a man—this man—added to her little family.

"Will you come back and visit me again, Lynell?" a beaming

353

Heather asked as he sat and reluctantly swung his long legs into the rented Ford.

Lynell turned, struggled out of the low-slung automobile, and lifted the child off her feet, squeezing her in a parting bear hug. "You bet I will, Heather. You can count on it."

"Nana thinks we're lovers," Catherine told him as they pulled out of the driveway, waving and tooting the horn.

"And what did you tell her?"

"I told her it wasn't true, but I don't think she believed me."

Lynell continued waving over his shoulder until they were out of sight of the house. "I suppose there's no harm done," he said when he turned forward to face the flat expanse of Interstate 35 stretching out for miles before them.

"I suppose," she said. "After all, lovers do come and go."

"Yes," he agreed softly. "Lovers do come and go."

The drive to the airport was extremely quiet, though neither of them knew precisely why.

21

A bone-chilling rain fell on Boston on the first day of spring, as though Mother Nature wished to avoid any lingering doubt New Englanders might have had, that winter, for them, was over only on the calendar.

Aimée Harris crossed Alston Avenue on foot that evening and turned up Marlboro Street toward her apartment, thinking again, as she so often did, of Lynell Alan. She would never be a meaningful part of his life. She had known that six months ago when she left New York. It might have taken nearly five years to figure it out, but at least she finally had. So she'd risked an abortion when she knew he'd have married her on the spot if she'd just told him. But it never would have worked for them, and nothing reaffirmed her decision more than the drastic upswing both of their lives had taken in the brief time they had been apart.

Boston breathed a new and exciting spirit into her each time she returned, and each time she left she missed it more. She missed the friendly strangers who passed her on the street. She missed the clean, crisp salt air drifting in off Boston Harbor. She missed the apple trees lining Marlboro Street, trees that in the fleeting days of spring blossomed pink and white with flowers all the more beautiful for their transiency. She would never live in another place again.

Once back in Boston, the first time she had seen Lynell on television, alone in her small new apartment, she had hyperventilated for fully an hour after the 60-second spot was finished. At least she was

355

over that part of it now. Libby was right: It would probably have been better never to have experienced great sex, because then you could never miss it.

Todd Thornton was the other side of the coin from Lynell. He had matured into an even-tempered, dispassionately practical man: no hills or valleys, just a steadiness she'd come to rely on. It was better for her that Todd was so different from Lynell. Fewer memories that way. Todd was a man she could probably live with, if not ecstatically, at least comfortably. Perhaps she would even fall in love with him some day. And now she would have to make that decision, because the question Lynell hadn't ventured to ask in five years had taken Todd only five months to raise.

At her apartment she slid last night's casserole into the oven, then took a leisurely bubble-bath, nodding off several times before being awakened by the smell of burning chicken. Well, she wasn't particularly hungry anyway. At 8:30 she slipped into bed naked, feeling the sting of the cool sheets against her warm skin. Finally, a good night's sleep. When the telephone rang, it seemed she'd been sleeping for days. It was 8:50.

"Turn on Channel 5," Libby said excitedly.

"What?" Aimée made a groggy attempt to snatch herself back from sleep.

"Channel 5," Libby repeated. "He's on!"

"What? Who's . . . who's on?" But sleep wouldn't let go.

"Lynell, asshole! He's on 'The Merv Griffin Show!' "

She fumbled for the remote-control box in the darkness and flipped on the small color television at the foot of her bed. The picture came on before the sound, and she saw Mary Cline sitting four chairs to Merv's right, elegant in an expensive black chemise. To her immediate left was Mark Collins, who had probably caused epidemic heart failure among the nation's women when he had come on in his neatly tailored tuxedo. He sported his trademark five-day growth along with a reddish-brown tan she imagined he had picked up on an exotic location-shoot, where the sun had also bleached out his pale yellow hair and frosted the ends of his sandy whiskers as white as snow. He was nothing less than devastating. Catherine Ward, strikingly beautiful in a simple suede skirt and a white silk blouse, her long, willowy legs crossed casually in front of her, sat to Mark's left. Lynell, who must have come on last, sat to Merv's immediate right, dressed in the ubiquitous faded Levi's, red plaid cotton shirt, and tan corduroy sport coat.

"We asked Mary to bring us her favorite photographs of Mark and

356

Cathy and Lyn," Merv was telling the audience. "If you'll check the monitors, we'll let you be the judge."

The shot of Mark came up first, and the women in the studio audience *oohe*d and *ahhe*d at Mark in jeans and an aviator's fleece-lined leather jacket, collar turned up against an invisible wind that riffled his long, straight hair, a murderously sexy scowl set into his broad, whiskered jaw.

When the cameras returned to the group on stage, a smattering of applause soon rose to a crescendo.

"*Very* nice," Merv said. "Wow!" He mimicked Mark's scowl and glanced down the line of models at Mary Cline. "Well, what do you think, Mary? Do I have a future?"

A wave of laughter rippled through the studio.

"Don't call us, Merv . . . ," Mary began.

"We'll call you," the two finished in unison.

"And next," Merv said simply. "Catherine Ward."

When the shot came up on the monitors—and on television screens across the country—the studio audience gasped audibly, then applauded at the full-length photograph of Catherine in a sky blue, one-piece, French-cut swimsuit, leaning seductively against a bathhouse, tongue licking her upper lip, and yellow blonde hair caught in a stiff ocean breeze.

"Jesus Christ," Aimée muttered under her breath in awed appreciation.

"Catherine Ward. Breathtaking," Merv said in a masterful understatement when he and his guests came back on screen. "Absolutely breathtaking."

Catherine Ward was laughing and shaking her head modestly. Mary Cline smiled and looked at her understandingly. "That's not Cathy's favorite," she admitted.

"You don't like it, Cathy?" Merv asked incredulously.

"I prefer shots where I'm less . . . ," Catherine began.

"Exposed?" Lynell finished for her, to appreciative laughter.

"Well," Merv added sincerely, "it certainly displays all of your many charms."

"Thank you. But I'd hoped Mary would pick one that didn't display *quite* so many."

The young woman was bantering with Merv as easily as though she were sitting around her own living room. Aimée was impressed.

"And here's Mary's favorite shot of Lynell Alan," Merv announced to the audience.

It was the Boulet advertisement with Lynell reclining on one elbow in a pair of bikini briefs, a fully exposed example of slim, well-defined musculature.

"Mary, you didn't," Lynell was protesting half-heartedly to rising laughter as the camera returned to the stage.

"At least we're even now," Catherine said. She gripped Lynell's sleeve fondly, and Aimée felt a distant jealousy rising in her.

"I don't know what he's complaining about," Mary told Merv. "That shot made Lyn famous in Europe. They actually had to remove it from a billboard at a rotary in Paris, because so many women were driving off the road."

There was a final photograph from a Now Shampoo advertisement of Lynell and Catherine together, and then Merv quizzed the models on their family backgrounds. He seemed fascinated by Lynell's Ivy League education. "How do your parents feel about your career in what is more traditionally a female profession—and one in which you didn't put your expensive education to use?" he asked.

"My mother loves it. She brags to all of her friends that I'm in this or that magazine or television ad. In fact, she's probably raised your ratings on today's show ten points all by herself."

"How about your father?"

"Well, as you might imagine, he's a bit less convinced. Sometimes I get to play tennis with him and a couple of his friends when I'm in Connecticut for the weekend, and I get the feeling he's kind of embarrassed by what I do."

"Do any of his friends ever give you a hard time?"

"Once in a while—not often anymore, though."

"You probably earn more money than most of them."

"Probably, but I never throw that up to them."

"Do you mind if I ask what Lynell Alan is worth a day?" Merv asked tentatively.

Lynell looked down at Mary, who shook her head and said, "It's no secret."

"Well," Lynell answered, "I'm *paid* two thousand dollars a day. I'm probably *worth* about fifty." Warm laughter filled the studio.

"There you have it," Merv announced to his audience. "If you happen to have a spare two thousand dollars lying around the house, you too can hire Lynell Alan or Catherine Ward or Mark Collins for the day."

Aimée shook her head. Two thousand dollars a day. It was ridiculous. And his accountant still sent her four hundred of each two thousand—utterly ridiculous. Well, that was okay. If he had another year

358

like this one, the cottage on Martha's Vineyard would be totally paid for. She had never wanted his money. What she had once wanted she would never have—at least not with Lynell Alan.

Several minutes of small talk ensued, including Merv's best wishes on upcoming projects for each of the four: Cline Models' expansion into television film production, Mark Collins's new exclusive with Calvin Klein, and Catherine Ward's with Chanel No. 5 perfume. For Aimée, it was all ho-hum until the last.

"And best of luck, Lyn, on your upcoming role on 'General Hospital.' Another model moves on," Merv added with his signature oh-so-sincere grin.

Lynell Alan was in an obviously unrehearsed state of shock. Mary Cline sat smiling smugly. "The call just came in the other day," she explained. "There wasn't time to tell you."

Next to Lynell, Catherine Ward was grinning as gleefully as a child. Between Catherine and Mary Cline, and unnoticed by most viewers amid the excitement of the moment but not by Aimée Harris, Mark Collins scowled his patented scowl. But this one was less sexy than frightening.

"A scoop, folks," Merv said, as proudly as though he thought Johnny Carson might be watching.

If Mark Collins had a gun, Aimée thought, *Merv would have a real scoop.*

"This must be incredibly exciting news, Lyn," Merv went on.

"Exciting . . . Yes . . ."

"Well, tell us how it feels suddenly to become an actor. Do you have any acting experience?"

"None professionally," Lynell answered, struggling to regain his composure. "A couple of small roles in college plays. You know, the usual stuff: *Glass Menagerie, Oklahoma* . . ."

"Well, then," Merv said, "acting will certainly represent a new challenge for you."

"It certainly will," Lynell agreed. "But I enjoy modeling, and after all the work I've put in, and the support I've gotten," he added with an acknowledging nod in Mary Cline's direction, "I wouldn't want to give it up."

"But isn't acting every model's dream?"

"I guess it's supposed to be. I know it's in vogue to knock modeling, to say it's only a springboard to bigger and better things, but I'm grateful to modeling and I'll keep doing it as long as they'll have me. Of course, the problem there is the age factor, which you don't have so much in acting. So if I had the opportunity to do both—modeling and acting—it would be wonderful but . . ." He shrugged. "Anyway, as you know, in this business one never records the credits until the job is finished. So far, I know as little as you do about this, Merv."

"Well, we'll keep our fingers crossed for you, Lyn," Merv said solicitously. "Thank you all again for being with us."

The four rose and departed to a tumultuous chorus of applause and whistles, and overcome by the inescapable irony of Lynell's belated success, Aimée sat back against the headboard of her bed, stunned.

When he stepped behind the curtain a stagehand held aside for them, Lynell breathed a deep sigh of combined elation and relief. As she followed him offstage, Catherine squeezed his arm excitedly and affectionately faked a punch to his jaw. "Knocked 'em dead," she said proudly.

"We've got to talk," he said with deadly seriousness as Mark strode wordlessly past them.

"Good job, kids," Mary Cline complimented as she walked by on Mark's heels.

"You aced him again," Catherine whispered when Mark and Mary were out of earshot.

But he ignored the comment. "Let's go get a drink someplace"

"Sure. I'm going to change clothes and lie down for a few minutes first, though," Catherine said as they continued toward their adjoining dressing rooms. "I'm beat."

"Sounds good," Lynell agreed. "I'll come by your room—say in a half hour or so?—and we'll go then."

"Great."

Lynell turned on the monitor in his dressing room. They were taping a standup comedian named Steve Wright. He enjoyed the short routine, but a performance by a modern dance troupe followed and he quickly became bored. He tried to nap but was too restless, so he went out into the hallway, checked his watch, and though it had been less than twenty minutes, went to Catherine's door, knocked, and went in.

"Cath . . ." But her name caught in his throat. "I . . . thought you were going to try to quit," he said disappointedly.

"I am trying."

"Apparently not very hard. For Christ's sake, Catherine, are you going to be a coke head your whole . . ." Hearing the harsh, unsympathetic words coming from his own mouth, he stopped short. But too late. "Oh God, Catherine, I'm sorry. . . ."

360

"Don't be. And don't be so naive, Lynell," she snapped, snorting the second line and sniffing deeply to clear her nasal passages. "I *can't* quit. And all your half-hearted good intentions won't make the slightest bit of difference."

"But, Catherine, I . . ." But the words wouldn't come. It seemed they never came—because he was never quite sure what they should be, or if he felt them or would ever feel them.

"No, Lynell," she said, cutting abruptly into his hesitation. "I've got to straighten out my own life—my own way. I've got to make *myself* happy."

"But I can help you, Catherine. I *want* to help you."

Her ironic chuckle mocked him, though she didn't mean to be cruel. "No, Lynell, it's too late for that. Just leave me alone. You've got problems of your own. I don't think you feel, Lynell—really feel. I don't think you *can* feel. No commitments, no ties, just breeze in and out of people's lives without a care. No, forget the social-worker act. Let's keep our relationship strictly professional. It's always worked out well that way." Why she said what she heard herself say next, she wasn't exactly sure. Why she felt so alone and hurt, she wasn't exactly sure, either. "Lynell," she said in a voice so low it was almost a whisper, "in your own confused way you're almost more pathetic than I am." And she shouldered her way past him and out the door.

Any hopes Lynell had for an immediate reconciliation were dashed when Catherine didn't show up for the return flight to New York.

After a sleepless night, Lynell called Catherine's apartment, but there was no answer. Then, on a hunch, he called the agency, but she hadn't checked in. Finally, in desperation, he called Constance Ward.

"I wouldn't tell another soul, Lynell," Constance confided, "but I think I should tell you. In fact, I've picked up the telephone to call you half a dozen times. Catherine's checked herself into the Manhattan Women's Hospital, the drug rehabilitation program. Lynell," she continued hesitantly, "I know Catherine told me you two are just friends, but I have a feeling that a friend is exactly what she needs right now."

But Catherine refused to see him, and his flowers and cards went unacknowledged. And the airing of the American Express advertisement in the major markets didn't seem so exciting, and the soap opera deal in the works with ABC didn't seem so exciting. And all he felt when "The Merv Griffin Show" aired was an emptiness that couldn't even be filled when his family called to congratulate him. There was more to life than a successful modeling career. He was only beginning to realize it now that he had one. He had no friends, no woman in his life, nothing.

When Catherine Ward awoke in the Manhattan Women's Hospital the morning after she had watched their segment on "The Merv Griffin Show," she felt like death. She was so incredibly lonely she thought for a moment her heart might break. When the nurse brought the flowers, a dozen white orchids this time, and Catherine read the card, she was *sure* it would: "Catherine, I'm proud of you. Your friend as ever, Lynell." He had been sending flowers—usually a dozen roses—and the same card for four days, and she hadn't seen or spoken with him in all that time. She didn't need him—or anyone else—to be proud of her, she thought as she began dressing in her street clothes. She needed to be proud of herself. She wondered if she ever could be.

362

22

"Do you know me?"

Eunice Blair was the picture of concentration. She stopped pacing and moved around in front of her high-backed swivel chair, never taking her eyes from the television screen.

"You might not recognize me wearing my own clothes, with dry hair, or without . . . what's her name." The man shrugged bewilderedly. Eunice chewed her lower lip and watched as though for the first time as the young man crossed the busy London intersection, the backwash from the heavy traffic frothing his curly hair.

"Even in Europe . . . ," he went on with an easy, natural, unforced delivery. As he stood at the curb, a red double-decker bus pulled to a stop behind him and he glanced over his shoulder at its side, its full length adorned by a huge poster advertisement of himself in bikini briefs reclining on one elbow. Then he looked quickly back at the camera. "Even in Europe," he repeated with a shrug, "where my name is a household . . . uh . . . face . . ."

It was a clever advertisement to slip into the campaign, a reversal of American Express's usual theme of selecting someone like Jim Henson or Robert Ludlum or Paul Gallop, a person with a familiar *name* whose *face* was unknown, and Eunice Blair chuckled lightly. Her assistant, Beverly O'Neal, watched from behind her, wondering if her boss had forgotten she'd buzzed her three replays ago.

"Bev, get Abby down here, will you, please?" Eunice asked without looking up.

"Yes, Ms. Blair." And Bev O'Neal was off like a shot. She knew that tone of voice. It meant, "We're heading into action." And it meant now.

"The American Express Card . . . ," he said, hesitating as he stepped aboard the bus. On the bottom step he turned and grasped the brass pole for support. As the bus slowly pulled away from the curb, he looked again at his own larger-than-life likeness on its side and finished, ". . . don't leave home without it." The ubiquitous pale green card popped onto the screen, accompanied by the sound of an embossing machine chunking out the letters "L-Y-N-E-L-L A-L-A-N." In the final few frames a familiar young blonde woman appeared, jogging alongside the bus as it gathered speed. Grasping the brass pole for support, Lynell Alan reached out and helped the woman aboard. He took a long, appraising look at Catherine Ward, then turned back to the camera with a puzzled expression, then back to Catherine again. "Do I know you?" he asked as the bus whisked off screen.

Eunice stood abruptly, snapped in the "ON/OFF" button, then spun and addressed the younger woman. "Well?"

"It all depends," Abby Needler answered evenly.

"On what?"

"On exactly what you've got in mind for this guy." Abby Needler had been at *Vogue* for five and a half years and had worked her way up steadily, from assistant editor to associate editor to her present position of managing editor, through her previous journalistic experience with *Tennis* and *Family Circle* magazines, knowledge of the magazine business, and, in no small measure, anticipation of what her boss expected from her. With her eyes narrowing imperceptibly, she studiously regarded Eunice Blair, a tweed-suited spire of impatience.

"What I have in mind for 'this guy,'" Eunice answered, "is the cover of the June issue."

So *that* was it. That was why she had watched this advertisement with Eunice five times and why, Bev O'Neal had told her over the phone, Eunice had been watching it alone in her office for the better part of the past two days. A smile began to edge across her face. Eunice wanted her to disagree. She expected her to disagree, to analyze every subtle nuance. That was what made Abby invaluable to Eunice—she saw below the surface, to the deeper ramifications of decisions.

"Well?" Eunice Blair repeated the question impatiently.

"Perfect."

"What?" She was stunned, sure she had misheard the mistress of contrariness. *Bad idea,* Abby must really have answered. *A man on the cover of* Vogue *magazine? The other women's magazines would run us out of business. And why* this *guy?* She imagined Abby contemptuously spitting out the last two words.

"Perfect," Abby Needler repeated. "The time is right. Of course, we've never had a man on the cover. And the women recently . . . well, they all seem to look the same. Besides he's the perfect man—an up-and-comer. Those ads are great." She pointed at the television set as though it were still playing the American Express advertisement. "And the ad campaign with Catherine Ward has made Now the number one shampoo on the market in less than a year. He's highly visible, and with his recent appearance on 'General Hospital' . . ." She left the sentence hanging. "He's the perfect type, too: not *too* flashy, not *too* young, and his age matches our reader cross-section. The only man who could touch him right now is Mark Collins, but I don't know if our readers are ready for the whiskers—and without them he's almost as pretty as our cover *girls.*" She paused dramatically before raising her palms to deliver her final summation. "Lynell Alan is perfect."

"That's it!" Eunice said, beaming enthusiastically. "The Perfect Man."

They discussed his body—well-proportioned, though not overstated; his even white teeth, with one ever-so-slightly chipped incisor reminding you of the boy next door; the swarthy complexion highlighting almost royal-blue eyes; the prominent cheekbones and full, sensual lips; the all-American masculinity of his broken and imperceptibly crooked nose. But it was the eyes, Eunice decided, that made the man—the deep-set, sensitive eyes masking a mysterious complexity that drew you inexorably to him.

Abby Needler was leaving through Bev O'Neal's outer office. She slowed a half-step when the telephone rang. Bev answered it on the first ring. "Ms. Blair's office. Of course. One moment please." Then she buzzed the inner office. "Ms. Cline returning your call."

So the decision had already been made, Abby thought as she reached for the door, unable to hesitate longer without being obvious. Thursday's planning meeting would be another Eunice Blair show, and Eunice was so sure of herself on this one she would neither need nor want Abby's support. There would be objections, of course; some from the older, more conservative women on the staff—most from that stubborn new Doherty woman. But none would matter. As long as Eunice Blair was in charge, as long as she was the editor-in-chief of

Vogue, Lynell Alan would be on the cover of the June issue. And unless Abby Needler seriously misjudged the market, it would be the biggest newsstand sales flop in publishing history—and *Vogue*, as much as *People* and *Mademoiselle*, relied on newsstand sales. Christ, no one passing a newsstand would even *recognize* the magazine as *Vogue* without a woman on the cover. Lynell Alan was The Perfect Man, all right—the perfect man to get Abby Needler Eunice Blair's job. It would be a disaster. She knew it.

Three days after "The Merv Griffin Show," Mary Cline was back in her office in New York. The call came in at precisely 10:17 A.M., according to the Seth Thomas grandfather clock that stood in the middle of the wall opposite her desk. She liked being able to look up at it from where she sat. In business, timing was everything.

"Is it Eunice or her secretary?" she asked Thelma Preble.

"Her secretary."

"Tell her I'm with a client and I'll return her call as soon as possible."

"Yes, Ms. Cline."

Now it was 10:47 and Mary Cline hadn't thought of anything but Eunice Blair for half an hour. Why had she called—*herself?* For a model? An art assistant always did that, and did it through LeeAnn, not directly. It had to be something else, something important. But what?

"Thelma, get Eunice Blair on the phone for me and let me know when she's on the line. Her, Thelma, not her secretary.

Sixty seconds later Thelma buzzed Mary Cline back. "Ms. Blair on hold for you, Ms. Cline."

"Thank you." Mary Cline counted the swings of the pendulum. It didn't pay to appear overanxious.

Lynell flew back to Los Angeles two days before the taping of the episode that would mark his introduction—and probably his farewell—to the cast of "General Hospital." He spent the time visiting area sights: Disneyland, the Dodgers, the Angels. But even those didn't take his mind off Catherine. He should have insisted on seeing her, to straighten things out between them. Then again, maybe the time wasn't right. She needed some time to herself, time to think things out. Anyway, the show must go on and he had to get his mind off his personal problems. He had to give it his best shot. He wished he had someone to talk to. The night before the taping he called Mary Cline.

"Do they know I can't act?" he asked her nervously.

"It's not exactly *Othello*, Lynell. You only have one line."

"You've got to put my face back together, Doc."

That was it. His one pleading line. Nothing to it. What made it even easier were the bandages that covered both his face and his self-conscious anxiety, allowing him to remain safely anonymous. After a dramatic closeup of his gauze-wrapped head the scene ended, leaving both the victim's identity and the source of his injuries a mystery. Then they did an immediate fast-forward taping of a second scene of the same doctor removing the bandages, for a segment that would air two weeks later. Two weeks in ten minutes. Ah, the wonders of TV!

As the doctor slowly and dramatically—always dramatically—performed the unveiling, the camera shot from behind the victim, whose face remained unrevealed until the makeup artist had slipped in and done several minutes of touchup.

"Wonderful job," the nurse said adoringly as the camera came in for another angle, this time a closeup that would be worthy of all of his mother's bragging to her friends.

"That's a wrap," the director announced after the second take, signaling the end of Lynell's brief but illustrious acting career. A room at the Hyatt Regency for five nights—at $150 a night—first class airfare back to New York, and $3,000 plus expenses. All for three lousy takes. Of course everyone knew that television, and especially these phenomenally successful afternoon soaps, had money to throw away. If they wanted to throw a little of it in his direction, fine by him.

"Wonderful job," the nurse, an attractive redhead whose real name was Tanya Kirkland, said again, this time complimenting *him* as he swung his legs out of the hospital bed. Though the stagehands and director had been helpful and cooperative since his arrival, this was the first really amiable sign from any cast member.

He shrugged modestly. "Thanks, but you people did all the work. I just sort of lay there."

"Hey, don't sell yourself short. You did what you were supposed to do. That's more than I can say for most non . . . for most inexperienced actors," she said as they walked off the set.

"You were right the first time. I'm a non-actor."

"Actually I was going to say non-professional," she admitted sheepishly, pushing her wild, strawberry hair back from her face. "But the only thing that really makes an actor a professional is getting work. So now you're a professional." She stopped outside her dressing room and smiled up at him. "How about lunch if you're not busy?"

"Fine. I'm sure not busy."

If Tanya Kirkland wanted to impress him, The Ivy certainly did the trick. The exterior, under gray skies and a rare Southern California rain, seemed little more than modest. But the interior was dripping with ambience, with priceless antiques and big name producers, directors, agents, and movie stars. Lynell tried not to stare at Dolly Parton, who was wolfing a man-sized plate of chili at the very next table, or at John Travolta, who was devouring a thick swordfish steak three tables away, or at Tom Selleck, who couldn't possibly escape notice even at a table in the farthest corner.

"I see only us common folk come here," Lynell commented.

Tanya shrugged. "It's on me," she said. "My way of apologizing on behalf of everyone in the cast."

"Thank you, but that's not necessary."

"It sure is. We were beastly. It's just that actors sort of close ranks when outsiders come along. You know . . . I guess we all thought a *real* actor should have gotten this job. There are sure plenty of us out of work."

Lynell nodded apologetically.

"Hey, but it's not your fault. You had an opportunity and you made the most of it. You did a wonderful job, too," she said again. "And we could be seeing a lot of each other soon."

The instinctive tilting of his head alerted her, but too late.

"You didn't know?"

"Know what?" he asked suspiciously.

Tanya Kirkland bit her fingernail nervously for a moment. "What the hell, you'll find out soon enough anyway. The rumor around the set is that if you're any good you'll be worked into the regular cast. The feeling among the execs is that we need some new blood. That's another reason the cast members weren't too receptive to you—especially the men. They're all afraid that if you catch on, they'll be conveniently killed off in an automobile accident or become the victim of some fatal disease in an upcoming episode. That's the scuttlebutt, anyway . . . for what it's worth."

Whenever Lynell was nervous or frightened, he ate. At The Ivy he ate an absolutely scrumptious swordfish steak, fresh green beans, a baked potato with butter, sour cream, and chives, and two irresistible apple tortes. But he didn't taste any of it. He was terrified.

He returned to the Hyatt, but before he could get out the door for his run the telephone rang.

"Why didn't you *tell* me?" he screamed excitedly.

"Mary thought you'd be too nervous if you knew," LeeAnn answered. "Anyway, it's only talk so far. Why get your hopes up for nothing?"

"Hopes?" he asked, his voice quaking audibly. "Try fears." He was anxious to hit the streets for a long, introspective run. "So, what was it you were calling about, LeeAnn?"

In the first seconds after she told him about *Vogue*, he thought the only running he might do would be to the bathroom. "It's completely hush-hush until the issue comes out. The magazine business is super cutthroat and they don't want to risk being scooped. You understand? No one. Not even your mother. *Especially* not your mother," she added.

"Yes, yes, I understand," he answered absently, but he didn't at all. He didn't understand how his life could be changing so drastically, how it could have gotten so far out of his control. "I understand."

That same evening Lynell Alan was on a half-empty Northwest Orient red-eye flight from Los Angeles to New York. Though he wasn't due back for several days and couldn't even tell his family of his latest career break, he felt the need to be home again, if only for the weekend. Everything seemed to be unraveling, and even his professional successes couldn't tie things together. The only answer was family, and he thought again of Catherine.

As the flight crossed middle America at thirty thousand feet, he stood in the restroom of the first class lounge and leaned close to the mirror. Once again he could see all of the flaws. He was tired and it showed in the deepening lines gathering at the corners of his eyes and bracketing his unsmiling mouth.

An attractive young stewardess, the name "Joan" etched on her nameplate, had been pursuing him since takeoff and once again appeared at his side when he returned to his seat in the nearly empty first class section. And once again he politely rejected her.

"Well, if you're ever in Minneapolis," she offered, producing a small slip of paper on which were already scrawled her name, address, and telephone number, "give me a call. I'm based there."

It had been like this more and more since Aimée had left him. His career was riding high and he supposed this kind of thing was one of the inevitable perks. A month ago, maybe even a week ago, he'd have taken Joan up on her offer. Maybe Catherine was right about him. His life certainly had taken a new direction. It had just required six months for him to recognize that the new direction was down.

On Monday morning Lynell took the private elevator to the penthouse studio of Gene Tillman, the most famous portrait photographer in the United States, and maybe in the world. He had had to switch elevators at the eighteenth floor and now rode alone, with only his own heartbeat audible over the heavy rattle of the chains. He still couldn't believe it: *him* on the cover of *Vogue* magazine. And he hadn't even been able to tell his mother. He had considered breaking his vow to LeeAnn on his weekend visit to Pine Orchard. But then he remembered it had taken Liz Alan less than two hours to get word out along her maternal grapevine not only that he was going to be appearing in her favorite soap opera, but also on which dates the episodes would be aired. She would die when she saw *Vogue*, absolutely die. First her favorite soap—now her favorite glossy. She would never forgive him for not giving her advance notice.

There was no question he would have told Catherine, but she had made it abundantly clear she wanted nothing at all to do with him. He wished Billie Devlin would call them for another Now commercial soon. If he could just see Catherine he knew things would work themselves out.

When the elevator door opened onto the twenty-eighth floor studio, Lynell, his heart in his throat, stepped into the reception area and wondered for the thousandth anguished time: *Why me?* He supposed he should have gotten over second-guessing himself by now, especially in light of his recent success, which could only be described as phenomenal. But he doubted he ever would. There was always someone better looking out there, and though looks alone were not the source of his current popularity—at least so Mary Cline maintained—whatever popularity he enjoyed, he knew wouldn't last long. Mike Bradley's lecture outside On Stage flashed across his mind. Perhaps if he was able, with the continuing help of his accountant at Arthur Young & Company, to keep saving his money—and if he was able to keep his ego in check—perhaps then it wouldn't be so difficult when the trend reversed itself, as surely it would.

"Good morning, Mr. Alan. They're waiting for you in the studio." The casually dressed young receptionist pointed over her shoulder. "First door on your right."

"Thank you." When he opened the door of the studio, he was surprised—overwhelmed might have been a better word.

A dozen people scurried about attending to the details of the set, the camera, and the other supporting equipment. They all stopped what they were doing when he entered the room, and the hush that accompanied their measured appraisal was deafening. As one by one, they returned to their tasks, a sylphlike young woman approached and offered her hand.

"Sandy MacGregor." She grinned broadly as her eyes fell to his sneakered feet, then slowly rose along his denimed legs and royal blue, white-collared Marona pull over, and up to his smiling face.

"Lynell Alan."

"Not much question about that," she said flatly. Then she did a quick double-take over the length of him. "Professional curiosity," she explained. "I'm in charge of wardrobe. I hope the clothes fit."

"I'm sure if they don't, you'll make them fit."

"Here's a copy of the proposed layout. Coffee?"

"Love some," he answered, following her across the highly polished hardwood floor. The studio was sparsely furnished and immaculate, and they sat at a round butcherblock table in a corner that served as a small kitchenette. He liked Sandy MacGregor instinctively. She was the only one who kept him from feeling like a complete jerk. Everyone else ignored him as he waited for them to finish their preparations. Fifteen minutes after Lynell's arrival, David, the makeup artist, sent for him, and Lynell followed some assistant's assistant to a tiny, mirrored cubicle in the rear of the studio.

"I wish they'd given me more time," David said petulantly to no one, as Lynell sat in a hydraulic barber chair and looked into the row of mirrors at his own infinitely fading image. It was an optical illusion, he considered, that somehow served to summarize what his personal life had become.

"Maybe I should have come yesterday," Lynell said. When that failed to elicit so much as a grin, Lynell tried another tack. "Well, they always hire the best for the most difficult jobs."

"So true," said David evenly.

"I'll try not to sweat."

Rubbing a fine powder between his thumb and first two fingers, David stood back and announced regally. "Try not to talk, either. I work in silence."

David was a bitch but he was also an artist. He was, however, an artist who was used to working with women, and as Lynell silently watched him, he wondered if the heavily mascaraed young man had even the remotest idea of how a *man* was supposed to look.

David squeezed the thinnest trails of white accent cream over the almost indistinguishable character lines that had begun to insinuate themselves permanently into the once smooth skin under Lynell's deep-set eyes. Over a thin liquid base, David brushed on India Earth to highlight his already prominent cheekbones. Lighter tones brought up the bridge of his nose and darker shades diminished the sides. David spent fully thirty minutes on Lynell's eyes: darkening the light-brown brows, accenting the lids, and lengthening the lashes.

After applying the finishing touches, David quietly left his subject to Henrietta, the hairdresser, a middle-aged Isadora Duncan look-alike who was as talkative as David was mute. Where Lynell hadn't been *allowed* to speak to David, he couldn't get a word in edgewise with Henrietta. The woman never took a breath. As she aimlessly chattered on, dropping names and primping his hair with equal dexterity, Lynell suddenly realized there would be far less of him in the final product than there was of David and Henrietta. He felt like the "makeover" section in one of the women's magazines Aimée had chronically left lying around the apartment—it might even have been *Vogue*—where a plain-Jane was miraculously transformed into a raving beauty in a matter of minutes. As he had once heard Grandma Alan quip when he had told her how nice she looked, "A little powder and a little paint makes you what you ain't."

"Done," he heard Henrietta say finally, as she stood back to admire her work.

"What?" Lynell asked blankly when he realized she was speaking to him.

"Done. *Finis.* Take a good look, young man," she added as David re-entered the room with Eunice Blair at his side. "You'll never look as stunning again."

Lynell stared into the mirror at the finished product, acutely aware that the trio was awaiting his reaction to his own perfection. He looked smooth. He looked young. He looked perfect—almost too perfect. He looked like a fag. "Do you want me to be honest?" He already could tell they didn't. But what the hell. He'd gone this far, and David and Henrietta gave him an enormous pain in the ass. "I look like Shirley Temple in drag. I looked better when I came in."

Everyone seemed to move at once. Lynell was sure David would have lunged for his throat if Henrietta hadn't been standing belligerently between them. Eunice Blair had grabbed David by one skinny arm, and his own momentum spun him to face her.

372

"He's right, you know," Eunice said evenly.

"Well, then, I don't know *what* you want, Eunice. The man looks perfect."

"Yes, but the perfect man doesn't look perfect, David, sweet. Let's start over, leaving a bit more of Mr. Alan, shall we?" she offered solicitously. "After all, it's *him* we're selling on this cover, darling, not you."

David was steaming by this time, but Eunice kept up the onslaught, as though she were punishing him for her own poor judgment. "This is different from our usual job. We want him to look like a thirty-year-old man, not an eighteen-year-old girl."

"Well," said David, spinning on his heels, "why don't you try *Sports Illustrated*? Perhaps they could suggest someone who'll splash a little mud on his face." With that he stormed out, with Henrietta in his wake.

Eunice Blair looked to the barber chair where Lynell still sat, the relief on his handsome face visible even through David's heavy layers of paint. She shrugged fatalistically. Then she turned back toward the empty doorway and spoke as though to it. "David *is* very good," she said. "But temperamental. And women are his forte. I was afraid this might happen." She paused, sighing deeply. "So," she said, snapping a soft cloth from the shelf on which David had left the tools of his trade and flipping it to a literally blank-faced Lynell, "who is it who does the best makeup job in the business on Lynell Alan?"

"Lynell Alan," he answered sheepishly.

"I thought you might say that. Well," she said, indicating the shelf full of creams and powders with a sweep of her hand as she headed for the door, "knock yourself out."

No one knew his face the way he had come to know it over his years in the business—its highlights and its flaws—and in less than fifteen minutes he emerged from the back room, having wiped it clean with cold cream and cotton balls and started over, lightly accenting its features with a basic subtlety with which David was completely unacquainted.

Eunice Blair regarded his work with the same inanimate concentration with which he imagined she would inspect Gene Tillman's contact sheets. "Looks fine. That's what we should have done in the first place. Oh, well, David does a good deal of work for us. And I imagine his generous paycheck will smooth his ruffled feathers."

Sandy MacGregor outfitted him from the waist up in "after six" attire, which he wore over his Levi's, the cover calling for a head shot to be cropped high on the shoulders. He was positioned and, with the rest of the crew, left waiting for another ten minutes before the photographer made his entrance. He was worth the wait.

Gene Tillman was dark-complected and extremely tall. The photographer's graying hair had aged fifteen years beyond his boyish face, which, though smooth and unlined, was at best pleasantly attractive and already bore the suggestion of a double chin. He wore a faded Navy blue Yale T-shirt, left untucked as a concession to an expanding waistline, and snugly fitting khaki slacks that had about them the look of age. His gait, which was gracefully masculine, immediately put Lynell at ease.

"Sorry I'm late," he apologized, extending his hand and shaking Lynell's warmly.

"No problem," Lynell said, noting as he stood that Gene Tillman was at least four inches taller than he. "I get paid by the hour."

"I understand we're contemporaries of a sort," Tillman continued.

Lynell concentrated on the dark unlined face, squinting away the gray hair with effort. "Gene Tillman," he said suddenly, snapping his fingers with the recollection. "You played basketball at Branford High."

Tillman nodded. "And you beat the crap out of us all three years."

Lynell grinned at the pleasant memory.

"Well, buddy," Tillman offered, "I'll try my best to make you look good again."

Catherine Ward awoke in her own bed at around midnight—that is, if she had ever really been asleep and was not merely moving fitfully in and out of consciousness. She was not alone. Her daughter was sleeping soundly, snuggled up against her. Catherine had cut back her work schedule drastically in recent weeks and was now splitting her time between New York and Iowa. She had tried both in- and out-patient treatment for her drug problem—which she had at least finally acknowledged—but the only prescription that seemed to work was family.

At the moment she was peeling back the years, wondering what it was that had made her believe she could possibly have succeeded in the cutthroat, dog-eat-dog world of modeling. She inhaled slowly, deeply, held her breath for several seconds, and exhaled in a tension-releasing rush, feeling her muscles relax in waves. After a few such exercises the waves extended along her arms to her fingers, down her legs, and to her feet. Then she rubbed the middle fingers of both hands in

374

tight, gentle circles against the throbbing at her temples. Only when she was completely relaxed and the throbbing had subsided did the names begin spinning in her head: Revlon, Closeup, *Mademoiselle*, Jantzen, Halston, Dior, Now—damn you, Lynell—Black Velvet, *Glamour*, Bill Blass, Coca-Cola, Oil of Olay, American Express— damn you to hell, Lynell Alan.

John Butler Hoben, her recently acquired New York shrink, had warned her the nights would be the most difficult. Dr. Hoben—he of the obligatory neatly-trimmed gray-streaked beard, thinning hair, horn-rimmed glasses, and voice so soft she had to strain to hear it. "You'll wake up and there will be nothing to do. Take two of these," he'd added, handing her the illegible prescription, "and if you still can't sleep—read, or watch 'The Late Show,' or go out to . . ."

"Iowa."

"Go out to Iowa and hug your kid."

So that was what she was doing, and in her sleep Heather squirmed out of her mother's unconsciously tightening grasp.

It was now May of 1984, over three years since she had first left for New York, and by any standards she was a success in her profession. She had in those three years earned perhaps a million dollars, but in spite of her basically simple tastes and the fact that virtually everything she wore had been donated to her wardrobe by one client or another, she had very little in her bank account to show for it. Uncle Sam had skimmed nearly fifty percent off the top; perhaps thirty percent had paid for general living expenses: food, shelter, utilities, insurance, and the like; she had sent ten percent to her Nana. And probably another ten percent had gone up her nose. Life in Manhattan was expensive.

So, indeed, she had been on the covers of *Gentleman's Quarterly*, *Sports Illustrated*, and a dozen women's magazines. She had been, at various times, the Charley girl, the Black Velvet woman, the Noxema girl, the Closeup smile, and readily identifiable with untold other products and advertising slogans. So, why didn't she *feel* successful? She didn't feel successful because she *wasn't* successful—not on her own terms. And that had nothing to do with her career; had nothing to do with her being an expensive merchandising tool and nothing but that, like a label on a bottle, a clever tag line, or a catchy tune. She enjoyed most of what she did most of the time, and who could argue with being vastly overpaid merely for having been fortunate enough to have been born photogenic?

So, what made her a failure? Drugs. Drugs made her a failure as a functioning human being. It distressed her that just thinking of cocaine now made her nose twitch, even with her child lying here beside her. Lynell made her a failure as a friend. But first and foremost, she thought, holding Heather closer again, whatever it was that forced her away from her child made her a failure as a mother. Perhaps Heather and Nana would both be better off without her. She suddenly realized the kind of agony her own mother must have gone through. She bit her trembling lip. She was weak, so weak. Could nothing save her? Well, she was going back to New York in the morning. Maybe she'd get lucky and her plane would crash. Who knew? Maybe back in the city she'd muster the nerve to tie a rope around her neck. At least *her* daughter would never have to walk in and find *her*.

"But imagine the nerve of that self-important slut!" David fumed. "Where does she get off telling me how to do my job? You want to know what she's done? I'll tell you what she's done. She's doubled my fee to *Vogue*. That's what she's done. That hag wouldn't know a decent makeup job if it waltzed up and goosed her. For heaven's sake, just look at the puss on her. No, no, Franco, no more wine, thank you," he said, covering his crystal goblet with his hand."Just thinking about Eunice Blair has given me a splitting headache."

It was nine o'clock in the evening, almost a week after his curt dismissal from the makeup job for the cover of *Vogue's* June issue, and David was still furious every time he thought about it. Across the table from him at Tavern on the Green sat Franco Canero, who was still trying vainly to resurrect himself from photographic oblivion and just as vainly trying to get into David's tight pants. It made David sad even to look at the old queen. Although he had always been thin, Franco was now almost painfully so, with deep, dark circles under his small, sunken black eyes. David suspected that though Franco did all he could to maintain his business contacts with dinner invitations such as tonight's, his business, like his face—was sagging further and further every day.

"I mean, it's certainly not the job. I don't need the credits anymore, if that's what you're thinking. I've done a dozen covers for *Vogue*, and more for *Mademoiselle* and *Glamour*. Of course, I don't do them all, nor do I expect to. Christa Blair, the bitch, *must* have Alex, and that Belafonte woman insists I don't know black skin well enough to do her. What a joke—skin is skin. And I think that occasionally Eunice and the magazine like to spread the work around a little for variety, if not for quality. It wasn't losing the job, it was the *way* Eunice went about it. It was like . . . well . . . like giving Frank Sinatra the hook in the middle of 'New York, New York' and replacing him in midchorus with Liza Minelli, for heaven's sake!"

"Oh, darling David, everyone knows you're the best in the business. That's the main thing," Franco said with the slightest tinge of impatience. He wished David would get off this tired subject and on to something that could help *him*. "You have more work than you can possibly handle, I'm sure."

"That, my dear Franco, is immaterial. The unmitigated gall of that woman absolutely burns me up. Her whole attitude is simply unconscionable. I have half a mind to . . ."

"To what?"

"Nothing, nothing," David mumbled. The line was baited and set. There was no reason to reel it in before the fish was securely hooked. "Don't you agree that the decent, the professional thing to do under the circumstances would have been simply to suggest to me that what they had in mind for the model was somewhat different than usual? That the shading was to have been more understated? Doesn't she think I could have handled that? After all, clients often make specific requests, and I have always been able to satisfy their needs. But the implication that I couldn't have given them what they wanted . . ."

"Now, now, David. How about a nightcap? It might relax you." David seemed to be relenting.

"Oh, all right. Perhaps a snifter of Courvoisier *would* settle my nerves." David paused while the waiter took Franco's order. Then he continued. "It was just that she made me look such a fool. I mean, showing me up in front of Henrietta is one thing, but in front of a *model*? No telling how much work it will cost me. Every day—*every day*—for a solid week I've had a phone call about it. It's positively mortifying."

"Oh, David, I'm sure you're overreacting; it was just another job. I've heard nothing about it myself. It's probably long since forgotten." Franco *had* heard about it, of course, though he had enough tact not to mention it. Anyway, the story going around lacked the details David was slowly filling in, details which were taking an intriguing shape. Henrietta, who, as she told it, had made a futile attempt to calm David and then to intercede with Eunice Blair on his behalf, had been asked to finish the styling job. She hadn't even named the model when he had asked. "Just another from the Clines' stable," she had said.

"I wish you were right," David lamented, "but I'm afraid that fucking Henrietta has told half the town on her own. After pretending to be on my side, she actually sneaked back in there and worked on his

377

. . ." He stopped in midsentence, as though having let the pronoun slip out unwittingly, pausing calculatedly to let Franco absorb the idea completely. If indeed Henrietta had told half the town, he could count on Franco to tell the rest. "Oh, I'm afraid I've let the cat out of the bag," David went on, slapping his hand lightly against his cheek. "Oh, dear," he clucked, "if Eunice finds out that it was I who let out the secret, I'll never work at *Vogue* again." As if he gave a flying fuck! He'd be around long after that bitch's head rolled.

The excitement Franco Canero had felt when he had stealthily turned his camera away from the two-way mirror on the dressing room wall of his studio and pulled down the black background curtain, leaving Lynell Alan's sperm trickling down over Ginny's plump stomach, was an excitement so unrelenting that for months afterward the mere mention of the man's name gave him an erection, as it did now, over two years later. But in spite of the uncomfortable stiffness in his crotch, the excitement he felt now was not at all sexual—it was like that of the lion stalking in the coolest hours of the day. No, the excitement was not sexual at all. It was predatory.

With a well-chosen "slip" delivered with his unfailing sense of timing, David had touched a nerve in Franco Canero, an ugly nerve that lay constantly exposed. He was jealous—incurably jealous, not of Lynell Alan per se, but of the type: the healthy, scrubbed, oh-so-refined, born-with-a-silver-spoon-in-his-mouth type who'd never had to work for anything in his life, the type to whom everything had always come easily. Lynell Alan was the embodiment of them all: the rising young models and rising young agents and rising young photographers; the Richard Avedons and Francesco Scavullos and Gene Tillmans; the Davids and Esmés and Zolis, with their pretentious mononyms. The acrimony he felt for all of them focused on the person of Lynell Alan.

Now, after all the demeaning things he'd had to do, all the low-rate, half-day jobs he'd had to take to stay in business, to stay in the studio he'd occupied for over twenty years—now, he finally saw a dignified way out. Of course blackmail, as ugly as that sounded, might still prove to be more pragmatic, more financially rewarding. But if it didn't work, this was so simple, and so much more professional. It was so simple, in fact, that he wondered why it hadn't occurred to him before. But then the time had never been right before.

Canero threw back his brandy and called for the check over David's strenuous objections. After all, paying for dinner was the least he could do for the inspiration.

Within twenty minutes Franco Canero was in the bedroom of his modest Upper West Side apartment, with an eleven-by-fourteen manila folder open on his bed and the telephone in his hand. He was about to embark upon his first market venture in fifteen years. Only the stock certificates were eight-by-ten glossies. But first he had to check the latest quotations.

Oh, he was going to keep his studio running, all right, and running as a class operation—as always. After all, he held all the cards. Yes, he held all the cards—and they had Lynell Alan's picture on them.

"Hello, Paul?"

Two weeks before it was to hit the newsstands, Lynell received an advance copy of *Vogue*. There had been a time—before the Now commercials, before the notoriety—when every tearsheet meant excitement, when he would wait impatiently for every magazine ad or fashion layout, every catalogue, every Sunday newspaper department store supplement. He would stand excitedly at a drugstore counter with a magazine open to his ad and hope someone would recognize him. But time had changed all that—time and success.

Now he rarely saw print advertisements he'd modeled for unless he ran across them while reading *Sports Illustrated* or *Time* or *Playboy*, or unless he wanted a particular one for his portfolio. Of course, the Calvin Klein billboard loomed over him and everyone else who passed through Times Square; the vandalized Camel Cigarette posters snarled their magic-marker-mustachioed snarls at a million subway commuters each day; and he saw most of his television commercials, simply because, though he hated to admit it, he watched more and more television, especially since he had been living alone.

But when Eunice Blair's secretary sent him the *Vogue* issue in its heavy manila envelope, *that* generated the old excitement. He took the unopened envelope to his apartment, left it on the bed while he took a long, relaxing shower, and relished the anticipation of what he fully expected to be the best picture ever taken of him.

It would have been frosting on the cake to have been able to take Aimée out to dinner at a spectacular restaurant like The Four Seasons, or Windows on the World, to celebrate—but she was gone; or to call Catherine and meet somewhere to share the moment—but he doubted the wounds were healed. And it was too late to take the train to Pine Orchard and be back for tomorrow's early morning shooting. So there was no one.

A man eating alone in a restaurant was somehow even more pathetic-looking to him than a woman. He refused to feel pathetic at such a moment of personal victory—at least not in public. After all, what did he have to complain about? Almost any man in America would gladly have traded places with him. So he slipped on his faded Levi's, a forest green Dartmouth sweatshirt, and a pair of scuffed running shoes, and went out for a pizza and a six-pack of Saint Pauli Girl. What the hell, he'd run an extra mile each day for the next week to burn off the excess calories. He hadn't had a pizza for a year.

Back in his apartment, he anxiously opened the envelope and slid out the magazine that in two weeks would be on every newsstand, on every stationery store and drugstore magazine rack—not to mention in over one million mailboxes—in America.

He began to hyperventilate as he held the magazine. The corner was clipped diagonally and the sticker on the front read "First Bound." The cover picture was unbelievable. Imagine, he thought, millions of people were actually going to think he *looked* like that. They weren't going to consider Sandy MacGregor's impeccable wardrobe, or the tireless work of the lighting man, or his makeup job and Henrietta's hairstyling job, or the hundreds of photographs and different angles taken by "the world's greatest portrait photographer." They would only see the final product. To them it would be as though he had stood there and said "cheese" and been caught in all his natural splendor. What they were going to see was that close-up shot of his face: chin turned down and a bit to the left, so the bridge of his nose looked almost perfectly straight; left eyebrow raised, nostrils flared, and lips broken into a seductive smile that showed enough teeth to promise they'd be perfect and white.

"The illusion," he said to no one, with a chuckle. There was hardly a man alive—or a woman, for that matter—who could measure up under such scrutiny without a great deal of help. He was just the canvas that the *real* artist had made into a masterpiece, and he wouldn't begin to let himself think anything else. But he was bursting with pride even to have been a part of it.

He studied the cover for a full five minutes, sipping his beer slowly while the cheese congealed on his rapidly cooling pizza. He studied it from every angle, from every vantage point, and in every light. He ambled across his living room and glanced at it out of the corner of his eye, trying to guess if it would entice a woman into stopping to buy it. A model's worth was judged by how much of the product he sold. Though he and the artists—and mostly the latter—had done the best they could with what they had to work with, Lynell doubted the picture would stop traffic—foot or otherwise. He hoped the people at

Vogue didn't think, as he suddenly did, that they'd have been better off using a pretty-boy like Mark Collins, or someone else, anyone else.

The brief copy inside was flattering, not just to him but to all models:

> Lynell Alan is not the stereotypical male model, as a growing majority of men in this business in the eighties are not. Vapid and gay? Decidedly not. Mr. Alan has earned bachelor's and master's degrees from Dartmouth College, that prestigious Ivy League institution known as much for the quality of its men and women as for the quality of its education . . . previously occupied the eminently cerebral position of junior accountant at Arthur Young & Co. in Boston, one of the largest and most renowned in its field . . . linked with a gamut of sexy women, from a beautiful New York attorney to a glamorous soap opera star, and every gorgeous young model in between.

He wondered where they had manufactured that last line, but he supposed it made for good copy. Certainly it came with the territory.

On the same page were reduced shots from the Now (with Catherine), Calvin Klein, and American Express ads. On the facing page was the pièce de résistance: a full-page, full-length shot of him wearing khaki safari shorts and a royal blue golf shirt, under a heading that read: "The Perfect Man." He thought of Catherine, of Aimée, and of his family, and of how proud they would be when they saw this. He could barely wait the two weeks.

The full-length shot was, without a doubt, camp, like the "Nerd" and "Preppy" posters he'd seen all over town, but it was an ego trip just the same. Beneath the Topsiders it stated the facts: height 6'2", weight 175, waist 32, inseam 32, suit 40L. Arrows moved up the body, labeling a dozen or so parts from "thin ankles" to "soft brown curls," from "flat stomach" to "perceptive blue eyes," from "long athletic legs" to "nose broken playing basketball." An arrow pointing to his heart said "sensitive." The poster was definitely cute.

His pizza was stone cold. Just as well. He could make up the calories from the four beers he had already drunk, and the other two he'd finish by bedtime, by skipping dinner. *Vogue* certainly wasn't interested in fat cover boys.

After he slipped into bed, he devoured the magazine a final time. He hoped it sold well, if only to justify Eunice Blair's confidence in him. When he snapped off the light his head was spinning, partly from the alcohol and partly from elation. If there was never another memory, this one would be enough. But if there *were* other memories, he prayed he would have someone to share them with.

The mailman always came before he went running, so Lynell brought his key with him. But he only checked the box when he returned. It gave him something to look forward to, even if it was only bills or junk mail, and occasionally there would be a letter from Veronica or one from his mother and father.

Today the small metal box held another pleasant surprise, though he was more than a little bit exasperated that the manila envelope was folded and forced into it, irreparably creasing whatever was inside—probably photographs. The folder bore a New York City postmark but had no return address. He began tearing it open when the elevator stopped at his floor. As he walked along the hallway, the anticipation began to build. It had been almost two weeks since he had received his advance copy of *Vogue*. Perhaps someone thoughtful from the magazine, or even Gene Tillman himself—that would be like him—had sent him the outtakes from the shooting.

He stopped fumbling anxiously with the seal for just long enough to flip the three locks and turn the door knob, sliding the photographs out excitedly as he walked into the apartment.

His hand recoiled from the photographs as though they were on fire, and he staggered to the couch, falling into it with a thud. Holding only the semishredded remains of the manila folder, he stared blankly ahead with his vision focused inwardly—on his past, his present, and what little future he still had.

He saw the corner of the folded sheet of paper peeking out of the torn folder. Numbly he pulled it out, unfolded it.

"I'll be in touch."

The telephone began to ring almost immediately.

"Go to hell!" Lynell shouted into the telephone, almost before he recognized the effeminate voice at the other end of the line. Then he slammed down the receiver and, in a rare display of mindless violence, grabbed the telephone cord and ripped it from the wall. There was no way he was going to yield to blackmail, no way in the world. Let this be the end for him, then: *Vogue* magazine. He'd leave quietly, with what remained of his dignity, while he was still on top. There couldn't possibly be enough time for that little fruit to hurt him—or *Vogue* or anyone else—with those pictures.

So it was time. But still, he had been lucky. Sure, he had groveled and crawled and uncharacteristically clawed his way up the ladder, but somehow he had managed to stay one step ahead of the real shit for most of his brief career. Now that it was about to bury him, he suddenly realized he was ready. Ready to use more of himself than just his looks . . . ready to try to achieve a measure of success without having to walk over someone else's fallen corpse to do it . . . ready to let down his impenetrable guard and begin to put his trust in someone again. In short, he was ready to return to the real world.

He looked at the frayed end of the broken telephone cord he still held in his hand. "You can't fire me," he said as a peaceful smile crossed his handsome face. "I quit!"

23

Playboy arrived during the first week of each month, *Time* came on Tuesdays, and *Sports Illustrated* was in his mailbox like clockwork every Thursday afternoon; he counted on them all as he counted on the sun rising each morning. But *Vogue?* Lynell had had to ask Sandy MacGregor, because he knew that when it came out he'd be right there in the street, buying it off the rack, hoping someone might recognize him.

When the day came he was suddenly afraid he couldn't measure up. He didn't shave, dressed sloppily in cutoff jeans and a T-shirt, pulled his Red Sox cap low over his curly hair, donned his shades, and headed for the streets, having managed to repress Franco Canero and his photographs. Not having heard from him since that first telephone call, Lynell had just about convinced himself that Canero had been bluffing—and it seemed he was right. After all, who would *want* the photographs? Certainly no one could *publish* them.

It was a beautiful mid-May Saturday morning, already in the low seventies by 10:30 A.M., and the sun was high in the cloudless sky, almost as high as his soaring spirits. He thought of Aimée, as he often did, and of the first time, nearly two years ago, that he had appeared in a national publication, a full-page advertisement for Head tennis clothes in *Tennis* magazine. After Aimée had paid for a copy at the small drugstore, she had opened the magazine to his ad and pointed it out to the pretty teenage girl waiting on her. "He's gorgeous," the girl had said with a puzzled shrug.

When Aimée simply held out the page and pointed to the man at her side, the girl did a double-take, then stammered and spoke to Aimée as though Lynell wasn't there.

"It's him," she said. "It's really him!" Then she looked, disbelieving, from Lynell to the photograph and back again. "He's even prettier in person than he is in the picture," she said. "He has such beautiful blue eyes and the picture doesn't do them justice. And he should be smiling in the picture, too," she said of a now beaming Lynell. "He has such nice teeth."

More and more in recent days people looked at him with a flicker of recognition, as though they thought they might recognize him from another time and place. He passed the newsstand at Twenty-third and Lexington, leaned against the corner brownstone, and took in the activity.

A blue-haired, doddering matron walked an ancient gray poodle that looked too warm, wrapped in its red plaid vest. A lean black man in expensive running shoes stood lookout for the three-card monte game in the middle of the Twenty-third Street block. Two young punkers with bright orange Mohawk haircuts, each shouldering an enormous ghetto-blaster, bebopped by in leather and chains. But like a racehorse with blinders, Lynell kept focusing on the newsstand, on the man on the cover.

Eyes like blue diamonds sparkled from the smooth, tanned skin, and he wondered if anyone had eyes that blue or skin that smooth. From twenty feet away everything was a blur except that picture. Of all the fashion shows, of all the print ads, of all the television commercials, none compared to this. Not even "The Merv Griffin Show" or "General Hospital." It was the winning basket as time ran out, the home run in the bottom of the ninth. It was the pinnacle, the thrill of a lifetime. It was a first.

After fifteen minutes he stepped up to buy his copy. By his count five women had bought the magazine in those fifteen minutes. Two had tossed it haphazardly into shopping bags, but the other three had thumbed through it tentatively as they walked home, perhaps intrigued after all, as the decision-makers at *Vogue* had hoped they would be, that a man had finally made its prestigious cover. He didn't notice that three of the five who had bought *Vogue* had also bought the higher-priced, lower quality magazine displayed alongside it.

"Clever packaging" was the advertising phrase that came to mind

385

when his eye saw, before his mind registered, the double image of VOGUE'S PERFECT MAN in the same pale blue colors. *Nothing's sacred, no one's immune, any angle to sell more magazines at eight dollars a shot,* he thought, as he handed the vendor a twenty-dollar bill and removed a copy of *Vogue* from its place on the rack. As he did, his eyes drifted.

Cold steel pierced his chest, and he was only vaguely aware that twenty dollars would more than cover the cost of both magazines.

"Your change," the vendor called out.

As Lynell staggered from the newsstand he was bumped by the lean black man, who would have lifted his wallet if he had been carrying one. The newly-purchased *Vogue* fell to the ground unnoticed.

"You dropped your magazine." It would never in a lifetime have occurred to the attractive young woman passerby that this agonized face was the same one as that on the cover of the magazine she held out to him.

"How?" Eunice Blair asked no one. She still had not looked up.

Bev O'Neal's head shook slowly in sincere and silent mourning.

The magazine was folded open to the middle and doubled over so that only the lefthand page was showing. Technically, it was not a great picture: black and white, and a little fuzzy, the subject appearing to have been caught unaware. But there was no mistaking the identity. Eunice Blair saw her career wilting in that flawed photograph. *Funny,* she thought philosophically, *there's so little in this picture that hasn't already been seen by half the population of America—half the population of the frigging world. We've all seen the long, sleek legs; the hard, flat stomach; the well-proportioned arms; the broad muscular chest.* Even in that lousy print, who wouldn't recognize the wide, strong jaw, and the high-crested, finely chiseled cheekbones that tempered the severe masculinity of a slightly broken nose? The soft, curly hair? Eunice shook her head sadly and read the caption aloud: " *'Do you know me?'* Holy shit, Bev!"

Eunice Blair was not totally cold and unfeeling. If she had given Lynell Alan any thought at all, personally or professionally, she would have been sympathetic. But as yet, she hadn't had time even to consider all the business ramifications of her own situation. As one by one they came to her, she looked over her shoulder at Bev O'Neal and said, in a voice laced heavily with sarcasm, "At least they didn't refer to him as 'The Perfect Man.' Maybe no one will notice," she added without conviction.

Bev O'Neal's face twisted in sincere emotional pain. "Look at the cover."

"Oh God, don't tell me," Eunice hissed as she folded open the magazine. The only thing she noticed about the black-and-white photo of a nude Mark Collins on the facing page was that it wasn't another of Lynell. "But they couldn't have had time," she protested halfheartedly, trying frantically to find the cover, flipping the pages back through picture after full-color, full-page picture of thickly muscled men posed in various degrees of sexual arousal. Her head dropped in defeat when she found it. The picture was of a stranger, a stranger bulging threateningly from a pair of red nylon briefs below the name of the magazine, which was emblazoned across the top in royal blue: *Boyplay*. But it was the sticker that caught her eye and held it, the sticker plastered to the near right of the bulging briefs: "INSIDE: VOGUE'S PERFECT MAN UNWRAPPED." She looked up at Bev O'Neal with a pained expression on her face.

Bev nodded. "It's on every issue."

"Where the hell did you find this rag?" Eunice demanded, as though surprised that the staid Bev O'Neal would have stumbled onto this kind of smut.

"It wasn't difficult," Bev answered. "I'll bet every newsstand in the city has it on front display. The three I passed did. And what do you think it's being hawked next to?"

"Don't tell me."

"Bingo. And at four times the price of our magazine, they're going like the proverbial hotcakes. We've made their year."

"Good grief. Get Abby up he—"

"She's on her way, Ms. Blair."

As the two women stared at the untimely picture, Abby Needler was making her way to Eunice Blair's office, trying to think of other things. The shit was going to hit the fan on this one—and she, at least, was well out of range. Abby was trying to erase the smug grin from her face. But to do that she had to erase the picture of Lynell Alan, "The Perfect Man," from her mind—the picture she and everyone else in the city (Christ, everyone in the country by tomorrow), would have superimposed on the gorgeous Gene Tillman portrait that adorned the cover of the June issue of *Vogue*: the unflattering, black-and-white picture with the dazed expression on his face and the semierect organ standing out before him with the blatant suggestion of more.

That must be the way a person looks when they've had a heart attack, Abby thought when she saw Eunice slumped over her desk, ashen-faced, looking ten years older than she had only yesterday, when she had gloated over her apparent victory as initial newsstand sales soared. Bev O'Neal backpedaled silently as Abby approached. Good morning seemed inappropriate. It was not going to be a good morning at all, at least not for Eunice Blair.

"Have you seen this?" Eunice managed to croak when she felt, rather than saw, Abby Needler at her shoulder.

"Yes." Abby spoke evenly, betraying no emotion.

"What do you think now?"

After a long, thoughtful pause, Abby said, "They made him look so . . . big."

She felt terrible. Really terrible. The incredible rushes weren't there anymore—only the debilitating depressions. No longer did she sniff the drug to bring on the highs, but merely to erase the lows. It had been a month since she'd quit the rehabilitation program, and she really had cut back, she tried to convince herself.

Catherine Ward had not stopped thinking of Lynell Alan since her copy of *Vogue* had arrived the day before. Perhaps she had been too hard on him. Perhaps he needed her friendship as much as she now knew she needed his. But could the hurtful words ever be forgotten by either of them?

She'd brought her copy to the Dudleys' this morning and they had all agreed that the cover close-up brought out all the best in him: the bright, sparkling eyes, alive with questions; the kind, thoughtful face that searched for answers. She should have been there with him to celebrate his moment of victory. But then, he was probably with some new woman who could give him more than she offered, more than she could ever offer.

"You're not giving *me* any of it."

"What? I'm sorry, Mike. What did you say?"

Mike Dudley stood impatiently, hands on hips. One tail of his denim shirt hung haphazardly out of his wrinkled khaki slacks. "I said, 'You may have it all in there somewhere, but you're not giving *me* any of it.' Why don't we quit early and the four of us will take in the Ninth Avenue International Food Festival," he said. "What do you say?"

"Not yet, Mike. I'm sorry. I wasn't concentrating. Let's do it again." She adjusted the cups of her push-up bra, but no amount of wriggling or shoulder-hunching would keep even her small breasts from spilling out over the plunging neckline of the blue-and-gold-striped Danskin

388

she wore for the cover of Martin Bennett's latest Angela Stark novel, *The Aerobic Assassin*.

Martin Bennett, who, following Catherine's brief hospitalization for exhaustion, had reassumed his friendly-protector role in her life, leaned back lazily in his director's chair and cocked his beige fedora to a jaunty angle. "Trust me, doll," he said, doing his best Mickey Spillane, "we want the skin."

"Martin!" Catherine admonished, crossing her arms exasperatedly in front of her, which only served to aggravate the problem. Still, she couldn't help but join their good-natured laughter.

"I'm going to take a run down to the snack bar next door. How about some coffee, Catherine? You look like you could use a cup." The omnipresent Jayne Dudley was already rummaging through her purse for change.

"Sure. That would be nice," Catherine answered.

"Four regulars?" Jayne asked with a nod to her husband and Martin Bennett.

Catherine struggled desperately to get into it, to capture the mood. She even went so far as to do a few jumping jacks and run off a series of toe touches and trunk twisters. But before she managed to work up a sweat Jayne had returned—without the coffee.

"My God, take a look at our friend Lynell." She was gasping for breath, as though she hadn't waited for the elevator but had raced up the stairway, vaulting the two flights of steps by threes.

In spite of herself, Catherine broke into a proud, maternal smile. "Not *another* cover?" she asked as she eagerly reached for the magazine. "I hope they don't overexpose the boy."

"Poor choice of words," Jayne said. But Catherine didn't hear.

She had to find him.

There was no answer when she telephoned his apartment from the Dudleys' studio. "It'll take me about half an hour to get there. Please keep trying him, Jayne. If he answers, tell him I'm on my way."

"Just go, sweetheart," Bennett urged, practically pushing her out the door. "We'll take care of it. Go, go, go."

"Jesus, his career is kaput," Mike said when Catherine was gone.

Mike Dudley wasn't the only person in town with the same thought. Lynell Alan's career, which had skyrocketed him to a modest amount of fame and a tremendous annual income, would never have a chance to reach its apex and slide into a smooth and gentle decline like most.

He would never face the dilemma of quitting or hanging on as Mike Bradley had, as dozens of others had. His career would stop—dead— and he would be buried with it, and forgotten, as fast as an industry was capable of forgetting.

It was not yet noon when the extension phone range beside the tennis court behind the eight-bedroom mansion in the Riverside section of Greenwich. Nothing was as important as having your opponent on the run and finishing him off with a backhand winner down the line. If it was the Devlin woman, she'd keep ringing. If it wasn't Devlin . . . well, then, he just didn't give a flying fuck who it was or what it was about.

By the fourth ring Billie felt the sweat trickling from under her arms. She had always prided herself on her coolness under pressure, but then she'd never had to call the chief executive of the cosmetics division of Textron, Inc., at home before.

"Well?" Ralph Thompson asked curtly.

Thompson's abruptness knocked Billie even further off balance. She and the entire problem were merely a minor annoyance keeping him from something far more important. Through Billie's mind flashed the image of Ralph Thompson's, tight, bare behind poised on the outstroke over some topheavy, emptyheaded secretarial type.

"Ms. Devlin," he prompted impatiently. "I don't have all day. Let me be as direct as I can. Ivory Soap was able to dump Meg Brewster for breach of contract when those pictures appeared in *Playboy*. I just want you to tell me we can do the same with this Alan character."

"The head of our legal department has just finished reading the contract and says definitely yes."

"Then do it."

"Yes, sir, but . . . the last of the spots can't be pulled until tomorrow night."

"So I won't watch TV this weekend," Thompson snapped and the phone went dead.

Though it was a Saturday and one of the first summerlike days of 1984 in the northeast, several executives interrupted their days for similar discussions. It was true that each showed more concern over their connection with the suddenly infamous Lynell Alan than Ralph Thompson had, but it was also true that no corporation could afford to absorb the inevitable loss more easily than Textron, when an outraged, hypocritical, and fickle public, a public that thrived on watching the mighty fall, boycotted the fallen Lynell Alan and, coincidentally, all that he represented—both literally and figuratively.

Saturday was a working day at a network whose recent ratings had run a consistent third in a three-way race, a network that, last week, had not had a single program in the Nielsen Ratings' top fifteen.

Case Lawson was sipping coffee in his suite in the ABC Building when his assistant program director slid the issue of *Boyplay* across his cluttered desk. In the fifteen minutes the magazine had been in the building, Lawson was the tenth person to have seen it.

"Holy Jesus." It was the even, passive voice of one resigned to disaster. It was the voice of a man from whom, in the wake of loss upon loss, almost certain victory had been snatched at the final moment. "We can't get a break, can we?"

"You all right, Case?"

"Did we deliver the 'General Hospital' contract yesterday?" He stood and slowly paced to the wall-length window looking out over the sun-drenched city.

"No, I checked."

"Thank God for procrastination. Then I'm all right. Strike that. No, I'm not all right, but at least I won't jump."

"Too bad . . . I mean about the kid and this rag," the assistant program director added quickly. "I saw the test print. He was good."

"Good? He was *great*." Lawson paused, nodding absently. "In fact, he was perfect," he said with heavy irony.

Not everyone associated professionally with Lynell Alan dropped him that Saturday in May. Some waited until Monday.

He was too young to die, but what did he have left? His credibility as a professional—as a human being—was gone. Everyone—clients, friends, even family—had deserted him. Or maybe *he* had deserted *them*. It didn't matter now. He stood naked in the bathroom in front of the full-length mirror, eyes following the smooth lines of his body in the reflection, a body on which he had spent untold hours of sweat and pain. Somehow it was impossible to imagine this body moldering in a dark, dank grave. Maybe he should leave instructions for cremation.

Yes, he was certainly too young to die, but what choice was there left for him?

24

It was noon when the Checker Cab pulled up in front of Gramercy Towers. The man on the steps never looked up from his magazine, and Catherine paused deliberately before opening the cab door.

He stared into the magazine from behind dark glasses. Brown corkscrew curls sprang from underneath a Red Sox baseball cap pulled low over his forehead. His long, bare legs stretched out lazily in front of him, and he leaned back on one elbow, unconscious of the appreciative glances of a pair of young women passing by.

The cab pulled away from the curb and she stood on the sidewalk, still watching him. Lynell Alan was not a man to be pitied. He was bright, articulate, well-educated, charming. For him the end of a modeling career would not be the end of the world—not as it might be for, say . . . her . . . or Mark. She thought again of Mark. In her concern for Lynell she had nearly forgotten poor Mark.

When Lynell looked up, her heart pounded with anxiety. What, for one minute, had made her think he needed her? She wanted to run, wished she'd never come. But as she stood irresolute, Lynell, ever the gentleman, slid off his dark glasses. Her eyes met his, red-rimmed and hurt, and she wondered how long she'd been in love with him.

He was standing, walking slowly, deliberately toward her, was halfway to her before she even realized that her arms were held out to him.

Catherine stepped back, slipped the magazine from his hand,

walked the few steps to the corner, and dropped it ceremoniously into the trash basket. Then she took his hand and led him wordlessly into Gramercy Towers, past the doorman, smiling and unseen.

The phone was ringing when they walked down the eighteenth floor hallway. It was still ringing when they entered the apartment. "I'll take care of it," Catherine said. She walked to the kitchen and stood by his new wall phone, waiting, until she thought it would never stop ringing. When it did, she took the receiver off the hook, called Jayne Dudley to tell her they were all right, pressed the bar again to get a dial tone, and placed the receiver gently on the counter. "Can I get you a drink, a sandwich, anything?" she called from the doorway.

Lynell only shook his head absently, his mind still focused on the damning picture that had ruined his career.

She sat beside him on the couch and turned toward him. That face, that incredible face. She could read the emotions on it as clearly as words on a page.

"It was Canero," he stammered.

She put a finger to his lips. "Not now. It's not important now." She wrapped her arms around him and felt his shuddering sobs and ached to absorb his pain. "It's all right," she whispered, as she held the back of his head and pressed his damp face to her neck. "It's all right."

"My family—," he began through his sobs, but she cut him off gently.

"Your family is still your family." She drew a deep breath and sighed. "And your friends—if you forgive them—are still your friends."

As he calmed, he told her about Canero and Ginny. "You know," he said with a touch of irony, "I think it might have happened the day I first worked with you. Or, I don't know, maybe things just run together after a time. The great watercolor of life," he mused with mock drama. "How could I have been so stupid?" He thought reflectively of the young girls in San Francisco and of the others. "Of course, I guess you could say I haven't been all that difficult to seduce in recent years," he said apologetically.

"That really depends on how you look at it," Catherine said flatly.

Then he told her about Mark Collins—né Carl Howard—and about his ugly-duckling childhood. The story went on for over an hour, and as Catherine listened raptly, the weight of years of confusion and guilt gradually lifted from his chest. Through it all, Catherine did finally absorb some of his pain, and in hurting for him, knew that he hurt less. Only then did Lynell confront his final failure—Aimée.

"I've never talked about my relationships with women before or my

393

inability to commit myself to anything important—never. I've never really even thought seriously about it before."

"Maybe you didn't *want* to think about it—or *have* to."

"I've only joked about it, but I've never really thought about *why.*" Then he stiffened suddenly. "Jesus, I must seem like a real monster."

"Not at all," she whispered with a soft shake of her head. "Not at all. You seem like a human being." She reached to touch his whisker-rough cheek with her fingertips, then dropped her hand quickly, self-consciously, to his shoulder, then back to her own lap. "Not 'The Perfect Man.' Not the touched-up, airbrushed, flawless, mindless model of the American male. We *aren't* the illusion, Lynell. We're flesh and blood. We're human beings and we make mistakes. We have ugly scars even Revlon and Max Factor can't erase. And even worse, we bear the guilt of having scarred others. And we can't always make it better. All we can do is try."

They looked into each other's eyes as though each of them was starving and would find nourishment there. When Catherine clenched her eyes the tears ran unchecked down her cheeks. Lynell reached up and smoothed her soft hair to the nape of her neck, and held her, feeling the tenseness flow from her. "I know it must be hard to forget," he said. Then he held her tighter as he slowly pulled the stake from her heart. "And I know that I've been in love with you since the instant you first spoke to me."

It was an afternoon that should have lasted forever, and in their care to absorb even the most minute detail, for Lynell and Catherine it *would* last forever. Through the open kitchen window the unseasonable warmth of a bright May afternoon brought with it the song of the city—honking horns and blaring sirens and the screeching tires of speeding cars—a caroling now as sweetly subliminal as that of birds in a distant wood.

They talked of childhoods and of youth—which he reluctantly admitted to having had almost thirteen more years of than she. They talked of loves and hates, of wonders and horrors, feeling no constraint of time and wrapped in an intimacy neither of them understood or questioned.

In the waning light of afternoon, amid the unraveling of histories, she looked at him in a way that ended all conversation. "Why do you suppose it took us so long to get here?" she whispered.

"At least we did," he answered. When he kissed her it seemed not like a first kiss, but the first of a million kisses to come, and there was in it such a powerful sustaining force that he didn't feel constrained to have them all now, but wrapped her snugly in his arms and rocked her gently back on the couch. As they cuddled together, the falling dusk spread over them like a warm, soft blanket.

When they awoke the room was dark and cold, and Lynell went to the kitchen and shut out the draft. Then he returned to her and, taking her hand, led her wordlessly to his room, to the side of his bed, guided by the shadowy illumination of a full moon through the window. Her mouth was warm and soft and moist under his, and his lips trembled, barely able to withstand the near-pain of the pleasure that was suddenly magnified by his need for her. He unbuttoned her blouse slowly, slipped it over her shoulders, and heard it rustle to the floor. The dark shadows curved around her breasts like the disembodied fingers of his desire. It was a vision he had tried a thousand times to shut out of his dreams.

When he kissed her breast Catherine drew in her breath as though it had caused pain, and Lynell drew back instinctively. The last thing he wanted was to hurt her again.

"Please," she whispered, and again he pressed his lips into the soft warmth of her breast, then found the erect nipple and tugged on it with a delicious eroticism that made Catherine's knees tremble. He undressed her slowly, running his hands tenderly over each provocative new part of her—across her broad, strong back and down to the curve at the base of her spine, around her slim waist, cupping the swell of her round buttocks in his hands and gripping her to him, not lustfully but lovingly.

Catherine lay on the bed as he undressed himself. When he was beside her, she clutched him to her with a need so desperate it seemed it had been inside her forever. In their naked embrace he felt the security of her soft, warm breasts against his chest, and as she rocked him against her, he was mildly embarrassed by the aching stiffness that intruded between them.

For a long time they held each other that way—tightly, serenely, securely—and his sexual urgency, *their* sexual urgency, receded. When it rose again, it rose with an unbridled intensity that was released by three words they spoke simultaneously, words that never meant more to two lovers.

This man, so gentle, so tenderly loving, erased the lingering shadows with soft strokes of his hands on her body, erased them from every secret place, and she never thought of stopping him—never—because she had wished those shadows away for so long. When his hands caressed her breasts and moved gently, insistently down across her abdomen, each part of her was clean and new—her thighs, her calves, her toes. He suckled at her breasts and a tingling warmth spread through her. He probed her navel with his tongue and it was tantalizing. "Please, yes," she begged. All of the memories must be erased and somehow she knew that only this man could erase them. And he did, gently, soothingly, tenderly, tantalizingly, until uncontrollable shivers of ecstasy racked her and she cried out, releasing emotions locked inside her for years, for a lifetime—forever.

Lynell only entered her when her orgasm was over, easing into her with tortuous deliberation. He did not make love to her then but held her tightly, and swam in the burning pleasure of being inside her, of a oneness so complete her body was his, and his hers, and *she* was inside *him*. For a time they might have drifted into sleep, but for a time they were surely in another world, and when one of them moved they could not tell which one of them it was, and when they were both moving they were of the same sex, male-female, female-male, one primal organism anatomically fused, rocked to a rhythm that shook them as a single being. And they lay together in the stillness of the sensual aura of their oneness—silently—tasting the salt taste of one body, smelling the faint aroma of one body, feeling the suction of perspiration-soaked skin and hearing the deep, even breathing of one. There was no need to speak, no need to ask questions, no need because they had been, for that moment, one body, one soul.

It was clean and pure and absent of inhibition—intense, fulfilling, complete. When they awoke again, the words came more easily than she had imagined they would, came in whispers and in smiles and in laughter.

Time was a blur and ten minutes, ten hours, ten years later they stood in the antique bathtub under the soothing spray of the warm shower, soaping, kissing, teasing, embracing, and she was taking him in her mouth and she *enjoyed* it because his body was hers, and when she stood to kiss him her knees trembled with her joy and pleasure and she clung to him for support, her knees buckling as she sat on the edge of the tub, the warm spray tingling her skin, and he was between her spread knees and his tongue stabbed her with an ecstasy so intense it was pain, and when he carried her to the bed and dried her and they were warm beneath the covers in a tangle of unidentifiable limbs, both finally knew what it was to love and be loved, to need and be needed.

"What a day!" Mary Cline said with a sigh, falling into the middle of the leather couch in her office. "What an unbelievable day."

"I'd like to get my hands on that bastard," Albert spoke menacingly from behind the teak desk.

"Which one?" his sister asked cynically.

But Albert Cline's train of thought was focused on something else entirely. He had already reached Rocco DeMarco—though he would never tell Mary that. It would be easy to find out who was responsible for those photographs after Rocco put out the word. Then Al would go back into the leg-breaking business one last time—and this time for free. No one stole money from Al Cline's pocket. *No one.*

LeeAnn Schneider, called from a sunny Saturday she'd planned to spend window-shopping along Fifth Avenue, stood by the door at the ready—ready to be sent running for coffee . . . ready to be dismissed with an offhand wave . . . ready for the whim of either of the Clines.

"Which one, Albert, dear?" Mary asked again.

"Huh?"

"Why, dear, would you strangle our 'Perfect Man?' " Mary asked sarcastically, "or the fucker who took those pictures? Because as surely as I'm sitting here a couple of hundred thousand dollars poorer, there's somebody out there almost that much richer. You don't think for a minute Lynell posed for that picture, do you? No," Mary went on, answering her own question. "He's not the type. No, he wanted to be something in this business and he knew it wouldn't happen that way. He had nothing to gain. Now, take Mark. There's a man who'd do anything to make a buck. Not that it matters. He had probably just about peaked anyway. How long can you make a living on a five-o'clock shadow?"

LeeAnn's pulse rate was rising and her breathing quickened so that she was afraid she might hyperventilate. Her past rose up silently, bringing her, finally, to her senses. "You're talking about them as if they were dead," she blurted, surprised but proud that for once she'd spoken her mind.

"Ah, my dear," Mary said with a pensive nod, "but they *are* dead." She looked across the room at her brother, who was rolling an expensive Havana cigar sullenly between the thumb and first two fingers of his right hand, and a vindictive mask fell over her features, transforming her from a plain-looking, middle-aged woman to an ashen-faced hag. "*We'll* see to that. Won't we, dear? First things first, of course. Catherine Ward is too closely associated with Lynell Allen to survive unscathed, so she'll have to go down with the ship. She was on her way out anyway," Mary continued with a flick of her wrist she would have used to shoo away a mosquito. "But as for Mark Collins and your friend Lynell . . . We'll cover our asses. We want every connection

397

with them severed—immediately. Cancel all their bookings and get someone else of their types over to see the clients. I think we've lost Billie Devlin and Now. She was *extremely* agitated. And ABC and the soap opera are history. But we'll get someone over to the rest of them. I want a new headsheet without Lynell and Mark and Catherine. It's the models' money anyway. Then it's simply a question of how badly they want to stay in the business," Mary said with a cruel grin.

"Yeah," Albert added. "Which means how hard up they are."

"Precisely," said his sister.

LeeAnn could feel the heat searing the back of her neck, could feel the sweat trickle between her small breasts. But she was riveted to the thick carpet, paralyzed by a growing sense of outrage.

"Now," Mary began, rolling her eyes to the ceiling as though seized by a brainstorm. "Sooner or later Catherine will get the message and take a bus back to Iowa and conveniently disappear. As for the men: Our Perfect Man is one thing. He is undeniably bright and well-educated and, as I understand it, has a family business to fall back on. I very much doubt he'll take too many jobs walking floors at Macy's or handing out free cigarettes on street corners. . . ."

"Or pleasing some of our kinkier potential clients," her brother threw in.

"But," Mary said, "I believe our Mr. Collins is quite another story. I mean, after fucking and sucking one's way through life, what else is one qualified to do?" She turned to her brother with a smile that held in it a kind of perverted sense of victory. Mary Cline did not like to lose. "Albert, dear, would you care for a cup of coffee?"

He returned his sister's smile with a nod.

"LeeAnn," Mary said solicitously, "be a dear and get us some coffee."

LeeAnn's head was shaking in awed disbelief at the two grotesques who sat before her. Suddenly she dropped her pad and pencil to the floor and said in a voice of controlled rage, "Fuck you." And she spun on her heels and walked out, closing the door softly behind her . . . forever.

In the quiet of the office it was several minutes before Mary and Albert Cline actually believed that LeeAnn Schneider had finally found the nerve to break free. Albert turned to his sister, with the indulgent smile of the father of a particularly obstreperous child. "Well, dear, I suppose nothing's more replaceable than a booker."

"No, dear, I suppose not," Mary answered with a sigh. "Unless it's a model."

25

Mark Collins was still standing naked in front of his full-length bathroom mirror when the telephone began to ring insistently. Who was he kidding, anyway? There wasn't even the remotest chance he'd off himself. Maybe the possibility had been real when the thought had first occurred to him, in that moment of desperation when he'd first seen the photographs almost two weeks ago. Then Franco Canero had begun blackmailing him to the tune of fifteen thousand dollars, and he'd been naive enough to think that that would be the last he'd hear of it. Or maybe the possibility had been real minutes ago when he had again opened that porn rag—maybe if, at that precise moment, he'd had a pistol close by. . . . But the deadliest thing he had at hand was a seldom-used safety razor, and the urge had quickly given way to rational thought. There had to be plenty of alternatives for a man in his delicate situation, and when the dust cleared on this little mess, he'd take some time to figure out just what those alternatives were.

As it happened, the dust cleared as soon as the damned telephone stopped ringing.

It was after 9:00 P.M. when Catherine and Lynell awoke, still locked in an embrace. "Where were you on October 15, 1962?" Catherine asked as she stretched against him, her voice a sleep-scratchy impression of Sergeant Joe Friday.

"October 15, 1962? Morning or afternoon?"

"Hey, I'm serious. Where were you on October 15, 1962? At precisely 12:30 P.M., if you must know."

"Hmm, let's see. I was twelve years old, so I was probably at lunch with Miss Octoman's seventh-grade class. Except if it was a Saturday. Then I know for sure where I was. I would have been watching Looney Tunes. Why? Where were you?"

"I was in Ames, Iowa—being born," she said, her voice softening seriously. "And I'm sure I've been in love with you since that minute."

Lynell wrapped his arms around her in the darkness, hugged her with all his might, and marveled and the size and strength of her young body.

"Christ, it fits you better than it fits me," he said when Catherine went to the closet and pulled on the silk kimono he'd picked up when they'd gone to Tokyo for Now. She hadn't yet tied the sash or pulled the lapels over her breasts, and he wondered at the will that had kept him from wanting her from the moment they had met. "I hope it doesn't embarrass you that you turn me on so," he apologized, walking to her until he pressed himself against her.

"Oh, yes," she said, wrapping him in the silk with one hand and squeezing him gently with the other. "It embarrasses me to death." They stood with their eyes sparkling in the dim light of the bedside lamp, and she stroked him in the cool, smooth fabric until he expanded against her hand and she dropped the kimono, let go of him, and pulled his body to her, writhing with the heat of him between them, until he groaned and the hot, viscous fluid pulsed against her. "Oh yes, Lynell, it embarrasses me to death," she whispered, throwing her arms around his neck and kissing him ardently.

He scooped his moth-eaten gray sweatshirt off the floor, and she snatched it from his hands and wiped her abdomen with it before pulling the kimono around her again.

"Hey, I was going to wear that," he protested lamely.

"I know," Catherine answered sarcastically, throwing the sweatshirt in the already overflowing laundry basket in his closet, spinning, and walking to the door with the sprightly gait of one reborn. "How about something to eat?"

"Great. I'm starved."

She was gathering the makings of a gourmet omelette when he came into the kitchen in his worn terrycloth bathrobe, walked up behind her, reached around to grasp each breast, and hugged her to him tightly. "God, why does this feel so good?"

"Maybe it's so good because we were—and are—friends first. And just maybe it took love this long to overcome selfishness."

He held her for a long time, rocking her back against him. Then he kissed her cheek. "I think I'll give Mark a call—see how he's taking it."

"He'd probably do the same for you," she said sarcastically.

"I've worked with him a bunch of times in the past year or so . . . Bloomies, Calvin Klein . . . He's really not such a bad guy when you get to know him. Aggressive, but not a bad guy."

"I suppose so," Catherine agreed.

"I have a feeling Mark is really a lot nicer than he wants people to believe," Lynell continued as he reached for the telephone.

"You're right, Lynell. I guess I should be more charitable."

Lynell counted ten rings before hanging up. "No answer."

"Maybe he's out of town."

"Yes, out of town," Lynell agreed absently, as he remembered the poisonous thoughts that had possessed him up to the moment he had seen Catherine earlier in the day.

They were eating when the telephone rang. "Oh, shit," Lynell swore. "I forgot to leave it off the hook."

"Want me to get it?"

"Don't bother, Catherine. Let it ring. The only person in the world I want to talk to is right here." He covered her hand with his own, wrapping his fingers around it affectionately.

The telephone rang three times and stopped.

"Not very persistent," she said.

"It's a signal from my family," Lynell explained. "Three rings, hang up, call again. I'm not always big on answering the phone, so it's a way they can let me know that it's one of them."

The phone began to ring again. "Would you?" he asked. "I'd rather explain it in person. Tell them I'm fine and that we'll be out tomorrow. You *will* come with me?"

"Of course."

Aimée Harris had been calling since just after noon. It seemed ironic that only yesterday she'd called to congratulate him on *Vogue*. It was wonderful. It was beautiful. It was *him*. And now . . . ?

"Hello?"

"Hello . . . Catherine?" A brief but painful shock jolted Aimée's heart.

"Yes."

"This is Aimée. Oh, Catherine, I'm so glad you're there with him. I

401

know how much Lynell cares for you. I've been calling all day. How is he?"

"He's just fine under the circumstances. He took the phone off the hook so he wouldn't be bothered, but I know he'll want to talk to you. Just a second."

Lynell was shaking his head until Catherine cupped the receiver with her hand. "It's Aimée."

"Oh," he said softly.

Catherine smiled self-consciously as she handed him the phone. She felt as though she had been caught with another woman's man. When Lynell began talking she quietly left the room, a familiar ache beginning to rise in her chest.

"What will you do, Lynell?" Aimée asked finally.

"Find another line of work, I guess," he said, forcing a laugh. "But first I think I'll take that vacation. You're right, I need one."

"Somewhere quiet, private, far from the maddening crowd. Like that old place we used to rent on the Vineyard."

"Yeah, what a great place," he mused. "Christ, it's the middle of May, though. A place like that wouldn't still be available."

"No, it wouldn't," she agreed. "As a matter of fact, I checked on the house about six months ago. The owner had lowered the price a few thousand dollars and the realtor was finally able to sell it. The new owner hasn't shown the least bit of interest in renting it."

"Oh, does he live there, the lucky bastard?"

"No, but I happen to know him pretty well and he's definitely not the type who would want strangers living in his home."

"I don't blame him, I guess. I wouldn't either."

"That's what I thought. That's exactly why it's been vacant for six months."

There was a long, confused pause at Lynell's end of the line. It was as though she had just told him that two and two were five. "Aimée . . . what are you talking about?"

"I was waiting for your birthday, Lynell, but . . . what's another few days? . . . Lynell? . . . *You* own the house . . . Lynell? Lynell? Are you still there?"

"What?" he asked weakly.

"Are you still there?"

"Yes," he answered in a barely audible whisper.

"Except for the few hundred dollars that came out of my pocket when you first moved to New York, every penny you've given me has gone directly into a trust fund in your name, with me as trustee. Last November I made the down payment: fifty percent in cash. That's why they came down in the price. The interest and dividends on what's left in the trust fund support the mortgage, taxes, insurance, and upkeep, including a cleaning woman who goes in once a week. Happy Birthday!"

There was another long silence at Lynell's end of the telephone. Tears began to trickle, then to stream down his face. "Aimée . . . Thank you, but . . . I wanted *you* to have that money . . . to repay you for . . ."

"You did. You repaid me for everything . . . a thousand times over. The discoveries, the maturity, and the memories are worth far more than the money. Anyway, as I always said, 'I don't want it, I don't need it, and—' "

"I know," he broke in with a chuckle, "you make twice as much as I do in a good year."

She laughed. "Well, not any more, but I do all right."

"Aimée, I absolutely can't believe it. I can't begin to thank you. But I've always kind of thought of it as our place."

"Don't be silly. I've always thought of it as *your* place. I never really liked it very much," she lied. "Too remote."

"Aimée, I . . . Thank you."

Her next piece of news made him even happier, if possible, than the first—this time for her. "Lynell, Todd Thornton and I are going to be married."

There was an immediate tightening in his chest as his years with her flashed before him—good years, years of youth and hope and dreams, years of searching, years now irretrievably behind them. "That's wonderful, Aimée, wonderful." Aimée Harris and Todd Thornton were two of a kind. They seemed to fit together the way, well, the way he and Catherine fit together. In his mind he had her wedding present already picked out: a BMW—cornflower blue, of course, her favorite color.

"Lynell?" In the deafening silence he could hear her soft breathing at the other end of the line. "Lynell, I'll always love you."

"Yes, I know. And I'll always love you, Aimée."

He placed two calls after hanging up: one to Pine Orchard, Connecticut, and the other to Ames, Iowa. When he returned to the bedroom with two glasses of brandy, Catherine was sitting up against the headboard reading *Vogue*. The hurt look on her face changed his mind. There were more important things to discuss right now than his new house. "You'll go blind."

"I'm not reading. I'm just looking at the pictures."

"You made the bed," he said, handing her a glass of brandy.

403

"It seemed the appropriate thing to do." She looked up at him as ruefully as a puppy being left at the kennel. "Lynell? Are you still in love with her?"

He stood looking down at her for what seemed like an eternity. "I'm in love with the memory," he said, almost in a whisper. "Aimée is a warm, wonderful, caring person, and I'll always love her and what we once had. We had some great, growing years together. But it's over for Aimée and me." He clinked his glass against hers, and after each of them had sipped, he put both glasses on the bedside table and took her in his arms, kissing her hard and long, feeling her soft mouth open warm and moist against his.

When they awoke again Lynell turned on the small black-and-white television in the bedroom and flipped it to the eleven o'clock news on WXPTV, Channel 10. "I feel as though I've been on a desert island for a month," he said, adjusting the contrast and volume. Though Channel 10 was primarily a local news show, they frequently led with an important national or international item. Tonight it was the ongoing conflict in El Salvador.

"How about some orange juice or something?" he asked as he turned and started toward the kitchen."

"Lynell, wasn't that the door?"

"What?"

"The door. I thought I heard a knock."

This time he heard it, too. "Who the hell could that be?"

"I don't know," she answered. "But don't you think if someone bothered to come over you should answer it?"

"I guess," he said with a sigh. "Just a minute," he called out. Then he slipped into his jeans and a T-shirt and reluctantly left the bedroom, closing the door behind him.

"We can make this thing work for us," Mark Collins said excitedly, as he rushed past him into the apartment.

"I see you've come through this unscathed."

"*Unscathed?*" Mark said. "Man, we've achieved an actor's dream: instant notoriety."

"But I'm not an actor," Lynell pointed out as he sat tiredly in the chair across from Mark.

"*Everybody's* an actor. Only *you* have a lot more potential to get paid for it."

"Look, Mark, be sensible. Do you really think ABC is going to want me around after this episode?"

"If they don't, NBC will—or CBS. People are going to want to see us. We're famous!"

"Infamous."

"Even better," Mark said. "Soaps thrive on infamy—and scandal. So do the movies. And they thrive on personalities and the dirt that's written in *People* magazine and the *National Enquirer*. Man, you don't seem to understand—we're *big*."

"Okay, even if you're right," Lynell conceded, wariness and suspicion creeping into his voice. "Why tell me? I know you, Mark; at least, I know you well enough to know you're not into doing favors."

"I'm telling you because we're big but we can be even *bigger*. Imagine if we appeared together on 'Good Morning, America' or the 'CBS Morning News.' We'd have every housewife in America eating out of our hands. I've seen you in action, man. My looks and your charm . . . We've got it made. Then when the offers start rolling in . . . we go our separate ways . . . make it or break it on our own."

Lynell looked unconvinced.

"What do you say?" Mark prompted. "Don't be a sucker. This is the kind of break we've worked for, the kind of break we've been pimping ourselves for Al and Mary Cline for."

"I haven't been pimping myself," Lynell broke in.

"*Modeling* is pimping yourself," Mark sneered disdainfully.

"I'm getting out," Lynell said, "before they throw me out—if they haven't already. Catherine is, too, I think."

Mark nodded. "That's your first mistake, buddy. She's a loser. Mary Cline has already used her up. Nobody wants to take a risk on a coke head. Cut her loose, man. Keep away from her. Or if you have to have her, at least send her home. Go visit her out there. Keep a low profile."

Lynell shook his head in disbelief. "How can you say that, Mark? Catherine's my friend."

"Yeah," Mark said knowingly, "you're *my* friend, too." He stood and walked to the door, Lynell close behind him. Fuck Lynell Alan, he thought. He was a loser, too. It would have been better *with* him—splashier. But he could do it *without* him, too. He turned and faced Lynell.

It was in Mark's eyes, Lynell thought, shaking his head resolutely—a dullness, a blankness. Neither of them spoke for a long moment. "And I was just beginning to like you," Lynell said disappointedly. And he remembered something Catherine had said to him not too long ago: You don't *feel*, Lynell, she had said. "Mark, there's something inside you—an emptiness. Something died somewhere along the way."

"Well, if there is something inside me that's dead, they killed it: the Clines and the Caneros and the clients and the advertising agents"— he interrupted himself suddenly to grin and shake his head— "and all the other users. Well," he said, extending his hand, "if you change your mind . . . But it has to be soon. Strike while the iron's hot and all that."

"Good luck," Lynell said icily as he closed the door behind him. As if Mark would need it.

"Who was it?" Catherine asked as Lynell slowly took off his jeans and T-shirt.

"Mark."

"Oh, good. Is he . . . ?"

"Fine," Lynell broke in. "He's fine."

Lynell turned off the television, returned to Catherine, and slipped wordlessly into bed beside her. They held each other tightly long into the night.

"Thank you, Sean." Franco Canero's eyes followed the tight little ass out of the room before he picked up the *New York Times* Sunday morning edition and scanned the front page. A small item on the bottom righthand side of the page caught his eye: "Fashion Model Overdose Victim." He held his breath as he read, realizing he was doubtless one of the very few who had read the headline and didn't assume it was going to be about a woman. Before he noticed the Los Angeles dateline it had actually occurred to him that it was Lynell Alan or, more probably, Mark Collins, and guilt welled up inside him as his desire for the two men once had. Then he thought of the $175,000 that would get him on firm footing again, that would help him return himself to world renown, that would procure for him an unlimited number of sweet, delectable young lovers like Sean.

He quickly read the article, only to discover it was about a Nina Blanchard protegé, one Tommy Bristol. . . . Still, the image lingered. But there was no conceivable way anyone could, or would, connect him to those pictures—no one with any credibility, that is. So why did he have the uneasy feeling recently that he was being followed? "Just my overactive imagination," he said out loud, dismissing the thought.

He took the eight-by-ten original print of Mark Collins from the drawer of his bedside table. It was far from perfect, but a hell of a lot clearer than the reprint in that sleazy rag.

When he heard Sean returning from the bathroom, Canero slid the picture back into its manila folder and closed the drawer. Under the sheets he was rock hard, the necrophiliac fantasy reeling in his brain. "Sean, sweets? How are you at playing dead?"

In Pine Orchard the Alan clan was gathered in full force: Oliver and Liz, Veronica and her husband, Jack, and their two young children. It had taken two cars to transport them all to New Haven and still have enough room on the return trip for Lynell and his guest. "*Vogue* was wonderful," his father conceded grudgingly.

"Did you see the other?"

"No one will give it any notice at all. It was obviously taken from concealment by some pervert. Why," he continued, his voice rising suddenly in outrage, "it may as well have been taken while you were at a urinal in a public men's room." Then he turned to Catherine apologetically. "Excuse me, young lady," he said with a bow.

"*Everyone* has noticed," Lynell said after introducing Catherine. "I've been axed by clients I didn't even know I had. I'm finished as a model. What'll I do?" he asked finally in frustration, turning to his mother, who scanned the faces of her family and Lynell's friend and spoke for the first time.

"You don't need them, Lynell. You've got us. You know what we always say . . ." Then she smiled genteelly and said with a shrug, "Fuck 'em!"

It wasn't until late afternoon, when they were able to extract themselves from the near-party atmosphere his family had thrown around them like a protective shield, that Lynell and Catherine sat quietly on the deserted beach.

"This whole thing is just so unbelievable," Catherine said with a shiver. "Why would anyone do it?"

"Money," Lynell answered simply.

A desperate depression washed over Catherine like the cool afternoon breeze whistling through her sweater, and she felt herself slipping helplessly into a familiar abyss. She glanced to her right where Lynell dangled a long cattail above L.C., who leapt at it playfully, batting its fluffy spores into the light sea breeze. "I think I'll go inside and take a nap," she said, leaning to kiss him on the cheek. He looked so content, so serene in this moment she could easily have cried for its passing.

"Good idea. Your lips are ice cold. I'm going to stay and watch the sun go down."

Upstairs in the guest room, behind her closed door, Catherine rummaged through her small overnight bag until she'd found what she was looking for, what she was aching for. She opened the vial, placed it on the bureau, and dipped the long fingernail of her little finger into the powder. As she slowly, tantalizing brought it up under her nose, there was nothing on her mind—nothing but getting that white powder into her nostrils, into her brain.

The suddenness with which he came into the room so startled her that she knocked the entire contents of the vial into a fan-shaped arc across the polished top of the mahogany bureau. There it lay like the pure white sand of a broken hourglass, like the scattered particles of her life, like time irretrievable.

"I'm sorry," he said, the shock of his discovery matching his embarrassment at having violated her privacy. "Liz sent me up with clean towels and . . . and I thought you were out on the beach with Lynell."

"It's I who should be sorry, Mr. Alan." She sighed deeply, trying to catch her breath. "Please don't tell him," she said, as he lay the towels on the foot of her bed.

"I won't tell him, my dear. That's up to you." Oliver Alan walked to the door, turning at the last moment. "Catherine, Liz and I are extremely grateful that our son had you to help him through this rough time. You know," he said, "help works best when it goes both ways." Then he closed the door softly behind him.

Liz Alan stood at the kitchen window, putting the finishing touches on a dinner on which even she had to admit she had outdone herself. The family gathered so seldom these days. But she felt the pride and warmth of a mother hen, watching from the window as Lynell sat on the beach with the gently undulating Sound behind him and the distant cliffs of Greenport lining the horizon in a scene reminiscent of so many of his television commercials.

She's such a beautiful girl, Liz thought, when Catherine walked out onto the beach to rejoin him, *inside and out. And as Lynell said on the telephone last night, they will be good for each other.*

But something was wrong. Something was suddenly dreadfully wrong, and Liz Alan fought an uncontrollable urge to run out on that beach and hug her son protectively, as she had when the family had met him today at dilapidated Union Station. Since childhood he had always been the vulnerable one—homely, good-natured little Lynell—protecting himself with a smile.

As Liz watched anxiously, Catherine said something and Lynell turned and walked wordlessly away, and Liz recalled the days when she and Oliver had watched him let Veronica take away his toy cars without a fight. *My poor, sad, confused baby,* Liz thought, *still holding everything inside.*

When Lynell reached the high-water mark he stopped suddenly. For a long moment he stood absently toeing the damp sand. Then he slowly turned around and held out his arms, and Catherine ran to him without hesitation.

"Oh, yes, they'll be *so* good for each other," Liz said as her husband walked up behind her. "She's a lovely girl, isn't she?"

"Yes, she is. It looks as though he's finally found something worth fighting for after all," Oliver agreed as they watched the young couple stroll hand-in-hand down the beach until they disappeared around the point toward Indian Neck.

"You've watched a lot of that boy's life from this kitchen window," Oliver said, hugging her around the waist. He would not betray Catherine's confidence. There was no need. Catherine and Lynell had found each other. They were halfway there. Together they could find their way home.

It was Dan Buford who reached Lynell in Connecticut to tell him of the death of their former roommate, Tommy Bristol. "I thought, what with your own problems, you might not have heard."

"I'm glad you called, Dan. Of course I'll be there."

The memorial service, in New Jersey, three days later, was simple and private, a peaceful thirty-minute interlude in the hectic media blitz sparked by Mark Collins's frenetic self-promotion. Lynell tried desperately to think only of Tommy, but it was difficult, knowing all the while that when he left the chapel he would face the same relentless reporters who had confronted him when he and Catherine had arrived.

"Mark Collins has already appeared on 'Good Morning, America.' How do you think this will affect your career?"

"Miss Ward, will you stay with Cline Models now that they've dropped Mr. Alan?"

"Are you aware the June issue of *Vogue* has enjoyed record over-the-counter sales?"

"Not to mention *Boyplay.*"

He nervously straightened his tie and spoke passively. "I'm here to pay my last respects to a friend and colleague. Nothing else is important at this time." He was poised and unflappable as he looked into the camera, once the face of an ally, now turned enemy.

More than one middle-aged woman saw him on the six o'clock news and was touched by his dignity and his warmth. More than one young woman stared enviously at Catherine Ward and dreamed of what it would be like to be loved by such a man. The world had done him wrong, and it wasn't fair. It just wasn't fair.

Epilogue

JULY 1984

The cold, sweeping wind balled the Atlantic into a tight fist that pummeled the West Tisbury shore. The pounding of the surf and its echo off the cliffs below were the strong, steady heartbeat of the Island, and he was sure Martha's Vineyard would sink into the ocean and die without it.

Fourth of July weekend had come and gone with the same peaceful tranquillity as the two weekends before it, far from the fickle tide of public opinion. His three-bedroom colonial retreat was nestled in a thick grove of firs above the beach, a mile and a half—by car-width dirt road—south of West Tisbury Road, and at least that far from the nearest neighbor on either side. They saw no sign of life but an occasional distant fishing boat, heard no sign of life at all over the pugnacious sea.

Lynell dropped three more logs on the fire and poked at them absently while L.C. stood, stretched, and moved several feet farther from the hearth in anticipation of the rising heat. Catherine's lovely eyes flashed in the incandescent glow. This time he had stood close by her through the month-long in-patient rehabilitation program at Fairfield County Hospital, and she looked younger, healthier, more radiantly beautiful than he had ever seen her.

When he sat beside her on the oriental rug, stretching his legs and reclining against the worn, musty-smelling ottoman, Catherine leaned

413

and kissed his cheek gently. "You should get the place winterized. Don't you think it would be great fun in February?"

"Great fun," he said sarcastically. "We'd have to be airlifted in."

"Buy a plane."

"You're optimistic."

"Why not? LeeAnn said you could live pretty comfortably for quite a while off the royalties from your Perfect Man Poster alone. They're selling out all over the country. And the ABC deal? Triple what they were going to offer you only eight weeks ago—*if* you want it."

The crackling of the logs rose over the whistling wind, amplifying the stillness. "I'd still like to find out how LeeAnn got this phone number," he said knowingly.

A sly grin lit Catherine's beautiful young face. "*I'm* not a hermit. I wanted someone reliable to have a number where I could be reached. Anyway, you said it once yourself: I've got this business all figured out. The hero with clay feet. That's *today's* perfect man. Of course, then there's LeeAnn's proposition. With her connections and knowledge of the business and your financial background—not to mention me as your first model," she added kiddingly, "you two would be a natural to open your own agency."

"I guess you've got a couple of decent years left," he joked. "But first things first. Then we'll decide about my career."

"*We* nothing. It's your life. It's your decision. *You've* got to decide what *you* want."

"I've been meaning to speak to you about that. I know what I want, Catherine. For the first time in my life I know *exactly* what I want." The rising enthusiasm in his voice woke the little girl, who drowsed tiredly on the blanket between them. She stood slowly and leaned against her mother, yawning and rubbing her sleepy eyes.

"I want a family," Lynell said softly, gathering Heather between them into a bear hug. "I want *this* family." Then he sat back and looked from Catherine to a smiling Heather, and asked in a whisper barely audible over the wind and the surf and the crackling fire, "Will you two please marry me?"